Louise Allen loves i[...] landscapes and plac[...] Burgundy and the C[...] Louise lives on the [...] gardening, researching family [...] inspiration. www.louiseallenregency.co.uk, @LouiseRegency http://janeaustenslondon.com

Linda Sole started writing in 1976 and, writing as **Anne Herries**, won the 2004 RNA Romance Award and the Betty Neels Trophy. Linda loves to write about the beauty of nature, though they are mostly about love and romance. She writes for her own enjoyment and loves to give pleasure to her readers. In her spare time, she enjoys watching the wildlife that visits her garden. Anne has now written more than fifty books for Mills & Boon. You can visit her website at: www.lindasole.co.uk

Regency Christmas Courtship

LOUISE ALLEN
ANNE HERRIES

MILLS & BOON

First Published in Great Britain 2019
by Mills & Boon, an imprint of HarperCollins*Publishers*
1 London Bridge Street, London, SE1 9GF

REGENCY CHRISTMAS COURTSHIP © 2019 Harlequin Books S. A.

His Christmas Countess © 2015 Melanie Hilton
The Mistress of Hanover Square © 2009 Anne Herries

ISBN: 978-0-263-27944-3

1119

MIX
Paper from
responsible sources
FSC C007454
FSC
www.fsc.org

This book is produced from independently certified FSC™ paper to ensure responsible forest management.

For more information visit: www.harpercollins.co.uk/green

Printed and bound in Spain
by CPI, Barcelona

HIS CHRISTMAS COUNTESS

LOUISE ALLEN

Chapter One

December 24, 1819—the Scottish Borders

Becoming pregnant had been so easy, so catastrophically simple. An unaccustomed glass of champagne, a little unfamiliar flattery, a night made for romance, a careless, innocent tumble from virtue to ruin.

Somehow that ease increased the shock of discovering just how hard giving birth to the baby was. *It is because I'm alone, I'm cold, I'm frightened,* Kate told herself. *In a moment, when these pains stop, I will feel stronger, I'll get up and light the fire. If I can get there, if there is any dry kindling, if I can strike a spark.*

'Stop it.' She spoke aloud, her voice echoing in the chill space of the half-ruined bothy. 'I *will* do it because I have to, because I must, for the baby.' It was her fault her child would be born in a tumbledown cottage on a winter's day, her miscalculation in leaving it so late to run away, her lack of attention that had allowed the pickpocket to slip her purse from her reticule in the inn yard, leaving her penniless. She should have gone to the workhouse rather than think she could walk on, hoping for some miracle and safe shelter at the end of the rough, muddy road.

Her mind seemed to have turned to mush these past few days. Only one message had been clear: *get away before Henry can take my baby from me.* And she would do anything, anything at all, for this child, to keep him or her safe from her brother's clutches. Now was the time to move, while there was still some light left in the lowering sky. She tried to stand up from the heap of musty straw, but found she could not. 'Pull yourself together, Catherine Harding. Women give birth every day and in far worse conditions than this.' Beyond caring that she was reduced to a lumbering, clumsy creature, she managed to get on to her hands and knees and began to crawl towards the hearth and the broken remains of the fire grate.

The weakness caught her before she could move more than a few feet. It must be because she had eaten so little in the past day and night. Shaking, she dug her fingers into the dirt floor and hung on. She would gather a little strength in a moment, then she could crawl nearer to the cold hearth. Surely giving birth could not take much longer? Learning some basic facts of life would be far more useful to young women than the art of watercolours and playing the harp. Learning the wiles of hardened rakes and the consequences of a moonlit dalliance would be even more valuable. Most of all, learning that one could not trust anyone, not even your closest kin, was a lesson Kate had learned too late.

If the mother she could not remember had survived Henry's birth… *No.* She caught herself up before the wishful thinking could weaken her, before the haunting fear of what her own fate might be overwhelmed her. She was still in the middle of the floor. How much time had passed since she had thought to light the fire? Hours? Only minutes, from the unchanging light. Kate inched closer to the hearth.

Something struck a stone outside, then the sound of footsteps muffled by the wet turf, the snort of a horse and a man's voice.

'This will have to do. You're lame, I'm lost, it is going to snow and this is the first roof I've seen for the past ten miles.' English, educated. Not an old man, not a youth. *Hide.*

She backed towards the heap of straw, animal instinct urging her to ungainly speed. A plank table had collapsed, two legs eaten through by rats or damp, and she burrowed behind it, her breath sobbing out of her lungs. Kate stuffed her clenched fist into her mouth and bit down.

'At least water's the one thing we're not short of.' Grant Rivers dug a broken-handled bucket from the rubbish heap outside the tumbledown cottage and scooped it into the small burn that rushed and chattered at the side of the track. His new horse, bought in Edinburgh, twitched an ear, apparently unused to forming part of a one-sided conversation.

Grant carried the bucket inside the part of the building that had once been a byre. The place was technically a but and ben, he supposed, one half for the beasts, one half for the family, the steaming animals helping them keep warm through the long Border winters. There was enough of the heather thatch to provide some shelter for the horse and the dwelling section had only a few holes in the roof, although the window and door had long gone. At least the solid wall turned its back on the prevailing wind. He could keep warm, rest up. He was enough of a doctor to know he should not ignore the headache and the occasional dizziness, the legacy of that near-fatal accident a week ago.

He lifted off the saddle, took off the bridle, used the reins as a tether and tipped the bag of oats from his saddlebag on to a dry patch of ground. 'Don't eat it all at once,' he advised the chestnut gelding. 'It's all you are getting until we reach civilisation and I've half a mind to steal it to make myself porridge.'

There was sufficient light to see by to clean out the big hooves and find the angular stone that had wedged itself into the off-hind. It looked sore. He gave an apologetic rub to the soft muzzle that nudged at him. His fault for pressing on so hard even though he suspected he would be too late for his grandfather. At least he had been able to send a letter saying the things in his heart to the man who had brought him up, letting the old man know that only dire necessity kept him from his side at the end.

He must also get back to Abbeywell for Charlie's sake. It was the last place he wanted to be, but the boy needed his father. And Grant needed his son, for that matter. Christmas was always going to be grim this year with his grandfather's health failing, but he had not expected it to be this bad—him bedridden in Edinburgh with his head cracked open and Charlie left with his dying great-grandfather. Grant had planned to leave the city on the seventeenth, but that was the day a labourer, careless with a scaffolding plank in the New Town, had almost killed him. As soon as he had regained consciousness and realised he was incapable of walking across the room, let alone travelling, Grant had written the letter. The reply had arrived from the steward two days ago. His grandfather was not expected to last the night.

Grant had hoped to be with his son for Christmas Day. Now he might make it by that evening if the gelding was sound and the weather held. 'We'll rest up, let the bruising ease, stay the night if I can get a fire going.' Talking to a horse might be a sign of concussion, but at least it made something to listen to beyond the wind whistling up this treeless Borders valley. Unless the direction of that wind changed, the makeshift stable was fairly sheltered and the horse was used to Scottish weather.

And for him the familiar cold of a Northumberland winter was no different from this. There was enough rubbish lying about the place to burn. He'd make a fire, pass the night with the food in his saddlebags and allow himself a dram from his brandy flask, or the illicit whisky James Whittaker had handed him as they'd parted yesterday in Edinburgh's New Town.

Something in the air... Grant straightened, arms full of dry scraps of wood, nostrils flaring to catch that faint rumour of scent. Blood? Blood and fear. He knew the smell of both from those weeks in the summer of '15. The killing days when he and his friends had volunteered to join the fight to see Napoleon finally defeated. The memory of them had saved his neck in more than a few dark alleyways before now.

A low moan made the horse shift uneasily. The wind or an animal? No, there had been something human in that faint wisp of sound. He did not believe in ghosts and that left someone hurt or in distress. Or a trap. The cottage would make a handy refuge for footpads. 'Eat your oats,' he said as he eased the knife from his left boot and tossed the armful of wood away.

He moved fast as the wood clattered into the far corner, then eased around the splintered jamb of the inner door to scan the single living room. It was shadowed and empty—a glance showed a broken chair, a scattered pile of mouldy straw, an overturned table, cobwebs and shadows. There was that soft, desperate sound again and the scent of fear was stronger here. Caution discarded, he took three strides across the earth floor and pulled away the table, the only hiding place.

It did not take several years of medical training to tell him that he was looking at a woman in labour and a desperate one at that. Of all the medical emergencies he might have confronted, this was the one from his nightmares. Literally. Her gaze flickered from his face to the knife in his hand as she scrabbled back into the straw.

'Go away.' Her voice was thready, defiant, and there was blood around her mouth and on the back of the hand resting protectively on the mound of her belly. She had bitten her fist in an attempt to muffle her cries. His stomach lurched at the sight. 'One step more and I'll—'

'Deposit a baby on my boots?' He slid the knife back into its sheath, made himself smile and saw her relax infinitesimally at his light tone. When he tossed his low-crowned hat on to the chair, exposing the rakish bandage across his forehead, she tensed again.

'Don't be ridiculous.' Her voice was English, educated, out of place in this hovel. She closed her eyes for a moment and when she opened them again the effort to stay focused and alert was palpable. 'This baby is *never* coming out.'

'First one?' Grant knelt beside her. 'I'm a doctor, it is going to be all right, trust me.' *There's two lies to begin with—how many more will I need? I'm not qualified, I've never delivered a baby and I have no idea whether* anything *is going to be all right.* He had, however, delivered any number of foals. Between theoretical knowledge, practical experience of female anatomy and years of managing a breeding stables, he would be better than nothing. But this child had better hurry up and get born, because he was trapped here until it was.

He was big, he was male, he seemed to fill the space and the bandage made him look like a brigand, despite the well-made clothes. But his quiet confidence and deep, calm voice seeped through Kate's cramped body like a dose of laudanum. *A doctor.* The answer to her incoherent prayers. There were miracles after all.

'Yes, this is my first child.' *And my last. No amount of pleasure is worth this.*

'Then let's get this place warm.' He shrugged out of his greatcoat and laid it over her. It smelt of horse, leather and man, all strangely soothing. 'We'll make you more comfortable when the fire's lit.'

'Dr...?'

'Grantham Rivers, at your service. Call me Grant.' He poked at the grate, went into the stable and came back with wood. His voice was pleasant, his expression, what she could see of it, unruffled, but she could sense he was not happy about this situation. For all the easy movement, the calm voice, he was on edge.

'Grantham?' Incredible the effect of a little warmth and a lot of reassurance, even if she was all too aware that her rescuer wished he was somewhere else entirely.

'I was conceived there, apparently, in the course of a passionate wedding night at the Bull Inn.' He was striking a flint on a steel cupped in his palm and surrounded by some sort of tinder. It flared up and he eased it into the wood, nursing the flame with steady, competent hands. 'It could have been worse. It might have been Biggleswade.'

She had never imagined laughing again, ever, at any-thing. Her snort of amusement turned into a moan as the contraction hit her.

'Breathe,' he said, still tending the fire. 'Breathe and relax.'

'Relax? Are you mad?' Kate lay back, panting. Breath-ing was hard enough.

'No, just male and therefore designed to be unsatis-factory at times like this.' His mouth curved into a smile that she could have sworn was bitter, but it had gone too fast to be certain. 'What is your name?'

Caution resurfaced. She was at his mercy now. If he were not the good man he appeared to be, then there was nothing she could do about it. Her instincts, sharp-ened by the desperate need to protect her baby, told her to gamble and trust him. But with her life, not with her secrets. Should she lie about her name? But that would serve no purpose. 'Catherine Harding. Miss,' she added as an afterthought. Might as well be clear about that. 'My friends call me Kate.'

Dr Rivers began to break the legs off the table and heap the pieces by the fire. Either it was very rotten or he was very strong. She studied the broad shoulders flexing as he worked and decided it was the latter.

'Where's the baby's father?' He did not seem too shocked by her situation, but doctors must be used to maintaining a neutral front, whatever their patients' em-barrassing predicaments.

'Dead.' That *was* a lie and it came without the need for thought. Then, hard on the heels of the single word, the wariness resurfaced. This man seemed kind and promised to help her, but he could still betray her if he knew who she was. And, almost certainly, if he knew what she had been part of. He was a gentleman from his voice, his clothes, his manner. And gentlemen not only helped ladies in distress—or she hoped they did—but they also stuck together, protected each other against criminal conspiracies.

'I'm sorry about that.' Grant Rivers laid the tabletop on the earth floor, heaping up the drier straw on it. He was asking her something. She jerked her mind back to dealing with the present. 'Have you any linen with you? Shifts, petticoats?'

'In my portmanteau. There isn't much.' It had been all she could carry.

He dug into it, efficiently sorting through. A nightgown went on one side, then he began to spread linen over the straw, rolling her two gowns into a pillow.

'Dr—'

'Grant.'

'You are very efficient.' A contraction passed, easier than before. He was making her relax, just as he had said.

'I had a short spell in the army. Even with a batman, one learns to shift for oneself. Now, then.' He eyed her and she felt herself tense again. 'Let's get you into something more comfortable and on to this luxurious bed.' It was getting darker and she could not read his expression. 'Kate, I'm sorry I'm a man, I'm sorry I'm a complete stranger, but we have got to get you into a nightgown and I have got to examine you.' He was brisk, verging on the impatient. 'You're a patient and just now you can't afford to be shy or modest.'

Think of the baby, she told herself. *Think of Grant Rivers as a guardian angel. A Christmas angel, sexless, dispassionate. I have no choice but to trust him.* 'Very well.'

He undressed her like a man who knew his way around

the fastenings of women's clothing. *Not sexless, then.* She was out of her stained, crumpled gown and underclothing before she had time to be embarrassed. He'd placed the nightgown so it had caught a little warmth from the fire and soon she was into that and on to the bed, sighing with relief at the simple comfort of it, before she had the chance to realise her nightgown was up around her waist.

'There, we just place this so.' Grant swung the greatcoat over her. 'Now a light, something hot to drink. Lie back, concentrate on getting warm.'

Kate watched from between slitted eyes as he built up the fire, brought in a bucket of water and set it by the hearth. He lit a small lantern, then dipped water into a mug, adding something from a flask balanced on a brick by the flames, and washed his hands in the bucket. His actions were rapid, yet smooth. *Efficient* was probably the word. A man who wanted to get things done and who wouldn't waste time. A man who was forced to wait on this baby's schedule. Both his efficiency and, strangely, his impatience were reassuring. She was seeing the essence of this man.

'Where did the lantern come from?'

'I carry one in my saddlebags. I'll just find something else for water. We'll need a fair bit before we're done. Luckily the last occupants were fairly untidy and there's a promising rubbish heap outside.'

He ought to seem less than masculine, coping so handily with domestic tasks, but he merely appeared practical. Kate studied the broad shoulders and narrow hips, the easy movement, the tight buckskin breeches. She never expected to feel the slightest flutter of sensual need for a man again as long as she lived, but if she did, purely theoretically, of course, Grant Rivers was more than equipped to provoke it. He was definitely very— *'Ooh!'*

'Hang on, I'll be with you in a minute.' He came back in carrying an assortment of pots, water sloshing out on to the floor. He held out his hands to the fire. 'My fingers are cold again.'

What has that got to do with...? Kate sucked in an outraged breath as, lantern in hand, he knelt at her feet and dived under the greatcoat tented over her knees.

'It is remarkable how one can adapt to circumstances,' she managed after five somewhat stressful minutes. Incredibly she sounded quite rational and not, as she felt, mildly hysterical.

Grant emerged, tousled but composed, and sat back on his heels, shaking thick, dark brown hair back out of his eyes. He smiled, transforming a face she had thought pattern-book handsome into something approaching charming. 'Childbirth tends to result in some unavoidable intimacies,' he said. 'But everything seems to be proceeding as it should.' The smile vanished as he took a pocket watch from his waistcoat and studied it.

'How much longer?' She tried not to make it sound like a demand, but feared it had.

'Hours, I should think. First babies tend to be slow.' He was at the fire, washing his hands in yet another container of water, then pouring something from a flask into a battered kettle with no handle.

'Hours?'

'Drink this.' He offered the brew in a horn beaker, another of the seemingly inexhaustible contents of his saddlebags. 'I'll get some food in a minute. When did you last eat?'

That needed some thought. 'Yesterday. I had break-fast at an inn.'

Grant made no reply, but when he brought her bread and cheese made into a rough sandwich, she noticed he ate nothing. 'What are you going to eat? This is all the food you have with you, isn't it?'

He shrugged and took a mouthful of the liquid in the horn beaker. 'You need the energy. I can live on my fat.'

He rested his head against the rough stone wall behind him and closed his eyes. *What fat?* With a less straight-forward man she might have suspected he was fishing for compliments, but it did not seem to be Grant Riv-ers's style.

What was he doing as a doctor? She puzzled over him, beginning to slip into a doze now the food was warm in her stomach. He was educated, he had been in the army. There was no wedding ring on his finger—not that there was anything to be deduced from that—and there was an engraved signet on his left hand. His clothes were good. And yet he was riding over the Marches without a ser-vant and prepared for a night of rough living.

A piece of wood slipped into the fire with a crackle, jerking her fully awake again. 'How did you hurt your head?' Was he fleeing from something?

'A stupid accident in Edinburgh. I'd been staying with a friend in the New Town and the place is covered in building sites. Some fool of a labourer dropped a plank on me. I was out cold for a couple of days and in no state to move much after that, but there's nothing broken.'

He closed his eyes and she did the same. She let her-self drift off, reassured. She was safe while he was there.

Chapter Two

The night passed with intervals of sleep interrupted by increasing waves of contractions. At some point Kate was conscious of simply abandoning herself to Grant Rivers, to the competent hands, the confident, reassuring voice, the strength of the man. There was no choice now, but her instincts told her this was a good man, and if she was mistaken, there was nothing she could do about it. As time passed, on leaden feet, her trust grew.

She held on to his fingers, squeezing until she felt his bones shift under her grip, but he never complained. He was going to deliver her baby, he was going to save her so she could hold her child in her arms. He was her miracle. She was tired beyond anything she had ever experienced, this was more difficult than she could have imagined and she seemed to have been in this place for years. But it would be all right. Grant Rivers would make it all right.

It was taking too long. Kate was exhausted, the light was dreadful and he had no instruments. He knew full well that if there were complications, he did not have the knowledge to deal with them.

As dawn light filtered through the cobwebbed windows, Grant took a gulp of the neat whisky, scrubbed his hands over his face and faced down the fear. She was *not* going to die, nor was the baby. This time, at this crisis, he could save both mother and child. There was no decision to be made about it, no choice. He had only to hold his nerve, use his brain, and he would cheat death. This time. He stretched, went out to check on the horse, then saw the tree growing at the back of the bothy and smiled.

'Talk to me, Kate. Where do you come from, why are you here, alone on Christmas morning?'

'Not alone.' She opened her eyes. 'You're here, too. Is it really Christmas?'

'Yes. The season's greetings to you.' He showed her the little bunch of berried holly he had plucked from the stunted tree and was rewarded with a smile. *Hell, but she looks dreadful.* Her face was white and lined with strain, her hair was lank and tangled, her eyes bloodshot. She was too thin and had been for some time, he suspected, but she was a fighter.

'How old are you?'

'Twenty-three.'

'Talk to me,' he repeated. 'Where are you from? I live just over the Border in Northumberland.'

'I'm from—' She grimaced and clutched at his bruised hand. 'Suffolk. My brother is a…a country squire. My mother died when he was born, my father was killed in a hunting accident a few years ago. He was a real countryman and didn't care for London. Henry's different, but he's not important or rich or well connected, although he wishes he was. He wanted me to marry well.'

A gentlewoman, then, as he had thought. 'You're of age.' Grant wiped her face with a damp cloth and gave her some more of the warm watered brandy to sip. It should be hot sweet tea, but this was all he had.

She was silent and he guessed she was deciding how much to tell him, how much she trusted him. 'He controls all my money until I marry with his blessing. I fell in love and I was reckless. Naive. I suppose I had a very quiet, sheltered country life until I met Jonathan.' She gave a twisted shrug. 'Jonathan's…dead. Henry said that until I had the baby I must stay at the lodge near Edinburgh that he inherited from an uncle, and then he would… He *said* he would find a good home. But I don't trust him. He'll leave my child at a workhouse or give her to some family who won't love her…' Her voice trailed away. 'I don't trust him.'

It wasn't the entire story. Kate, he was certain, was editing it as she went along. He couldn't blame her. This probably happened all the time, well-bred young women finding themselves in a difficult situation and the family stepping in to deal with the embarrassment, hoping they could find her an unsuspecting husband to take her off their hands later. It was a pity in this case, because Kate, with her fierce determination, would make a good mother, he was sure of that.

He settled back against the wall, her hand in his so he would know when another contraction came, even if he drifted off. He was tired enough to sleep without even the usual nightmares waking him, but Kate's fierce grip would rouse him. How much time was this going to add to his journey? Charlie knew he was coming and he was a sensible boy for his age, but he'd been through too much and he needed his father. *He needs a mother, too.*

There was nothing he could do to hasten things now. He shifted, trying to find a smooth place on the craggy wall, and prodded at the other weight on his conscience, the one he could do nothing about now. Grant had disappointed his grandfather. Not in himself, but in his reluctance to remarry. Over and over again as he grew frailer the old man had repeated his desire to see Grant married. *The boy's a fine lad,* he'd say. *But he needs brothers, he needs a mother... You need a wife.*

Time and time again Grant had repeated the same weary excuses. He needed more time, he had to find the right woman, to get it right this time. He just needed *time.* To do what? Somehow learn to read the character of the pretty young things paraded on the marriage mart? Discover insights he hadn't possessed before, so he didn't make another disastrous mistake? His own happiness didn't matter, not any more, but he couldn't risk Charlie. *I promise,* he had said the last time he parted from his grandfather. *I promise I will find someone.* And he had left for the Continent, yet again.

He neither needed nor wanted a wife, not for himself, but Abbeywell needed a chatelaine and Charlie needed a woman's care.

'What will you do when the baby is born?' he asked, focusing on the exhausted woman beside him.

'Do next? I don't know,' she said. 'I can't think beyond this. There is no one. But I'll manage...somehow.'

She's not a conventional beauty, but she's got courage, she's maternal. Time seemed to have collapsed, the past and the present ran together. Two women in childbed, one infant he could not help, one perhaps he would save. But even if he did, nothing would prevent this child being born illegitimate, with all the penalties that imposed.

The germ of an idea stirred. Kate needed shelter, security for her child. Would she make a good governess for Charlie? He pursued the idea around. Charlie had a tutor, he did not need someone with the ability or knowledge to teach him academic studies. But he did need the softer things. Grant remembered his own mother, who had died, along with his father, of a summer fever when he had not been much older than his own son was now. She had instilled ideas about kindliness and beauty, she had been there with a swift hug and a kiss when male discipline and bracing advice was just that bit too harsh.

A mother's touch, a mother's instinct. Kate was not a mother yet, but he sensed that nurturing disposition in her. Charlie didn't need a governess, he needed a mother. Logic said…*marry her.*

What was he thinking? *I'm too tired to think straight, my brain's still scrambled.*

In the stable the gelding snorted, gave a piercing whinny. Grant got to his feet, went to the outer door and peered through the faint mist the drizzle had left behind it. A couple of men, agricultural workers by the looks of them, were plodding along the track beside a donkey cart. He went back inside and Kate looked up at him. Her smile was faint, but it was there. *Brave girl. Are you wishing for the impossible? Because I think it is walking towards us now.*

'We're still in Scotland,' he said, realising that his mad idea was possible to achieve. *Am I insane? Or are those strangers out there, appearing right on the heels of that wild thought, some kind of sign?* 'There are two men, farmers, coming along the track.' *Witnesses.* 'Kate—marry me.'

'Marry you?'

It was hard to concentrate on anything except what was happening to her, anything beyond the life inside that was struggling to be free. Kate dragged her mind back from its desperate focus on breathing, on the baby, on keeping them both alive. She remembered the mix of truth and lies she had told him and stared at Grant.

In the gloom of early-morning light he did not appear to have lost his mind, despite the blow to the head. He still looked as much like a respectable, handsome English gentleman as might be expected after a sleepless night in a hovel tending to a woman in childbed.

'I am not married, I am not promised to another. I can support a wife, I can support the baby. And if you marry me before the child is born, then it will be legitimate.' His voice was urgent, his expression in the morning light intent. He smiled, as though to reassure her, but the warmth did not reach his eyes.

'Legitimate.' *Legitimate.* Her child would have a name, a future, respectability. They would both be safe and Grant could protect her from the results of Henry's scheming. Probably. Kate rode out another contraction, tried to think beyond the moment, recall *why* she couldn't simply solve this problem by marrying a complete stranger. He could certainly hide her, even if unwittingly. She would have a new name, a new home, and that was all that mattered for the baby.

She was so very tired now, nothing else except her child seemed important. Grant was a doctor living in the wilds of Northumberland, hundreds of miles from London. That should be safe enough. But why would he? Why would he want her and her baby, another man's child? *Legitimate. We would be hidden.* The tempting words swirled through her tired brain, caution fighting desperation and instinct. 'But there's no time.'

'This is Scotland,' Grant said. 'All we have to do is to declare ourselves married before witnesses—and two are heading this way. Say *yes*, Kate, and I'll fetch them and it will be done.'

'Yes.' He was gone before she could call the words back. She heard his voice raised to hail someone. *Yes, I will do it. Another miracle to go with my good angel of a doctor. A Christmas miracle. He never need find out the truth, so it can't hurt him. What is the term? An accessory after the fact. But if he doesn't know...*

'Aye, we'll help you and gladly, at that. I'm Tam Johnson of the Red House up yonder and this is my eldest son, Willie.' The accent was broad Border Scots. 'You're lucky to catch us. We're only going this way to do a favour for a neighbour.'

There was the sound of shuffling feet outside and Grant ducked back in. 'May they come through now?' Kate nodded and he stood aside for two short, burly, black-haired men to enter.

They seemed to fill the space and brought with them the smell of wet sheep and heather and peat smoke. 'Good morning to you, mistress.' The elder stood there, stolid and placid. Perhaps he attended marriages in tumbledown cottages every day of the week. Beside him the younger one twisted his cap in his hands, less at ease than the man who was obviously his father.

'Good day,' she managed, beyond embarrassment or social awkwardness now.

Grant produced a notebook, presumably from his capacious saddlebags. She wondered vaguely if he had a packhorse out there. 'I assume we need a written record that you can sign?'

'Aye, that'll be best. You'll be English, then? All you both need to do is declare yourselves married. To each other, that is.' The older Mr Johnson gave a snort of amusement at his own wit.

'Right.' Grant crossed the small distance and knelt beside her, took her hand in his. 'I, Grantham Phillip Hale Rivers, declare before these witnesses that I take you, Catherine—'

'Jane Penelope Harding,' she whispered. He was only a doctor. They did not put announcements of their marriages in London newspapers.

'Catherine Jane Penelope Harding, as my wife.'

Another contraction was coming. She gritted her teeth and managed, 'Before these witnesses, I, Catherine Jane Penelope Harding, declare that I take you, Grantham Phillip…Hale Rivers, to be my husband.'

'We'll write the record outside, I think.'

She was vaguely conscious of Grant standing, moving the Johnsons out of the room, then her awareness shrank to the pain and the effort. Something was happening, something different…

Where was Grant? She listened and heard him, still in the stable.

'Thank you, gentlemen.' There was the chink of coins. 'I hope you'll drink to our health. You'll bring the donkey cart back down here after noon?'

'Aye, we will, no trouble at all.' That was the older man, Tam Johnson. 'You'll not find it far to Jedburgh now the rain's stopped. You'll be there by nightfall. Thank you kindly, sir, and blessings on your wife and bairn.'

'Grant!'

He ducked under the low lintel and back into the inner room. 'I'm here.'

'Something's happening.'

'I should hope so.' He took up the lamp. 'Let's see what this child of ours is doing.'

Grant made her feel secure, Kate thought hazily. Even in those last hectic minutes she had felt safe and when the first indignant wails rent the air he had known just what to do.

'Here she is,' he'd said, laying the squirming, slippery, red-faced baby on her stomach. 'The most beautiful little girl in the world at this minute and very cross with the pair of us by the sound of her.'

Time had passed, the world had gone by somewhere outside the bubble that contained her and the child in her arms. She was conscious of Grant moving purposefully about. At some point he took the baby and washed her and wrapped her up in one of his clean shirts, then washed Kate and helped her into a clean nightgown and wrapped them both up in his coat.

There was something hot to drink, porridge to eat. Perhaps the Johnsons had left food or had come back. She neither knew nor cared. When Grant had spoken to her, asked her if she could bear to travel, she had nodded. He had sounded urgent, so she made herself agree, told herself that he would take care of them and all she had to do was hold her baby safe at her breast.

It was bumpy at first, and her nose, about all that was exposed, was cold, but that was all right because Grant was there. Then they were in his arms again and there was noise and people talking, women's voices, warmth and a soft bed. They must have stopped at an inn to rest.

Kate looked up at him standing over her, looking dishevelled and very tired. And...*sad*? This was the man she had married. It seemed unreal. 'Thank you.'

'My pleasure.' He sounded almost convincing. 'What are we going to call her?'

'Anna, after my mother.' She'd decided that in the course of the bumpy journey. *Anna Rivers. And I am Mrs Rivers now. We are safe and all at the cost of a few lies.* Not little, not white, but she would be a good wife to him, be happy in her modest home. He would never know.

'Anna Rosalind, then, for my mother.' When she looked up, surprised by the possessive note in Grant's voice, he shrugged. 'She's an important small person, she needs at least two names. I've found you a nursemaid. She's used to newborns.' A cheerful freckled face appeared at his side. 'This is Jeannie Tranter and she's happy to adventure into England with us. It isn't far now, only across the border into Northumberland.'

'Oh, good.'

I wonder whereabouts in Northumberland Grant lives...but it doesn't matter, we're safe now, both of us, hundreds of miles away from Henry, hundreds of miles away from a vengeful earl and the law. We can go anywhere and no one will take her away from me because she belongs to Grant now. That was all that mattered. *We both belong to him.*

The thought drifted in and she frowned. Her baby had a father, but she had a husband. A man she did not know, a man who had total control over her life, her future.

Something touched her hair and she opened her eyes. Grant was still looking down at them. She remembered to smile at him, then turned her attention back to the baby.

* * *

'I'll take a bath, then I'll be in the parlour if you need me,' Grant said to Jeannie Tranter.

The girl nodded briskly, her attention on the woman and baby in the bed. 'Aye, sir, I'm sure we won't need to disturb you.'

And that's put me in my place as an unnecessary male. It had been the same the last time. *Don't think about the last time.* The bathwater in front of the fire was still hot, the pleasure of scrubbing away the grime of the past twenty-four hours or so blissful. He soaped his hair, ducked under and came up streaming, then found he had no inclination to get out. Baths were good places to think.

Grant had dozed a little, then woke without any sensible thinking done at all to find the water cool. He splashed out to dry off and find something from his depleted wardrobe to change into. A childbirth used up an inordinate amount of clean linen.

By the time he was in the private parlour pouring a glass of wine, his legs stretched out on the hearthrug, his brain had woken up. Just what had he done? A good deed? Perhaps, although tying a woman, a complete stranger, to him for life was a risky act of charity. Or was it an entirely selfish act, a gesture to his guilty conscience, as though he could somehow appease his grandfather's shade by doing what the old man had so wanted and thus fulfilling his promise? The uncomfortable notion intruded that he had found himself a wife and a stepmother for Charlie without any effort at courtship, without any agonising about choices.

The easy way out? Too late to worry about motives, I've done it now. And the child's a girl, so no need to worry about the inheritance, should it ever arise, God forbid. He'd married a plain woman of genteel birth with a social-climbing brother who was going to be very pleased indeed when he discovered who his new brother-in-law was. That could be a problem if he wasn't careful. Grant rolled the wine around his mouth as he thought it all through.

Pushing doubts aside, he had someone to look after the household, someone who appeared to be bright enough not to be a dead bore on the occasions when he was at home. And Kate had courage and determination, that was obvious enough. He had a wife and only time would tell if it had been a wise decision or a reckless gamble.

There were fifty miles to cover tomorrow, over moorland and open country. If the roads were good and the weather held, they'd do it in the day and he would be only one day later than he had hoped. The inn had a decent chaise for hire, the stables held some strong horses by the looks of them—and they'd be needed, because there wouldn't be a change to be had until they were over the border. The gelding was sound now, it had only been a bruised hoof.

The rhyme 'For Want of a Nail' ran through his head. In that old poem the loss of the nail meant the loss of the shoe, the loss of the horse and its rider and, eventually, the loss of the battle and a kingdom. Because of his own haste his horse had been lamed, he'd had to stop and he'd gained a wife and child. Grant got up and rang for his supper and another bottle. He was maundering, comparing a disaster to—what? What crazy optimism made him think this marriage between two desperate strangers could be anything *but* a disaster?

Chapter Three

'Mr Rivers is a very good rider, is he not, ma'am?'

'Hmm?' From her position lying full length Kate couldn't see more than the occasional treetop passing by. 'Is he?'

Jeannie, the nursemaid, stared at her. 'But surely you've seen him riding, ma'am?'

'Yes. Yes, of course. I don't know what is the matter with me.'

'Not to worry, Mrs Rivers. My nana, who taught me all about looking after mothers and babies, she always said that the mother's mind is off with the fairies for days after the birth.'

My mind is certainly somewhere and I wish it would come back, because I need to think. Anna was sleeping soundly in the nurse's arms and Jeannie seemed exceedingly competent. The chaise had an extension at the front so that when the wall section below the front window was removed it could be placed in front of the seat to make a bed where a passenger could stretch out almost full length. Kate had slept heavily and although she felt weak and shaky she was, surely, in a fit state to take responsibility for herself. She should be thinking about what she had done and what the consequences would be.

I have married the man, for goodness' sake! A complete stranger. What is his family going to say? Grant was persuasive enough, but surely he couldn't convince them that he was the legitimate father of this child by a mother they'd heard nothing about before?

'I want to sit up.' Lying like this made her feel feeble and dependent. Besides, she wanted to see what Mr Rivers—what her husband—looked like on a horse.

Jeannie handed her Anna and helped her sit up. That was better. Two days of being flat on her back like a stranded turtle probably accounted for her disorientation. Kate studied the view from the chaise window. It consisted of miles of sodden moorland, four horses with two postilions and one husband cantering alongside.

Jeannie was a good judge of horsemanship. Grant Rivers was relaxed in the saddle, displaying an impressive length of leg, a straight back and a steady gaze on the road ahead. His profile was austere and, she thought, very English. Brown hair was visible below his hat brim. What colour were his eyes? Surely she should have noticed them? Hazel, or perhaps green. For some reason she had a lingering memory of sadness. But then she'd hardly been in a fit state to notice anything. Or anyone.

But she had better start noticing now. This was her husband. Husbands were for life and she had begun this marriage with a few critical untruths. But they could do Grant no harm, she told herself as she lay down again and let Jeannie tuck her in. There was this one day to regain some strength and get some sleep, then there would be a family to face and Anna to look after in the midst of strangers. But by then she would have her story quite clear in her head and she would be safe in the rustic isolation of the far north of England.

They stopped at three inns—small, isolated, primitive. Jeannie helped her out to the privy, encouraged her to eat and drink, cradled the baby between feeds. Her new husband came to look at her, took her pulse, frowned. Looked at Anna, frowned. Swung back on to his horse, frowned as he urged the postilions to greater speed. What was so urgent? Anyone would think it was life and death.

'I think we must be here, ma'am.' The post-chaise rocked to a halt. Kate struggled up into a sitting position and looked around. Darkness had fallen, but the house was lit and lanterns hung by the front door. Away from the light, the building seemed to loom in the darkness. Surely this was bigger than the modest home a country gentleman-doctor might aspire to?

She looked for Grant, but he was already out of the saddle, the reins trailing on the ground as he strode up the front steps. The doors opened, more light flooded out, she heard the sound of voices. She dropped the window and heard him say, 'When?' sharply and another voice replied, 'In the morning, the day before yesterday.'

Grant came back down the steps. 'In you come.'

'Where are we?' But he was already lifting her out, carrying her in his arms across to the steps. 'Anna—'

'I have her, Mrs Rivers. I'm right behind you, ma'am.'

'This is Abbeywell Grange, your new home.'

There was a tall, lean man, all in black, who bowed as Grant swept her in through the front door. A butler, she supposed, fleetingly conscious of a well-lit hall, a scurry of footmen. The smell of burning applewood, a trace of dried rose petals, beeswax polish, leather. There

were evergreen wreaths on the newel posts of the stairs,
the glow of red berries in a jug. She remembered Grant's
offering of the holly sprig and smiled. This was an old,
loved home, its aura sending messages of reassurance.
She wanted to relax and dared not.

'Welcome home, my lord. We are all very relieved
to see you. The staff join me in expressing our deepest
condolences.'

Condolences? On a marriage? Then the whole sentence hit her. 'My lord? Grant, he called you *my lord*.
Who are you?'

But the butler was already striding ahead towards the
end of the hall, Grant on his heels. 'Master Charles…
Lord Brooke, I should say, will be happy to see you, my
lord. It has been quite impossible to get him to go to bed.'

'Who is Lord Brooke?' she asked in a whisper as the
butler opened the door into a drawing room. A fire crackled in the grate, an aged pointer dog rose creakily to its
feet, tail waving, and, on the sofa, a small boy sat up,
rubbing his eyes.

'Papa!'

'Charlie, why aren't you in bed? You're keeping Rambler up.' Grant snapped his fingers at the dog. It was obviously an old joke. The boy grinned, then his eyes widened
as he saw what his father was carrying.

Grant settled Kate in a deep armchair by the hearthside and Jeannie, with Anna in her arms, effaced herself
somewhere in the shadows.

'Charlie.' There was deep affection in Grant's voice
as he crouched down and the boy hurled himself into
his arms. So, this was why he had been so impatient to
get back, this was what the discovery of a woman in labour had been keeping him from. *He has a son. He was*

married? A lord? This was a disaster and she had no inkling how to deal with it.

'You got my letter explaining about the accident?' The boy nodded, pushed back Grant's hair and touched the bandage with tentative fingers. She saw his eyes were reddened and heavy. The child had been crying. 'It's all right now, but I'm sorry I wasn't here when you needed me. Then on my way from Edinburgh my horse picked up a stone and was lamed with a bruised hoof, so I lost a day and a night.'

'Great-Grandpapa died on Christmas Eve,' Charlie said. His lower lip trembled. 'And you didn't come and I thought perhaps you'd… Your head… That they'd been lying to me and you were going to…'

'I'm here.' Grant pulled the boy into a fierce hug, then stood him back so he could look him squarely in the face. 'I'm a bit battered and there were a couple of days when I was unconscious, which is why I couldn't travel, but we've hard heads, we Rivers men, haven't we?'

The lip stopped trembling. 'Like rocks,' the boy said stoutly. 'I'm glad you're home, though. It was a pretty rotten Christmas.' His gaze left his father's face, slid round to Kate. 'Papa?'

Grant got up from his knees, one hand on his son's shoulder, and turned towards her, but Kate had already started to rise. She walked forward and stopped beside Grant.

'My dear, allow me to introduce Charles Francis Ellmont Rivers, Lord Brooke. My son.'

Kate retrieved a smile from somewhere. 'I… Good evening, Charles. I am very pleased to meet you.'

He bowed, a very creditable effort for a lad of— what? Six? 'Madam.' He tugged at Grant's hand. 'Papa, you haven't said who this lady is, so I cannot greet her properly.'

'This is Catherine Rivers, my wife. Your stepmama.'

Kate felt the smile congeal on her lips. Of course, if Charles was Grant's son, then she was his...

'Stepmama?' The boy had turned pale. 'You didn't say that you were going to get married again, Papa.'

'No. I am allowed some secrets.' Grant apparently agreed with the Duke of Wellington's approach: never explain, never apologise. 'You have a new half-sister as well, Charlie.' He beckoned to Jeannie and she came forward and placed Anna in his arms. 'Come and meet her, she is just two days old.'

The boy peered at the little bundle. 'She's very small and her face is all screwed up and red.'

'So was yours when you were born, I expect,' Kate said with a glare for Grant over Charlie's head. 'Why didn't you tell me?' she mouthed. *The boy isn't a love child. He's the product of a first marriage. I married a widower. And a nobleman.* She wrestled with the implications of Charlie having a title. It meant Grant was an earl, at least. Which meant that Anna was Lady Anna, and she was—what?

Earls put marriage announcements in newspapers. Earls had wide social circles and sat in the House of Lords. In London.

'There never seemed to be a good time.' Grant gave a half shrug that suddenly made her furious. He should have warned her, explained. She would never have agreed to marry him.

'What is her name?' Charlie asked, oblivious to the byplay. Anna woke up and waved a fist at him and he took it, very carefully.

'Anna Rosalind.' One starfish hand had closed on Charlie's finger. His face was a mixture of panic and delight. 'Would you like to hold her?'

'Yes, please.'

Grant placed her in Charlie's arms.

'Very carefully,' Kate said, trying not to panic. 'Firm but gentle, and don't let her head flop. That's it—you are obviously a natural as a big brother.' She was rewarded by a huge grin. She could only admire Grant's tactics. The surprise of a new baby sister had apparently driven Charlie's doubts about a stepmama right out of his head.

'Grant,' she said, soft-voiced, urgent, as Jeannie helped the boy to sit securely on the sofa and held back the inquisitive hound. 'Who *are* you?'

'The fourth Earl of Allundale. As of two days ago.'

'I suppose that was something else that there was no time to mention?' Again that shrug, the taut line of his lips that warned her against discussing this now.

Her husband was an earl. But he was also a doctor, and heirs to earldoms did not become doctors, she knew that. It was a conundrum she was too weary to try to understand now. All she could grasp was that she had married far above her wildest expectations, into a role she had no idea how to fill, into a position that was dangerously exposed and public. Even in her home village the social pages in the newspapers were studied and gossiped about, the business of the aristocracy known about, from the gowns worn at drawing rooms to the latest scandals. How could the wife of an earl hide away? But Grant had no need to fear she would make a scene in front of his son: unless they were thrown out into the dark, she found she was beyond caring about anything but warmth, shelter and Anna's safety this night.

'You are worn out. Charlie, give your sister back to her nurse and off you go to bed. I'll come and see you are asleep later.' Grant reached for the bell pull and the butler appeared so rapidly that he must have been standing right outside the door. 'Grimswade, can you dispatch Master Charles to his tutor? And you will have prepared my wife's rooms by now, I've no doubt.'

Grimswade stood aside as Charlie made a very correct bow to Kate, then ducked through the open door. 'Certainly, my lord. His late lordship had some renovation work done. In anticipation,' he added.

Grant stilled with his hand on the bell pull. 'Not the old suite?' His voice was sharp.

'No, my lord, not the old suite. The one on the other side of your own chambers. The doors have been changed. One blocked up, another cut through. His late lordship anticipated that you would wish to retain your old rooms even after he had…gone.'

Kate wondered if she would have to stand there all night while they discussed the interior layout of the house. She didn't care where she slept as long as it had a bed, somewhere for Anna, and the roof was not actually leaking.

'Very well. Have you made arrangements for the child and her nurse?'

'Yes, my lord.' Without any change in voice or expression Grimswade managed to express mild affront at the suggestion that he was in any way unprepared. 'My lady, if you would care to follow me.'

That is me. I am—what? A countess?

'I'll carry you.' Grant was halfway across the room.

'Thank you, no. Do stay here.' Something, Kate was not sure what, revolted at the thought of being carried. Grant

Rivers's arms—her *husband's* arms—were temptingly strong, but she was tired of being helpless and he was altogether too inclined to take charge. She had to start thinking for herself again and being held so easily against that broad chest seemed to knock rational thought out of her brain.

In a daze she managed the stairs, the long corridor, then the shock of the sitting room, elegant and feminine, all for her.

'I will have a light supper served, my lady. The men are filling your bath in the bathing chamber next to the dressing room through there.' Grimswade gestured towards the double doors that opened on to a bedchamber, one larger than she had ever slept in. 'And this is Wilson, your maid.'

'Luxury,' Kate murmured to Jeannie as the butler bowed himself out and the maid, a thin, middle-aged woman, advanced purposefully across the room. 'Too much. This is not real.' Fortunately the sofa was directly behind her as she sank back on to it, her legs refusing to hold her up any longer.

'You're just worn out, ma'am—my lady—that's all.' Jeannie's soft brogue was comforting. With a sigh Kate allowed herself to be comforted. 'It will all come back to you.'

The next hour was a blur that slowly, slowly came back into focus. Firm hands undressing her, supportive arms to help her to the bathing room, the bliss of hot water and being completely clean. The same hands drying and dressing her as though she was as helpless as little Anna. A table with food, apparently appearing from thin air. The effort to eat.

And then, as she lay back on the piled pillows of a

soft bed, there was Anna in her arms, grizzling a little because she was hungry, and Kate found she was awake, feeling stronger and, for the first time in days, more like herself.

'We might be confused and out of place,' Kate said as she handed the baby back to Jeannie after the feed, 'but Anna seems perfectly content.'

'You've not stayed here before, then, my lady?'

'No. I'm a stranger to this house.' *And to my husband.* 'Where are you to sleep, Jeannie?'

'They've set up a bed for me in the dressing room, my lady, just for tonight. It's bigger than the whole of the upstairs of our cottage,' she confided with glee. 'And there's a proper cradle for Lady Anna.'

'Then you take yourself off and get some rest now. I expect she'll be waking you up again soon enough.'

The canopy over the bed was lined with pleated seagreen silk, the curtains around the bed and at the windows were a deeper shade, the walls, paler. The furniture was light and, to Kate's admittedly inexperienced eye, modern and fashionable. The paintings and the pieces of china arranged around the room seemed very new, too. Strange, in such an old house. The drawing room, the hallway and stairs had an antique air, of generations of careful choices of quality pieces and then attentive housekeeping to deepen the polished patina.

Kate threw back the covers and slid out of bed. Deep-pile carpet underfoot, the colours fresh and springlike in the candlelight. Grant had reacted sharply when her chambers were mentioned. Interior decoration seemed a strange thing to be concerned about, given the circumstances— surely a new wife who was a stranger, another man's baby

carrying his own name, a bereavement and a son to comfort must be enough to worry about. *Another puzzle.*

She moved on unsteady legs about the room, admiring
it, absorbing the warmth and luxury as she had with the
food earlier, feeling the weariness steal over her again. In
a moment she would return to the big bed and be able to
sleep. Tomorrow she would think. There was a murmur of
voices, just audible. Idly curious, Kate followed the sound
until she reached a jib door, papered and trimmed so it
looked at first glance like part of the wall it was cut into.

The handle moved easily, soundlessly, under the pressure of her hand, and it swung inwards to show her a
segment of another bedchamber. Masculine, deep-red
hangings, old panelling polished to a glow, the glint of
gilded picture frames. Grant's bedchamber. For the first
time the words *husband* and *bed* came together in her
mind and her breathing hitched.

On the table beside the door was a small pile of pack-
ages wrapped in silver paper. She glanced down and read
the label on the top one. *Papa, all my love for Christmas.
Charlie.* It was obviously his very best handwriting. Her
vision blurred.

Grant's voice jerked her back. He must be speaking to
his valet. She began to ease the door closed. 'Thank you
for coming by. Tomorrow I'd be grateful if you'd take a
look at my wife and the baby. They both seem well to my
eye, especially given the circumstances—Kate must be
very tired—but I won't be easy until a doctor has confirmed it.'

Another doctor? Kate left the door an inch ajar. There
was a chuckle, amused, masculine, with an edge of teasing to it. 'It seems to me that you did very well, given

that you've never been trained for a childbirth. Or were you, in the year you left Edinburgh?'

'I observed one. I had, thank Asclepius and any other gods that look after inept medical students, studied the relevant sections of the textbooks before I did so and some of it must have stuck. I'd just about reached the limits of my book learning, though, and after the last time—'

The other man made some comment, his voice low and reassuring, but Kate did not register the words. *Grant is not qualified? He is not a doctor.* The embossed metal of the door handle bit into her fingers. *He lied to me.* The irony of her indignation at the deception struck her, which did nothing for her temper.

'I thought perhaps so much experience with brood mares might have helped, but I can tell you, it didn't,' Grant confessed.

Brood mares. He thought he could deliver my baby as though she were a foal.

She heard Grant say goodnight to his visitor as she set foot in his bedchamber. He turned from closing the door and saw her. 'Kate, what's wrong? Can't you sleep?'

'You are not a doctor.' He came towards her and it took only two steps to be close enough to jab an accusing finger into his chest. 'You delivered my baby, you told me not to worry. You fraud!'

Chapter Four

Grant stepped back sharply, the concern wiped from his expression. 'I have two years of medical training, which is more than anyone else within reach had. There *was* no one else to deliver your baby.'

'You might have told me.' She sat down abruptly on the nearest chair. 'You thought you could treat me like a brood mare.'

'Ah, you heard that. Damn. Look, Kate, you were frightened, in pain, and you hadn't the first idea what to do. You needed to be calm, to conserve your strength. If I had told you I had never delivered a baby before, would that have helped you relax? Would that have helped you be calm?'

She glared at him, furious that he was being perfectly reasonable, when something inside her, the same something that had latched on to those words, *husband* and *bed*, wanted nothing more than to panic and make a fuss. And run away.

Grant stood there, patient—and yet impatient, just as he had been in the bothy. He was good at self-control, she realised. If he wasn't so distracted by grief for his grandfather and worry for his son, she would not be allowed a glimpse of that edginess. And he was right, perfectly right. He had some knowledge and that was better than none. He had kept her calm and safe. Alive. Anna was healthy. Kate swallowed. 'I am sorry. You are quite correct, of course. I am just...'

'Embarrassed, very tired and somewhat emotional.'

'Yes,' she agreed. *And confused. Damn him for being so logical and practical and right, when I just want to hit out at something. Someone.* 'You did not tell me you are an earl.' She had wanted to hide, go to ground. Now she was in the sort of marriage that appeared in society pages, was the stuff of gossip.

Grant ran his hand through his hair. He was tired, she realised. Very tired. How much sleep had he had since he had walked into that hovel and found her? Little, she supposed, and he was travelling with a recent head injury. 'I didn't think it relevant and you weren't in any fit state for conversation.' His mouth twisted. 'My grandfather was dying, or had just died. I was not there and I did not want to talk about it. Or think about it. All I wanted was to get back to Charlie.'

'Were you too late to see your grandfather because of me?'

Grant shook his head and sat down opposite her. It was more of a controlled collapse than anything, long legs sprawled out, his head tipped back, eyes closed. The bandage gave him a rakish air, the look of a pirate after a battle. 'No, I wouldn't have reached him in time, not after the accident in Edinburgh. But even so, there was no choice but to stay with you—he would have expected it himself.'

No, she supposed there hadn't been a decision to make. No one could walk away from someone in the situation she had been in. No decent person, at any rate. She had married a decent man. Her agitation calmed as she looked at him, studied his face properly for the first time. She was thinking only of herself and Anna, but she owed him a debt. The least she could do was to think about his needs. 'I'm sorry. Go to bed. You are worn out.'

Grant shook his head and opened his eyes. They were green, she realised with a jolt, seeing the man and not simply her rescuer. But a warm green verging on hazel, not the clear green of a gemstone under water... 'Soon. I need to look in on Charlie.'

She was not going to exhaust him more by complaining about the fact he had not told her he had been married, that he had a son as well as a title. That could keep until the morning. She was certainly not going to look for any more resemblances to Jonathan. 'I will go back to bed, then. Goodnight.'

There was silence until she was through the jib door. She wondered if he had fallen asleep after all. Then, 'Goodnight, Kate.' She closed the door softly behind her.

'Goodnight, Kate. Goodnight, *wife*,' Grant added in a whisper as the door closed. Perhaps he should have kissed her. Poor creature, she looked dreadful. Pale, with dark shadows under bloodshot eyes, her hair pulled back into a mousy tail, her face pinched with exhaustion and a confusion of embarrassment and uncertainty. He could only hope that when she was recovered and suitably dressed she would at least look like a lady, if not a countess.

He hauled himself to his feet and stripped off his clothes with a grimace of relief. He felt as if he'd spent the past year in them. Naked, he stood and washed rapidly, then rummaged in the clothes press and pulled out loose trousers, a shirt and a robe, dressing without conscious thought. Comfort, something he could catnap in if Charlie needed him to stay and chase away nightmares, these would do. His eye caught the glint of silver paper and he went to investigate. Christmas presents. He picked them up, torn between grief and pleasure.

When he slid quietly into Charlie's room the mounded covers on the bed heaved and a mop of dark blond hair emerged. 'Papa!'

'I had hoped you were asleep by now.' Grant sat on the edge of the bed and indulged himself with a hug that threatened to strangle him. 'Urgh! You're too strong for me.'

Charlie chuckled, a six-year-old's naughty laugh, and let go. He looked up at Grant from under his lashes. 'I'm glad you're home.'

'So am I. I'm sorry I was not here when Great-Grandpapa died.'

'Dr Meldreth took me in to see him. He was very sleepy and he told me that he was very old, so he was all worn out and he wanted to go and be with Great-Grandmama, so I mustn't be sad when he left. But I am.'

'I know, Charlie, so am I. And we will be for a while, then we'll remember all the good times we had, and all the things we used to talk about and do, and you won't feel so bad. What did you do on Christmas Day?'

'We went for a walk and to church, and then I opened my presents because Great-Grandpapa said I must do so.' He sniffed. 'He gave me his watch. I...I blubbed a bit, but it made me really proud, so I'm glad. And thank you very much for the model soldiers and the castle and the new boots. Then we had Christmas dinner and Mr

Gough showed me how to make a toast. So I toasted *absent friends*, for both you and Great-Grandpapa.'

'It sounds to me as if the household was in very good hands with you in charge, Charlie.' Grant managed to get his voice under control, somehow. 'I found my presents— shall I open them now?'

Grant went to retrieve the gifts and they opened them together. His grandfather had given him a miniature of his parents, newly painted, he realised, from the large in-dividual portraits that hung in the Long Gallery. He read the note that accompanied it, blew his nose without any attempt to conceal his emotion and turned to Charlie's gift, which he had set aside.

'This is excellent!' It was a large, enthusiastic and al-most recognisable portrait of Rambler, his old pointer dog, framed in a somewhat lopsided, and obviously home-made, frame. 'I will hang it in my study next to the desk. Thank you, Charlie. You go to sleep now. Do you want me to spend the night here?'

'I'm all right now you are home, Papa. And Mr Gough let me talk to him all I wanted. He thought it would be better after the funeral when we can say goodbye again.'

The tutor had proved as sensitive as he had hoped when he hired him. 'You know where I am if you want to come along in the night.' Grant tucked his son in, bent down and gave him a kiss that, for once, didn't have his son squirming away in embarrassment. He seemed to understand and to be taking it well, but he was so young. Grant felt a pang of anxiety through the haze of weari-ness that was closing in like fog. Perhaps he would sleep without nightmares if he was this tired.

'I didn't know you were going to get married again,

Papa.' The voice from under the blankets was already drowsy.

Neither did I. 'Go to sleep, Charlie. I'll explain in the morning.' *Somehow. And I hope to heaven that you take to your new mother and sister, and she takes to you, because if not I've created the most damnable mess.*

'She's being a little angel, my lady.' Jeannie tucked the sleeping baby back into the crib she had brought into the sitting room while Kate was feeding Anna. Fed, clean and cuddled, she truly was sleeping like a small, rather red-faced cherub.

Kate, fresh from Wilson's best, and exhausting, efforts to turn her into something approaching a respectable lady, retreated to the sanctuary of the sofa next to the crib. Wilson was handicapped by an absence of any gowns to dress her in, to say nothing of Kate's figure, which, it was obvious, was not going to spring back instantly into what had been before. A drab, ill-fitting gown that was seriously the worse for wear was not helped by a headful of fine mousy hair that was in dire need of the attentions of a hairdresser.

She looked a frump, and an unhealthy one at that, she knew. Her husband, once rested and with a view of her in a good light, was going to be bitterly rueing his impetuous, gallant gesture.

His knock came on the thought and Kate twitched at the shawl Wilson had found in an effort to drape her body as flatteringly as possible. A harassed glance at her reflection in the glass over the fireplace confirmed that the wrap's shades of green and brown did nothing to help her complexion.

'Good morning. May I come in? Did you sleep well?'

The dark smudges were stark under Grant's eyes and the strong-boned face seemed fined down to its essentials. The rakish bandage had gone, leaving the half-healed cut and angry bruising plain across his forehead.

'Good morning. Yes, of course.'

She was not going to huddle on the sofa, trying to hide. She might look a fright, but she had her pride. Kate swung her feet down to the floor, pushed her shoulders back, lifted her chin and curved the corners of her mouth up. That felt very strange, as though she had not smiled properly in months. Perhaps she had not, except at Anna.

'Dr Meldreth is here, Kate. I think it would be a good idea if he checked you and Anna over.'

'He studied with you in Edinburgh, I gather?' He nodded. 'But unlike you is actually qualified?' That was a sharp retort—she could have bitten her tongue. If it were not for Grant's time at the university, he would have been far less capable of helping her bring Anna safely into the world.

'Exceedingly well qualified,' Grant said before she had a chance to soften her words. He kept any annoyance out of his voice, but his expression hardened. He must think he had married a shrew. 'I'll show him in, shall I?'

He didn't wait for her nod, but ushered in a short, freckled, cheerful man about his age. 'My dear, Dr Meldreth. Meldreth—Lady Allundale. I'll leave you together and I'll be in my study when you've finished, Meldreth.'

Kate summoned her two female supporters and managed to produce a calm, friendly smile for the doctor. He examined Anna and then, swiftly and tactfully, Kate, maintaining a steady flow of conversation while he did so. *Excellent bedside manner,* Kate decided. She felt confident in having him as their doctor.

'You are both in excellent health and the little one is just as she should be,' he assured her when she rejoined him in the sitting room. 'But you need to rest, Lady Allundale. Rivers told me what a rough time you've had of it and I don't think you have been eating very well, have you? Not for quite a while.'

'Probably not, Doctor.'

He closed his bag and straightened his cuffs with a glance at Wilson and Jeannie. It seemed he wanted privacy. Kate nodded to the other women. 'Thank you, I will ring when I need you.' When they were alone she made herself look him in the eye. 'There was something you wished to say to me?'

'I will be frank. I am aware that your marriage only just preceded little Anna's birth. I am also aware that Grant will fudge the issue, making it seem that yours was a long-standing relationship and that the marriage took place some time ago, but was kept quiet. Probably his grandfather's ill health can be made to account for that.'

'I assume that, as a doctor, you will exercise professional discretion.'

'Certainly.' He did not appear surprised by the chill in her voice. 'I simply wished to make the point that—' He broke off and cursed softly under his breath. 'This is more difficult than I thought it would be. I wanted to assure you that I will give you all the support I can. I also wonder just how much of Grant's past history you are aware of.'

She could freeze him out, look down her nose and assume the air of a thoroughly affronted countess or she could take the hand of friendship he appeared to be offering her. She needed a friend.

'I know nothing. I was not even aware that he was the

heir to an earldom when I married him. Nor that he was a widower with a child.'

'He will tell you himself, I am sure. But he was close to the old earl—Grant's parents died when he was not much older than Charlie is now. His grandfather brought him up and did a good job of it, for all that he probably leaned too much on the side of tradition and duty. Grant married a suitable young lady, to please his grandfather and do what it seemed was his duty, and talked himself into believing that was how marriage should be.' He pushed his hand through his sandy hair. 'I am saying too much, but you have to know this—Madeleine was a disaster. Possibly the only thing that could have made the situation worse was the way she died.'

'What happened?' Somehow Kate made herself sit quietly attentive for the answer. She had thought she was coming to some safe, comfortable home. A doctor's household, decent and respectable. Modestly prosperous. Instead she found herself married to an earl, with his unburied predecessor somewhere in the house. Her husband had married tragically, she had a stepson—and a new baby. And she had the overwhelming feeling that she could not cope with any of this. But she had to. Grant had thrown her a lifeline and she had a duty to repay him by being a proper wife, a good stepmother to Charlie— and, somehow, a passable countess.

'There was a fire. Rivers was…injured, but he managed to get Charlie out. They couldn't save Madeleine.'

'When?'

'Four years ago. We do not think Charlie remembers any of it, thank God.'

'That is a blessing.' *Poor little boy.* 'Thank you.

Forewarned, at least I can try not to blunder into sensitive areas.'

'Some blundering might be a good thing, frankly.' Dr Meldreth stood up. 'Rivers took it too well, too stoically, for the child's sake. I am not sure he ever really put it behind him. And now he is bone-weary, he's exerted himself sooner than he should after a blow to the head and he's feeling as guilty as hell because he didn't get back in time to see his grandfather before he died.'

'I will try to make him rest and hope he feels able to talk to me.' Kate rose and held out her hand to the doctor. 'Thank you. It is good to know he has a friend close by.'

'I'll be back in a couple of days, unless you send for me earlier.' Meldreth shook hands briskly. 'I wasn't sure whether to mention anything, but Rivers said you've got courage, so…' He shrugged. 'I'll see myself down to the study. Good day, Lady Allundale.'

After that it was hard to sit with any composure. So, the situation was such that the good doctor would not have said anything unless he thought she had courage. That was hardly reassuring.

But perhaps it was time she started drawing on that courage, assuming she did actually possess any. If only she did not feel so ignorant. She had experienced the upbringing of any country gentlewoman, with the neighbouring wives doing their best to support a motherless girl. But, although her manners would not disgrace her, she had no experience of the kind of social life Grant would be used to. Now she was presumably expected to know how to greet a duke, curtsy to a queen, organise a reception and look after scores of tenants and staff.

Well, there was no time like the present to begin. Kate rang for Wilson. 'I do not know when the funeral will be, but I must have respectable mourning clothes.' If they were going to have to improvise and dye something with black ink, then the sooner they started, the better.

'It is tomorrow, my lady. His lordship said not to disturb you about it. There'll just be gentlemen there, no ladies, so you can stay in your rooms.'

Her little burst of energy deflected, Kate sat down again and gazed out at the grey skies, trying to make sense of the world she found herself in and her place in it, and failing miserably. Luncheon was brought up. Grimswade delivered a pile of novels, journals and newspapers. She fed Anna and cuddled her, dozed a little, tried to pay attention when Wilson suggested they make a list of all the essentials she needed to buy. Dinner arrived, a succession of perfect, luxurious little courses. Kate refused the red wine, but found she had the appetite to demolish virtually everything else that was put in front of her. The doctor had been correct. She had been neglecting herself out of worry.

Grimswade appeared as the footman was carrying out the dishes. 'Is there anything else you require, my lady?' Butlers, she knew, cultivated a bland serenity under all circumstances, but she thought he looked strained. The whole household seemed to be holding its breath.

Was there anything she could do? *Nothing,* Kate concluded as the door closed behind the butler. Just keep out of the way. Charlie was with his father and a stranger's clumsy sympathy would be no help to them. She should have asked Grimswade when the rest of the family would arrive. At least they could take some of the burden off Grant's shoulders. How lonely this felt, to be in the middle of so many people and yet completely cut off from their fears, their hopes.

She gave herself a brisk mental shake for the self-pity. She and her child were safe, protected and, at least for a few days, hidden. They had a future, even if it was shrouded in a fog of unknowns. Grant and Charlie were mourning the loss of someone dear to them and the best thing she could do was to intrude as little as possible. Grant had made it clear he did not want her involved or he would have confided in her, wouldn't he?

Chapter Five

She had slept well, Kate realised as she woke to the sound of curtain rings being pulled back. In the intervals when Jeannie had brought her Anna to feed she had listened for sounds from Grant's bedchamber, but none had reached her.

The light was different. She sat up and saw the heavy snow blanketing the formal gardens under a clear, pale grey sky. 'What a heavy fall there must have been in the night, Wilson. Is the house cut off?'

The maid turned and Kate saw her eyes were rimmed with red. She had been crying. *Of course, the funeral.* She felt helpless.

'Very heavy, but the turnpike road is open, my lady, and the men have cleared the path to the church.' Wilson brought a small tray with a cup of chocolate and set it on the bedside table, then went to make up the fire. 'I'll be back with your bathwater in half an hour, my lady.'

The luxury, the unobtrusive, smooth service, suddenly unnerved her. She was a countess now, yet she was the daughter of an obscure baronet, a girl who had never had a Season, who had been to London only three times in her life, who was the mother of a child conceived out of wedlock and the sister of a man who had embroiled her in unscrupulous criminality. *I can't do this...*

The door opened as she took an incautious gulp of hot chocolate and burned the inside of her mouth. 'Wilson?'

'It is us. Good morning.' The deep voice held grief and weariness under the conventional greeting. 'I came to tell you that we will be leaving for the church at ten o'clock. The procession will go past the window, if you wish to watch.' Grant stood just inside the room, one hand resting on Charlie's shoulder, the boy pulled close to his side. Charlie's eyes were red and he leaned in tight to his father, but his chin was set and his head high. Grant looked beyond exhausted, although he was clean-shaven, his dark clothes and black neckcloth immaculate.

'I am so very sorry.' The cup clattered in the saucer as Kate set it down and Grant winced. She threw back the covers, slid out of bed and then just stood there in her nightgown. What could she do, what right had she to think she could even find the comforting words? Her instinct was to put her arms around the pair of them, hug them tight, try to take some of the pain and the weariness from them, but she was a stranger. They would not want her.

'There will be local gentlemen in church, those who can make it through the snow. And the staff, tenants and so on. There will be a small group returning for luncheon, but the staff have that well in hand and you should not be disturbed.' He might as well be speaking to some stray guest who deserved consideration, but was, essentially, an interloper. 'There will be no relatives, no one to stay. We only have cousins in the West Country, too far to attend in this weather, and a great-aunt in London, who likewise could not travel.'

Kate sat down on the edge of the bed. 'I am so sorry,' she repeated. 'Is there anything I can do? Letters to write, perhaps? You will want to spend your time with Charlie.'

'Thank you. My grandfather's... *My* secretary, Andrew Bolton, will handle all the correspondence. There is nothing for you to do.' Grant looked down at the boy as they turned towards the door. 'Ready? We should go down to the hallway now.'

'I'm ready.' Charlie's straight back, the determined tilt of his head, were the image of his father's. He paused and looked back at Kate. 'Good morning, Stepmama.'

Kate watched the procession from her window. The black-draped coffin was carried on the shoulders of six sturdy men, cushions resting on it with decorations and orders glittering in the pale sunlight. Grant walked behind, his hand on Charlie's shoulder, the two of them rigidly composed and dignified. Behind paced a crocodile of gentlemen in mourning clothes followed by tenants in Sunday best and a contingent of the male staff.

She found a prayer book on a shelf in the sitting room and sat to read the burial service through quietly.

By the time luncheon had been cleared away Kate decided that she was going to have to do something. She had cracked the jib door into Grant's bedchamber open a fraction so that she would know if he had come up to rest, and by four o'clock he had not. She handed a fed, gurgling Anna to Jeannie, cast a despairing glance in the mirror at her appearance and set off downstairs.

'Have the guests left?' she asked the first footman she

encountered. He was wearing a black armband, she noticed with an inward wince for her own lack of mourning.

'Yes, my lady.'

'And where is my husband?'

'In his study, my lady.'

'Will you show me the way, please?'

He paused at the end of the hallway outside a dark oak door. 'Shall I knock, my lady?'

It looked very much closed. Forbiddingly so. 'No, I will. Thank you…'

'Giles, my lady.'

She tapped and entered without waiting for a response. The room was warm, the fire flickering in the grate, the curtains closed against the winter chill. There were two pools of light, one over a battered old leather armchair where Charlie slept, curled into a ball like a tired puppy, the other illuminating the papers spread on the desk.

It lit the hands of the man behind the desk, but left his face in shadow. 'Grant, will you not come to bed?' she asked, keeping her voice low.

There was a chuckle, a trifle rusty. 'My dear, that is a most direct suggestion.'

Kate felt her cheeks flame. 'I was not trying to flirt, my lord.' *I would not know how and certainly not with you.* 'Surely you need to rest, spend a few hours lying down. You must be exhausted.' She moved closer, narrowing her eyes against the light of the green-shaded reading lamp. The quill pen was lying on its side on top of the standish, the ink dry and matte on the nib. Grant had run out of energy, she realised, and was simply sitting there, too tired to move.

'Perhaps I am.' Grant sounded surprised, as though

he had not realised why his body had given up. He made no attempt to stand.

'Why did you marry me, if you will not allow me to help you?' Kate sat down opposite him, her eyes on the long-fingered, bruised hands lying lax on the litter of papers. They flexed, then were still. Beautiful hands, capable and clever. She had put those discoloured patches on the left one. She had a sudden vision of them on her skin, gently caressing. Not a doctor's hands any longer, but a lover's, a husband's. Could he see her blush? She hated the way she coloured up so easily, was always consumed with envy for those porcelain-fair damsels who could hide their emotions with ease.

'You felt sorry for me, I can see that. It was a very generous act of mercy, for me and my child,' she went on, thinking aloud when he did not answer. 'And, for some reason, your grandfather was anxious to see you married again and you would do anything to make him happy.' Still silence. Perhaps he had fallen asleep. 'But I cannot sit upstairs in my suite for the rest of my days.'

'Not for ever, no. But for now you are still a new mother. You also require rest. Is there anything you need?' he asked.

At least he was not sleeping where he sat. Kate did not wish to bother him with trivial matters, but he was talking to her, maybe she could distract him enough to consider sleep... 'I have no clothes.' His expressive fingers moved, curled across a virgin sheet of paper. 'Other than two gowns in a sad state and a few changes of linen,' she added repressively. 'I need mourning.'

'It can wait.' The words dropped like small stones into the silence, not expecting an answer.

At least he was not sleeping where he sat. If she could

rouse him enough, she might persuade him to get up and go to his bed. 'Not for much longer. I cannot appear like this, even if it is only in front of the servants.'

He focused on her problem with a visible effort. 'The turnpike is clear. Tomorrow, if the snow holds off, Wilson can go into Hexham and purchase enough to tide you over until you are strong enough for a trip into Newcastle.'

'Thank you.' Kate folded her own hands in her lap and settled back in the chair. If he thought he could send her back to her room with that, he was mistaken. The silence dragged on, filled with the child's breathing, the soft collapse of a log into ash, her own pulse.

'Are you going to sit there for the rest of the afternoon and evening?' Grant enquired evenly when another log fell into the heart of the fire.

'Yes, if you will not go and rest.' She kept her tone as reasonable as his. 'You will be no good to Charlie if you make yourself ill with exhaustion.'

'So wise a parent after so few days?' There was an edge there now.

'One needs no expertise, only to be a human being, to know that the boy will need your attention, your presence, while he grieves. You are in no fit state for anything now, after so many days without proper rest. And you cannot deal with your own grief by drugging yourself with tiredness.'

'How very astringent you are, my dear.' Grant moved suddenly, sat up in his chair and gathered together the papers in front of him. 'No soft feminine wiles to lure me upstairs, no soft words, only common-sense advice?'

'If you wanted the sort of wife who deals with a crisis by feminine fluttering, who feels it necessary to coax and wheedle, then you have married the wrong woman,

my lord.' She kept her voice low, conscious of Charlie
so close. But she could not rein in the anger entirely and
she knew it showed. 'I do not know what your first wife
was like, although I am sure she was raised to be a far
more satisfactory countess than I will be, I am afraid.
But I will try to enact little scenes of wifely devotion for
you from time to time, as you obviously seem to expect
them.' *His first wife was a disaster, Dr Meldreth said. I
will be one, too, although a very different kind of disaster.*

'Demonstrations of wifely devotion would certainly
be a novelty. However, if you can refrain from enact-
ing scenes of any kind, I would be most grateful.' Grant
pushed back his chair, went to lift Charlie in his arms and
murmured, 'If I could trouble you for the door?'

*I must make allowances for his exhaustion, for his
bereavement,* Kate told herself as she followed the tall
figure through the hallway and up the stairs. Giles the
footman was lurking in the shadows and she beckoned
him over. 'His lordship is going to rest. Please let the
rest of the household know that he is not to be disturbed
until he rings. It may well be that this disrupts mealtimes,
so please pass my apologies to Cook if that is the case.
Perhaps she can be ready to provide something light but
sustaining at short notice?'

The footman's gaze flickered to Grant's unresponsive
back. Kate waited, eyebrows raised as though she found
it hard to understand his hesitation. She had never had
to deal with superior domestic staff of this calibre and
she suspected he knew it. The way she looked wouldn't
help. But, like it or not, it seemed she was mistress of
this household now and she must exert some authority
or she would never regain it.

'My lady.'

'Thank you, Giles.' She nodded as though never doubting his obedience for a moment and climbed the stairs. By the time she reached the landing Grant had turned off down a side passage. She followed him to the doorway of what must be the boy's bedchamber. A tall, fair-haired young man came out of an inner doorway and turned down the covers. Between them they got the child out of most of his clothes and into bed, exchanged a few words, and then Grant came out.

'That's his tutor, Gough. He'll sleep in the side chamber in case Charlie wakes.' Grant kept going into his own rooms. Without conscious thought Kate followed him. '*I* do not require tucking up in bed, Kate.'

'I do not know *what* you require, my lord.' She turned abruptly, in a way that should have sent her skirts whirling in a dramatic statement of just how strained her nerves felt. They flopped limply about her ankles, adding to her sense of drabness. 'Your son has both more sense and better manners, from what I can see.'

She reached the jib door to her room, pulled it open, and a hand caught the edge of it, pushed it back closed. Grant frowned down at her. 'What is wrong?'

'*Wrong?*' Would the man never give up and just lie down and sleep? Kate turned back, raised one hand and began to count off on her fingers. 'Let me see. You do not tell me you had just inherited an earldom. You do not tell me you are a widower with a son. You drive yourself to the brink of collapse trying to do everything yourself. I find myself mistress of a great house, but the servants do not appear to expect me to give them orders...' *I need to hide and I find myself a member of the aristocracy.*

'You have just given birth, you should be resting.' Grant pushed the hair out of his eyes with one hand, the other still splayed on the door. She rather suspected he was holding himself up.

'I am quite well and I have a personal maid and an excellent nursery maid. I do not expect to talk about all those things now, but I do expect my *husband* to go and rest so we can discuss them sensibly in the morning.'

'Very well.' He turned back through the door with all the focus of a man who was very, very drunk with lack of sleep. He walked to the bed. Kate followed him and watched as he sat down and just stared at his boots as though he was not certain what they were.

'Let me.' Without waiting she straddled his left leg with her back to him and drew off the boot. Then switched to the other leg. 'Now your coat.'

Grant's mouth twitched into the first sign she had seen of a smile for days. 'Undressing me, wife? I warn you, it is a waste of effort just now.'

Is he flirting again? Impossible. She caught a glimpse of herself in the mirror, a drab creature with a lumpy figure, a blotchy complexion and a frightful gown, next to Grant's elegant good looks. Mocking her was more likely. 'Stand up. I am not going to clamber about on the bed.'

He stood, meekly enough, while she reached up to push the coat from his shoulders. She was slightly above average height for a woman, but he was larger than she had realised, now she was standing so close. No wonder he had lifted her so easily. She found herself a little breathless. Fortunately the coat, like the boots, was comfortable country wear and did not require a shoehorn to lever off. The fine white linen of his shirt clung to his arms, defining the musculature. He had stripped off his coat in the bothy, she recalled vaguely. Doubtless the other things she had to focus on had stopped her noticing those muscles. Ridiculously she felt the heat of a rising blush. Kate unbuttoned his waistcoat, pushed that off, then reached for his neckcloth.

Grant's hand came up and covered her fingers as she struggled with the knot. She looked up and met his gaze, heavy-lidded, intent. 'You have very lovely blue eyes,' he murmured. 'Why haven't I noticed before?'

He was, it seemed, awake. Or part of him was, a sensual, masculine part she was not ready to consider, although something fundamentally feminine in her was certainly paying attention.

It is my imagination. He is beyond exhausted, too tired to be flirting. Certainly not flirting with me. Kate shot another glance at the mirror and resisted the urge to retort that at least there was something about her that he approved of.

'I was quite right about you.'

'What?' she demanded ungrammatically as she tugged the neckcloth off with rather more force than necessary, pulling the shirt button free. The neck gaped open, revealing a vee of skin, a curl of dark hair. It looked…silky.

'You have courage and determination.'

Kate began to fold up the length of muslin with concentration. 'I am trying to get you to rest. What about that requires courage?'

'You don't know me.' He sat down. 'I might have a vicious temper. I might hit out at a wife who provoked me.'

'I think I am a reasonable judge of character.' She had wound the neckcloth into a tight knot around her own hand. Patiently, so she did not have to look at him, Kate began to unravel it. This close she could smell his skin, the herbal, astringent soap he used, the tang of ink on his hands, the faint musk that she recognised as *male*. But Grant smelt different, smelt of himself.

She walked to the dresser and placed the neckcloth on the top, distancing herself from the sudden, insane urge to step in close, lay her head on his chest, wrap her arms around the lean, weary body. *Why?* To comfort him perhaps, or because she wanted comfort herself, or perhaps a mixture of the two.

When she turned back Grant was lying down on top of the covers, still in shirt and breeches. He was deep, deep asleep. She stood looking down at him for a moment, studied the fine-drawn face relaxed into a vulnerability that took years off his age. How old was he? Not thirty-two or -three, as she had thought. Twenty-eight, perhaps. His hair flopped across his forehead, just as Charlie's did, but she resisted the temptation to brush it back from the bruised skin. The long body did not stir when she laid a light blanket over him, nor when she drew the curtains closed slowly to muffle the rattle of the rings, nor when she made up the fire and drew the guard around it.

My husband is a disturbingly attractive man, she thought as she closed the jib door carefully behind her. Anna was crying in the dressing room, she could hear Jeannie soothing her.

'Mama will be back soon, little one. Yes, she will, now don't you fret.'

A husband, a stepson, a baby. Her family. She had a *family* when just days before all she had was a scheming brother who had always seen her as wilful and difficult and the babe inside her, loved already, but unknown.

Anna, Charlie, Grant. When her husband woke, refreshed, he would see her differently, realise he had a partner he could rely on. She owed him that, she owed Anna the opportunity to grow up happily here. The anxiety and the exhaustion had made her nervy, angry, but she must try to learn this new life, learn to fit in. As the pain of the funeral eased, she would be there for them all. Charlie would learn to like her, perhaps one day to love her. And somehow she would learn how to be a countess. She shivered. How could a countess stay out of the public eye?

When tomorrow comes, it will not seem so overwhelming, I'll think of something. 'Is that a hungry little girl I can hear? Mama's coming.'

Chapter Six

Hunger woke Grant. One minute he had been fathoms down, the next, awake, alert, conscious of an empty stomach and silence. Gradually the soft sounds of the household began to penetrate. The subdued crackle of the fire, someone trudging past in the snow, the distant sound of light, racing feet and the heavier tread of an adult in pursuit. Charlie exercising his long-suffering tutor, no doubt. Close at hand an infant began to cry, then stopped. *Anna. I have a daughter.* And a wife.

There was daylight between the gap in the curtains, falling in a bright snow-reflecting bar across the blanket someone had draped over his legs. Grant pushed the hair out of his eyes, winced and sat up, too relaxed to tug the bell pull and summon food and hot water.

Now, today, he must take up the reins of the earldom. That was perhaps the least of the duties looming before him. He had known for nearly twenty years, ever since his father died, that he would inherit. His grandfather had run a tight ship, but had taught Grant, shared decisions as he grew older, explained his thinking, given him increasing responsibilities. There were

no mysteries to discover about the estates, the investments or the tenants and he had inherited an excellent
bailiff and solicitor along with the title.

Charlie was going to be all right, given time and loving attention. Which left Kate. His new wife. What had
he been thinking of, to marry her out of hand like that?
She was certainly in deep trouble, all alone with a new
baby and no means of support, but he could have found
her a cottage somewhere on one of the estates, settled
some money on her. Forgotten her.

His grandfather had been fretting himself into a state
over Grant's first marriage. Blaming himself for ever introducing Grant to Madeleine Ellmont, worrying that Grant
was lonely, that Charlie had no mother, that the future of
the earldom relied on a healthy quiverful of children. So
much so that Grant had come to hate the house that had
always been his home. But he could have lied to him, made
up a charming and eligible young woman whom he was
about to propose to, settled the old man's worries that way.

What had prompted that impetuous proposal when
he already knew his grandfather must be beyond caring about his marital state? Something about Kate had
told him he could trust her, that she was somehow *right*.
He had glimpsed it again yesterday when he had looked
into her eyes and seen a spark there that had caught his
breath for an instant.

A clock struck ten. Lord, he'd slept more than twelve
hours. Grant leaned out of bed and yanked the bell pull.
He had to somehow get everything right with Kate. She
was unsettled to discover she was a countess with a stepson and that was understandable. He had an edgy feeling that he had disconcerted her when she was helping
him to undress. He kept forgetting that while she might

be a mother she seemed quite sheltered, not very experienced. What had he said? Nothing out of line, he hoped. For the first time he wondered about Anna's father and just what that love affair had been—a sudden moment of madness, a lengthy, illicit relationship, or...

'You rang, my lord?' said Giles the footman.

Grant frowned at him for a second. It took some getting used to, being *my lord* now. 'Hot water, coffee. Ask Cook to send up some bacon, sausage... Everything. She'll know.'

When the water came he washed and then shaved himself while Giles found him clean linen and laid out plain, dark clothes. That was something else to add to the list, a valet.

When he tapped on the jib door and went through into Kate's suite he found her in the sitting room, the baby in the crib by her side, her hands full of a tangle of fine wool. She was muttering what sounded like curses under her breath.

'Good morning. Cat's cradles?'

'Oh!' She dropped the wool and two needles fell out of it. 'Mrs Havers, the housekeeper, brought me this wool and the knitting needles. She thought I might like to make a cot blanket, which was very thoughtful of her. I didn't like to tell her I haven't tried to knit since I was six.' She grimaced at the tangle. 'And *tried* was the correct word, even then. Did you need me, my lord?'

'Grant, please. I came to see how you are and to thank you for persuading me into bed yesterday. I had gone beyond being entirely rational on the subject.' There was colour up over her cheeks and he remembered making some insinuating comment about luring him into bed. *Damn.*

'I hope you feel better this morning.' She bent her head over the knitting once more, catching up the dropped stitches. 'Charlie was up and about quite early, testing the bounds of his tutor's patience. He seems a pleasant young man, Mr Gough.'

'He's the younger brother of a friend from university. I thought he would be a good choice as a first tutor—he has plenty of energy and Charlie seems to have taken to him.'

Kate picked up the wool and began to wind it back into a ball, her gaze fixed on her hands. 'You slept well?'

'Yes, excellently. How is Anna this morning?'

Grant sat down and retrieved a knitting needle from the floor as Kate answered. He might as well order the teapot to be brought and some fancy biscuits—this seemed like a morning call, complete with stilted, meaningless polite chat, achieving nothing.

'Tomorrow, I intend going down to London. I must present myself at the House of Lords, the College of Heralds and at Court.' He was escaping.

'Oh.' She set down the wool and sat up in the chair as though bracing herself. 'I am sorry, I had not realised we would be leaving so soon. I am not certain I feel up to the journey yet.'

Surely that was not panic he saw in her eyes? He shook his head and realised Kate had taken that as a refusal to listen to her objection.

'But…if we must, may we stop in Newcastle on the way? Then I can buy a respectable gown or two to tide me over.' She looked around, determined, it seemed, to obey his wishes. 'Where have Jeannie and Wilson got to? I am sure we can be ready in time.'

'There is no need for you to disturb yourself. I had no intention of dragging you away. I will take Charlie and

Gough with me, I don't want to leave the boy without me yet. They can come back on the mail after a few weeks, once I am certain he is all right.' Kate closed her eyes for a moment and he felt a jab of conscience at not realising how exhausted she must be. 'When you feel up to it you will find Newcastle will serve for all your needs while you require only mourning clothes.'

'Very well. As you wish, my lord.' Kate picked up the wool and needles again with a polite smile that seemed to mask something deeper than relief. 'And you will send Charlie back, you say?'

'The moment I am certain he doesn't need me. In the longer term I will be too occupied with business to give him the company he needs and the house and servants will be unfamiliar to him. He will be better here, where he feels secure. I will send for him again after a month or two—travelling long distances will be no hardship for him, he'll find it an adventure—but I want him based here.'

'Of course. As you think best. I can see that London might not be a good place for a small boy in the longer term if you cannot be with him most of the time.'

Grant told himself he should be pleased to have such a conformable wife, such an untemperamental, obliging one. Perversely, he felt decidedly put out. Through yesterday's fog of tiredness he seemed to recall the sparkle that temper had put in Kate's eyes, the flush on her cheeks, the stimulus of a clash of wills. Women were moody after childbirth, he knew that. This placidity was obviously Kate's natural character.

'Grant?' She was biting her lip now. 'Grant, will you put a notice about the marriage in the newspapers? Only, I wish you would not. I feel so awkward about things…'

Newspaper announcements had been the last thing on his mind, but he could see she was embarrassed. 'No, I won't. An announcement of the birth, yes, but it will give no indication of the date of the marriage. "To the Countess of Allundale, a daughter." All right?' Kate nodded and he hesitated, concerned at how pale she had gone. Then she smiled and he told himself he was imagining things. 'If you'll excuse me, my dear, I have a great deal to do.' She would no doubt be delighted to see the back of him—and why should it be otherwise?

May 5, 1820

Home. Warmth on his back, clean air in his lungs, the sun bathing the green slopes of the Tyne Valley spread out before him. Grant stood in his stirrups to stretch, relishing the ache of well-exercised muscles. However ambiguous his feelings about Abbeywell, he had been happy here once and perhaps he could be again, if only he could blank out his memories and find some sort of peace with his new wife.

His staff had obviously thought he was out of his mind to decide to ride from London to Northumberland instead of taking a post-chaise, but he knew exactly what had motivated him. This had been a holiday from responsibility, from meetings and parties, from political negotiating and social duty. And a buffer between the realities and reason of London and the ghosts that haunted this place.

If he was honest, it had also been a way of delaying his return to his new wife and facing up to exactly what his impulse on that cold Christmas Day had led to.

'I like her,' Charlie had pronounced on being questioned when he came on a month's visit to the London house in March. But he was too overexcited from his adventurous trip on the mail coach with Mr Gough to focus on things back in Northumberland. He wanted to talk to his papa, to go with him to the menagerie, to see the soldiers and the Tower. And Astley's again, and…

'You get on together all right?' Grant had prompted.

'Of course. She doesn't fuss and she lets me play with Anna, who is nice, although she's not much fun yet. May we go to Tatt's? Papa, please?'

Doesn't fuss. Well, that would seem to accord with Kate's letters. One a week, each precisely three pages long in a small, neat hand. Each contained a scrupulous report on Charlie's health and scholastic progress, a paragraph about Anna—she can hold her head up, she can copy sounds, she can throw her little knitted bunny— and a few facts about the house and estate. *Millie in the kitchen has broken her ankle, the stable cat caught the biggest rat anyone had seen and brought it into the kitchen on Sunday morning and Cook dropped the roast, it has rained for a week solidly...*

They were always signed *Your obedient wife, Catherine Rivers*, each almost as formalised and lacking in emotion as Gough's reports on Charlie or his bailiff's lengthy letters about estate business. And never once did she ask to come to London or reproach him for leaving her alone.

He replied, of course, sending a package north weekly, with a long letter for Charlie, a note for Gough, answers to Wilkinson's estate queries. And there would always be a letter one page long for Kate, with the kind of gossip that Madeleine, his first wife, had expected. What the royal family were doing, what the latest society scandal was— omitting the crim. con. cases, naturally—the latest fads in hem lengths and bonnets as observed in Hyde Park. Signed *Your affct. husband, Grantham Rivers.*

The parkland rolled before him like a welcome carpet and the road forked, the right hand to the house, the left to the rise crowned with the mausoleum his greatgrandfather had built in the 1750s. The chestnut gelding was trotting along the left-hand way before Grant was conscious of applying the reins. No rush, it was only just noon, no one was expecting him to arrive on any particular day.

The classical monument sat perfectly on its hillock, turning the view into a scene in an Arcadian painting. It was a Greek temple with its portico facing south, its basement full of the ancestors his great-grandfather had removed from the church vault, its inner walls made with niches for the future generations of Rivers. 'So we can admire the view,' the first earl had reportedly announced. 'I'm damned if I'm spending eternity in that damp vault with some dullard of a preacher sermonising on top of me.' The countess of the day had had mild hysterics at the sentiment and had been ignored and now she, too, shared the prospect.

Grant tied the gelding to a ring on the rear wall of the building and strolled round to the front. There were stone benches set under the portico and it would be good to rest there awhile and think about his grandfather.

The sound of laughter stopped him in mid-stride. He recognised Charlie's uninhibited shrieks, but there was a light, happy laugh he did not recognise at all. He walked on, his boots silent on the sheep-cropped turf, and stopped again at the corner.

A rug was spread out on the grassy flat area in front of the temple steps and a woman in a dark grey gown was sitting on it, her arms wrapped around her knees, her eyes shaded by a wide straw hat as she watched Charlie chasing a ball. An open parasol was lying by her side.

'Maman, look!' Charlie hurled the ball high, then flung himself full length to catch it.

The woman clapped, the enthusiasm of her applause tipping her hat back off her head to roll away down the slope. Long brown hair, the colour of milky coffee, glossy in the sunlight, tumbled free from the confining pins and she laughed. 'Catch my hat, Charlie!'

Maman? Grant started forward as Charlie caught the hat, turned and saw him. He rushed uphill shrieking, 'Papa! Papa! Look, Maman—Papa's home.'

The woman swung round on the rug as Charlie thudded into Grant, his hard little head butting into his stomach. He scooped him up, tucked him under his arm and strode down to her. She tilted her head back, sending the waves of hair slithering like unfolding silk and giving him an unimpeded view of an oval face, blue eyes, a decided chin and pink lips open in surprise.

'My…my lord, we did not expect to see you for another day at least.' Her face lost its colour, her relaxed body seemed to tighten in on itself.

Kate? Of course it is Kate, but… He did something about his own dropped jaw, gave himself a mental shake and managed to utter a coherent sentence. 'I made good time.' He set Charlie on his feet. 'Maman?'

'Stepmamas are in fairy stories and they are always wicked. So I asked Mr Gough for the words for *mama* in lots of languages and we looked them up and I chose *maman*. Maman likes it,' his son assured Grant earnestly. 'She said it was *elegant*.'

* * *

'Will you not sit down?' It was extraordinary how it was possible to sound quite calm outwardly when her insides were in a jumble of feelings, the overriding one of which was confusion. Kate gestured towards the open basket and managed what she hoped was a welcoming smile. 'Do have some luncheon. We have enough food to withstand a siege. Charlie, as always, assured Cook that we might be lost in the woods for days. We never are, but Cook does not like to take the risk.'

When in doubt when dealing with a man, feed the beast, her mother had always said with a chuckle. Kate kept her tone serious and was rewarded by the slight upward tilt of one corner of Grant's mouth. He had a sense of humour, then. It had not been possible to detect it in his dutiful letters, which had not been made any less dry by the fact they contained nothing but gossip. Presumably that was all wives were supposed to be interested in.

Wives, of course, were perfectly capable of reading the news-sheets and keeping informed that way, although that simple fact did not seem to occur to men. Her brother, Henry, had always been amazed when she revealed an opinion on anything from income tax to child labour and he firmly believed that thinking led to weakening of the feminine brain. Kate pushed away the resentment and watched her husband as he moved round to drop to the rug at her side and discovered Anna lying under the parasol, kicking her legs and chewing on a bone ring.

Grant reached over and tickled her and the resentment retreated some more. He was good with the children, she must remember that.

'She has grown and she looks to be thriving. As do you,' he added. 'I scarcely recognised you.'

From the way Grant shut his mouth with a snap he realised that was a less than tactful remark. Instead of saying so Kate wrestled her hair into a twist and jammed the hat back on top. 'Babies tend to grow in the natural course of things. But she is very well, as am I.' She sent him a considering, sideways glance, making sure he saw it. 'You look much better than I remembered.'

That very forward remark obviously caught him by surprise. Grant tossed his low-crowned hat aside and shifted round to look directly at her, eyes narrowing. 'Thank you. I think.'

She had known him to be a good-looking man when she married him, but not this attractive, with a London gloss on his hair and clothes, his face tanned from his long ride north. 'In December you looked haggard, bruised and exhausted. You were recovering from a blow to the head and you were grieving,' Kate said with a slight shrug. His eyes moved down to her breasts as she moved and she caught her breath at the answering flare of heat in her belly. The fact that she had a figure obviously interested him. No doubt it was the transformation of her bosom; men could be very predictable.

It was nearly five months since Anna's birth now. She had passed through exhaustion to a conviction that when she felt stronger she never wanted a man to touch her again. After all, her first, and only, experience had not been so pleasurable as to have her yearning for more.

And that comfortable state had lasted for three months until the moment when she had looked up from the dinner table to see Grant's portrait hanging on the opposite wall, just as it had since the day she arrived. It had been part of the decoration of the house, hardly regarded, but that evening she had felt a startling stab of attraction as she met the direct green gaze. The feeling had been so visceral, so unashamedly physical, that she'd choked on her fish terrine and Mr Gough had rushed round the table to offer her water.

Since the arrival of Grant's letter announcing his return she had been in an unseemly state of confusion, alarm and anticipation. This was her husband—and husbands expected their *rights*.

Chapter Seven

'After all, I was in the process of giving birth,' Kate continued calmly, hoping the frankness of her words accounted for the heat in her cheeks. The thought of Grant exercising his husbandly rights made her positively breathless. 'It is hardly surprising that we both now appear to be tolerably well looking in comparison. Of course, I could tell that you were a well-favoured man, even then, but it must be a relief for you to discover that I am not *quite* as bracket-faced as you feared.'

'It is difficult to know how to reply to that.' Grant was not used to being left at a loss for words, she could tell. Possibly he was slightly flattered, although he must be accustomed to being regarded as good-looking. Possibly also he was feeling a trifle awkward about letting her see what he had thought of her before.

'There is no need to say anything.' She was not a conventional beauty, she never had been, but she thought that these days she looked at least tolerable, and, if Grant now thought so, too, she was content with that.

'I have been away a long time, longer than I intended.' He had decided to get all the apologising over at once, it seemed. Kate wondered if the length of his absence had anything to do with his mental image of his new wife. Had he escaped to London and the arms of a beautiful mistress? As apologies went, it was not very effusive, more a statement of fact than of regret.

'We have managed very well and you were a most regular correspondent.' *Not that I understand you any better now than before you left. And you are a man, not a saint, so I must not feel jealous of a mistress—she is only to be expected. But if you take one up here, one that I know about, that will be a different matter.* The stab of jealousy was unexpected and she diverted it into a vicious cut at the pastry in front of her. 'Would you care for a slice of raised pie?' she enquired to cover the impulse to snap out a demand to know all about this theoretical other woman. 'It is chicken and ham.'

'Papa, are you home for long?' Charlie had been sitting almost on his father's feet, obviously on the point of bursting with the effort to Be Good and not interrupt the adults.

'For the summer. Ough!' Grant fell back on the rug under the impact of Charlie's flying leap and hug. 'You are too big for jumping on your poor father. Big enough to come out with me and start learning about the estate, I think, provided you keep up your lessons to Mr Gough's satisfaction. Now, sit quietly and eat your picnic while I talk to your stepmama.' Grant settled the boy between them and against her side Kate could feel her husband's encircling arm and the child's skinny little body quivering with happiness like an overexcited puppy.

The arm was warm and it was tempting to lean into it, to feel the muscled strength braced to support her.

Kate sat up straight and filled a plate for Grant from the picnic basket.

'Thank you. Have you heard from your brother yet?' he asked as he took the food from her.

'No. I have not written to him and I would, of course, have mentioned it in my letters if I had. I do not want him to know of this marriage. I do not want him to know where I am. To be perfectly frank, we were not close. We did not part on good terms and it would be awkward…' She'd scoured the newspapers daily, looking for the arrest or trial of Sir Henry Harding, baronet, for blackmail. But perhaps aristocrats had other ways of dealing with the potentially explosive matter of extortion. She shivered. But there had been no notice of Henry's death, either.

'Awkward to have him asking questions about our marriage?'

She nodded, grateful that he had jumped to the wrong conclusion. She did not want Henry to know about her marriage because, beside him embroiling her any deeper in his schemes, she had no idea how he would react. At best, he would attempt to borrow money from his new brother-in-law. At worst, he could cause the most dreadful scandal and she could not inflict that on Grant.

'I would be much happier if you did not make contact with him.' *And find out who Anna's father is and realise just how I came to lose my virginity to the man and became an accomplice in blackmail.* Grant was the kind of principled gentleman who would never allow such dishonesty to go unpunished, whatever the scandal. *Let sleeping dogs lie…*

Grant shrugged. 'We are going to have to deal with him sooner or later. In the meantime, are you opposed to entertaining a small house party? It had not occurred to me to propose it, but now I see you looking—'

'More the thing?' Kate suggested, swallowing the hurt. Had he really thought to shut her away up here, an unpaid housekeeper and guardian for his son, simply because he considered her plain and awkward? Now, it seemed, he did not fear she would embarrass him in front of his friends. The fact that she had welcomed the seclusion was neither here nor there.

'More rested,' Grant supplied smoothly. 'And from your letters it sounds as though you have the household well in hand.'

'Your staff are well chosen and well trained. Once they had accepted that I really was your wife, and not some stray you had picked up on the moors, they have proved most cooperative.' Not that she would have stood for any nonsense. She had been used to helping run a small household, so she knew the principles, and she was all too aware that if she did not secure the respect and loyalty of the staff of this much larger one right from the start, then she never would. It was another mark in Grant's favour, the loyalty and affection they showed for him.

'How small a house party?' she enquired, leaning away from him to give Anna a quick kiss and to hide the uncertainty that she could manage the sort of gathering an earl might hold. Provided it was here, on what had become her own turf, she was not too anxious.

'No more than three close friends of mine, potentially with partners. I've had enough formal socialising in London to last me several months. Charlie, do you remember Lord Weybourn?'

'Uncle Alex?'

'Yes. He was married in January. I thought to ask

him and his wife to stay. And, if they are still in the country, Lord Avenmore and Lord Edenbridge. They are old friends,' he added for Kate's benefit. 'The two bachelors might bring their unmarried sisters, perhaps, to balance out the men.'

'That sounds delightful.' Kate took a bread roll from the basket, then sat with it in her hands, wondering why she had picked it up. The longer Grant sat beside her, the more her appetite deserted her. It was nerves, that was all. She was happy that he was back, for Charlie's sake if nothing else—only, there was a hollow feeling of anticipation, as though the air had been sucked out of her lungs. This was her husband and he was going to expect to begin a normal married life, with all that entailed. Part of that hollowness was apprehension, but a good part was excitement and she had been making herself face that ever since the arrival of the letter announcing his return.

She put the bread roll back untasted, handed Charlie an apple turnover and smiled as he ran off, mouth full, to retrieve his ball. Beside her Grant was silent and she sought for small talk to fill the void. 'It has been…quiet. I am glad you are back. The children are very absorbing, of course.'

'But they are not adults. You have been lonely.' When she murmured agreement he asked, 'Have none of our neighbours called?'

'Dr Meldreth and his wife and the vicar and his sister, that is all. Please, do not make too much of it. I am in mourning, after all, and in the country people do observe that very rigorously. I see them in church on Sunday, naturally, and I usually dine with Mr Gough.'

'Now I am back I will visit all our neighbours, let the

ladies know we are not in strict mourning any longer.
You should get any number of calls within days.'

Charlie's voice floated down from the portico of the
mausoleum. '...and now Papa's back I will help him with
the estate, just like he helped you, Great-Grandpapa.
You'll be proud of me when I do that, I expect, Mama.'

'What the devil?' Grant swung round, sending the
lemonade jug rocking. 'Who is he talking to? My grandfather, his mother? Is the child delusional?'

'Of course not.' Kate grabbed his arm as he began to
get to his feet. Grant shot her a frowning look, but settled
back down beside her when she did not relax her grip.
'He missed his great-grandfather, so we started coming
down here so that he could talk to him. And then he realised that his mama was here, too. He understands that
we do not know what happens after death and he doesn't
think he is talking to ghosts or anything unhealthy like
that. But it comforts him, helps him to sort out his feelings. Rather like writing a diary, I suppose.' Kate came
up on her knees beside Grant, her hand on the unyield-
ing arm braced to push him to his feet. 'Did I do wrong?
He is not at all morbid about it and this is a lovely place.
A peaceful place, where he can remember happy times.'

'He cannot remember his mother, he never really knew
her, she died when he was only just two.' Grant stayed
where he was, but the tension radiated off him. Had he
loved his first wife so much that he could not bear any
mention of her? But that was not what Dr Meldreth had
implied. The staff in the house acted and spoke as though
Charlie's mother was a grief that could not be spoken
about, becoming thin-lipped and awkward if Kate made
any reference to her. There were no portraits, not even
in Charlie's room.

'He says he remembers her scent and the fact that she always wore blue, but that is all. I have no idea whether it is accurate, but it helps him to have that faint image. He is certain that she was beautiful.'

'She was.' Grant's voice softened. 'Blonde and blue-eyed, which is why she favoured blue in her dress. She always wore jasmine scent and on a warm evening it lingered in the air like the ghost of incense…' Kate closed her eyes at the hint of pain beneath the reminiscent tone. 'Charlie would do well to forget she ever existed,' he said and turned so his back was to the little temple.

'Grant!' Kate stared at him, then scooped up Anna as the baby began to cry, as unsettled by his abruptly harsh tone as she was.

'She was a disaster as a mother.'

And a disaster as a wife? 'He need not know that,' Kate said fiercely.

'Of course not, what do you take me for?'

'I do not know. I do not know *you*. But he needs the confidence of knowing he had a mother who loved him, even if she was not very good at it in your eyes. What does it matter if *you* do not like it, if it is best for Charlie?'

'Damn it, Kate. You presume to lecture me on my own child?'

'Yes, of course I do.' She glared back at him over the top of Anna's bonneted head, aware that she was bristling like a stable cat defending her kittens. Then she saw the darkness in Grant's eyes, the memory of goodness knew what past miseries. 'I am sorry, but I am his stepmother and you left him with me to look after. He is still only a little boy, not ready for harsh truths.' She rocked the baby, trying to soothe her. 'What did she do that was so unforgivable?'

Grant got to his feet in one fast movement, a controlled release of pent-up tension. 'I am sorry, but I have no intention of raking over old history. Madeleine is in the past and there is nothing you need to know.' He bent to pick up his hat. 'If you will excuse me, Kate, I will ride on to the house and take Charlie with me. I assume a footman is coming out in the gig to collect you and bring the basket back?'

'Yes, I expect him very soon.' Kate was glad of Anna grizzling in her arms, demanding her attention. She did not want to look into those shadowed eyes and see his anger with her, or his pain over his beautiful, lost wife.

He called to Charlie and the boy came running to be hoisted up into the saddle in front of his father. Grant gave him the reins. 'Wave goodbye to your stepmama.'

When the sound of hooves died away and Charlie's excited chatter faded amongst the trees, Kate fed and changed Anna, packed away the baby things in one basket and the remains of the picnic in the other and got to her feet, too restless to wait for the footman and the gig.

She had to think about Grant, but not about what would happen that night. If she began to imagine that, then she would be in more of a state of nerves than a virgin on her wedding night. The virgin might have a little theoretical knowledge, but Kate knew exactly what would happen and the thought of being in Grant's bed made her mind dizzy and her body ache.

She had lain with Jonathan just once and she had believed herself in love with him, a delusion she now knew was born out of ignorance, a desperation to get away from home and the lures of an accomplished rake. And the experience had been a sadly disappointing one, even though she had not truly understood what to expect. But she hardly knew Grant, the man, at all, he had never so much as kissed her hand and she was most certainly not tipsy with moonlight and champagne. And yet, just the thought of him made her breath come short and an ache, somewhere between fear and anticipation, form low down. Goodness knew how she had managed a rational conversation with him appearing like that.

Kate tucked Anna more snugly into her little blanket, settled her into the folds of her shawl to make a sling and began to walk back to the house. It would take almost half an hour with her arms full of her wriggling, chubby baby. Time enough to think about something other than how long Grant's legs had looked, stretched out on the rug, how the ends of his hair had turned golden brown in the sunlight.

Time, in fact, to consider that locked door on the other side of Grant's suite of rooms in the light of what he had said about Madeleine, the beautiful wife who had been such a bad mother and who had died in a fire.

She had realised almost from the beginning that the forbidden suite must have been her predecessor's rooms. She could understand that the chambers would hold difficult memories for Grant, but even so, it was surely long past the time when they should have been opened up, aired, redecorated and put to use. What would happen when Charlie was old enough to be curious about the locked door? It was unhealthy to make a mystery out of his mother like that, and if he ever discovered that was where she had died, he might well have nightmares about it.

None of the keys on her chatelaine fitted the lock and all the servants denied having the right one, either. Eventually Grimswade told her that neither his late lordship nor his young lordship had wanted the rooms opened. 'The earl holds the only key, my lady,' he told her, his gaze fixed at a point over her head.

Since then Kate had tried hard not to allow the locked room to become a Bluebeard's chamber in her imagination, applying rigorous common sense to keep her own nightmares at bay. She had found her way around the house without looking at the door if she could help it, she had asked no further questions of the staff, but it refused to be forgotten. There were times when she seriously considered picking the lock with a bent hairpin, or seeing if a slender paperknife would trip the catch, then told herself to not even think about something so unseemly.

Now she wondered just what Madeleine's crimes had been. *A disaster as a mother.* That, somehow, did not make sense. Surely she could not have beaten the child— neither Grant nor his grandfather would have allowed her unsupervised access if they feared violence. And being a distant and cold mother was nothing unusual amongst the nobility, Kate knew. Many a child was raised almost entirely by servants without anyone accusing the parents of being a disaster.

The only explanation Kate could think of was that she was a failure as a wife and therefore morally unfit to be a mother. Had she taken a lover—had Grant found them together in her bedchamber? It was an explanation, but it was difficult to imagine Grant being cuckolded. In fact, her mind refused to produce an image of a more attractive alternative who might have tempted his wife to stray.

'Which is very shallow of me,' she admitted to Anna. The baby stared back at her with wide green eyes. 'Grant is intelligent, good-looking, and he was the heir to an earldom when she married him. But good looks and position are not everything. If Madeleine had found her soulmate…'

Then she should have resisted temptation. Madeleine was married, she had made vows, she had a child. Which is easy enough for me to say. Despite being a well-brought-up, respectable young lady, I gave my virtue easily enough. Of course, having a scheming brother who put her in the way of a man who could be trusted to yield to temptation when it was offered and who could not afford a scandal had helped her along the path to ruination. Her becoming pregnant was, as far as Henry was concerned, the perfect gilding on his plan to blackmail her lover. *What if Jonathan came back now, walked around that bend in the path ahead?*

Kate watched the bend approach. No one appeared around it, of course, least of all the rakish Lord Baybrook. And if he did, he would not be coming with protestations of undying love, with explanations of how she had entirely misunderstood his flat refusal to marry her when Henry had confronted him two months later, after she had been forced to confess her predicament.

Not that she had seen him then, of course. Henry, as befitted the male head of the household, had taken himself off to London to, as he put it, *deal with the matter.* Only, he had not dealt with it, not brought her a husband back. At the time it had struck her as strange that her brother had not been more angry, but she had decided that perhaps he had been relieved that he had not found himself facing the viscount at dawn on Hampstead Heath. Then she had found the letter in Henry's desk, the coldly furious response to blackmail, the counter-threats. But Lord Baybrook had not called Henry's bluff. He would pay, she thought, reading the letter. Pay—and then she was certain that one day he would find some way to make Henry pay and Kate, too, the woman Jonathan thought had deliberately set out to ensnare him.

Anna gurgled and Kate stopped, her feet sinking into the soft mulch of the path. There was nothing to be gained by brooding on it, fretting over the long arm of a vengeful aristocrat or wincing in shame at her own part in her brother's schemes. Most certainly, she was in no position to judge Grant's first wife on moral grounds. Equally certainly, if she had the choice between Grant Rivers, Lord Allundale, and Jonathan Arnold, Lord Baybrook, she had no doubt which man she would choose now.

Chapter Eight

Grant sat up in the marble bath and considered the tricky, but eminently safe, subject of plumbing. His grandfather had installed baths with a cold-water supply and drains for the main bedchambers, but he had not risked the newfangled systems of boilers and piped hot water. Grant had agreed with him at the time, but lugging the cans of hot water upstairs and along endless corridors certainly made a great deal of work for the servants.

He lathered the long-handled brush and scrubbed his back while calculating the safe location for boilers and the length of pipework one would need. It was technical, complicated, and was entirely failing to stop him brooding on the subject of his wife. His second wife.

He had been deep in discussion with his secretary and the steward when he heard her voice in the hallway that afternoon. Six months ago Mr Rivers would have pushed aside the piles of paperwork and asked the men to wait while he went out to greet her. But the Earl of Allundale could not do anything as unfashionable and demonstrative as interrupting an important meeting in order to speak to his wife for no reason whatsoever. A few months in London society had reminded him forcefully of that.

Madeleine had always said he was far too casual, not sufficiently aware of his own consequence, or of hers. Now he was the earl he should behave like one, and, given the circumstances of their marriage, Kate was going to need all the consequence he could bring her, he was very conscious of that.

Now he put aside the brush and lay back to critically survey what he could see of his body as he stretched out under the water. Toes, kneecaps and a moderately hairy chest broke the surface. No stomach rising above the soap suds, thank goodness. The London Season was enough to put inches on anyone foolish enough to eat and drink all that was on offer during interminable dinner parties, suppers at balls, buffets at receptions. But with rigorous attendance at the boxing salons, sessions with the fencing master and long rides in the parks, at least the elegant new clothes he'd ordered when he'd first arrived still fitted him by the end.

Alex had laughed at him for having a fashionable crop, but he had hardly noticed the teasing—contemplating his old friend Alex Tempest married to the woman he had believed on first sight to be a nun was enough to distract any man.

Alex and Tess had seemed happy. Blissfully so and physically, too. Shockingly they hardly seemed able to keep their hands off each other—Lord and Lady Weybourn appeared to have no reservations about appearing unfashionably in love.

Grant reached out and pulled the plug out, then, when the bath emptied, he put it back and turned on the cold-water tap. He made himself lie still until it reached his shoulders. It had dawned on him when he reached London that he was a married man again. Which meant that he should be faithful to his wife. It was not something that had entered his head when he made that rash proposal, and sex had not been exactly at the forefront of his mind for at least a month before that, what with the anxiety about his grandfather and then so much travelling, culminating in his accident in Edinburgh.

Now he lay in the cold water and made himself calculate. This was May. It had been mid-November when he had ended that pleasant little dalliance with the Bulgarian attaché's wife in Vienna. Nearly six months. Despite the chill of the bath, blood was definitely heading downwards with the realisation of such prolonged celibacy. Damnation. He could hardly sling a towel round his hips and stride off to his wife's bedchamber to deal with the matter. That was not the way to approach one's first night in the marriage bed. And what were Kate's expectations of that marriage bed anyway?

Grant climbed from the bath and stood in front of the fire while he towelled himself dry. The logical way to discover her feelings and views on any subject was simply to ask her. On the other hand, he hardly knew the woman. Wife or not, he could not just sit down and have a frank and open discussion about sex. She would be shocked.

He had been away a devil of a long time and he had a guilty conscience about that, he realised as he towelled his back. He could expect to receive, at the very least, some wifely remonstrance on the subject before he was forgiven. Yet when they had met in front of the mausoleum Kate had simply not acknowledged that there had been anything wrong, so he could neither justify himself nor be forgiven. Maddening. The question was, did she realise how awkward that was and was she administering a particularly subtle punishment? Or did she care too little to be annoyed with him? Probably the latter.

The faint sound of splashing stopped him, the towel still stretched across his shoulder blades. Of course, when the suites had been changed around, the two new bathing rooms had been carved out of a small, little-used retiring room and the walls must be simply lath and plaster. He padded across and applied his ear to the panelling. Definite splashing and the sound of Kate's voice.

Grant stepped back with a grimace. The next thing, he would be peering through the keyhole at his own wife. The sounds were certainly exercising his imagination in a thoroughly arousing way, as though his body needed any more encouragement. He gave his back one sharp slap with the towel and went out to the dressing room, where Griffin, his smart new London valet, was laying out his smart new London clothes. If nothing else, his wife would not be confronted by the travel-worn, battered, weary, grief-stricken man she had married. He gave a grunt of satisfaction as he lowered his chin the half-inch to perfect the set of the waterfall knot in his neckcloth, nodded his thanks to Griffin and headed for the drawing room and the start of his new marriage.

Kate paused at the head of the stairs for one last calming breath, twitched her black silk skirts into order and descended the staircase in a manner befitting a countess. She had waited nearly four and a half months for this evening and the unexpected encounter with Grant that morning had done nothing to make this any easier. The exhausted, kind, patient stranger she had married was now an alert, attractive, impatient, secretive stranger.

Nothing had changed for him, it seemed, except for the fact that he'd had nearly four and a half months' worth of town bronze, the status of an earl and an endless amount of time to regret marrying her. She had her looks back, her confidence as the mistress of a large country house and an inconvenient attack of physical attraction for the aforesaid stranger.

I want a proper marriage, not simply make-believe for the rest of our lives. But what does he want? She smiled at Giles as the footman opened the door for her and then checked on the threshold as Grant turned from the contemplation of a landscape painting she had placed over the hearth, a replacement for one of the old earl's more bloodthirsty hunting scenes.

'A definite improvement.'

For a moment she thought he meant her appearance, then he gestured to the painting. *At least he is smiling.* 'I am glad you think so.' Kate went to her usual armchair by the fireplace. The distance across the room had never felt so long, nor her limbs so clumsy. Grant moved as though he would intercept her, touch her, but she sat down before he could reach her side. With a feeling of relief that she recognised as sheer nerves she picked up her embroidery frame from the basket beside the chair. She wanted this man, but she had no idea how to cope with him.

'Naturally, I would not remove any portraits, but I found that sitting here every evening under the glazed eyes of a slaughtered stag was somewhat dampening to the spirits,' she said as she found the needle, then dropped her thimble.

Grant stooped to retrieve it and handed it to her. He moved back, but remained opposite her, one elbow on the end of the mantelpiece. In any other man she would have supposed the pose was intended to draw attention to his clothes or his figure, and it certainly did that, but Grant's attention seemed to be all on her.

'That is a charming gown. Have you been sending to London for the latest fashions?'

She had been pleased with it, although a trifle nervous of the low neckline, which the dressmaker assured her was high by London standards. 'No, merely for the latest fashionable journals. I have discovered a most accomplished dressmaker in Newcastle and an excellent fabrics warehouse.'

'In that case you might wish to accompany me into the city next week and choose something for half mourning. I imagine you are weary of unrelieved black and grey and the six months isn't too far away. I hardly feel the need to apply the strictest rules, do you?'

'We are mourning *your* grandfather, it is for you to decide, but I must confess that some colour would be welcome.' It would be a delight, to be truthful, even if it was only shades of lavender and lilac. She placed a careful row of French knots. 'Were your friends very surprised at the news of your marriage?'

Grant's eyebrows rose at the abrupt change of subject and it seemed to Kate that in moving to take the chair opposite her he was taking the time to compose his reply with care. 'My three closest friends know something of the truth.' He shrugged. 'I could hardly deceive them that our relationship was of long-standing, they know my movements too well. But I would trust them with my life and you may rely on their absolute discretion. As far as acquaintances in town are concerned, I confided in a few incorrigible gossips that Grandfather had not approved of the match, hence a secret Scottish wedding and no announcement. They were titillated enough by the disapproval not to question the date and one or two were obviously on the verge of remarking that it was convenient that his death precluded an uncomfortable confession to him following the birth of our child.'

'How...distasteful.'

'Society can be like that, I find. The prospect of gossip and scandal sharpens even the most respectable tongue.' He shrugged. 'But it plays into our hands. They'll spread the tale and provided no one has the effrontery to demand to know the date of the wedding it will soon become of no matter, and even if some conclude that we anticipated the wedding, no one will hold that against you. It will soon be old history.'

'They won't hold it against me because too many of them have done the same, no doubt.' His lips twitched at the tartness of her tone. 'Did you tell people who I am?' she asked, trying not to sound as worried as she was. 'And what is supposed to be the reason for your grandfather's disapproval?'

'I mentioned that you were from a respectable minor gentry family in Suffolk.' She managed not to let out a long sigh of relief. 'The fact that your father was merely a country squire without connections or an established place in society was sufficient explanation for Grandfather to oppose the match. The old man was a product of his generation—nothing less than the daughter of an earl, and one bringing a substantial dowry and influence with her into the bargain, was good enough for the Earl of Allundale.'

'I see.' Kate unpicked the knot she had just set, which had become unaccountably tangled. *So presumably*

Madeleine had been Lady Madeleine, even though she was married to a mere Mr Rivers.

'That was his view,' Grant said. 'I do not share it. Having married a lady with just those qualifications as my first wife, I know all too well they are no guarantee of anything. However, it makes a perfectly plausible reason.'

'Of course,' she agreed. *And the old earl was quite correct—what do I bring to this marriage? We could have a good marriage, as long as I can keep my secrets, but if they become public knowledge, it will make a scandal that would rebound on Grant and on the children.* She was pleased at how composed she sounded.

'Kate, you must write to your brother soon,' Grant said.

'No. I will not write to him. I do not want him knowing anything of my marriage.'

'Kate, why ever not? I would have asked you for his direction and done so myself if I had realised you would neglect to do so. I need to talk to him about the settlements,' Grant said. 'And I assume he is holding money for you that will be released on your marriage. I seem to recall you saying something.'

Did I? How foolish. 'There is virtually nothing. I do not want to make a fuss about it. He has control until I marry with his approval, that is all.'

'You think he will object to me? He may not know me by reputation, but he is hardly likely to turn up his nose at an earl.'

'He would be delighted with an earl,' Kate said drily. 'But he will be unpleasant. If you must have the truth, Henry has an expensive wife and ambitions beyond his means. He is quite unscrupulous.' That was all true enough. 'If he discovers who I have married, he would ask to borrow money—which I doubt you would ever see again. To encourage him to sponge off you would not be right.'

That was harsh, but it was a mild version of the truth. Henry would hold the scandal of Anna's parentage over Grant, try to entangle him in that mire. He would get a surprise if he tried it, she thought grimly. Grant would probably throttle him. But then there was the blackmail. What if Grant thought he must inform the magistrate? He was an honest, straightforward man. There was no way he could ignore it, surely? Then he would be smeared by association, by his marriage.

'He is my brother-in-law. I would not like to be unreasonable. Do not sound so apologetic, my dear. Brothers-in-law are almost expected to hang on one's coat-tails.' The tolerant amusement in Grant's voice was no help. 'Besides, there is the matter of the settlements, which I really should discuss with him. You should have what is yours.'

'It is very little, a few hundreds.'

'Settle it on Anna if you do not want it. It is always a mistake to neglect financial matters, however minor.'

Kate wondered suddenly just how wealthy Grant was. There was no stinting about the household, the land was obviously in good heart. But that might simply be because he was expending all he had on keeping things just so. Now, on top of the risk of her dubious brother touching him for loans, which would never be repaid, she had saddled him with the expense of a wife and a child. She had removed his opportunity for a much more advantageous marriage and all she could offer were the skills of any competent mistress of a country house.

For how much longer could she put Grant off about

contacting Henry? Or could she add to her deceit, tell Grant that she had written to her brother, but that he had cut the connection?

But then Grant would still want to pursue her money for her and, she suspected, he would try to heal the breach. And behind those fears was the lurking terror that sooner or later he would ask her to accompany him to London, take her place beside him in society as his hostess. Inwardly she quailed. A country mouse contemplating life amidst the birds of prey of fashionable London could not have felt as inadequate. She could not even dance the waltz, Kate reflected with a descent into gloom. The faint smile felt as though it was pinned to her face. She would manage if she had to. Somehow. But if Lord Baybrook was there…

'Kate, is something wrong?' Grant had obviously noticed the artificiality of her expression.

'No, of course not.' She made the effort to smile with her eyes when all she felt was queasiness.

'There is no need to be anxious.' There was something warm in his expression, some meaning in his tone. Kate stared back, puzzled, as he added, 'About tonight, I mean.'

He is talking about bed, about making love. Does he mean not to be anxious because he will come to me… or that he will not? I hope he comes. There was no hiding the truth from herself that she was attracted to this man, this stranger-husband. She felt the blush rising up her face and with it the shame that Grant would see her eagerness, think her a wanton. Or perhaps he would welcome that, expect her to be very experienced and to possess sophisticated skills in bed.

It was difficult to understand this feeling. After all, her

skills were non-existent and she had no idea what would be involved in sophisticated lovemaking.

'I am not anxious about tonight,' she said, rather too loudly.

'Dinner is served, my lady.' Grimswade somehow managed to sound even more smoothly efficient and bland than normal. When had he appeared in the doorway behind her? Had he heard? She wondered if it was possible to pass out from sheer embarrassment. Henry always said that one should treat the servants as though they were furniture and would discuss anything and everything in front of them—from an embarrassing rash to his gaming losses.

'Thank you, Grimswade.' She found a smile for the butler as she began to rise to her feet, then almost jumped in surprise to find her husband by her side, his hand outstretched.

'My dear.'

My dear. A conventional phrase, that is all. He means nothing by it. She put her fingertips on his wrist and resisted the urge to curl them around the strong tendons, to feel the jut of his wristbone. When she had seen him this morning her eyes had been drawn to his bare, tanned hands, a sharp contrast with her smaller, paler hands beside his on the rug. What would those long fingers look like on her body? How would they feel? Now she told herself that she could detect nothing through the fine kid of her evening gloves, not his body heat, not the pulse of his blood.

'I do hope you like the new recipe for veal ragout Cook has been trying,' Kate remarked as they walked through to the dining room. 'It is an old family one I remembered.' Discussing the food was utterly banal. He would think her so dull. But it was safe.

Giles the footman stepped forward to pull out her chair
at the foot of the table for her, but Grant was before him.
He pushed it in carefully as she sat, then laid one hand
on her shoulder in a fleeting caress before taking his own
place at the head of the long board. 'I am certain that
whatever you suggest will be delightful.' That warmth
was back in his eyes and behind it a question that had
not been there before. Or perhaps a doubt.

Conscious of the attendant footmen, of Grimswade
bringing the decanter to fill Grant's wine glass, Kate
closed her lips on the impulsive questions—*What do you
want of me? What do you expect of me?*—and focused
her attention on the dishes arrayed on the table. At least
her husband would have no reason to complain of her
supervision of the kitchen, whatever he felt about her
presence in his bed.

Chapter Nine

Kate was nervous. That blush when he had mentioned *tonight* had not been the faint glow of anticipated pleasure, but the embarrassment or nerves that Grant might have expected from a virgin. But she was not untouched— the presence of little Anna was proof enough of that. So what was it? An aversion to him, or painful shyness? One would be easy enough to overcome, the other, less so.

'Have you been dining here in lonely state every night?' he asked, casting round for some innocuous topic to discuss in front of the servants. He could send them away, of course, but that might only aggravate whatever fears Kate was harbouring.

'Usually I invite Mr Gough to join me. I find he is an intelligent conversationalist. Once a week we have an early supper with Charlie in the small dining room with all the leaves taken out of the table. He enjoys the grown-up treat.'

Grant felt a jab of something unpleasantly like jealousy and instantly regretted it. His wife had been lonely, Gough was a gentleman, intelligent and doubtless pleasant company, and he, too, was probably lonely and welcomed the opportunity for conversation.

But something in his expression must have betrayed that instinctive, possessive reaction. Kate bit her lip and glanced uneasily at the footmen as though expecting a rebuke in front of them.

'An excellent idea,' Grant said with casual approval. 'My grandfather would dine with Gough when he did not have company visiting and often when he did. I am glad you had congenial adult companionship.'

'We had a lot to discuss about Charlie's lessons. Mr Gough follows your instructions carefully, of course, but there is so much day-to-day detail. I hope you do not feel I am encroaching?'

It was a question, not an apology, and Grant was careful to keep his own tone light. 'Certainly not. You are his stepmama, after all, as I am sure you would have reminded me if I had objected to your involvement.'

Kate flushed up at that, but her voice was confident as she raised it to give an order. 'Grimswade, that will be all. We will serve ourselves and ring when we require dessert.'

'My lady.' The butler gestured to the footmen and closed the door softly behind the last liveried back.

Kate put down her fork and fixed him with a direct gaze, compelling his attention. 'My lord, I think we should be frank. I have a great deal of experience of being a daughter and a sister and of the limits of my authority and freedom in those roles. Since I have been here at Abbeywell I have gained several months' worth of knowledge of how to run a large country house. But I have no experience of a husband, of the limits he will impose on my actions, of his expectations of me.'

Ah, so now the recriminations come. Grant chewed his mouthful of beef, swallowed and decided that dodging the issue would not help. 'In effect you feel I abandoned you.' He had done just that, but he was damned if he was going to justify himself. Which was a good thing, because he was not certain that he could. He had left Abbeywell because he knew, once he was not drugged with exhaustion and grief, that he could not bear to be there. Now he was going to have to make himself endure. He owed it to Charlie, to the estate and to his neglected wife.

Part of him had been running away from confronting what he had done by marrying a woman without the qualifications necessary for a countess. He was beginning to suspect he was wrong about that judgement, but confessing that he had believed it could only be deeply wounding to Kate.

'You had a great deal to do in London, many responsibilities in connection with the earldom. I am not reproaching you, my lord.' Her smile was sudden, vivid, and took him completely by surprise. 'I merely explain my own…limitations.'

'I wish you would use my given name.' Grant smiled back, charmed, and realised he had never seen that open, uncomplicated smile from Kate before. She smiled at the children, at the servants, but never at him.

But why would she? He had hardly seen her except as a desperate woman in the throes of labour, or an exhausted one in its aftermath. Even that morning her smile had been polite and dutiful. But this expression transformed her. Strangely it did not enhance her beauty, as a smile usually did for a woman. Instead it emphasised the slight irregularity of her face, it crinkled up her blue eyes and showed the little gap between very white, otherwise even, front teeth. And yet…*charmed* was the only word for his reaction. This was a real woman, not a pretty, regimented society doll. A real woman he knew not at all.

'I see no limitations, Kate. There is nothing we cannot deal with by a little discussion, an exchange of views, greater familiarity.' He chose the final word deliberately.

That produced a blush that he had no difficulty interpreting as anything but one of sensual awareness. Kate's lips were parted and she did not meet his gaze, but glanced up, above his head, blushed even more rosily and reached for her water glass.

Grant suppressed the instinctive movement to turn and look at the wall behind his chair. Of course, that was where his own portrait hung. So what was there about that to make her colour up? Unless she had spent every mealtime sitting just there, looking at his image and liking what she saw. He bit his lip to repress a grin that could only be unworthily smug. He was used to hearing himself described as a good-looking man, women seemed to like to flirt with him, but he felt no conceit about that. He looked like his grandfather at the same age, which was good fortune and no merit of his. He could feel some satisfaction at the appreciation shown by his lovers, however, because he was confident that was due to practice and an interest in his partner's pleasure as well as his own, rather than to heredity.

His first wife had been more prone to burst into tears or tantrums at the sight of him than to blush prettily. The marriage had been an arranged one and they had hardly known each other before it. Grant had come to the conclusion that Madeleine was simply averse to sex and hoped that he was not the cause, but that it was something inbuilt in her character. She had been stiff and unresponsive in bed from the first, informing him, when he had asked her what was the matter, that her mama had explained to her that she must endure her marital duty and that was what she was doing. Enduring. It was hard work being a sensitive and imaginative lover in the face of that. And then he had made the grave tactical error of getting her pregnant too soon...

Grant pushed away the memory and focused on the very different wife facing him down six foot of polished mahogany. It occurred to him that it would be a pleasant novelty to be wed to a woman who took an interest in the physical side of marriage. He allowed himself to smile and decided that Kate was decidedly flustered.

Slowly, slowly, don't startle her, you are almost a stranger in her eyes, he reminded himself. Just because she showed sensual awareness did not mean that she was not shy. He must court this woman even though she was already his countess. 'I hope you will always feel free to discuss any thoughts you have about Charlie. As for the household, it is yours to command, and if the allowances I give you for those expenses and your own expenditure are inadequate, I will certainly amend them.'

'Thank you.' Kate had recovered her composure, it seemed. She took a sip of wine. 'It would be helpful to know when we might have regular discussions about day-to-day issues.'

'Of course. Would around ten each morning suit you? I am usually back from my morning ride about then and the steward and estate manager come to see me after luncheon.' She nodded, apparently happy with the proposal. 'Of course, we will have much more time together to discuss more...intimate matters.'

The charming smile vanished, but the equally charming blush persisted. How far down did it go? Below the decorous dip of her black silk evening gown? Down far enough to tint those sweet curves with rose? Grant shifted in his chair, feeling again the lash of his own arousal. Slowly, slowly might be wise, but the seduction of his countess promised to be a leisurely pleasure.

Kate watched her husband's face and tried to read the thoughts behind that handsome, intelligent surface. She suspected that he was clever enough to hide whatever emotions he did not want her to read, although the warmth in his gaze and the faint curve of his lips when that gaze strayed downwards from her face were less revealing of deep thoughts than of basic masculine instincts, that was certain.

She wanted him, although now the man was before her in the flesh and not simply as a fantasy fuelled by a two-dimensional image, that wanting was tinged again with apprehension. Kate reached for the silver bell that stood before her place. 'Time for dessert, I think, my lord.'

One dark brow lifted.

'In front of the servants I should not be too familiar, Grant,' Kate said repressively and was rewarded by a fleeting, wicked smile that vanished into an expression of aristocratic calm when the footmen re-entered.

Somehow Kate's increasingly fevered imagination had carried her directly from the dining table to the bed-chamber and it came as a shock to see Grimswade setting the decanters on the sideboard when the dessert dishes were cleared, just as he always did when Mr Gough dined with her.

'I will leave you to your port, my lord.' She rose and Grant stood, too. She caught his reflection in the glass of the watercolour that hung by the door as she left and saw he was still on his feet, watching her. The glimpse of dark, shadowed eyes made her shiver deliciously.

Now what? Mr Gough would linger only long enough to drink one glass, more out of custom than pleasure, she suspected. Then he would join her for an hour, bringing journals with items he thought might interest her, or some written exercise of Charlie's that he knew she would approve.

She had come to enjoy the harmless, companionable interludes that were such a pleasant novelty. Her brother had never scrupled to leave the ladies waiting for him if he had a male companion to talk to or when he found a female guest tiresome. Sometimes, he would not join his wife and sister at all, disappearing to a cockfight in the village or to join his cronies for a game of cards without as much as a by-your-leave.

Kate picked up her embroidery, regarded the unsteady line of French knots with dismay and began to unpick them.

'If you scowl at that unfortunate piece of work much longer, it will scorch,' a deep voice remarked from just behind her.

She jumped, drove the needle into the ball of her index finger and said a naughty word under her breath. She switched the glare to Grant, who moved, soft-footed, to stand in front of her.

'You have pricked yourself. My fault for startling you.' He hunkered down, the silk of his evening knee breeches straining tight over muscular thighs, and took the wounded hand in his. 'Let me kiss it better.'

'I— Oh!' He lifted her hand, pressed his lips to the tiny bead of blood and then sucked the whole top joint of her finger into his mouth. Kate stared down at the fashionably barbered dark head bent over her hand, the wide shoulders in their blue superfine, the elegance of the man performing a small, insignificant, utterly indecent act.

Because it was indecent, she had not the slightest doubt of it. His fingers clasped lightly around her wrist, the ends over her pulse as if to monitor the effect he was having on her. She was shackled by the encircling grip as securely as if by iron manacles, because she could no more have moved her hand away than flown.

The sensitive tip of her finger was encased in the wet heat of Grant's mouth. His tongue caressed the pad until the sting of the needle prick was lost in the soft touch. She could sense the sharp edge of his teeth, carefully kept from her flesh as gradually, so very gradually, he drew her finger into his mouth as far as the middle joint. The suction pulsed, moving it in and out, his tongue tip curled and the heat rose through her as she realised what this action mimicked.

She needed to move, to squirm in her chair and push him away, draw him closer. She needed—

Grant sat back and she jerked her hand back against her bodice, the damp finger leaving a mark on the silk for a moment. 'Has that taken the sting away?' His lids were half closed, his eyes dark, his parted lips a little moist.

As if he has been kissing me, she thought wildly. *This is what he will look like when he holds me in his arms, when his body comes down over mine, pressing it into the bed. His* naked *body over mine, hot and hard and aroused.*

Somehow she found the composure to murmur, 'Perfectly, thank you', as though he had merely dabbed at the little puncture with his handkerchief. 'So careless of me. I might have got blood on the linen.'

Grant's lids lifted, his lips closed as he smiled and he stood up, looming over her for a moment. Kate found her eye level was precisely right for her to see that whatever he said, however coolly he might smile at her and however steadily he got to his feet, he was aroused. Impressively, alarmingly, aroused. *Just like my fantasies.*

'I think I will retire now.' It was the instinct to escape, to be alone to come to terms with what his touch was doing to her, but as soon as the words were out of her mouth she saw that Grant had interpreted them as an invitation, a direct response to what had just happened. Kate folded her embroidery into a careful square, put it into the sewing box and made herself rise with leisurely grace. Anything but let Grant see how excited and panicked he made her. Why she must hide it, she was not sure, because instinct told her he would welcome her awareness. It was pride, perhaps, or apprehension of her own limited experience disappointing him. Or was it fear that her own confused and heated fantasies would prove false and she would feel as let-down and unsatisfied as she had with Jonathan?

'Goodnight, my… Goodnight, Grant.'

His crooked smile was teasing. 'Goodnight, Kate.'

He doesn't mean it as a farewell. He'll come to my room, she told herself as she climbed the stairs and hurried to the nursery for Anna's goodnight kiss and a quick word with Jeannie. Then to Charlie's room, her fingers crossed that he would be asleep and there would be no battle over lights out. But he hardly stirred as she brushed the hair back from his forehead, kissed the smooth skin and pulled his tumbled covers back over his sprawled body.

Wilson, her maid, was already in Kate's bedchamber, alerted by the downstairs staff. 'The new lawn nightgown—' Kate began, then saw that it was already laid out on the bed, its matching robe beside it. Of Kate's usual comfortable plain cotton nightgown there was no sign. 'You already have it,' she observed lamely.

'Yes, my lady. With his lordship being home, I assumed this would be the right one.' The woman said it without the slightest hint of embarrassment. Apparently she took it as a matter of course that her master would visit his wife's bedchamber and that her mistress would want to look her best.

And why shouldn't she? Kate told herself, attempting to look as nonchalant as the maid about the fact she was preparing to receive her husband. *She thinks we are an established married couple who have been separated for months, not two virtual strangers who have not even exchanged a kiss.*

She submitted to the bath and the hair brush, made a choice at random from the array of scent bottles presented to her, rejected the robe and climbed into bed, wishing she had not read so many Gothic tales where the heroine, a virgin sacrifice clad all in white, awaits the arrival of the mysterious dark man, who may be the villain, or, perhaps, the hero.

She tried to calm herself with thoughts of her youthful fantasies about marriage. It had been a sheltered life in the Essex countryside. Motherless, her behaviour had been subject to more scrutiny by her father and brother and the neighbouring matrons than it might otherwise have been. So flirtations were very mild, her social circle limited, her daydreams of a husband vague and romantic. No wonder she had fallen so hard for Jonathan.

Minutes passed. Kate reached for the novel she had been reading and tried to focus on it so that she would not look too eager, or too nervous, when Grant came in. She read the same page four times. The clock struck the half hour. He would have gone to look in on Charlie and perhaps also Anna. He would have bathed, or at least washed. Shaved, perhaps. He was, she suspected, a fastidious man. *Another half hour, he'll come within the next half hour,* she told herself and frowned at the small print that seemed to dance before her eyes.

She pushed one shoulder strap down, then pulled it back. *Ting,* went the clock on the mantelshelf. *Ting, ting...* Kate counted to eleven. Grant was not coming. She tossed aside the book and made herself go through all the perfectly acceptable reasons why he might not. Then she threw back the covers and slid out of bed.

No patience with slippers, no patience with a wrapper and certainly no patience with a husband who'd left her for months, then behaved in a manner enough to fluster a nun, let alone a wife, and who then left the aforesaid wife to a lonely bed and a very silly novel.

Kate opened the connecting door without bothering to knock. Grant was sitting up in bed, bare-chested, the evening beard still shadowing his chin and what appeared to be a most absorbing book in his hands.

He looked up as she stepped into the room, but he did not let go of the book.

'What are you reading?' Kate demanded.

'Constitutional procedure,' he said so calmly that she wished she was wearing slippers so she could throw one. How dared he be all relaxed when she was a positive tangle of emotions? 'I am attempting to get my head around some of the trickier aspects of the working of Parliament.'

He closed the volume. 'Why? Are you looking for something interesting to read?'

'No. I am attempting to get my head around the trickier aspects of marriage,' Kate retorted. 'I see I may have to consult an encyclopaedia.' The door, when she turned and stalked back into her bedchamber, slammed with the most satisfying bang.

It opened again before she reached the bed. 'Perhaps I might assist,' her husband offered.

Chapter Ten

Kate kept walking on shaky legs, climbed into bed and only then turned. Grant was dressed, somewhat sketchily, in a heavy green silk robe, belted loosely at the waist over what appeared to be nothing but bare skin.

She took a strengthening breath down to her diaphragm. 'Assist? You, my lord, are the source of my confusion.'

'Because I did not come to your bed?' He moved to the foot of it, sat with his back against the post, legs stretched out parallel with hers, and studied her face.

Kate made herself lie still and not acknowledge the insidious pressure of his body. One long, bare, elegant foot pressed against her hip bone. She wanted to run a finger along the sharp cords of tendon, the curve of his instep. Instead she said, 'I told myself that Charlie might have had a nightmare, or that you were so tired after your journey that you had fallen asleep or that a crisis might have occurred on the estate. All those were perfectly reasonable excuses for flirting with a wife you had not seen for months and then failing to…to join her. But constitutional procedure? I am not a vain woman, but really, I had not placed myself below turgid reading matter of that sort.'

'I was employing it to take my mind off your presence in the next room. It was not very successful, and
if I had been aware of that nightgown, it would have
been even less so.' As Grant leaned back, the front of his
robe gaped open to reveal the side of his muscular chest,
dusted in dark hair.

'Why?' It seemed she was only capable of enough
breath for one word at a time.

'I thought you were nervous. Shy. Flustered.' He
shrugged and the robe gaped more. Kate held her breath.
'I did not want to pressure you.'

'Of course I was…*am* shy. I do not know you. We
have never even kissed, let alone…that. How am I supposed to feel?'

'You are not a virgin,' Grant pointed out. He looked
faintly wary, she was glad to see. *So he should be. He is
lucky I am not throwing* The Caledonian Bandit *by Miss
Smith at his head. It is all it is fit for.*

'Clearly not.' She had her breath back now the robe
had ceased its descent. 'But I am not at all experienced.
I…I became pregnant very quickly.' She tried to recall
what she had told him about her lover. Lying was so alien
and so difficult. 'And we could not meet often.'

'I'm not a virgin, either, of course. I don't expect you
to hold that against me. But you are not at all experienced?' He seemed to be pleased by that. Men were
strange creatures.

'Yes. I mean, no.' It had been lovely to be in Jonathan's
arms, to be able to show her feelings for him, of course
it had. While it lasted, before disillusion set in. But even
at the height of her short-lived infatuation he had never
made her feel so agitated, so confused as this did. And it
had not been such a wonderful experience that she was

desperate to repeat it, so why did she want Grant to shrug off that robe, come to bed and just— 'So, yes, I was apprehensive. I am still. But now I think it would be better to simply get it over with.'

'Get it over with,' Grant repeated, his voice flat. 'Your expectations do not appear to be very high.' His hands had gone to the ties of his robe. Now they stilled.

'I am sure you make love very nicely,' Kate said politely, wishing the soft feather mattress would simply swallow her up. Now she had insulted him. No man was going to take well the suggestion that his lovemaking was anything but magnificent. *Very nicely? Of all the things to say...*

'I have not had any complaints recently.' Grant straightened up from his relaxed slouch against the bedpost.

Recently? From his mistress, I suppose. Does that mean his late wife... Pride made her bite back the question. 'I just thought it would be better to—'

'Get it over with. Yes, I grasp the point that flirting and courting and giving you time to get accustomed to me may not be the best way to go about this and that you really wish it was all over.' He stood up and tugged the knot in the sash free. 'But you do wish me to come to your bed?'

'Yes. Of course. Lights?' It came out as a squeak. The branch of candles was still alight on her dressing table and the little oil lamp by the bed cast a warm, but revealing, glow over the snowy expanse of sheets.

'We have confided that neither of us is a virgin. I think we can cope with the shock of nudity.' Grant shrugged off the robe. He sounded less than happy.

Kate closed her eyes, then, when there was no sound of movement, opened them again. Grant was standing there, hands on lean hips, waiting, she supposed, for her to faint, scream or dive under the covers. She did none of those things, just stared at his admirably flat stomach, then, when she thought her breathing was under control, let her gaze slide lower.

He was not as aroused as he had been in the drawing room when he had been sucking her finger, but then he was probably finding her so infuriating that it was killing his desire. Kate realised suddenly that she did not want that. She wanted Grant to make love to her, here, now and with enthusiasm. His eyebrows lifted as she threw back the covers, reached for the hem of her nightgown and dragged it over her head in one ungainly movement.

When she made herself meet his gaze she found he had not moved, but the green eyes were dark beneath lowered lids and his mouth was curved into a crooked smile that held both approval and a promise.

'Right from when we first met, I knew you had courage,' Grant said as he closed the distance between them. He lay down beside her and, to her enormous relief, pulled the covers up over their bare bodies. She was very aware that the last time she had lain with a man she had not given birth to a child and that this man had once been married to a woman who, if Kate had discovered nothing else about her, had been a beauty.

The warmth of his body as he lay beside her was comforting, but her nerves were jangling and she just wished he would get on with it. 'Have you changed your mind?' she asked.

'No.' Grant turned so he was on his side facing her and moved closer, until the evidence of just how much he had *not* thought better of this was branding itself to her hip. 'I was giving you the opportunity to dive out of the other side of the bed if you had changed yours.'

Afterwards Kate had no idea whether it had been nerves, hysteria or simply her old sense of the ridiculous reasserting itself, but she found herself laughing. 'Like a scene in a French farce,' she managed between gasps of mirth. 'In and out of bedrooms, in and out of bed…'

'You have obviously been watching far more *risqué* farces than I have,' Grant said with a grin, and then, before she had stopped laughing, before the nerves could seize her again, he rolled her on to her back and kissed her.

Kate was open-mouthed on a gasp of laughter and Grant took advantage of her parted lips to take possession, his tongue sliding in to stroke hers, his lips warm and firm and demanding. For a first kiss it was anything but tentative, but nor was it impatiently demanding. *Here I am,* Grant seemed to be saying. *I want you, you want me. Shall we?*

Her body knew the answer, it seemed. Her arms curled around his neck, pulling him closer as her tongue stroked against his. *Yes.* He felt so different, so new. Taller and more muscular than Jonathan, his hands slower, yet more assured, his taste absolutely new and very arousing. Her hands slid over his shoulder and the right one encountered long, rough tracks of scar tissue. Grant shrugged away from her touch and she took the hint, curling her fingers around his neck instead. Then she forgot all about scars.

When Grant broke the kiss, gathering her in against his chest, she rubbed her cheek against the dusting of coarse hair, learning his scent. Citrus from the soap he had washed with, a faint hint of leather, a distant tang of brandy, a musk that was very male, very much him. The scent she remembered from that long desperate night when he had sat close beside her and she had clung to his hand, patterning it with bruises, spiced now with arousal.

'That tickles,' he said, his voice a rumble under her cheek. His hands were beginning to stray, down over her hips, up across her ribs, curving around her buttocks. Kate let her own fingers wander, exploring the flat stomach, dipping into his naval, which made him gasp with laughter, running up and down the thicker line of hair, not daring to follow it all the way.

Grant seemed content to let her roam, but his own hands became more purposeful, stroking up over the curve of her breasts, rubbing across her nipples just enough to make them peak and tingle, then down to brush the curls at the apex of her thighs.

Kate began to move, restless, and found her fingers were gripping Grant's hips. Jonathan had been faster, more urgent, rougher. Did Grant not want her with the same desire?

His lips closed over one aching nipple and she moaned, arching up against him. She felt his lips curve into a smile and then shivered with nerves as he shifted and pressed one hand gently between her thighs, opening her.

'Oh, yes,' he said, the words vibrating against the puckered skin of her nipple, and his teeth nipped gently as he slid one finger into her. Then his thumb found the place that Jonathan had rubbed against so impatiently. Only, Grant was gentle, teasing, and the raw, almost intolerable sensation became one of pulsing sweetness mixed with a desperation that had her squirming against his hand.

'Shh, slowly, slowly,' he murmured against her neck. But she did not want to be slow. She wanted him now, wanted the *more* that she could sense, just out of her reach. Her right hand moved from his hip, stroked down, touched the heated flesh and stroked again until he groaned aloud.

'If you do that—'

'Yes,' Kate urged. 'I want… I don't know. I need…'

Grant's weight was a fresh arousal as their bodies touched down their entire lengths, hot skin against hot skin. He shifted, lifted on his elbows and then, holding her gaze with his, sheathed himself within her.

'Ah…sweet Kate.' He closed his eyes, dropped his head so his forehead rested on hers and held still. She felt the tension vibrating through him as she grasped the broad shoulders, tilted her head so her lips found his. The urgent need to move became a longing for peace as she lay there, so close, so much at one with him. She let her body encompass his, ease around it, holding him within her.

When he began to move it was at first so slow, so gentle, that she hardly realised that her own body was rocking with his, yielding to the slow thrusts, the need building again as she released the hard flesh only to accept him back with a soft gasp of pleasure. The rhythm increased until she was clinging to him, gasping as they rode the gathering, building storm together.

Grant shifted, lifted her against him, and the pressure built until she was curled around him, her ankles locked at the small of his back, striving desperately to catch hold of whatever it was that was tormenting her so deliciously, promising something that was just out of reach. And suddenly she broke apart, heard herself cry out, felt Grant tense and arch over her, and then the world went black, save for the lights in the darkness behind her lids as she let go and flew.

What had just happened? Kate lay in the circle of Grant's arm, her cheek against his chest. His skin was damp, his heartbeat strong, rapid, but slowing as she sensed him drifting into sleep.

What had *happened*? she asked herself again, lying wide-eyed in the flickering candlelight. She hardly knew this man except as the Good Samaritan who had saved her that bleak Christmas. Saved her, saved her child, turned her life upside down. Yes, he was an attractive man, but a man with secrets, a man with barely hidden darkness in his soul.

She had married him, accepted the protection of his name, his status and his wealth. Accepted, too, that she had a duty as his wife to lie with him and perhaps, if she was fortunate, to bear a child of his. *And I had become excited by the thought of him,* she admitted to herself. *Aroused.* Which was good, because it would have been hard to accept lovemaking with a man for whom she could feel no attraction.

But this wonderful physical experience—where had that come from? She had known Jonathan a little, liked him, thought she loved him, considered him a handsome man and had been eager to go to his arms. Yet his passion had left her strangely untouched, unsatisfied, confused. *I talked myself into love with him, didn't I?* Kate told herself. But she did not love this man, either, so what was the difference? *Why did I not burn up in Jonathan's arms as I did with Grant?*

Because Grant is the better lover, of course. So it was all a matter of technique, of arousal, and in her imaginings when she met Jonathan she had told herself the romantic lies that it was all about love.

Kate turned away from the comfort of the warm, strong body beside her to lie on the edge of the bed on cold sheets. *I deserve the chill,* the nagging little voice of her conscience chided. *Wanton.* 'Jonathan,' she whispered. What a fool she had been, how eager to experience love, when really what she had been seeking was this, this physical delight. And as a result of her naivety and Henry's cynical scheming she had been ruined and was now hundreds of miles from home, living a lie.

That had been…incredible. Grant let himself drift in utterly relaxed drowsiness, his body boneless with sensual pleasure. He had never expected it, never thought that Kate would catch alight in his hands, that her body would answer his with that joyful, urgent sensuality.

She curled against him now, warm, soft. Kate, his wife, who did not react to his kisses and caresses as though forcing herself to yield to her duty, but as though she wanted to join him in creating magic. To find a compatible lover was not such a novelty, but to find that, quite by chance, he had married a woman who took and gave with such sweet, almost innocent, eroticism, that was a miracle.

Kate moved, turned away, and he woke fully to see she was lying, her back to him, on the edge of the bed. 'Oh, Jonathan…' He caught the faint whisper and even with that thread of sound, the unhappiness.

Something cold and heavy lodged in his stomach. Disappointment? Jealousy? So, Kate was still in love with Anna's father, still mourning him, which must explain her shyness and confusion earlier. Now she was feeling guilty for enjoying making love with her husband.

Because she had enjoyed it, that was not arrogance on his part—even the most accomplished courtesan could not have feigned that reaction. Grant reached out his hand to touch her shoulder, then drew it back before his fingers reached the curve of exposed skin. Reluctant to intrude, he turned on his side away from Kate's tense body and pulled the covers up over both of them. If he touched her now, she would think it was a demand for more sex. If he tried to console her, then she would know he had heard that whisper. He had no idea what to say to make things any better. At least now he understood her strange mood, the evidence of interest, of arousal, and yet the fear that forced her to ask for his presence in her bed had driven her to want to *get it over with*.

Grant got up, went to snuff the candles, doused the bedside lamp, pretended that he believed Kate was fast asleep as he fought down the dark mood that threatened to grip him. It was unreasonable, to feel...hurt. He was not in love with Kate and she had made no pretence of marrying him for anything other than the protection of his name for her child, so in no sense was he betrayed or deceived. She did not dislike him, he was certain, and she was certainly not repelled by him. It was simply that she had been in love with someone else, someone for ever out of her reach. And now she was making the best of the circumstances. In effect he had married a widow and done so before she'd had a proper chance to mourn.

But how to mend this marriage? He had the summer and the autumn, that was all. Then they must go to London, he would take his seat in the House of Lords and Kate must learn to be a peer's wife, a society hostess.

They could do it as virtual strangers—after all, many marriages functioned like that—but it was not how he wanted his marriage to be and it was not how he wanted the children to grow up, in a household with parents who were distant and cool with each other.

A hideous accident had taken Madeleine before Charlie's life could be blighted by his parents' unhappiness, but Grant was not prepared to risk it again. He could live without a wife's affection, certainly without her love, but somehow, for the sake of the children, he was going to have to make this work and make Kate happy, or, at the very least, content.

Chapter Eleven

When Grant opened his eyes on to the dawn light he found that, against all expectation, he had slept without his dreams being full of heat and flames and he had woken knowing how he was going to deal with his marriage. He would not let Kate guess he had heard her last night, he would not mention her lover, he would apologise for his long absence in London and then he would simply carry on as though everything was normal. He would make love to his wife, he would talk to his wife, he would ask his wife's opinions—and he would keep her so busy out of bed, so well satisfied in it, that she would not have the energy to mope over the man who had fathered Anna.

Beside him Kate stirred. He curled his arm around her and pulled her round to face him. She mumbled sleepily, eyes still closed, hair tousled, but she did not resist. Grant tightened his grip and bent to kiss her. 'Good morning, Lady Allundale.'

If she seems the slightest bit reluctant, then we'll have to talk... But Kate's lips opened under the pressure of his and her arms came up around his neck, her fingers sliding into the hair at his nape in a way that made him shiver with anticipation. It was a start. *Make love to her until she's dizzy,* he told himself, inhaling the scent of warm, sleepy woman. That would be no hardship.

Kate woke, stretched, blushed. She was alone in her bed, but Grant was still a powerful presence in the room. Her body ached pleasurably in the most intimate places, the musk of their lovemaking was heady in the air, the bedclothes were a tangle and, when she turned her head to look at the pillow where his head had rested, there was a single dark brown hair that curled around her finger when she touched it.

So, last night had not been a dream. They had made love twice and Grant had seemed to be very satisfied with the result. She most certainly was—physically satisfied, that was. Mentally she felt happy, guilty, confused and apprehensive. Happy, because to take that much pleasure in one's husband's arms must be a blessing—and the greatest good fortune. But she did not understand how it could be that she could do so. She did not love Grant and he did not love her. Would this last, or had it been a fluke? She wished she could talk to him about it, but how could she?

The conversation would be impossible. *I am overwhelmed by how good it is to make love with you. But why did I not feel like that with the man who took my virginity? Is it always going to be like that? Am I very ignorant and unskilled? Will you become tired of me soon? Am I disgracefully wanton?*

What if he agreed that, yes, she was lacking skill and sophistication, yes, the experience had been nothing out of the ordinary for him? 'I would sink with shame,' she murmured.

'My lady?' Wilson had entered from the dressing room with her usual quiet efficiency. The mistress of the household might have had the most wonderful and confusing night of her life, but the routine continued as usual.

'Nothing.' Kate cast a despairing glance around the bedchamber as the curtains were drawn back and light flooded in, revealing the wrecked bed, the sash of Grant's robe, her own nightgown tossed to the floor. Wilson merely glided around, gathering things up. She folded the sash neatly and set it aside.

'Would you care for breakfast here in your room, my lady? Or will you be taking it in the breakfast parlour?' That was where Kate normally took it, along with Charlie and his tutor.

'His lordship—'

'His lordship rode out about an hour ago, my lady. I understand from his man that it is his usual habit when in residence here.' There was not the faintest suggestion in her voice that his wife might be expected to know this. But of course, Grant had spoken of it last night and she had forgotten. For the past few months she had felt in control of herself, of this household. Now the arrival of one man meant, it seemed, that she could not even recall last night's conversation.

'I will take breakfast as usual in the parlour, after I have seen Lady Anna.' And Grant had suggested that they meet at ten to discuss practical matters. That had seemed an excellent idea at the time, now she could not imagine producing one coherent word when she had to face him again.

* * *

The harmless meeting still did not seem anything but an ordeal to be survived when she tapped on the study door on the stroke of ten.

'Come in!'

She pushed the door open and Grant came to his feet behind the big desk. 'My dear Kate, you have no need to knock.'

My dear Kate. 'Thank you.' She made herself meet Grant's eyes and smile. She at least felt rather more composed now she was dressed and had made a neat list of things to talk about. It was amazing how clothes made a barrier to hide behind. Last night she had been naked with this man, clawing at his muscled back, revelling in the hard thrust of his body.

Kate took a firm hold on her imagination and forced herself to be practical. This was broad daylight. She was the mistress of the house, coming to discuss harmless domestic matters. She should not feel awkward—after all, up until yesterday she had not needed to knock on any door in this house. Except for the one Grant kept locked. Bluebeard's chamber. Madeleine's rooms. She took the seat on the other side of the expanse of polished oak. 'I have several things I would like to discuss.'

'So do I. An early ride gives me the opportunity for some uninterrupted thinking, so I made some notes.' Grant picked up the sheet of paper from the blotter in front of him, frowned at it, then abruptly screwed it up and tossed it into the hearth. 'And I thought I had worked it all out, a plan for this marriage.'

'A plan? Why do we need a plan?'

'I did not think we did. I thought I would come back

here for the summer, join my wife and family, spend a pleasant few months getting to grips with the estate and then take us all back to London after Christmas when Parliament reconvenes. Then you could enjoy the Season.'

'And that is no longer your intention?' *Please, not London.*

'Certainly it is. And I thought that it would be easy enough to find a way to live together, to coexist and form a household, despite the way our marriage started.'

Her mouth felt dry. Kate willed herself to say calmly, 'So what has changed?' *What had gone wrong that he had brooded about on his morning ride?*

'Last night—' He broke off, looked out of the window and then back at her as though making the effort to meet her gaze. 'I was not going to say anything. I thought we could coexist, work together and simply put the past behind us. But in the light of day, I wonder if that is the best way forward for us.' He picked up a quill without looking at it and Kate watched as it bent in his grip. When it snapped Grant glanced down as though he was unaware he had been holding it.

'I see.' She could hear that her voice was colourless, but for the life of her she did not know how to inject any warmth into it. 'You must find me inexperienced, lacking in...sophistication.'

'In bed? Oh, hell.' Grant got to his feet, came round the desk and sat on the edge of it, close to her. 'No, that is *not* what I mean. Last night was very pleasurable for me, Kate. Very. But I heard what you whispered afterwards. You are still in love with him, aren't you? You are doing your duty as my wife, but you still love Anna's father.' He said *duty* as though it was a dirty word.

'I... No, I don't.' She realised how important it was

to make Grant understand that. He did not love her, he was not asking or expecting her to love *him*, but he must loathe the thought that he had taken to his bed a woman who was gritting her teeth and doing her duty—even if she discovered she enjoyed it.

If Jonathan had been a groom from the stables, a local farmer, a merchant from King's Lynn—any of those—she could tell the truth, admit he was alive and had refused to marry her. But how could she confess that her lover had been an aristocrat who was in all probability known to Grant? The awful thought struck her that they might be friends. What if Jonathan had confided in him? *I'm being blackmailed by some dirty little worm and his two-faced bitch of a sister.*

She had to keep lying even though she hated it. 'I had thought I must still love him, but I am not in love and perhaps I never was.' She stared up at Grant, trying to find the right words, create a safe fiction that would protect her—and him—from the humiliation of the discovery that he had married not just another man's cast-off lover, that he had given his name, not to some fatherless baby, but a child with a parent who could very well support it. A man who would probably want to see her and her brother tried for blackmail.

Kate tried to find a story that would satisfy him. 'Jonathan was going to America, and then he would send for me. But when no letter came, when I realised he must be dead, lost at sea, then I was frantic with worry. But not with grief. I was sad, but I wasn't devastated. And I would have been, wouldn't I, if I loved him?'

It was partly true. When Henry told her that Lord Baybrook had refused to marry her she had been frightened, but she had been more fearful that Henry would challenge him to a duel rather than shattered by his betrayal. If she had loved him, truly loved him, his refusal to protect her should have broken her heart. And when she had found out Henry's infamy, if she had loved Jonathan she would have gone to him, done everything in her power to put things right. As it was, to her shame, she had done nothing until she realised that Henry was a threat to her unborn child.

'I see.' Grant lifted a hand as though to touch her, then let it fall back to rest on his thigh. The broad hand gripped the buckskin-covered muscle and the movement sparked a dull gleam from the signet on his finger.

She could not raise her gaze from his hand. 'You are shocked.' Of course he was, what did she expect? 'It was scandalous enough that I slept with him, but if I did not even have the excuse of loving him… And now, to find such pleasure with a man I hardly know? You must think I am a wanton.'

'I think I am a lucky man.' Kate jerked up her head and saw Grant's smile—sudden, dazzling. Confusing. Then he bent down, pulled her into his arms and up to perch on the desk beside him. 'You are not wanton, Kate. You are sensual, passionate and desirable. I thought I was marrying a woman with courage and intelligence who would be a good stepmother to Charlie. I rather think I have been more fortunate than I deserve.'

'Desirable?' She was no traditional beauty, she knew that. And childbirth had made changes to her body, even though she had ridden and walked until her figure was trim again and her muscles taut.

'Desirable,' Grant confirmed and bent his head to snatch a kiss from her lips. 'Did you not notice how much pleasure you gave me last night?'

Kate felt ready to sink, but Grant was being frank with her, and very understanding, so she owed it to him to be equally frank. Besides, his arm around her waist, the pressure of his body against hers, gave her courage. 'I thought men didn't mind very much who they were with, once they were actually making love. That any woman would do.'

Beside her Grant made a sudden, suppressed sound. Laughter or outrage? 'Believe me, we mind.' It had been laughter. 'And, no, any woman will not do. Except for the sort of rutting beasts whom I hope you will never encounter.'

'You do not find being married to me as bad as you feared, then?' She let herself lean into him, reading his mood through the feel of the big body more easily than she could interpret his expression.

Grant stiffened, then she felt him relax. *He has decided to carry on being truthful.* 'I foresaw difficulties, and the bedchamber was one of them. I am much reassured.'

'And the others included the fact that you thought me plain, awkward and unfit to be an earl's wife?' Kate prodded.

'As you observed yesterday, neither of us was at their best last Christmas.'

'So you left me here rather than allow London society to see who you'd married.' As soon as she said it, she knew the fact that he had left her here had been a blow to her pride, even as she had been so relieved that he had done so. And it was very poor tactics to make him think she wanted to go there now.

Grant got to his feet and began to pace around the study. 'I could not... It was too soon after the birth for you to travel.' Perhaps he was not prepared for total honesty after all. At least, she pondered, he was careful not to hurt her feelings.

'You could have sent for me when Charlie went to London for the second time.'

'I told myself that Anna was too young, that she was better here in the country air.'

'You told yourself?'

Grant swung round and she saw his expression was rueful, not angry. 'You listen to what is behind the words, don't you? Yes, I *told myself* we were better apart. My reasons for marrying you were good, I knew that. But the risks, the drawbacks, seemed greater the longer I was away from you.'

And you did not come back, you left it months. Why?
'And now?' *This is the rest of our lives, the choice between happiness or, at best, a bitter toleration.*

'Now I wish I had come back sooner, begun to know my wife sooner. London and the Season may be a trifle… sticky, but we have months to build this marriage to be too strong for gossip to break it and for you to become a confident countess.'

It is to be happiness, then. She pushed away the thought of the Season, the threat implicit in those words. 'I have a list,' Kate said and smiled at her husband. For the first time since she had woken up to the enormity of what she had done, the word *husband* did not fill her with apprehension. And London was a long way away, time to worry about that later.

'And what is on this list? An increased dress allowance? I'm to make numerous morning calls with you?' He was teasing her, but his eyes held that familiar reserve. What did he think she would demand?

'I want you to show me the house and the estate

yourself. Tell me about it and what it means to you. Let me see it through your eyes.' That was what she had wanted, for all those months. She needed to understand Abbeywell and its importance to Grant and Charlie, then she would know how to live here, not as a visitor, but as part of it. There were changes she could see that needed making, projects that would improve the life of the tenants, the ease of using the house, the beauty of the estate, but she had no right to make them without consultation and some she would not even suggest if her idea for diverting the stream to make a water garden meant drowning Grant's favourite boyhood hideout or the suggestion for building a communal laundry for the village was simply too expensive. Opening the door to Madeleine's rooms was far down the list of what she could venture upon, even though it was becoming something dangerously like an obsession.

'You want me to show you around? But you have been here for months, running the household. Charlie must have dragged you all over the grounds, Mrs Havers will have covered the domestic side of things.'

'Yes, but it is your *home*, you grew up here. Now I am your wife I need to understand it as you do, if that is possible.' Grant still seemed surprised. 'It will help me understand you, too.'

'If that is what you would like, then of course.' He sounded merely polite, but Kate thought he was pleased. 'You realise that you will be undermining the main complaint of husbands everywhere—*my wife does not understand me*?'

'Is that what you men say to each other in your clubs to justify lurking there, drinking and gaming, or is it what you whisper in the ears of ladies who you hope will take pity on you and share their favours?'

Her relief at the change of mood between them had carried her into dangerous waters. Grant raised one dark brow and was suddenly no longer the amused, slightly flirtatious husband of a moment ago. 'Are you asking me if I am faithful to you?'

Kate slid from her perch on the desk. It was no longer the time and place to sit swinging her feet, behaving like a milkmaid with her swain. She must remember that she was a countess. 'No, I am not asking you that question and I do not think I ever would. But if you are asking if I wonder about other women, then, yes, of course I do. I know that men are not designed to be celibate, even the best of husbands.'

'I keep forgetting that you do not know me,' Grant said and she saw from the set of his mouth that she had managed to insult him again. 'I take marriage seriously. I may not have made vows to you in church, but I will act as though I have. I will be faithful to you and I have been since we wed, if you are wondering about a mistress in London, or even less reputable arrangements.'

'Thank you...' Kate managed. Her sister-in-law, Jane, had confided that no man could be trusted to be faithful, that it was in their very nature to seek out new excitements, new women. She had shrugged in the face of Kate's shocked disbelief and incoherent protests about honour and love matches. Men, Jane maintained, were all tomcats by nature and male honour did not preclude infidelity. Either her sister-in-law was wrong, or Grant was telling her what she wanted to hear. She trusted his honour, she realised. Grant would keep his vows.

'And I am sure I do not need to say that I do not

subscribe to any fashionable tolerance in regards to my wife.' He waved a dismissive hand when she opened her mouth to protest. 'I am sure you will be as faithful as a wife can be, Kate. I am just saying, for the record, that I will call out any man who lays a finger on you—and do my damnedest to kill him. And if your Jonathan had abandoned you and not drowned, then I would go after him and kill him, too.'

They stared at each other for a long moment, then Kate said, slowly, 'You may trust me with your honour and mine and I trust you in the same way.' She would never betray him with another man—but the pit was gaping at her feet. She had lied to him, she continued to lie to him, and if he realised that her lover was alive and was being blackmailed by her brother, she did not know what he would do.

'Enough of this serious stuff.' Grant's sudden grin caught her off balance as it had done every time he had surprised her with it. 'What is the first place you want to explore with me?'

'The water garden.'

'We do not have a water garden,' Grant pointed out.

'I know. I think we should, don't you?' *He need never find out.* She forced herself to smile and found it was real. Tomorrow might never come, Christmas was a long way off and, for now, they were happy.

Chapter Twelve

Grant came with her to visit Anna, who delighted him by smiling and gurgling and gripping his fingers. He picked her up, despite the nursemaid's warnings about babies who have recently been fed, and tossed her up to make her laugh.

'Never mind, my lord,' Jeannie said consolingly, ten seconds later. 'I'm sure it will sponge off.'

By the time Kate had found her bonnet and cloak, Grant had surrendered his milky coat to a silently disapproving valet and changed to a battered old shooting jacket and well-worn boots. 'I have a suspicion that water gardens mean bogs,' he said as he joined her on the steps down to the rear garden. 'At least the sun is shining.'

Kate led the way across the formal parterre to the lower level where a lawn, uneven and rank despite the gardeners' best efforts with scythe and roller, sloped away from the woods.

'The view from the parterre in this direction is dull and this lawn leads nowhere except to that boggy patch just inside the woodland. See, where all the alders are, and those rushes, beyond the bank?'

'There's a spring there. I remember that it used to be a good place to find frogs. I think Grandfather had the bank thrown up to keep the water from the lawn.' Grant strode towards the woodland, then stopped as his foot sank into mud. 'And not very effectively, by the looks of it!'

'We can skirt round.' Kate was already leading the way and scrambled up the bank. 'I thought if the bank was breached and the spring water channelled, then it would come out here. We could excavate a chain of ponds across this lawned area and puddle the bottoms.'

Grant had walked further along the top of the bank, but he turned to look back at her. 'And what do you know about puddling bottoms, Lady Allundale?'

'I read about it in a book I ordered on making artificial water features. You need a great deal of stiff clay, then it is spread across the bottom of the hollow and trampled down by lots of men in stout boots.'

'Lots of men?' Grant was frowning now.

'I thought it would be valuable employment for the local people. But if you think it would be too costly, of course I understand.' How foolish to allow her imagination to run away with her when she had no idea how far Grant's resources would stretch. He had this estate and a London house to maintain, a son to educate and now a wife and daughter.

'It sounds like an excellent idea. I was simply disappointed that when you said *we*, you meant a gang of hefty labourers. I had assumed you and I would be puddling in the mud.'

'Us?'

'Mmm.' Grant seemed oblivious to her gasp of scandalised laughter as he looked around the boggy patch and then further into the woods to where a shaft of sunlight lit up one of Kate's favourite places, a glade of soft grass spangled with wild flowers. 'I like the idea of getting very wet and very muddy with you. I appreciate your eye for landscape as well, my dear. What do you make of that sunlit patch through there?'

'It is lovely and usually quite dry underfoot because it is on a slight slope. I would not like to damage it if we do make the water garden.'

'It merits further inspection.' Grant held out his right hand. 'Let me help you around the edge of the mire.' Intrigued, Kate followed. 'How very wise of you to bring a cloak,' he observed as he turned to face her and she caught her breath at the wicked intent in his expression.

'Why?' Although she could already guess and his fingers were at the ties at her neck.

'Because we do not want grass stains on the back of that charming walking dress, do we?'

'Grant! In the open? What if someone sees us?'

'Who?' He looked up from spreading the cloak on the grass. 'No one can see this spot from the house—I used to hide here often enough as a boy.'

'I don't know! Gardeners, gamekeepers. Poachers,' she added wildly as her husband tossed aside his coat and began to untie his neckcloth.

'The gardeners are scything the front lawns. The gamekeepers are chasing the poachers over there.' Grant knelt down and gestured vaguely to the east. 'I am tired of being serious and sensible. I am tired of duty. I want to be utterly frivolous with my wife.' He held out his hand. 'Do you want to be frivolous with your husband?' he asked as his fingers went to the fastenings of his falls.

* * *

An hour later Kate flopped back on to her crumpled cloak beside the long, naked body of her husband as he sprawled face down, half on and half off the cloak.

'That,' he observed without moving, 'was excellently frivolous.'

'I would never have thought it.' Kate snuggled against Grant's flank, glad of the heat of his skin. The breeze was cool through the trees, despite the sun almost reaching its height. 'If I had been asked to describe you, *frivolous* would be one of the last words I would have thought of.'

'I used to be wild, a rakehell in training, my grandfather always said.' Grant rolled over on to his back. 'When I was at university with Gabe and Alex and Cris they called us the Four Disgraces. That's why he did not oppose my attending medical school. He said a few years in cold, dour Edinburgh delving into cadavers would sober me up better than anything short of a spell in the army and with less chance of him losing his heir.'

'Did it sober you?' Kate buried the chilly tip of her nose in the angle of his neck and shoulder and smiled as he muttered in protest. He stopped complaining when she slid her hand, palm down, across the flat planes of his chest and began to play with the curls of hair.

'Coming home and finding my grandfather recovering from a heart seizure did that. I was needed here and I couldn't expect him to carry the burden of the estate and all its business while I pursued an interest that could only ever be that—an interest.'

She sat up, but stayed close to his warmth as she admired the lean, masculine beauty of the body lying beside her. The only flaws were the raking scars from his right shoulder, disappearing down to his shoulder blade. That was what she had felt the first time they had lain together.

Kate leaned over and touched them. 'You said you were in the army for a while. When was that?' She could feel him bracing himself against the desire to shrug her hand away.

'I volunteered in '15, when Bonaparte escaped from Elba. I was at Waterloo and escaped with my life and a healthy horror of warfare.'

'So you were wounded and these are battle scars?'

'No.'

She stared at them. There was something familiar about them, the way the flesh had been damaged, the way the weapon had raked through the flesh. Then she remembered Jason Smith, who had been Henry's groom years ago. He would get drunk and pick fights and he was, from all the rumours, a nasty dirty fighter when he'd taken drink. Then one evening he had come staggering into the kitchen, pouring blood, and Kate had helped the housekeeper dress the wounds. Long, raking parallel cuts like these, the result of a slashing blow from a broken bottle. Surely Grant was not the kind of man who got involved in barroom brawls? But that flat negative had been a clear warning, and if he had wanted to explain the scars, then he would.

'And then you married?' she asked as though her questions had not interrupted the story of his life.

'Yes.' There was no change in Grant's tone, but he sat up and reached for his clothes. The affirmative had been as flat as the negative and just as clear a warning. *No trespassing.* 'You are getting chilled, best to get dressed before the gardeners decide to scythe the back lawns, as well.'

He helped Kate with laces and pins, exhibiting the facility with feminine garments that she had noticed back in the bothy. If she had felt a little more confident, she might have twitted him gently on the subject, but she had strayed far enough into dangerous waters with that question about his first marriage.

'We need a summer house, you know.' Grant sat on a tree stump to pull on his boots. He pointed at a flat area in the centre of the clearing. 'If we built one there, it would have a view down to your new water gardens.' He stood and stamped his feet firmly into the battered old boots. 'Then we can be frivolous whatever the weather and with less chance of scandalising our innocent staff and the not-so-innocent poachers.'

'Classical or rustic?' Kate laced her half-boots, determined to be as sophisticated about the prospect of future al fresco lovemaking as Grant was. The prospect was delicious in itself, but most of all she treasured the fact that he was becoming so relaxed with her. Surely, soon, the scars from his unhappy first marriage would fade?

'Classical,' Grant said. 'A little temple in the woods. It will have a fireplace and an inner chamber we can lock and a room for picnics on warm rainy days.'

They strolled back up to the parterre, hand in hand, bickering gently about how a chimney could be incorporated into a classical temple, and were met by Charlie, his tutor at his heels.

'There you are, Papa! Have you fallen off your horse? Your hair is on end and your hat has gone. And, Maman, did you know your cloak is inside out?'

'Lord Brooke, we have discussed the fact that a gentleman does not pass personal comments on the appearance of others, have we not?' Mr Gough was so straight-faced that Kate was certain he had a very good idea of just what his employers had been doing.

Charlie grimaced at the formal address, the signal that he was in the wrong. 'I am sorry, Maman, Papa. Only, I was looking for you. The post has come and there are letters with Uncle Alex's seal on, and Uncle Cris's and a very splodgy one that must be from Uncle Gabriel, I think, because he told me he had lost his signet ring whilst dicing with a German count and—'

Mr Gough cast up his gaze as though in search of heavenly assistance. 'Lord Brooke, we will return to the schoolroom and you will translate *I must not speculate on other people's business* into Latin and then write it out twenty times in a fair hand.'

'Ouch,' Grant remarked when his son had departed with the air of a condemned man heading for the gallows. 'I am not certain I could translate that with any elegance these days.' He ran a hand through his tousled hair, twitched off Kate's cloak, shook it out, draped it over his arm and opened the door for her. 'Those letters, I hope, are the replies to my invitations to our first house party.'

Kate was conscious that he was watching her for a reaction. Did he fear she would be unable to manage a small, informal gathering, or was it his guests' reactions to her that gave him more concern? No man would want his closest friends to think he had made a poor marriage, that his wife was not good enough for him.

I am good enough, she told herself. *Good enough for him and for his friends. And I can manage a country house party more easily than he thinks.* The thought of confounding Grant with her ability gave her an inner glow of unworthy satisfaction, even if it was only a small thing. Henry liked to entertain his friends and his wife,

Jane, uncomfortable with country gentlemen and their hearty manners and unsophisticated pleasures, had been more than happy to unload the burden of organisation on to Kate.

If truth be told, it was the thought of female guests that gave her the most apprehension. Men, if they were comfortable, well fed and provided with plenty of sport, tended to be uncritical of their hostess. Ladies, on the other hand, were not. Polite, charming—and if they sensed a weakness, as relentless as a flock of pigeons pecking away at a pile of wheat grains until there was nothing left but the husks.

'Let's hurry and open them,' she said and was through the doorway into the shadowed hall with, surely, enough enthusiasm to convince Grant that she was not nervous in the slightest.

'Alex and his wife can come,' he said, studying the first letter. He opened the others. 'So can Cris and Gabriel. But they both say they will not be accompanied by their sisters. Gabe, in language I will not use to my respectable wife, assures me he will inflict neither his latest *chère amie* upon us, nor a respectable fiancée—which it is unimaginable that he will ever have, by the way—and certainly not his unmarried sister.' Grant folded the sheet with its sprawling black handwriting and grimaced. 'Now I come to think about my last encounter with her, that is probably a good thing. She can talk the hind leg off a donkey and needs diluting with a very large pool of other guests. Cris merely thanks me most properly for the suggestion, but tells me that he will be unaccompanied, as his sister is newly betrothed and will be staying with her future in-laws.'

Grant handed her that letter and Kate scanned the

elegantly written page. 'He sounds somewhat cool,' she ventured. 'Is it the prospect of meeting me?'

'He always sounds cool, although this does seem more detached than usual.' Grant took the letter back and read it again. 'It isn't us, it is him. Something's wrong, I think. He's been in Russia or Denmark or somewhere in that direction, doing a vaguely diplomatic job for the Foreign Office.'

'Not as an ambassador?'

'No, far more undefined than that.' Grant looked thoughtful and Kate did not probe. If his friend was engaged in espionage, he certainly would not want to speak of it. The poor man probably needed some peace and quiet and homely comforts after the stress of a foreign court.

'I suggested May 20 and they all say they can make that. Is it convenient for you?'

Two weeks? 'Certainly,' Kate said with a sense of fizzing excitement. Her first house party as mistress of Abbeywell and the chance to understand Grant much better through his friends. She could hardly wait. 'That will be no problem at all.'

The house was quiet, finally. Grant leaned back against the door of his bedroom and yawned. Charlie, still overexcited from the day before at the prospect of all his favourite honorary uncles arriving at the same time, had been difficult to get to bed. Anna, with the knack of small children for knowing when adults were tired and distracted, decided to wail endlessly and Kate had been absent-minded throughout dinner. And, to put the cap on a wearisome evening, she had indicated in an embarrassed murmur that it would not be a good time for him to visit her bedchamber.

So now he was feeling selfish for feeling disappointed when she was obviously self-conscious and uncomfortable. The decanters had been set out and he went to pour himself out a finger of brandy, shifting his shoulders under the heavy silk of his robe in an effort to ease the ache in the right one, which always complained when the weather turned cold and damp.

He'd been short with Kate yesterday when she had asked a perfectly reasonable question about the scars. On an impulse he tossed back the brandy and strode to the door, stopping only to remove the key from its hiding place in the indented base of a Japanese bronze figure and to pick up a three-branch candlestick.

It was over a year since he had been in the empty suite. The door swung open with a faint creak and the cold, stale air hardly moved the candle flames. He could still smell burning, he was convinced, even though all the fabrics and carpets had been torn out and destroyed, the walls and floor scrubbed. The seat of the fire was obvious from the heavy charring of the floorboards in front of the hearth and near the door where the edge of the rug had been was a dark patch. His blood.

He made himself walk further into the room, telling himself that he could not hear the crackle of the fire, the screams, the child's wailing cries. He could not smell the smoke, the burning brandy… But they were there, in his head, the memories mixed with the sounds and stench of the battlefield, the screams of the dying, and afterwards, those hideous pyres…

Then he was through into the bedchamber. It was still furnished, for the door had been closed that night and the smoke and flame had not penetrated here. It smelt of dust and old polish and faintly, unmistakably, there was the scent of jasmine in the air.

There were sounds here, too. A woman crying. Screaming. Sobs and reproaches. Pain and grief. To pull himself back into the present left him sick, but he made himself walk around the room checking coldly, methodically, for damage, signs of damp, of mice or mould. These chambers were spaces, that was all. They had no memory, no life of their own. The phantom sounds and smells were all in his head and he could overcome them, drive them out with the laughter of a son who was healthy and happy, the scent of a woman who found joy in his lovemaking, the smiles of a baby who reached out when she saw him. He had experienced no nightmares since he had returned to Abbeywell—he was healing, even if his lacerated shoulder never would.

He walked back, locked the door behind him, returned to his room. Yes, he could sleep now.

Chapter Thirteen

Kate woke, blinking at the darkness. Something had roused her. A shout? All was quiet, but instinct made her get up and tiptoe to the dressing room door, which stood ajar. Anna was fast asleep and there was no sound from Jeannie, who slept in a small room just along the corridor.

It must have been an owl, or a vixen's strange cry. Then she heard it again, distinctly now, unmistakably a human voice.

'Charlie!' It was Grant and she ran to the connecting door, threw it open expecting to find some emergency—a sick child, sleepwalking, an accident—her mind ran through the possibilities. But the room was dark and still, except for the sound of muttering and movement from the bed.

'Grant?' There was no reply. A cold finger of unease moved down her spine. Kate backed away into her own chamber, found by touch the candle and tinderbox by the bed and, hands shaking, struck a light. 'Grant?' This time she could see him naked on the bed, the sheets a tangle around his legs, trapping him. He seemed to be trying to drag himself towards the edge of the bed.

'Charlie. I'm coming. Charlie…' He was deep in the throes of a nightmare.

Kate bent over him, put her arms around his shoulders and tried to make him lie down, but he was too strong for her. 'We have Charlie. He is safe, quite safe,' she murmured, then repeated it loudly, but it did nothing to calm him.

Then something in the tension of Grant's body changed. 'Dream,' he muttered. 'No.'

He knew he was in a nightmare, Kate realised, and he was fighting against it, forcing it back with the strength of his mind as much as his body. She held on tightly, pulling the rigid body against hers, stroking down his back. When she touched the scarred shoulder she felt him flinch as though the wounds were raw.

With a heave Grant threw off her restraining hands, fell back against the pillows. 'Couldn't help her,' he muttered. 'Charlie…'

'He is here. You saved him. Charlie is safe.'

'I know,' he answered her rationally, irritably, even though he was asleep. 'Damned dreams…' And then he was still, relaxed, deeply asleep.

Shaken, Kate backed away from the bed, the candle flame wavering. She put up a hand to shield it and realised it was her own panting breath that made it move. Grant had been dreaming about the fire that killed his wife, she was certain. Dr Meldreth had said something about Grant being injured during the fire, but the only scars she could see on his body were the slashes on his shoulder and they were not burns. How could a fire cause those? But a weapon could, a broken bottle could.

None of it made sense. Kate stood watching her sleeping husband, then, once she was certain he was deeply unconscious, she pulled the covers up over him. Should she stay? No, she decided, staring down at his profile, stark against the white of the pillows. He had dragged himself out of that nightmare by sheer willpower, as far as she could tell. He would hate to know she had been watching his struggles against it.

But what had triggered it? she wondered as she turned away. She had seen no sign of bad dreams when they had slept together. The candlelight caught a glint of something metallic on the little table by the door and, curious, she went to see what it was. A key. A door key very much in the style of those for all of the bedchambers on this floor. It was in her hand before she realised that she had moved to pick it up. It was not the key to this room, that was protruding from the lock right in front of her, Charlie's room was never locked, in case of accidents. Hers, too, was unlocked.

Madeleine's suite. It had to be. Kate hesitated for perhaps ten seconds. Grant did not want her, or anyone, in those rooms. But whatever had happened there had scarred him, mentally and perhaps physically. It was giving him nightmares and the experience had been so bad he could not tolerate any mention of it. How could she help him if she did not understand?

The door opened with a faint creak like the protest of her conscience, but Kate kept going. This was the lesser of two evils and Grant need never know she had been in the rooms, she told herself.

The forbidden door opened easily and she stepped on to bare boards. The air was cold and dry and, stripped of its furniture, the room seemed enormous and overscale, like something from a fairy tale. *Bluebeard's chamber.* The light of the single candle that she held created deep pools of shadow in the corners, the edges swaying as her hand trembled. Something dark spilled like a puddle in front of the hearth and for a moment Kate thought it was a body fallen there, draped in a black velvet cloak.

'Nonsense,' she muttered and shook off the superstitious dread. 'Too many Gothic novels, you will be seeing ghosts next.' Even so, it took resolution to walk towards the pool of blackness. She stopped, her toes at the edge, and saw that the boards at her feet were charred by the heat of an intense fire. Instinctively she stepped back, repelled by the thought of her bare skin touching the blackness. There was another patch of darkness by the door and she made herself walk to that. There was no charring here, the boards were intact, although scrubbed until the grain showed. She had the cold certainty that this was blood, but there was no way of telling in the dim light.

The bedchamber door was closed. It yielded to her cautious push and Kate stepped into Madeleine Rivers's most intimate world. The room was feminine, exquisite in every detail, decorated in shades of blue with touches of silver, tarnished now, but still catching the light from the candle flame.

The dressing table held its array of bottles and jars, a silver-backed hairbrush and hand mirror. There was just the lightest film of dust, so whatever Grimswade said, one of the servants was coming in to keep the rooms clean. Then Kate saw a single line, fresh-traced through the dust. She held the candle flame close. It looked like the mark of a fingertip that had come close to one perfume flask. *Essence de Jasmine.*

There was a large mirror on a stand and Kate looked up to see herself reflected in it—pale-faced, pretty enough, dressed for warmth and comfort in a sensible nightgown, bare feet showing beneath the hem. The woman whose room this was would have scorned to look like this, she sensed. She glanced at the dressing room door, but did not try to open it. The thought of prying into the other woman's clothes was abhorrent.

Slowly, forcing herself not to run, Kate closed the door, crossed the sitting room and let herself out into the familiar world again. She turned the key in the lock and tiptoed back to Grant's bedchamber, laid the key down where she had found it and retreated to her own room.

What had that taught her? *Nothing,* she concluded as she climbed into bed and pulled the covers up tight to her chin, although the room was not cold. There were marks of a fire, possibly of blood. But she had known that already. She had intruded into Grant's private nightmare, against his wishes, and she had discovered nothing that might help.

Let that be a lesson to you, she would have said to Charlie if she had caught him prying. Now she had a guilty conscience, a definite case of the shivers and another secret to keep from Grant.

May 20—Abbeywell Grange

Grant strolled through the rooms of his home and shook his head with bemused pleasure. Kate had seemed understandably nervous when he had first come home, not just of him, but at the thought of making any changes to the house. With the confirmation of the house party all that reserve seemed to have been swept away, although he worried that she was overdoing things. It was almost as though she had flung herself into the preparations as a way of burying her nerves.

After he had visited Madeleine's rooms the nightmare had resulted in the inevitable headache and bad dreams every night afterwards. He fought both nightmares and the pain as he always had, but the relief when Kate shyly asked him back to her bed was acute. Somehow making love to his wife kept the demons at bay and he had not dreamed again.

But Kate was working too hard and he worried about that. When he waylaid her in the corridor and swept her into either his or her bedchamber, lists and note tablets would scatter along with her stockings and petticoats as he undressed her. Whichever room he walked into appeared to have a member of staff—some of them unfamiliar to him—working away. The billiard table was brushed to a perfect nap, while new blocks of chalk stood aligned under the racks of cues. His study acquired three more comfortable leather armchairs.

Grimswade was found in solemn consultation with his mistress on the correct number of packs of cards to order and brand-new umbrellas were set in stands by all the outer doors, along with every walking stick the house could muster. When Grant caught his wife emerging from the backstairs and kissed her, she tasted of sugar and cinnamon, but when he began to kiss with more enthusiasm, and the intention of licking it all off, she batted him away and scurried off muttering, 'New recipes!'

Charlie entertained them before his bedtime every evening with an entire repertoire of poems and recitations, Anna acquired at least half a dozen new dresses and the small drawing room was declared out of bounds to men as it was transformed into a ladies' boudoir.

'Grant! Oh, there you are.' Kate hurried in, seized his

hand and began to pull him towards the door. 'I need you to come upstairs immediately.'

'An admirable idea,' he agreed, allowing himself to be steered towards the stairs. 'But have we time? I expect they will begin arriving in about an hour or so, and your hair looks dashed complicated to fix if it comes down.' As it would, if what he had in mind—

'*Grant.* I want you to look at the guest bedchambers, not to…well, not to do anything else.'

He loved the way he could make her blush, while at the same time she threw herself into whatever amorous idea he had in the most enthusiastic way. And she was beginning to have ideas of her own. Grant paused on the landing, happily recalling the uses to which a set of library steps could be put, and was ruthlessly tugged to the first set of rooms.

'Is this all right for Lord Avenmore? He is the one I am most worried about. Lord and Lady Weybourn are newlyweds, so I thought what we would like and arranged their suite accordingly.' That produced an intriguing pink glow over her cheeks. Grant thought again how satisfying it was that he could make Kate blush. It made him think about making love to her…

'Grant, are you attending?'

'Yes, my dear.' It was his best husbandly voice and it usually worked whenever he had lost track of the conversation in erotic daydreams.

Kate gave him a decidedly old-fashioned look. 'And by the sound of it, Lord Edenbridge values comfort and informality, so his rooms were easy. But Lord Avenmore…'

Grant surveyed the room. It had always been an elegant chamber, but now it was decidedly masculine, with the landscapes replaced with large architectural engravings and all the Dresden china swept away to be replaced by Chinese blue-and-white export porcelain. It would suit Cris de Feaux's austere tastes very well and he said so.

'I didn't know what to do about books, so I have selected a mixture for all of the rooms. But I think we should consider redecorating some more suites very soon, because the rooms I have allocated to Lord Edenbridge are really almost shabby, and if you want to entertain larger parties in the future, it will be difficult. There are your grandfather's rooms, of course—but I hardly like to suggest making changes there if you would find that upsetting.'

'No, you are quite right. They would turn into three respectable guest rooms. I'll have the personal items moved to my rooms and the study. The study and the library are the places that remind me most of him anyway. I have no sentimental attachments to the bedroom suite.'

He was rewarded by a warm smile and glanced at the clock on the overmantel. Perhaps there was just time.

'And then there is the suite next to yours,' Kate said with the air of a woman steeling herself. 'The one with the locked door.'

'No!' He swung round away from her, his vision blurred by the smoke, his ears full of the obscene crackling laughter of the fire, the screams…the screams and the air full of the smell of brandy and burning and the pain in his shoulder and head so bad he could not focus, could not make that hellish decision…

'I realise there are sentimental reasons why it would be difficult, but it is a large suite, and if we were thoughtful with the decoration and furnishing, there need be nothing to remind you,' Kate continued. The sensible, slightly nervous voice flowed on, the remarks perfectly reasonable. Grant hauled himself back from the edge of his waking nightmare and made himself stand still, listen to her.

'How do you know it is a large suite? Have you been in there? I told the servants that the door was never to be opened except for a monthly cleaning.'

'I know.' He realised that Kate was standing her ground with an effort of will, that he was probably frightening her. He made himself step back, widening the space between them, and saw her make the effort to relax her hands from their tight grip on her skirts. 'But…I assumed, from the space I have been given for my suite. And it is obvious the areas that those rooms occupy, one only has to look at the adjoining rooms.'

'No,' Grant said. 'No, it is not obvious.' The angle of the external walls was deceptive at that point, the arrangement of the inner rooms, confusing.

Kate was not blushing now. She was pale and stammering, the picture of guilt. She made no attempt to deny that she had entered the suite. 'But…sooner or later Charlie is going to wonder why that door is locked. What will you tell him? Do you want to make it into some s-secret chamber of horrors to give him nightmares?' Kate was regaining her confidence now, he saw, driven by the force of her argument. She took two rapid steps forward, caught his hands in hers. 'Grant—'

'That room *is* a chamber of horrors,' he said between lips that seemed frozen. 'And it gives *me* nightmares. You've been in there, I don't know how, but you have been, against my expressed wishes. Now, do you want to probe any more? Do you want to dig out secrets that don't concern you, pry into my feelings and thoughts? Because the answer will be *no*, I tell you now.' He flung his hands apart, dislodging hers. 'You had no right, *have—*'

Grant broke off at the sound of a very heavy footstep outside the door. As he turned, Grimswade appeared in the opening. Somehow he bit back the demand that the butler go to the devil. 'Yes?'

'A carriage is approaching, my lord. I believe it is Lord Weybourn's conveyance.'

'Thank you. We will be down directly.' He followed Grimswade along the corridor without turning to see if Kate was following him, without a word to her. He was dimly aware, through the crashing headache that had descended as he lost his temper, that he should go back, apologise to her. Try to forgive her, if he could, for that intrusion. He kept going, down the curves of the front stairs, across the marble floor, the percussion of his boot heels on the stone like daggers stabbing behind his eyes.

Footmen flung back the double doors as he approached and sunlight streamed in, blinding him. Instinct took him out on to the top step, the swirling lights that distorted his vision revealing the shape of the approaching carriage like an image that had been torn across and reassembled out of true.

He was conscious of a presence at his side, of Kate's delicate scent. She made no move to touch him. Then the shape that was the carriage stopped. Footmen hurried down the steps, Grant fixed a smile of welcome on his lips. His vision was failing as the circle of broken, dancing lights enclosing nothing but blackness moved inexorably outwards. In a moment he would be blind.

'Grant! Are we the first?' It was Alex.

'Yes, you are. Welcome.' A figure in green wavered beside Alex and he broadened the smile, painfully. 'Tess, you are more than welcome to Abbeywell. Come and meet my wife.'

Then they were up the steps and beside them. He managed not to retch at the waft of rose scent as Tess stood on tiptoe to kiss his cheek. Alex gripped his hand and, turning, tucked it through his own. 'Migraine?' he murmured. Then he raised his voice. 'And this must be Lady Allundale, you clever devil, Grant. Ma'am, I am Alex Tempest and this is my wife, Tess. I am delighted to meet you at last.'

Alex swung round, taking Grant with him to stroll into the hall. 'Ladies, you will excuse us, but I must be off to consult Grant's valet this minute—I have a hideously uncomfortable nail working through the sole of these new boots.'

Grant found himself climbing the stairs and managed to get out, 'What the blazes—'

'You are blind with a migraine, Lady Allundale is as white as a sheet and Grimswade looks as though he has sat on a poker. What's wrong? No, don't try to talk. Same room as usual?'

Alex steered Grant into his bedchamber, pushed him on to the bed, pulled off his boots. 'Lie down, I'll send your valet in.'

Grant tried to sit up and was ruthlessly shoved back. 'I can't… You are guests, Cris and Gabe will be arriving…'

'We're friends, not guests. Leave it to me.' There was a rattle of curtain rings, the light against his eyelids was reduced. Then silence, broken only by the soft-footed entrance of Griffin, who pressed a glass into Grant's hand.

'Willow-bark powder, my lord.'

He gulped it down, wincing at the bitter taste, lay back

and tried to make his mind blank, relax his tense muscles. As soon as he could see, he would have to go downstairs and, somehow, come to terms with Kate.

Chapter Fourteen

'Here they are.' Lady Weybourn turned to the door. 'Or, rather, here is mine. Where is Grant, Alex? I didn't think he looked well.'

'Migraine.' Alex Tempest strolled in to the drawing room and smiled reassuringly at Kate. 'Haven't seen him blind with one for a while. I've sent his valet to him,' he added as Kate jumped to her feet with a murmur of distress. 'He'll be fine as long as he's quiet. There's nothing to be done.'

With him on his feet the only courteous thing to do was sit down. Griffin would send for her if she was needed and probably the last thing Grant wanted was his unsatisfactory wife fussing over him. She sat and Alex dropped his elegant length into a chair. 'He is subject to migraines? I did not know.' It was his anger at discovering her trespass into the forbidden rooms that had triggered it. And Lord Weybourn said he was *blind* with it.

'Only occasionally. It is very stressful situations when he can't act to resolve things, that's what usually sets them off. If he can act and *do* something, then Grant copes with anything.' Alex Tempest smiled his lazy, reassuring smile again. 'And he's a stubborn so-and-so. He'll be on his feet the minute he can see clearly, even if his head still hurts. I don't expect that blow he got in New Town helped any.'

'No, probably not.' She wrenched her thoughts away from guilt and worry and focused on her guests. 'Now, would you like to take some refreshment, or shall I show you to your rooms first?'

'Some tea would be very welcome.' Lady Weybourn unpinned her hat and set it aside, then peeled off her gloves as Kate rang for Grimswade.

'Tea and some food, Grimswade. Do you know where Lord Brooke has got to?'

'I do not, I regret to say, my lady. However, I venture to suggest that the production of cake will cause him to appear.'

'Uncle Alex!' Charlie erupted into the room and leapt at Lord Weybourn, who caught him, stood up and held him upside down by his heels.

'Good afternoon, Lord Brooke.'

His wife rolled her eyes at Kate. 'Do put him down, darling. He'll be sick.'

Eventually order was restored, Charlie was silenced by the threat of the withdrawal of cake and Kate once more embarked on making polite conversation with these two very informal strangers.

'You have known Grant for a long time, Lord Weybourn?'

'Alex, please. Yes, since university, along with Cris de Feaux and Gabriel Stone. We were known as the Four Disgraces, but I assure you we are sober and responsible now.'

Lady Weybourn snorted inelegantly. 'Nonsense, darling. You are merely better at hiding the insobriety and irresponsibility these days.' She turned to Kate. 'I think we are very brave, taking on two of them. We must see what we can do about finding nice civilising wives for the others, don't you think, Lady Allundale?'

'Oh, Kate, please. I don't know the others, so I really can't say.' The thought of Grant being a Disgrace would be funny if she wasn't feeling so apprehensive and guilty.

'These days we think of ourselves more as the Four Elementals, because of our names,' Alex continued, ignoring a whisper of, *And because that's the name of the inn in Ghent they meet up in,* from Tess. 'Tempest—wind, de Feaux—fire, Stone—earth, and Rivers—'

'Water,' Kate finished, relaxing a little. It was almost impossible not to, around these two. They would be good for Grant, she knew it.

'Two more carriages are approaching, my lady.'

'Thank you, Grimswade. We had better have more tea and cake brought in.'

'I'll come out with you,' Alex offered as she stood up with a murmur of apology. 'You can't be expected to greet those two by yourself.'

'They are quite safe really.' Tess walked beside her to the front door. 'At least, *mostly* safe. Gabriel is unsettling and Cris is terrifying, but just pretend you don't notice.' She waved enthusiastically as the two coaches, both driving at breakneck speed, came to a crashing halt.

Pretend I don't notice? How? Kate waited with butterflies somersaulting below her diaphragm as a footman opened one door and the other was thrown wide. The man who climbed languidly down with a nod to the footman was, Kate realised, probably the most handsome man she had ever seen. He was also glacially blond, blue-eyed and dangerously composed. Why dangerous?

'That's Crispin de Feaux?' she whispered to Tess.

'Indeed it is,' the other woman whispered back. 'I always think of archangels and flaming swords.'

He strode up the steps and bowed over the hand that Kate, expecting to shake hands, had extended. 'Lady Allundale, I am delighted to meet you at last.'

'Kate, allow me to introduce the Marquess of Avenmore,' Alex drawled. 'Cris, Lady Allundale. Grant's flat on his back with a migraine.'

'The prospect of losing to me at cards again, I assume.' The dark, loose-limbed man one step below the marquess needed a shave, a haircut, and had obviously chosen his expensive clothing for comfort. He smiled at Kate, a wolfish baring of his teeth that had her stiffening her spine before she offered her hand.

'Edenbridge, at your service.' He took her hand and neither kissed nor shook it. 'Clever, clever, Grant,' he remarked, closing his long fingers possessively around hers.

Oh, yes, this is definitely the unsettling one. 'Do come in.' Kate tried to look sophisticated, as though dark-eyed men with feral smiles murmured ambiguous compliments to her every day. He released her hand and she even managed not to snatch it back and hide it behind her back. 'There are refreshments in the drawing room, unless either of you would like to be shown to your rooms first?'

They all voted for refreshments, trooping after her into the drawing room, as much at home as she was. *More so,* she thought, nerves jangling as she worried about Grant, fretted about her marriage, restrained Charlie from causing havoc and somehow made conversation. She was certain it was thoroughly banal and that four people who obviously knew each other well would much prefer to be talking amongst themselves rather than answering her polite enquiries about their journeys.

And upstairs her husband, whom she had tried to deceive, was lying blinded by pain and she could do nothing to help him.

'Do have another ginger biscuit, Lord Avenmore. Such fortunate weather for your journey, was it not?'

Grant lay with hard-learned patience and watched the plaster details of the ceiling over his bed gradually come into focus. His head still felt as though it was gripped in a vice and pain stabbed behind his eyes, but the worst was over. The attacks were always short and savage and it took a while before bright light and loud noises were tolerable.

Normally he would sleep for several hours until the sickness and nausea were gone, but somewhere downstairs Kate was greeting his three best friends and he understood her well enough now to guess that she was doing so with poise and grace despite the ordeal. Because it would be an ordeal, meeting people who knew him better than anyone and far better than she did.

And then there was her unfamiliarity with high society. Cris, simply by standing around, had been known to make dukes run a nervous finger around their neckcloths. Gabe was enough to make any relatively unsophisticated lady flustered and Alex and Tess were so head over heels in love that they could only serve to point up the deficiencies in his own marriage.

And Alex had seen at once that something was wrong. Grant shifted cautiously and, ignoring the way it made the room move about, sat up. He had to get down to Kate. The acid anger still churned in his stomach as he forced himself to his feet and he stopped his unsteady progress across the room to his boots to analyse it.

His wife had disobeyed him, deceived him, so why did he feel guilty about being angry with her? He stared into the mirror at his narrow-pupilled eyes and rigid mouth. The sight made him feel considerably worse. He needed to think, but it was hard enough staying on his feet. Yet instinct told him to move. He reached for his boots, winced as he bent his head and made the effort to pull them on. Grant got to his feet and made his way downstairs, steeling himself against the tide of talk and laughter, punctuated by Charlie's whoops, that rose to meet him.

'Grant.' There was anxiety on Kate's face, as well as relief in her voice. She half rose from the chair, then sat down again, and he realised that, thankfully, she was not going to make a fuss over him.

Neither Cris nor Gabe stood. They knew too well that getting up, slapping him on the back or shaking his hand just now would make his head feel as though it had fallen off. Cris waved a greeting with a stylish turn of his wrist, Gabe merely smiled his pirate's smile. Charlie opened his mouth and was promptly scooped up by Alex, who wagged a finger at him until he subsided.

'My apologies for not receiving you. One of those confounded migraines.' They had left his usual chair for him, so he sat down and tried to focus.

'Charlie, take your father his tea, please.' Kate handed the boy a cup and turned back to her interrupted conversation with Gabe, which, to Grant's amazement, appeared to be about *vingt-et-un* and the calculation of odds. Perhaps he was hearing things.

Ten minutes later Mr Gough came down to remove a

reluctant Charlie and give the adults some peace. Then his guests decided that they should retire and wash off the dust of the road. They left, waving him back into his chair when he would have risen. 'We're family, remember,' Alex said airily. 'We'll find our way, Kate, never fear.'

It left him, head still pounding, sitting opposite his wife. She looked decidedly pale now the animation of talking had left her. 'Kate.' He realised he had no idea how he felt about her.

'Please don't. You could not reproach me half as much as I am reproaching myself. We were building trust between us, weren't we? And I destroyed it.' Bravely, she kept her gaze on his face and he remembered that it was her courage that had first impressed him.

'No, we were not.' It came out more harshly than he had intended, a snarl at himself as much as at her. Kate bit her lip and Grant closed his mouth before he said anything else unconsidered.

'I am not going to apologise any more.' She levelled a steady look at him across the teacups. Grant looked down and saw her hands were shaking. When Kate saw the direction of his gaze she curled them loosely in her lap as though willing them to stillness. 'I have said I am sorry, and I am, but my motives were good. Mostly. I cannot acquit myself of some curiosity.'

She admitted inquisitiveness and he knew she wanted to remodel that part of the house, but neither of those could be described as a *good* motive. Grant almost said as much, and then he saw the anxiety in her eyes, stopped thinking about his own feelings and saw hers. *Because if the positions were reversed, I'd have done the same thing.* Of course he would.

If Kate had been hiding some secret that gave her

nightmares, made her short-tempered and laid her low with migraines, he would have done anything that he could to discover what it was and try to set it right, whether she said she wanted him to or not. She was too important to him now—he would not have shrugged and ignored her pain, left her to carry the burden alone. Which meant that he was important to her. He knew himself well enough to recognise that when he was angry it took nerve to stand up to him. Kate had risked his anger and so he must forgive what she had done.

Forgive. And that meant telling her the truth, because otherwise she was going to fret herself to flinders over him. *Hell.* The thought made him nauseous all over again, his shoulder seemed to flare with remembered pain. What would she think of him? That he was as good as a murderer? It was, after all, what he thought of himself often enough as he lay awake long into the night, because that was better than sleeping and the dreams that came with sleep.

With another woman he would never have the confidence in her discretion and her understanding, but he could trust Kate, he realised.

'Yes, I can see that your motives were good.'

Kate's expression changed subtly. Relief, possibly. Anxiety about what he would reveal? Or regret that she had pushed things this far? He had always known her to be self-contained, now he could not read her thoughts, interpret her emotions, and he knew he should be able to. This was his *wife*, he should be able to understand her because that was what happened in real marriages and he wanted this one to be real.

Grant forced his reluctant tongue to form the words. 'I would not let you in to my secrets. Where's the trust in that? And you were not idly curious, I know that. You wanted to help, despite my best efforts to keep you out.'

'Most husbands would maintain that a wife must obey them,' Kate ventured. He thought of someone edging out on to thin ice, testing each step, listening for the ominous cracking. He had failed her by not trusting her before. Now she was wary of how far this tolerance went.

'Even if they are wrong. Yes, I know. I do not want to be a husband like that. Will you come here, Kate?'

She stood up, looking demure, except for the hint of a smile, and he realised with a flash of insight that she was relieved and something more positive than that. Happy? The relief at being able to understand her made his own lips curve in response.

'You have a headache,' she said.

'So don't bounce.' Grant opened his arms and Kate curled up on his lap, her head on his shoulder, and he gathered her in tight, tucked her head under his chin and thought how right she felt there, how perfect her weight on him was.

'Have you had these headaches all the time we have been married?'

'No. When we first got here I was so busy that I was too tired to dream. I had them in London, now and again, but they are always worse here.' He felt the familiar guilt at his own weakness, even as the rational part of his brain, the part that had studied medicine, told him that it was not something he could control by willpower.

He could almost hear Kate working it out. 'You have slept with me every night since you returned from London and you have not had nightmares, not ones that disturbed your sleep and woke me.'

'I suspect that sex helps,' Grant said, hoping he had

not shocked her. It had occurred to him, these past few days when he woke refreshed after a solid night's sleep.

'Of course!' Kate sat up, bumped his chin with her head, murmured an apology. 'The night you woke me up because you were dreaming and I went into your bedchamber and found the key was the first time since we had been sleeping together that we…haven't…' She seemed to find it difficult to select the right word. 'Made love.'

'Well, there's the answer,' he said, feeling, for the first time since that confrontation upstairs, like smiling. 'Lovemaking as often as possible.'

'It will cure the symptoms,' Kate said seriously, apparently not ready to joke about it. 'But not the cause. Have you talked to anyone about what happened when Madeleine died?'

'My grandfather, when it first happened. The other three.' He gestured at the ceiling, but she knew what he meant. The other three of the close band of four friends.

'Did you tell them what happened or how you feel?' Kate asked.

'How I feel? No, of course not. I told them the facts.'

Kate pushed at his chest until she was sitting upright, her expression wry. 'Men! Tonight, when we go to bed, tell me what happened and tell me how you felt, how you still feel.'

'I realise I owe you an explanation, that I can't make a mystery of this any longer, but what the devil do my feelings have to do with it?'

'I want to understand,' she said as she slid off his knee and stood up. 'How is your migraine now?'

'Better.' He rolled his head and flexed his shoulders. 'My neck's stiff, but that's usual afterwards.'

'You should take a hot bath.' He almost smiled again at the confident tone. Planning and making decisions seemed to cheer Kate up as much as it did him. 'And we'll take our time changing for dinner. Let's look in on Anna and Charlie on our way up,' she suggested. 'With our guests and our plans for later, I think this should be an evening for adults, don't you?'

'Oh, yes,' Grant agreed. 'Most definitely.'

Chapter Fifteen

Kate accepted a shelled walnut from Cris de Feaux, who was cracking them with one hand while moving the cruets around the table to demonstrate some obscure point about the Schleswig-Holstein question that her husband and Gabriel were arguing about.

'Thank you,' she murmured, too engaged with the argument to feel shy with him any more. He was beginning to intrigue her, with his sharp intelligence and sardonic observations. But he was unhappy, she sensed. It was hard to tell with such a controlled, contained man, but she thought he was acting, putting on a false front of normality for his friends. She wondered whether he resented the fact that two of them had married and there was certainly something in his eyes when he looked at Alex and Tess, but she thought it was pain rather than resentment or jealousy.

'The convolutions in a walnut are as nothing compared to Gabriel's mental processes,' Cris observed, breaking into her musings. 'Of course the Danes have a good claim to the territory,' he added as Alex joined in the argument. 'But the German states…'

Kate met Tess's eyes and smiled. She had been pleased with herself for remembering to rise and nod to Tess when everyone had finished dessert and she had been taken aback when the other woman said airily, 'Must we? It is only us after all.'

'Why, no, I would be happy to stay if the gentlemen are not inhibited by our presence.' They certainly would not be removing a chamber pot from the sideboard to relieve themselves, as she knew Henry and his male guests did as soon as the ladies were out of the way, because her wary inspection had revealed that was not done in this household. On the other hand she had always assumed that the men liked the freedom to discuss sport, politics and women.

'I would wager that you and I know quite enough about politics to keep our end up in a discussion,' Tess had announced. 'And if they want to talk about bare-knuckle boxing or duels, then I am all agog to hear about them, too.'

'But that means we won't be able to discuss opera dancers or our latest flirts,' Alex Tempest said plaintively and was punished with a well-aimed walnut thrown by his wife.

But, despite the teasing, the arguments were anything but frivolous. From her hours of lonely reading Kate realised that they were all travellers who knew the Continent well—and that included Grant, although she knew he had not been abroad since their marriage and she had no idea why he would be travelling across the Channel in any case.

'After the way we treated Denmark during the war, I am surprised they are a friendly nation now,' she remarked, making herself join in the discussion and not spend the evening silently puzzling over her husband.

'The fact that we bombarded Copenhagen twice?' Grant asked. 'Things in that part of the world are so complicated, even after the Treaty of Vienna, that they are probably grateful for a friendly trading partner who doesn't want to realign their boundaries.'

'You've never had any problem buying horses in Holstein, have you?' Gabriel Stone reached for the decanter and refilled all the glasses within reach.

'None. You'll have to come down to the stables and look at my latest crosses with Yorkshire coach horses. They are going to be the carriage horse of choice if I have anything to do with it.'

So that was what the handsome bay horses down at the stables were. They were not riding horses, she knew that, but not being a good horsewoman herself, she had never been curious enough to ask about them. Now it seemed that Grant was enthusiastic about horse breeding and she'd had no idea. Another side of her husband that was unknown.

The men got up, lost in an intense argument about something new that had escaped Kate's notice whilst she was brooding. 'Come and look at the atlas,' Grant was suggesting as he headed towards the door. 'It should be clear on a large-scale map.'

She and Tess were alone, one at each end of the table. 'That's done it,' Lady Weybourn remarked. 'They are off on the subject of Waterloo and we probably won't see them until breakfast time now. I shudder with relief every time I remember they were all four in that hell and none of them was wounded.'

'Shall we go into the drawing room?' Kate suggested and was surprised, and pleased, when the other woman took her arm in a companionable manner.

'Is Grant better now? He looks it.' Tess kicked off her shoes and curled up in an armchair in a scandalously casual manner.

Kate remembered something that Grant had said about Alex's wife being born on the wrong side of the blanket and never having a come-out. Despite that, she seemed relaxed enough about her place in society, which was encouraging. If she could do it, so could Kate. And then she remembered that she would have to negotiate London society while avoiding one particular aristocrat and it all seemed impossibly difficult again.

'Grant is much better, I think.'

'Had you had a row?' Tess asked with a cheerful lack of restraint. 'I thought you both looked positively stony with each other when we arrived, but of course that might have been his headache and your nerves at the thought of us all descending on you.'

'A row?' Kate temporised. She was not going to be indiscreet about Grant, but she did wish she had someone to confide in, at least about her husband.

'He's not like Alex. We have rows at least once a week and no one's any the worse for it and we usually end up laughing our heads off, or in bed. Or both,' she added with a wicked smile, apparently not noticing Kate's flushed cheeks. 'But Grant is so self-contained. Alex says he virtually never loses his temper—not to show, in any case. But you are obviously doing him good.'

'I am?' Kate murmured, lost in the face of so much frankness.

'When I first met him I had sprained my ankle and he was very kind to me, but his eyes held so much sadness, even when he was smiling. That's gone now.'

There was the fleeting memory of that look in his eyes

when they were in the bothy and, afterwards, when they reached Abbeywell. She had thought that the haunting sadness had gone because he was home again, and with Charlie, but Tess implied that it had been there for longer than just that difficult journey from Scotland. 'I know the look you mean. And you are right, it isn't there now.'

'That's love for you,' Tess said, her smile tender and secret.

'But it isn't,' Kate protested. 'We're not in love. Surely Grant told you all in London about how we met, why he married me? This is not a romance, this is a marriage of practicality.'

'Well, yes.' Tess sat up straighter, the smile gone. 'But he did not have to *marry* you to get you out of the fix you were in. There were all sorts of things he could have done to help you. He must have been attracted to you right from the beginning. And the way you look at him...'

'He needed a stepmother for Charlie,' Kate said stiffly. 'I needed a father for Anna and there was no time to discuss all the options, she was about to be born. And I don't love him.' *Do I?* Tess arched one dark brow. 'And Grant does not love me,' she added with rather more certainty.

'I am sure you know better than I,' Tess said, but the smile was back.

'Knows better than you about what, my darling?' The men were back in the room before Kate could answer that sly remark. 'Surely no one knows better than you about anything,' Alex Tempest added.

'Wretch.' Tess tilted her head back to look up at her husband. 'Have you men finished fighting the battle again to your own satisfaction? Because if Kate will excuse me, I am for my bed. It has been a long day.' She paused as she passed Kate. 'But I am right, you know, about at least one of you.'

Tess's departure broke the party up. Alex, it seemed, was not prepared to let her go up to bed without him, Gabriel suggested that Lord Avenmore come up with him so he could lend him a book he had just finished and, with the departure of her guests, Kate wanted nothing more than to get Grant alone upstairs.

'My chamber or yours?' he asked as they climbed the stairs.

'Yours.' He would be more relaxed there, she sensed. *I don't love him, I am not in love. I like him, I desire him, I am so very grateful to him, but...love? I still hardly know him and, anyway, I am not very good at recognising love.*

'I like your friends,' Kate said and went to help him out of his coat when he dismissed the waiting valet. 'Let me untie your neckcloth.' She enjoyed the closeness of standing toe to toe, unwinding the body-warmed muslin from around his neck, exposing a glimpse of skin beneath.

'Good.' Grant bent to nuzzle her temple as she stood folding the cloth. 'They like you, but then I knew they would, all being men of taste and discrimination.'

They undressed slowly, helping each other, pausing between garments for a lingering caress, a kiss. But without any spoken agreement Grant reached for his heavy silk robe when they were naked, while Kate retrieved her own robe from her room. She sat down facing him across the width of the hearth, studying the austere profile, the straight nose and firm mouth. He was a handsome man, her husband, and, yes, she looked at him and enjoyed doing so, just as Tess had observed. That did not mean she was in love with him.

'I married very suitably and far too young,' Grant said without preamble. 'We were *both* too young and I had very little experience of well-bred young ladies beyond the ballroom. I was disappointed that Madeleine seemed so cool, but she had seemed willing enough to marry me, and neither of us had been brought up to expect some passionate love match. We rubbed along well enough until Charlie was born and, naturally, I would not have dreamed of returning to the bedchamber for quite a while after that.'

'It sounds like a very lonely marriage,' Kate ventured.

Grant's shoulders moved in the ghost of a shrug. 'It is what we both expected, what I had grown up with. Then I visited her room one night and was told that she had done her duty by bearing me an heir and surely, if I wanted to *indulge my male lusts*, I could set up a mistress. I pointed out that sex within marriage was not a question of lust, and besides, I wanted more children and surely she did, too.'

He turned his head against the back of the chair until he was staring into the cold grate. 'I asked myself if I had been clumsy or insensitive in bed, I thought about Charlie's birth. I wondered, even, if there was another man she loved, had loved all the time we had been married. But she denied there was anything. Sex, she thought, was squalid and *animal*. Childbirth was *horrid*, especially as she really had little interest in children. Of course there was no one else—she had been reared to do her duty and she thought she was doing it. But if I felt she was not, then, naturally, she would resign herself.'

'Not very encouraging,' Kate murmured, secretly appalled. She could understand Madeleine's fears about childbirth, but why hadn't she confided in Grant, talked about it, rather than erected that wall of icy rejection between them? And her husband might have acquired a little more experience since his first marriage, but surely his lovemaking could not have changed *that* much? Perhaps, she mused, some women simply did not enjoy the physical side of marriage.

'No, and in retrospect I can understand her. She had been raised with no expectations of marriage beyond status—that was how she measured a successful match. A good wife gave her husband an heir, and, she reluctantly accepted, a spare. Her mother had instilled in her the belief that men were essentially bestial in their desires and that a lady endured their attentions out of duty. From the beginning she was expecting it to be a painful, distasteful, messy business. But the rest of her duty came easily to her. She knew how to behave impeccably in public, she enjoyed enhancing my standing, and with it her own. She loved to spend my money to make herself a decorative and fitting accessory at my side. But I failed to see all that. I thought another child would kindle warmer feelings, both for it and for me. Madeleine became pregnant within months and the birth was complicated. She lost the baby.'

'I am so sorry.' And he had lost a child, too, although she doubted anyone had comforted him about that.

'After that she became…difficult. She began to drink, to behave wildly. In public she was as impeccable as always, but in private it was a nightmare. The staff tried to keep drink from her, but she would find it. I never left her alone with Charlie and I certainly did not go to her bedchamber again. Grandfather would lecture her on her duty and she consigned duty to the devil.'

'You must have been tempted to have her committed to some form of care.'

'She was my wife so I did my best to look after her. I blame myself for getting her with child too soon, for not being able to save the baby.' He closed his eyes as though trying to block a vivid memory. 'I worked with Meldreth, did what I could, but he had to try to turn the baby and they were both so exhausted, mother and child. It was a miracle Madeleine lived. She was so angry with me for getting her pregnant again, it was as though she was fighting me. Every time she cried out it felt as though I had just, that moment, inflicted the pain on her. I still do not know whether it would have been better to have left the room, got out of her sight. Was I there because of my conscience, flagellating myself, or was I doing the right thing? I still do not know.'

His expression was so bleak it was hard to speak. Kate reached for the right words. 'Of course it was the right thing to do. You had some medical training, Dr Meldreth needed your help, your strength. But how could you be expected to have succeeded when an experienced prac-titioner could not?' She remembered the strain on his face, the shadows in his eyes as he worked to save Anna through that long night in the bothy. 'It must have been so hard for you to help me as you did.'

'No. That was a blessing, something I could do. There was no one else, I could hardly make things worse and I might make things better. And once she was born and I knew it would be all right, then it felt so good, as though I had been given a second chance. Up to that point, I admit, it was difficult to push the fears away.'

'But you kept on trying, you kept my spirits up and never let me see you were afraid of the outcome.' He smiled at that and she sensed it was a comfort. 'In the end, what happened?' she prompted when Grant fell silent.

'Come to her rooms.' Grant stood, took a key she recognised from his pocket and led the way the short distance along the passage. Kate saw his hands were steady as the key turned and the door swung open. They both carried branches of candles and she set hers on the hearth, while Grant placed his near the door.

'My wife died in this room,' he said, his face stark, his voice harsh. 'She died in front of my eyes and I did nothing to save her.'

'And that is only half the story,' Kate said when she could speak again. 'I know there is more to it than that, there has to be. Tell me.'

'I came home one night from dinner at a neighbour's house. Grandfather was beginning to fret because it was late and Madeleine had Charlie with her and when the nursemaid went to take him to bed she wouldn't let the girl in. I knew then there was something very wrong, because she hardly ever kept him with her or spent any time playing with him. The door was locked. I could hear him crying, so I broke it open.'

Grant walked into the room, towards the cold, empty hearth, where Kate waited, silent. 'It was hot, the fire was roaring in the chimney. Charlie was crying on the sofa that was over there, but it was angled away from me so I couldn't see him.' He gestured towards the side of the room away from the chimney. 'He sounded fretful and hungry, but not frightened.

'Madeleine was standing there, just where you are. The tray with the spirits was turned over at her feet, the liquid soaking the carpet. She had a cut-glass decanter in her hand.' He closed his eyes again and spoke without opening them. 'I think she had been drinking directly from it. She was certainly drunk. I walked across.' He moved as he spoke, blind, lost in the memory. 'I tried to take the decanter from her and she swung it at me. It hit the side of my head and smashed.' His left hand, fingers spread, speared into his hair. 'And then she must have panicked, I think. I tried not to hurt her, to take it from her gently, but I was half stunned. She swung it again and it hit my shoulder, cut down through my coat to the skin, and I fell.'

Kate glanced at the dark patch on the boards that endless scrubbing had not removed. She had been right. It was blood. Grant was still speaking, eyes still closed.

'I think I was knocked out for a moment. When I came to there was blood everywhere and there was screaming and Charlie crying. For a moment I was back on the battlefield with the noise and the smoke and the dreadful smells...' He stopped and opened his eyes. 'You do not need to hear it all. The brandy had splashed all down Madeleine's muslin gown, the carpet was already soaked. She must have staggered back towards the fire and her skirts caught. The carpet was ablaze. I crawled across, got Charlie and dragged him back. The door burst open and help was there, but it was too late for her.'

What to say? *How terrible. How tragic. Poor woman.* All so obvious and so meaningless. She would say what she thought, what concerned her, even if it was not the comforting platitudes that convention expected. 'You know you did the right thing, don't you? To go to Charlie and not to try to save Madeleine?'

'Yes.' Grant almost smiled at her. 'Yes, I know. I only had so much strength, I was bleeding like a stuck pig and she was probably beyond saving, even if I had gone directly to her. I had to get the child to safety.'

'Then, if you know that, accept it—'

'What is the problem? The problem, my dear, is that while my rational brain accepts it while I'm awake, my dreaming mind does not, it seems. A policy of *out of sight, out of mind* has worked to an extent so far, but you are right, I cannot continue like that, ignoring the existence of this room, ignoring that night.'

He stood up and held out his hand to her. 'Come, sweetheart. Let us go to bed, lock this door on the horrors of this room for another night.'

Chapter Sixteen

Grant kissed her, gently, sweetly, when they reached his bedchamber again. They shed their night robes and Kate climbed into bed beside him and lay on her stomach, her chin propped on her hands as she frowned at the harmless stack of pillows. 'So, what do you want to do? Leave the door locked for ever?'

'No. You are right, I cannot risk Charlie becoming curious.' He began to play with the ends of her hair as it spilled across the sheets. 'He is growing up and I need to deal with this for all our sakes.'

'Let us be practical, then,' Kate said, lifting her chin to look at him. He was stretched out, hands behind his head, the muscles of his upper arms and shoulders in strong relief. A wave of desire washed over her and she suppressed it. They could make love when this was decided. 'Pull the house down?' she suggested to shock him into suggesting a counter-solution.

'Demolish it? Rather an extreme solution—besides, I am fond of all the rest of the old place, so is Charlie.'

'Rip out those rooms, tear up the floorboards, get rid of the fireplace and everything in the bedchamber, put new dividing walls in to change the space completely.'

'That would work,' Grant said thoughtfully. 'And what do I tell Charlie?'

'Woodworm?'

'That's a lie.'

And Grant hates lies. 'Tell him that the floor is dangerous. And it is. Dangerous to your peace of mind, dangerous to his if he ever sees it and asks what the marks of fire are, what that dark stain is.'

'Clever.'

'Of course.' Kate said it smugly to make him laugh and, to her great relief, he did.

'Come here.' He hauled her up unceremoniously to lie on top of him. 'Thank you. I was beginning to think I was losing my mind. A man ought to be able to cope with such things.'

'Not everything, not horrors, not unless he is an unfeeling brute.' She laid her cheek against his chest and blew gently into the dark hair, smiling as his nipples contracted tightly. 'I think you feel more guilty because you did not love her.' It was dangerous to talk of love. As soon as she used the word, she had a horrid feeling that Grant might think she was fishing for him to say that he loved *her*. Which of course he didn't. Nor did she expect it. It was not as though…

'Is that some feminine logic that escapes me?'

'You cannot mourn her, only her unhappiness and the unhappiness she caused you. You dare not think too much about her in case you find you are relieved at her death.'

Beneath her the long, hard body had become very still. Kate could feel the thud of his heart, the slight rise and fall of his breathing. Then Grant said, 'You hit hard, do you not, honest Kate? You drag out thoughts that I had not even acknowledged.'

'I like you,' she said and raised her head to look deep into the troubled green eyes, half shielded by dark lashes. 'I hope I am your friend as well as your wife and your lover. Who can be honest if not your friends?'

'My closest male friends do not suggest such things.'

'Because they are male. Does Alex confide how much he loves Tess? Does Cris admit that he is in love?'

'Is he?' Surprise seemed to jerk Grant out of his inward-looking thoughts.

'I think so. He is certainly not happy, although he hides it well. I cannot be certain, of course, but there is something in his expression when he looks at Alex and Tess, and I saw it once, reflected in a mirror, when he was looking at us. Happy marriages. I cannot believe that he would be unhappy over not being married, because he could remedy that soon enough, he is so very eligible after all. Which makes me think he loves someone and it is not returned. Will he tell you about it?'

'Poor devil. I never thought to say that about Cris, and as for confiding, at knife point, possibly, otherwise, not,' he admitted with a faint smile that vanished as he frowned, back searching into his memory. 'I was not relieved she died. No, never that. If I could have gone back in time, never married Madeleine, then perhaps I would have done—but then I would not have Charlie, would I?'

Kate felt him relax as he thought of his son, then he smiled properly and she sensed the loosening of his taut body. 'We'll turn that space into rooms for the children. A bedroom each, a schoolroom, a nursery. That will chase the ghosts away better than any exorcism.'

'Grant, that's a brilliant idea.' Kate wriggled up to kiss him and realised that he had relaxed enough to be thinking of his new wife, not his old—or perhaps it was just his body that was doing so. She slid her tongue between his lips and snuggled her hips closer against his and smiled as her husband rolled her over with a possessive growl. He would not have nightmares tonight.

But, as she went down into the whirlpool of sensation with him, the thought flickered through her mind that they were making love without restraint and without care for the consequences. Strange that she had never given it a thought before tonight. The children's suite might need more rooms one day…

'You are happy.' Tess linked her arm through Kate's as they strolled across the parterre.

'Yes,' she admitted. 'We…confronted our problem. Look, you see that rough lawn down there? We are going to turn that into a water garden.'

'I'm so glad—about both the problem and the water garden.' Tess was not easily diverted from her theme. 'And I am happy for both of you. I only met Grant fleetingly before I married Alex, but I liked him very much. I am so glad he has found someone to love, someone who loves him.'

'I…' *Oh, why deny it? You are head over heels in love with the man.* 'Grant does not love me. I told you the truth, that it was a marriage of convenience. We hardly know each other yet.'

'Alex and I did not know each other very long before I knew that I loved him. Mind you, it took an awful lot to make him realise that he loved me, even when I set about seducing him,' Tess admitted with a candour that made Kate smile despite everything. 'Men are not very bright about emotions of that sort.'

'Nor am I. I don't want to have my heart broken. I

thought I was in love before, with Anna's father, but I was not. Now I feel like this about Grant and it can be wonderful in… I mean, it is wonderful being with him.' She must be the colour of a peony.

'Wonderful in bed?' Tess teased. 'For me, too. Aren't we lucky? Such *talented* men.'

'Yes. But Grant doesn't expect love in marriage. He certainly didn't find it with his first wife and that was a disaster that's haunting him still. He really did not want to marry again, not for himself. He did it because he wanted to rescue me, and because Charlie needed a step-mother and because he had promised his grandfather.' She watched a rabbit hop across the grass, stop to eat something, then, suddenly alarmed, make for the woods. That was how she felt—calm and content, then frightened by fears she could not quite name, doubts she could not express.

'I should be happy with what I have—a good man, two lovely children, security, physical bliss. And yet…'

'And yet you want it all and it will hurt all the more if he does not love you, because you can see so clearly how it could be.'

'And Grant says that *I* hit hard,' Kate said with a rueful smile.

'I was brought up by nuns to be painfully honest and it is difficult to remember tact sometimes. Are you sure he does not love you?'

'Quite sure. I believe he thinks he did the right thing in marrying me, which is something. But if I vanished off the face of the earth tomorrow?' She shrugged. 'He would be truly sorry, but his heart would not be broken.'

'What will you do?' Tess took off her bonnet and

began to swing it from its ribbons, turning her face up to the sky.

'You will get freckles,' Kate warned. 'Do? Why, nothing. I can't imagine ever having the courage to tell him. He would be so kind about it.' She shivered.

'Yes. Horrible,' Tess agreed. 'He would pussyfoot around being nice to you and you would never know what he really felt.'

'I think we should go through the things in Madeleine's bedchamber,' Kate suggested as she and Grant found themselves alone in the dining room waiting for their guests to join them for luncheon. 'Do you think there might be items you could give to Charlie as a memento of his mother? He would treasure that.'

'You wouldn't be jealous?' Grant seemed puzzled. 'He's never known her, he can't really remember her and he loves you. Why do you risk that by making her more real for him?'

'What he feels for me cannot be diluted by what he feels for anyone else. He loves you, he loves me, he loves his grandfather's memory and he can love his mother— that makes more love, not less.' *Tess was right,* she thought, *men really are confused about love.*

'I suppose that is true.' Grant caught Kate around the waist and pulled her into his embrace, to the imminent danger of the nearest place setting. 'He won't love you less—you are here and you are easy to love, Kate.' He said it with a smile as he dipped his head to kiss her and Kate lurched back clumsily, sending a knife clattering to the floor.

There was the sound of someone clearing their throat and Cris de Feaux remarked, 'My dear Grant, we are more than happy to take luncheon on the terrace—you only had to drop a hint, you know. But I'm sure a fully laid table is a most uncomfortable place to...er...bill and coo.'

Grant released her, scooped up the knife and waved the others into the room. 'If a man cannot kiss his own wife in his own dining room without being accused of disgusting practices, things have come to a sorry pass,' he remarked as he held a chair for Kate, then walked around to take his own place. 'Billing and cooing indeed. Where on earth did you pick up such a bourgeois expression?'

Gabriel Stone sat down next to Kate and gave a snort of laughter. 'I would pay good money to see the Marquess of Avenmore billing and cooing.'

Kate kicked him sharply on the ankle.

'Ouch,' he murmured. 'My dear Lady Allundale, if you wish to flirt, might I suggest that firstly you *caress* with your delightful foot and secondly that we do it away from your husband's jealous eye? I have no desire to face him at dawn. The man is too good with a firearm.'

'Oh, stop it,' Kate whispered back. 'I do not want to flirt with you, Lord Edenbridge, and you know it. Kindly do not tease the marquess.'

'Why ever not?' He turned his wicked smile on her. 'Teasing Cris keeps him human. He'd be too perfect to be true if we didn't.'

'He has feelings,' she said vehemently. 'Even if you do not.'

'Ah, Lady Allundale, just because you are in love, you do not need to wish the affliction on everyone.'

'It is not an affliction,' Kate snapped.

'No?' The dark, knowing gaze moved from her to Grant, who was engaged in an energetic argument with

Alex Tempest at the other end of the table. 'If you say so, sweet Kate, I must believe you.'

Infuriating man. Kate passed Gabriel the bread and butter with more force than elegance. *He knows I love Grant. Which means if both Tess and he can see it, then Grant must be able to see how I feel, as well. On the other hand,* she mused, pushing a slice of cold chicken around her plate, *perhaps Grant doesn't see, any more than he and Lord Edenbridge can perceive that Lord Avenmore is suffering.*

She was making herself dizzy, going in circles. Kate made a superhuman effort, pushed all thoughts of her marriage to the back of her mind and enquired about Lord Edenbridge's family home in repressive tones that managed to curtail even *his* tendency to tease.

'We need a builder,' Grant said a week later as they stood and waved goodbye to the three carriages.

'Not an architect?' Kate shifted Anna into a more comfortable position and kept an eye on Charlie, racing down the drive for a last wave to his favourite 'uncles'.

'No, the sketches we did will be enough for a good joiner to work from.' Grant turned back to the house. 'I thought to ask Wilson to sort all the personal items from the bedroom. The gowns, perfume bottles, the curtains, all of that kind of thing will go anonymously to charities in Newcastle for them to sell.' He hesitated. 'There's a miniature of Madeleine. Should I give it to Charlie now, do you think, or wait until he is older?'

'Now, I think.' Kate moved close to his side. 'You remember that tomorrow I have a number of ladies visiting for tea? I met them at Mrs Lowndes's charity sewing circle. Some of them are bringing children with them, which will keep Charlie occupied. That will give Wilson the opportunity to tackle the room.'

She stopped in the doorway and called to Charlie, who came racing back with Rambler, the elderly pointer, at his heels. The secrets and ghosts would soon be gone from this house and from Grant's heart, driven out by sawdust and hammering, plasterers and cheerful, noisy builders. Summer was coming, the valley was blossoming and her children were, too. Her husband seemed happy and she was learning to live with loving him in secret.

Christmas, and London, were a very long way away, Kate thought as she turned back to the hallway and her waiting husband. A long way. Grant would see how happy they all were here and it could only get better. When autumn came he would not want to leave this place for the dirt and noise and artificiality of London.

She held out her hand and he took it and, as he bent to kiss her, there was nothing but warmth in the green eyes that smiled into hers.

November 23—Abbeywell

'Lady Mortenson is holding a party and we are invited.' Kate waved the letter in Grant's direction.

'What date is it?' Grant looked up from the copy of the *Times* that was folded beside his plate.

'The eighteenth of December.' Kate spread damson preserve on her toast and passed her wardrobe in mental review. She would definitely need a new gown and probably some evening slippers, as well.

'That's a pity, we'll miss it.' Grant was still intent on the Parliamentary news.

'Why?'

'We will be in London by then, of course.' He looked up as if surprised she even had to ask.

'*London?* But you never said anything about London.'

'I most certainly did.' Grant tossed the newssheet aside. 'When I came back in May I said we would have the summer here, then go back to London.'

'After Christmas.' Somehow she stopped her voice rising to a shriek. 'You said *after* Christmas.'

'Yes, but the building work is proving far more disruptive than we thought with all the work they are doing on the chimney flues.' He was using what Kate thought of as his *husband being reasonable* voice. It usually amused her, especially as she won half of the battles that necessitated the use of it. Now she dropped the toast, jam-side down, on to the plate and stared at him as he continued, just as reasonably. 'We can't use half the downstairs rooms because we can't light fires there and the house is getting colder and colder. And you said yourself only the other day that it is making a lot of work for the staff, trying to keep all the dust under control. If we weren't here, they could shut up all the rooms, put dust covers on the furniture, retreat into the warm part and let the builders get on with it. I thought we could go down next week.'

'Next week?' Kate echoed faintly. Over Christmas week London would be quiet and starved of fashionable company because most of the *ton* would be at their country estates. But at the beginning of December she was sure the capital would seem as busy as always. It might not be the Season, but society would still be there in force.

'I'm sure I said something.' Grant shrugged. 'Perhaps I just remarked about it to Grimswade and Bolton. And

Wilkinson.' He picked up the paper again. 'I'm sure I mentioned it to Wilkinson.'

'My lord.' Kate kept her voice level because it would not do to shout in front of the footmen. 'You may have told your butler, your secretary and your bailiff, but you did not tell your *wife.*'

'There is no need to worry, my dear.' Grant seemed blissfully unaware that he was within an inch of having the jam pot thrown at him. 'The staff are well practised in getting packed up for London. We'll take the chaise for ourselves and the travelling coach for the children and Jeannie and Gough, and then another coach for the luggage. This fine dry weather seems set to hold.'

'Thank you, Giles, that will be all.' Kate waited until the footmen had gone out and the door had closed. 'My lord, I do not want to go to London.'

'Why ever not?' Finally she had his full attention. Probably the repeated use of his title gave him an inkling that all was not well.

'Because—' *My lover will be there. Anna's father. The man who ruined me and who has every cause to wish to see me in prison. My brother might be there and will try his damnedest to ensnare you in his schemes. Because you'll find out that I told you a pack of lies. Because I am terrified that everything we have built is going to fall apart.* And she could say none of that.

The six months that Grant had been at Abbeywell had been months of contentment. They had grown closer and had fallen into a domestic routine that appeared to please both of them. Their nights were filled with passionate lovemaking and Grant showed no sign of tiring of her, even though he had not declared any feeling for her beyond affection. The children were flourishing.

We have become a family, Kate thought, *but it is all founded on lies. My lies.* They were companionable, but sometimes that companionship felt merely polite and distant and Kate knew there was an invisible barrier between them that stopped them achieving the closeness that might lead to a mutual love. She suspected it was her own guilty conscience that had raised that sheet of glass. She dared not break it and the more time went past, the harder it became to even contemplate telling him the truth. It was as though the right moment had slipped through her fingers and was now vanishing, too far gone to catch.

The marriage was like a house built of cards. If Grant discovered the truth, then it would all come tumbling down—their family life, the children's security, Grant's reputation if, as she suspected he would, he insisted on confronting the criminality of what Henry had done. At some level Grant must sense that she was holding something back from him, but he was too much the gentleman to force the issue.

Or perhaps he does not care enough, she thought in her darker moments. He must have had enough drama and emotion with Madeleine not to want to demand a confrontation with her. Surely now he wanted only a quiet life with a wife who satisfied him in bed and loved his children. *But it is so lonely sometimes.*

'Why are you so reluctant to go to London?' Grant asked.

'Charlie will miss Christmas at home.'

'The town house is familiar to him now—besides, this house at Christmastide can only hold bad memories for him. Let him have this year somewhere entirely different and then the following year the recollections will be dimmer, the house will be much changed and we can enjoy the festive season here.'

That was perfectly, unarguably, reasonable. Kate tried another tack. 'I'm shy of London. I won't know how to go on there.'

'Of course you will.' Grant was beginning to look impatient now. 'You are quite at ease with company in the neighbourhood, you are well informed on the issues of the day, you make excellent conversation and you dance very well and you'll have fashionable gowns—there is nothing at all to be alarmed about.'

'I can't help it,' she said. 'I am.'

He was puzzled now, she could tell, and in a moment he was going to move from puzzlement to suspicion. 'Where is the courageous woman I found in that bothy?'

There was nothing for it. Unless she developed a disfiguring rash or broke a leg, she was going to have to face London society. 'Facing critical leaders of fashion is far more alarming than giving birth, believe me,' Kate said with a laugh that she hoped rang true.

Grant visibly relaxed. 'I will be there by your side.'

That is what I am afraid of. 'Of course.'

Chapter Seventeen

Something was wrong with Kate. Grant paced along the terrace, welcoming the cold, rolling his shoulders to relax them after two hours of solid work in the study with his bailiff and secretary, sorting estate matters out so that he could safely go away for a few months. Was whatever had made her so wary of London related to the reserve that was always present just below the surface, however cheerful she seemed, however lost in the passion of their lovemaking?

He wanted to trust her totally and yet, somehow, he could not. Was it the ghost of his first marriage haunting him, holding him back from that complete act of faith? He only wished she would tell him what it was that put the shadow in her eyes, those moments of constraint when he sensed she was holding back from telling him… something. It was hard not to think, *Confess something.* He told himself it was not jealousy that he felt, that she was not still pining for Anna's father. After all, she had told him she had not loved the man, and besides, what did it matter if she had? Theirs was a practical, companionable marriage, not a love match. Kate was passionate and responsive in bed, and that was what a man needed, not some foolish romantic fantasy with moonlight and roses. And heartbreak.

'My lord?'

He turned to find Jeannie standing outside the long window to the drawing room, Anna in her arms. 'Yes?' He strolled across to tickle the baby under her chin and she laughed at him and held out her arms.

'Could I leave Lady Anna with you a moment, my lord? I brought her down for an airing, but there's much more of a nip in the air than I realised and I want another shawl for her.'

'Of course. I'll wait with her in the drawing room.' He took Anna, who immediately fastened both chubby hands on his neckcloth and proceeded to demolish it as he carried her into the warmth.

'You, madam, are a menace to any gentleman with pretentions to elegance,' he chided and held her away while he went to examine the damage in the mirror. Not so bad, at least she hadn't chewed it this time. Anna laughed up at him and he smiled back, then sobered as a thought struck him. What if Kate's reluctance to go to London was a fear that a lack of resemblance between her husband and the child might be noticed? After all, Anna had reached the age when a proud mama might be expected to produce the child for a few minutes for morning callers to admire.

Their local acquaintance had known Anna as she grew up and, presumably, were used to her and accepted her as Grant's child without question. Now he shifted Anna until he could hold her up facing the mirror beside his own face and compared their features—straight brown hair in a shade nearer his dark tones than Kate's lighter tresses. A face that would, he was sure, echo her mother's as she grew out of babyhood and the promise of height that would fit well with both her assumed parents.

And green eyes. He shifted her round again so he could study them more carefully. Several doting matrons had remarked on those eyes—'Green, just like her papa's!' That was useful.

Anna was watching him now, eyes wide, and he realised that her eyes were not like his after all. They were a paler, clearer green with gold flecks and a dark rim around the iris. The effect was beautiful and unusual and when she grew up he imagined they would give her a unique charm. He checked his own eyes in the mirror—a darker green that verged towards hazel when he was tired or angry, so he'd been told. No gold flecks, no dark ring. But that was not a problem, Anna was like enough in various characteristics to both of them not to raise the slightest suspicions. It might be a different matter if she was a redhead or a pale blonde. He was conscious of disappointment that he had not found the reason for Kate's anxiety.

'Here we are, my lord, her warmest shawl. I'll take her now, shall I?'

Jeannie bore Anna away to the terrace, leaving Grant frowning at his own reflection in the mirror. Kate was perfectly competent socially, she was intelligent enough to learn and adapt quickly and she was usually confident enough to be aware of that. Could it be that she feared encountering her brother? He knew he should have insisted on making contact with the shadowy Mr Harding of somewhere in Suffolk, but he had managed to forget all about Kate's brother and she had done nothing to remind him. He should confront her about all of these things, but he sensed that if he did he would destroy the happiness they now had, perhaps simply for a phantom of his own imagination. He would watch and think and see how she took to London, see what clues he could discover.

He strode out of the drawing room and along to the little room Kate had claimed as her writing room, tapped and went in. 'Kate.'

She jumped, blotted her page and tutted irritably at him. Sometimes he made her cross simply because it was so rare to see her lose her self-control and he wanted to see the real woman that she kept so carefully hidden behind the facade of the good wife and mother. She revealed that face in bed, when she lost all inhibition with him, and she had shown it when she had helped him fight his demons over Madeleine, but there were times when he thought she was moving further and further away from him.

'I'm sorry.' He moved to stand behind her and ran the back of one finger down the exposed nape of her neck, enjoying the sensual little shiver she gave. 'Were you writing poetry? I am sorry if I have made you blot the final stanza.'

Kate gave a little snort of laughter, the irritation vanishing as fast as it always seemed to. 'No, I am not writing poetry. This is a shopping list for the linen warehouse. There hardly seems to be a decent sheet left in the house.' She twisted round to look up at him and he kept his hand where it was so that his fingers trailed round her neck as she moved. 'Do you think I should be writing odes to my husband's eyelashes?'

'Are they so worthy of praise?' He felt absurdly anxious that she should say so.

'They are indecently long and thick.'

'Are they indeed? Indecent, eh? All the better to tickle you with.' The confrontation he had come for was less interesting than the possibilities presented by a flustered wife, a comfortable chaise longue and the thought of how his eyelashes might be employed.

'Grant!' It was accompanied by a most encouraging blush. He turned the key in the lock, twitched the nearest curtain across the window and advanced on the desk.

'Grant—only half the window is covered.'

'If anyone is standing in the middle of the flower bed, on a box, contorting their neck in an effort to see in through the uncovered area of the window, all I can say is that we have more flexible staff than I imagined.' He stripped off his coat and waistcoat as he advanced. 'Am I going to have to chase you round the desk?'

'Do you want to?' Kate slipped off the chair and retreated to the far side. 'I warn you, I have a quill and I know how to use it.'

Grant hopped on one foot, then the other as he tugged off his boots. Kate was not making much of an effort to escape, which was interesting. He had never tried to make love to her downstairs and he had expected her to be shy of doing so in broad daylight. When he emerged from the folds of his shirt and prowled towards her clad only in his breeches she edged away around the desk, then, when he was within arm's reach, extended the quill like a rapier and flicked his right nipple with the point of the feather.

'*Touché,*' Grant conceded, moved his right hand and, when her eyes flickered to follow the movement, lunged, caught Kate around the waist and bore her off to the chaise. She tried to bounce up. He flipped her skirts up over her head and, as she struggled to extricate herself, pressed a kiss into the exposed triangle of curls at the junction of her thighs.

Kate went very still, but did not resist as he eased her knees apart, settled his shoulders between them, bent his head and brushed his lashes up the inside of her thigh, over the white, soft skin. There was a sudden heave and the skirts settled over his head plunging him into semi-darkness as he shifted the subtle caress to her other thigh.

That convulsive movement was all the resistance she gave as he worked his way up, fraction by fraction, towards his goal. She was aroused, there was no mistaking that. Grant parted the delicate folds, touched once with his tongue, and Kate came apart in his hands. He used his lips and mouth in a long, demanding kiss that had her writhing on the couch before he shook off the folds of her gown, pulled down his breeches and sheathed himself in her pulsing, hot body in one hard movement.

'*Grant.*' Her face was buried in the angle of his neck, her arms locked around his shoulders as he thrust. 'Grant, I—'

'Come again,' he demanded, controlling, somehow, his own need. 'Come for me again. *Now.*'

And she did, pulling him with her into the maelstrom.

I almost told him I loved him, Kate thought as she cradled her husband in her arms in blissful discomfort. The sofa cushion, a hard, cylindrical bolster, dug into the base of her spine, her corset was doing its best to stop her breathing and Grant, though without any spare flesh on him, was a significant dead weight on top of her. *Thank goodness I didn't.*

'Kate.' Grant's voice was muffled and he heaved

himself up until he was sitting on the end of the chaise. 'You were trying to say something just then.'

'Probably *more*, or *again*,' she temporised. 'Goodness, after that, how do you expect me to recall my own name?'

He grinned. 'Flatterer. Kate…' That change of tone from teasing to serious within the space of two words was ominous. She braced herself. 'Is the problem about going to London because you fear coming across your brother? I know you haven't written to him. Perhaps we should make contact now, before we go.'

'No.' She pushed down her skirts and scrambled to sit upright at the end of the chaise. 'Please, Grant. It will be too awkward. I cannot forgive him for how he behaved and he will not forgive me. Let sleeping dogs lie.' He still looked unconvinced as he refastened his breeches. 'It isn't as though my parents are alive, or that I have other siblings.' Which was true. She had cousins, but they were even more country mice than she was.

'If it upsets you so much, I will not insist.' Grant pushed his fingers through his hair, the habitual giveaway that he was frustrated. He would circle round, come back to this, she knew.

'And Henry would be a most unsuitable uncle for Charlie, a really bad influence.' That went home, she saw. 'May I have the carriage tomorrow? I need to go into Newcastle to have my hair done.'

'Surely the coiffeur will come here, or it can wait until you get to London?'

'Oh, did I not tell you?' She had not, quite deliberately. 'I saw an advertisement in the *Newcastle Courier* that Monsieur Ducasse, late of Monsieur Maurice's establishment in Bond Street, has set up in Newcastle. And Monsieur Maurice advertises in all the best journals—*La*

Belle Assemblée and so on. I would feel so much more comfortable with a fashionable style. I wrote to reserve a private parlour at the King's Head and he will attend me there.' Grant opened his mouth and she said hastily, 'Wilson will accompany me, of course.'

'Then of course you may have the carriage.' Grant got to his feet and lifted her hand to kiss the tips of her fingers. 'Not that you need any changes to make you look quite delightful, my dear.'

'Flatterer.' She laughed up at him and pulled his hand back to rest fleetingly against her own lips. *I love you and now I will lie and deceive and do whatever it takes to get through this ordeal without you ever discovering who the woman you married really is.*

'Kate?' Grant stopped dead in the hallway, then advanced slowly, like a cat who has seen something that may be prey, or may be something alien and dangerous. 'What have you done?' he demanded as he completed the circle.

Grimswade, who had appeared the moment the carriage drew up, effaced himself, closely followed by Wilson clutching Kate's bonnet, pelisse and reticule.

'Monsieur Ducasse gave me a new style.' She smiled brightly at him and fluffed the soft curls that framed her face. 'I think it's very dashing.'

'He's cut it.' Grant's green eyes were narrowed as he studied the effect.

'Just the front. I knew it would curl if he did that. The back is still long, so it can be put up. You see?' Kate turned right round, skirts belling out.

'It changes the shape of your face.'

She still couldn't work out whether he liked it or not,

or whether he realised that she had plucked her eyebrows into a finer arch. 'I think it shows off my cheekbones. I didn't know I had any before.'

'And the colour…' Grant was prowling again.

'Just a shade darker. Monsieur Ducasse said it would make my eyes look bigger.' He came to a halt in front of her and she widened her eyes at him. 'And bluer.' And he had stained her eyebrows to match. Wilson had the little brush and bottle safely tucked away.

'You look more sophisticated,' Grant said at last, when she thought she would go dizzy from holding her breath.

'Is that code for *older*?' She hoped it was. She wanted to look as different as possible from that wide-eyed, un-sophisticated girl who had been the bait to catch a lord in a blackmailer's snare.

'Just a trifle.' Grant seemed to have relaxed, lids heavy over his green eyes. 'It certainly makes you look more… experienced.' There was a wealth of hidden meaning in the one, drawled, word.

He likes it. That was a relief.

'Maman!' Charlie appeared, at the run as usual, skid-ded to a halt and stared. Then he circled her, just as his father had done, but with his mouth open.

Grant laughed. 'Your *maman* has had a haircut. Fancy, isn't it?'

'It's prime!' Charlie approved. 'Is it for London?'

'It is.' Grant's gaze met hers over the boy's head. 'I'm glad you are getting into the spirit of the London expedi-tion, Kate. It is past your bedtime, Charlie, off you go.'

'I'm doing my best.' She bent to kiss the boy before he ran off to the stairs, then slid her hand through the crook of her husband's elbow and leaned in a little, enjoying the smell of leather and the hint of coffee and the familiar, beloved scent that was simply *Grant*. She had been away all day and she had missed him, even for those few hours.

He turned his head from watching Charlie's retreating form, looked down at her and became very still. His eyes, which were usually green, darkened to hazel, as they did when he was tired, or angry or aroused. And this was definitely arousal, reacting to something he saw in her expression. 'Kate.'

Her chest was so tight that her lungs felt hollow. He was going to kiss her, here and now in the hallway, and she going to say it, tell him she loved him, and she could not, must not. Not when she was lying to him, deceiving him. 'Of course, it will mean a great strain on my dress allowance and my pin money.' She fluttered her eyelashes outrageously. 'Will you increase it, or will you be mean and beat me if I overspend?'

'I might do both,' Grant said, low-voiced. 'I might increase it so you may buy outrageous garments and then spank you just for the hell of it.' His expression promised considerably more pleasure than pain and she knew he was not a man who would raise a hand to a woman in anger. Was spanking another of those erotic games he was beginning to show her?

'That sounds interesting,' Kate murmured. 'But you'd have to chase me first.'

'That can be arranged.' Grant looked up. 'Yes, Grimswade, what is it?'

'Should I tell the kitchen to put dinner back, my lady, seeing as you have only just got in?'

'Goodness, is that the time?' For a moment she had thought the butler had overheard Grant and was suggesting delaying dinner while she was pursued around the bedchamber by a playful husband. Really, she must get a grip on her imagination! 'I'll go straight up now. Don't inconvenience Cook, thank you, Grimswade.'

'Thank you, my lady.'

'Coward,' Grant whispered in her ear as she passed him.

If only you knew, my love. Pray heaven that you never do.

Chapter Eighteen

December 15—Grosvenor Street, London

'More treasures?'

Kate nodded to Wilson and waited until the maid closed the bedchamber door behind her before she answered. Grant was standing at the foot of the bed and eyeing the heap of packets and bandboxes that the footmen had just brought up. She rather thought he was on the verge of smiling, but she could not be certain—after all, she had spent almost a week doing nothing else but shop.

'Yes. And you have bought a stack of neckcloths and at least two waistcoats, and a new evening suit and three pairs of boots.'

'I have.' Yes, his mouth was just twitching at the corner.

'One has to dress,' Kate drawled, risking it. 'At least that was what I heard one lady say to another while I was in the fitting room at Mrs Bell's.'

'That is absolutely true. Think what a spectacle Bond Street would be if one did not.'

'Especially if Prinny was on the strut.'

Grant shuddered. 'I did not need that image being put into my mind, thank you!' He picked up a large flat box from the floor. 'And what does this contain?'

'Um…I was hoping it was something you wouldn't see in broad daylight,' Kate confessed.

Grant weighed the box on the upturned palm of one hand and looked at the shop stamp on the lid. 'Ah, the cost of this, I imagine, is in inverse proportion to the amount of fabric it contains.'

'It was a *trifle* expensive. I was hoping it might be the sort of thing that would get me chased around the bedchamber.'

'But not spanked?' Grant had a speculative gleam in his eye. 'Try it on for me, and we'll see.'

'At four o'clock in the afternoon?' Her pulse was racing along with her imagination.

'I really cannot persuade you out of the idea that there are *respectable* times and places for lovemaking, can I?' Grant piled the parcels on the bed on to the floor, then sat down and pulled off his boots.

'I can be persuaded.' Kate picked up the box and whisked into the dressing room. 'Close your eyes.'

He was quite correct about the cost. If looked at dispassionately, the negligee consisted of nothing but floating panels of pale blue silk gauze, a large number of silver ribbons and dark blue silk flowers appliquéd in various strategic positions. Crushed up it would fit in a soup bowl and, as a garment, it was utterly impractical for anything except tormenting one's husband. She had thought it delicious the moment she saw it.

When she looked around the edge of the door Grant was leaning against a bedpost, arms crossed, eyes closed. He was wearing nothing but a severe expression. Once,

Kate would have been alarmed, now she could read him well enough to know she was being teased, especially as there was nothing to disguise the fact that he was finding this arousing.

She tiptoed up, swirled round so her gossamer skirts whispered across his legs and ran to the other side of the bed. Grant's reflexes were fast and he was on her heels, reaching for her as she scrambled across the bed, silk panels flying. Kate made it to the other side just as Grant somersaulted across the bed and landed on his feet in front of her.

'That is the most outrageously provoking garment I have even seen.' He was breathing far harder than the amount of activity justified.

'And you have seen many?'

Kate could have sworn he had actually growled, although as she found herself seized, upended and face down over Grant's knees, she could not be certain.

'Now, then, let's check the workmanship.' One large hand at the small of her back was more than enough to hold her down, even if she had wanted to struggle, which she did not. A wriggle or two, though...

There was a flurry of fabric, a whisper of silk, and then there was nothing over her buttocks but air. 'Quite impractical,' Grant observed. 'I cannot imagine how this would keep you warm on a chilly evening.' There was a tantalising pause, then one palm moved slowly over her right buttock. 'This would, though.'

It was only a light smack, more noise than anything. Kate squeaked, then gasped as he did the same to the other buttock.

'Warmer? Certainly pinker.'

What was warm was the thrust of his erection against

her stomach. Kate decided she liked this game. 'Beast! Savage!' She wriggled against him and was rewarded by a flurry of light open-handed slaps. She realised the wicked sensation of being powerless while Grant did what he liked was making her excited, breathless and very, very needy. 'Grant?'

'Hmm?' She felt the pressure of his lips on one sensitive buttock. 'Shall I stop? Perhaps you are right and this isn't the thing to be doing in the afternoon. We could get dressed and discuss the Parliamentary report in the *Times*.'

'You haven't checked the design of the front of the negligee. What if they stinted on ribbons?'

'What an appalling thought. I would have to wrap you in a cloak and take you straight back to the shop to demand a refund.' He turned her so she was sitting on his thighs and tipped up her chin. 'A very becoming shade of rose. Are you flushed because you enjoyed being spanked, or at the thought of being carried through the streets in nothing but this flimsy thing and a cloak?'

'Both,' she admitted as he began to untie the ribbons, counting as he went.

'…nine, ten…' His voice was not quite steady as he gave up on the little bows and lifted her, then brought her down so she was straddling him as he sat. 'I need to see it in motion,' he said, his voice husky as he lowered her with aching slowness until he was sheathed inside her. 'Like that.' She held him, burrowed close against him so the friction of the fine gauze fretted her nipples, and his, and felt the control he had been tantalising her with snap. *Kate.* He broke in six powerful strokes, took her with him into the whirlwind and then stayed, deep inside her, his arms around her, his forehead on her shoulder.

Just as she was sliding into sleep Grant murmured, 'I didn't hurt you, did I?'

'Of course not. I knew you would never hurt me.' She sat back, ran one finger down the straight line of his nose and smiled when, eyes still closed, he put out his tongue to catch the tip. 'And you aren't cross about all my shopping?'

'Of course not.' Grant opened his eyes and fell back on to the bed, bringing her with him. 'I've kept you locked up in Northumberland away from all the shops for months.'

'I've been extravagant, though.' He shook his head, but she persisted with her confession. 'I'm…nervous. It took my mind off things. It's quite dangerous really, spending all that money. It must be like gambling or drink.'

To her surprise he didn't laugh at the notion. 'You are probably right. But don't worry, if you can see the danger, then I doubt you are in it. But don't be nervous, Kate. I'll look after you. I won't let the society sharks near you.'

'I know.' *But you can't protect me from the monsters I've unleashed myself, my love.*

Grant climbed to the next step on the grand staircase leading to the ballroom of the Marquess of Larminster's ballroom, the setting for the marchioness's 'surprise' birthday reception for her husband. The event was a surprise for no one, least of all the long-suffering and newly sixty-year-old marquess, but he enjoyed indulging his wife and she enjoyed parties, the larger the better.

It was not the event that Grant would have chosen for Kate's introduction to London society, for the place was full to bursting and the noise level indescribable. It was also packed with the important people Kate needed to make a good impression upon if she were to obtain the entrée to the right circles and the friendship and approval of the ladies who made society go round. And they were married to the men Grant mixed with socially at his clubs and would be forming alliances with, and against, in the House of Lords.

As he stood with as much patience as he could muster in the receiving line, he looked down at his wife again, still coming to terms with how sophisticated and elegant she looked. It occurred to him that the height of his hopes had been that she would 'do', pass muster, not be a disaster. How little faith he'd had. Somewhere, always in the back of his mind, was the image of the bedraggled, exhausted, desperate woman in that bothy, the knowledge that she was not trained up for this world, that she carried scandal with her.

Despite coming to know her—her courage, her humour, her intelligence, her breathtaking natural eroticism—he had still taken it for granted that she could not cope with this world with its dagger-sharp criticism, its rivalries and sophisticated pleasures.

'Grant,' Kate murmured. 'We're moving again.'

Up another step, almost at the top now. She was still nervous, he could see the almost imperceptible tremor of the beading around the bodice of her gown, but she looked magnificent. Not a traditional beauty, she would never be that, but somehow something better. *Elegant, charming, warm,* he thought. *And sophisticated with her new hairstyle. And the minx has been colouring her lashes with lampblack and, if I'm not very much mistaken, she's using lip stain.*

Like a soldier she'd put on her armour to go into battle for him. *She makes me so happy.*

The realisation hit him as though someone behind him had punched him between the shoulder blades. Happy. He was actually, positively happy. Not just now and again, like when he was playing with Charlie, or feeling the wind in his hair when he galloped unchecked across the moor, or won a hand of cards against Gabriel, but bone-deep happy. That had come with this marriage. Somehow he had moved, without him realising it, from simply coping with life and snatching what pleasure he could, to a feeling of inner contentment. But he had not been conscious of feeling happy. *When did that happen? Just now? Yesterday? Weeks ago?*

A sharp elbow nudged him in the ribs. *'Grant, it's us.'*

'Sorry, air-dreaming.' Hell, in a minute he'd be shouting with laughter, capering like a fool for a fascinated audience. Grant found a social smile from somewhere, plastered it on and advanced on the marchioness. 'Lady Larminster, may I introduce my wife, Catherine?'

'Lady Allundale.' The marchioness raised artfully curved eyebrows as she studied Kate. 'Delightful,' she pronounced.

'Lady Larminster.' Kate's curtsy was perfectly modulated.

'Larminster, here's Allundale's wife at long last.' The marquess inclined his head and beamed at Kate, who curtsied again. 'You've taken long enough bringing her to town, Allundale.'

Grant had no trouble interpreting that as, *So what is wrong with her?* 'All due to my sins, ma'am. I'm greedy, jealous and possessive and don't want to share her.' As he spoke, he realised that was all quite true. He wanted to scoop Kate up in his arms and sweep her off back home. He wanted to do something about this strange fizzing joy inside him.

'Well, now, there's a declaration of the kind one doesn't hear enough of in these cynical days. Do you hear that, Larminster?'

Beside him he could almost feel the warmth of Kate's blushes, but when he walked her away from the receiving line and could look at her face he saw the light dusting of rice powder had subdued the colour, or else she was pale through nerves.

'She's a bossy old besom,' he said as he steered her into the reception room. 'But she means well.'

'I'm sure she does.' Kate's chin was up. 'That was very gallant of you, to say those things.'

'I meant them.' *You make me so happy. You have transformed my life.* How the blazes did one say these things to one's wife in the middle of this scrum? Surely there was a withdrawing room somewhere? Gabriel would have slipped a coin to a footman and would know the location of hidden nooks before he had even sized up the ladies at any social event. Alex, in the old days, wouldn't have been much slower. But Grant had never enjoyed dicing with scandal under the very noses of chaperons and sharp-eyed husbands and had always conducted his affaires with considerably more discretion.

'What is amusing you?' Kate obviously didn't find anything at all amusing about the hot, noisy throng and was eyeing them with a social smile on her lips and eyes as wary as any gladiator thrust into the arena, wondering where the lions hid and just how hungry they were.

'I'm regretting not bribing a footman, that's all,' he said vaguely. 'Come, let's circulate and I'll introduce you to some people you'll like.'

And, by a miracle, he managed to locate many of the acquaintances he had hoped to introduce to Kate. The pleasanter young matrons with small children of their own, the cheerful chaperons whose gossip was friendly, not vicious, and several gentlemen he could trust to treat her to polite and harmless flirtation or intelligent conversation.

After half an hour he felt she had relaxed enough to leave her with a group of his friends while he went to find her a glass of ratafia. When he got back she had Mr Whittaker choking with laughter over her description of their vicar confronted by the flock of sheep that wandered into the church during his sermon, pursued by a very amorous ram. By her side the Reverend Herbert, one of the Bishop of London's more irreverent curates, was extemporising a sermon of his own on the subject of lost lambs while making eyes at two young ladies who appeared very willing to stray in his direction.

Grant had never realised that Kate was a natural raconteur before, but she was holding her small audience gripped while, with perfect poise, she spun the tale in such a way that the poor vicar was described kindly and yet the scene was irresistibly funny.

'Do let me introduce you to my sister, Lady Allundale. She pines for witty conversation.' Whittaker took her arm, removed the ratafia glass from Grant's hand and steered Kate off into the crowd. She seemed more than happy to go with him.

'You look as nervous as a hopeful mama whose chick has just been launched into the stormy seas of the Season,' a familiar voice remarked.

'Alex.' Grant relaxed a trifle. If Alex was there, then Tess was as well, so that was two more allies. 'I don't know about looking like a hopeful matron, but I'm certainly nervous—Kate is painfully shy about all this.'

'She looks stunning. Very chic. I like the hair.' His friend was watching Kate with the eye of a connoisseur.

Grant narrowed his eyes at him, then told himself not to be ridiculous. This possessiveness played havoc with the common sense. 'She does, but she doesn't look like my Kate any more when she's dressed up like this.'

'Ah. *Your* Kate. I wondered how long it was going to take you to notice.' Alex's mouth twitched into its lazy smile as Grant frowned at him.

'Of course I notice. She's my wife.' He did his best to sound offhand. This new awareness of his feelings was too sensitive to discuss, even with Alex.

'No *of course* about it. Tess says we men have to be hit over the head with it before we realise it isn't lust or liking. When did you get hit with the brick?'

'An hour ago,' Grant admitted. 'At the top of the staircase, two couples from the head of the receiving line.'

Alex's hoot of laughter had heads turning, including Kate's. She raised her hand in a little wave, then turned back to her new acquaintances. 'No wonder you are looking vaguely concussed. Love does that. I assume Kate is aware of your feelings?'

'*What?* Don't be an idiot. Of course I'm not—' Grant managed to get his snarl down to a whisper. 'She makes me happy, that's all. I realised just now that I hadn't felt like this…for ever. And it is due to her. But that's contentment and liking and lus—er, compatibility in bed. It is not love. Ours is a marriage of convenience, you know that. And stop mopping your eyes, it isn't that funny.'

'No?'

'No, it is not.'

Alex rolled his eyes and returned his handkerchief to its pocket in the tails of his coat. 'There have been times when I've been deluded enough to think you quite intelligent, Rivers. I will leave you to stew and go and see who Tess is making eyes at and rescue them.'

'Don't say anything.'

'About what? The fact that you are *happy*? Or the fact that you're an idiot?' Alex strolled off, leaving Grant to practice deep breathing in the middle of the crowded floor in the intervals between greeting acquaintances, bowing to ladies and attempting to get his emotions and his brain into some kind of alignment.

He was an adult male with considerable experience of life and women. He had faced his man in a duel, he had fought at Waterloo and somehow got out of that intact, he had dealt with hysterical mistresses throwing the porcelain from under the bed before now. He wasn't a romantic youth desperate to transform simple liking, affection and desire into some hearts-and-flowers nonsense that could only end in disillusion and anticlimax. He was happy. His marriage made him happy. That was a wonderful realisation and now he could just get on with his life.

Chapter Nineteen

Kate was beginning to relax. In fact, she thought with a small start of surprise, she was actually beginning to enjoy herself. No one had pointed a finger at her, crying *Fallen woman!* or *Blackmailer's accomplice!* as they did in her worst dreams. She could see no one who looked even faintly familiar, except for Alex and Tess, and her new acquaintances were all pleasant and even positively friendly.

Grant had seemed a little strange for a moment while they had been waiting on the stairs, but perhaps he had been nervous for her, which was understandable. She had no idea how her shaky legs had got her up those stairs, but now she was happily answering questions about which days she was at home to visitors and promising to take Anna to call on Mrs Whiting, who had a baby girl almost the same age.

She sensed Grant with a prickling awareness that had her glancing back over her shoulder with a smile, even before he arrived at her side. Was he proud of her? She hoped so, because she thought she was doing very well indeed.

'My dear.' He rested his right hand at the small of her back, a possessive gesture that made her shiver pleasurably. 'I am afraid I must tear you away. If you will excuse us?' He nodded and smiled and was perfectly polite as he detached her from the group and began to walk her back towards the entrance.

'Grant, is something wrong? You haven't had a message about one of the children, have you?'

'No, nothing is wrong. I need to talk with you, that's all.'

So I must be doing something wrong... No, that can't be it. I know I have not put a finger out of line. Was he unwell? She looked up at his face as he took her arm as they descended the stairs, then sent a footman for their things. He looked tense, keyed up. It must be one of his wretched migraines, although it had been weeks since he had suffered one. Perhaps anxiety about her had triggered it.

Kate stayed silent and did not fuss, even when they were seated in their carriage. She was finally rewarded for her patience when Grant threw his hat on to the seat opposite, ran both hands through his hair and said, 'I am sorry to have dragged you away. You seemed to be enjoying yourself.'

'I was, very much. I have made some new acquaintances and that will make the next engagement even better. But it is no matter, there will be many other opportunities to talk with them.'

'There is something I need to speak to you about. Something important.'

Not a headache, then. Nor did he seem displeased. 'What is wrong?'

Grant had not put on his gloves and she peeled off her

own so she could slide her hand into his. It was warm and steady and closed around her fingers in a reassuring grip.

'Absolutely nothing is wrong, quite the opposite, in fact, but I think I will wait until we are home before I tell you.'

'Very well.' Comforted, she settled back and did her best to contain her curiosity.

In her bedchamber Kate handed over her evening cloak and gloves to Wilson and then dismissed the maid and waited with what patience she could muster.

Grant was normally reserved, she knew that from experience, but this seemed to be a secret out of the ordinary. Perhaps Prinny had offered him a diplomatic post and he was doubtful whether she was prepared to sail to Brazil. Or he had decided to take Holy Orders. Or buy a very large and expensive yacht. Or...

'Kate. I have never told you this... In fact, I have only just realised it, but this marriage makes me very happy. You make me very happy. I cannot recall ever feeling like this. Not all the time.'

She hadn't heard the door open and, lost in fantasies about sea voyages and cathedral closes, she could only stare at him. For a second she thought she heard him say *I love you*, then her brain made sense of what he had actually said and her pulse seemed to stutter. 'You... Grant, did you just say that I make you happy?'

'Yes.' He raised a quizzical eyebrow, seemingly expecting more of a reaction. 'I realise it is rather a sudden declaration, but is it so surprising?'

'When?' Her voice was strangely croaky. 'When did you realise it? I had no idea you had been feeling *un*happy.'

'I haven't.' He shrugged. 'Well, about Madeleine, of

course. But I had become used to thinking happiness was a matter of fleeting pleasures, of the absence of pain. This evening, at the top of the stairs just before we reached the receiving line, I realised that it is a positive thing, something that can fill me—and all because of you. Not the most convenient location for a revelation of that kind, you must admit.'

No wonder he had seemed so strange. Kate realised she was simply staring at Grant, unable to articulate a sensible response. Like, *I love you. And perhaps you are in love with me and don't realise it.*

'I'm sorry to be so dramatic about it.' He came further into the room and the door closed behind him with a click that made her jump. 'But I never speak to you about how I feel for you, how much I treasure what you have done at Abbeywell to make it into a home, how good you are with Charlie. I feel as though you have lifted a weight off my soul that I never realised was there. If that makes me sound ridiculous, I can't help it. I thought I ought to be open about how I felt.'

That was heaping coals of fire on her smarting conscience. Grant was offering her an honest declaration of his feelings when she did not deserve it, when she had lied to him in fact and by omission. But there was one thing she could be honest with him about, something she could give him, a response to his declaration. Not the full truth, of course, not that she loved him. She had been waiting too long for him to say it first, now she suspected he never would and her own love would be a burden to him.

Kate stood up and went to stand in front of him, linked her hands behind his neck and looked up into the steady green eyes. 'You make me happy, too. More than happy. With all my heart I am glad that you married me.'

He closed his eyes and rested his forehead against hers and sighed, a long, slow, difficult breath. 'Kate. Kate, I am sorry I never said these things before. I am not very good at emotions, I don't know how to be.'

'I understand.' She thought she did. He had grown up without his parents' marriage as a model. He had been raised by an elderly widower and married to a woman who had rejected and hurt him. Somewhere, deep inside, in a place he probably didn't even know existed, he had raised barriers to ever making himself as vulnerable as love would render him.

'You don't have to say things, to pretend to feelings you do not have. It is enough to know I make you happy. I just need you to know you make me happy, too,' Kate said, picking her way through, wary of saying anything that would make him suspect she loved him, force him to say the words that would be a lie. 'You were my Christmas miracle when you found me in that bothy and saved us. I am so glad I am your wife.' She stood on tiptoe and kissed him, and after the faintest hesitation he kissed her back, slowly, tenderly.

I must confess, tell him about Jonathan and Henry now. I can't deceive him any longer. It will hurt him that I have left it so long, but to leave it even longer can only make things worse.

He lifted one hand and began to pull the pins from her hair, drawing his fingers through it until it fell free on her shoulders. 'I am going to carry you off to bed and show you just how happy you make me, but before I do, I must tell you how proud I was of you tonight. I know you were nervous and unsure, but you did your best in spite of that and your best was magnificent.'

There was so much warmth and pride in his voice. If she did not know better, she might have added *love*. She didn't deserve any of those feelings, and if she told him the truth about Anna, the truth about her brother, then that pride would vanish, he would despise her.

'Thank you,' she murmured. 'It was far less daunting than I feared.' It had been—once she had assured herself that there was no sign of Viscount Baybrook, or of Sir Henry Harding, blackmailing baronet, either. Surely if Jonathan was in London he would have been invited to such a magnificent event as the Larminsters' reception? It was less likely that Henry would be there, but he might be in town if he had been both emboldened and enriched by extorting money from Jonathan, and it would be just like him to extract an invitation somehow.

Grant was working his way into the elaborate fastenings and folds of her gown and she arched her back to help him. *I will tell him tomorrow,* she resolved. *I cannot shatter this moment. I cannot, it is too precious.*

Grant used no erotic tricks, no titillating little games, only the magic of his mouth and his hands and his long, hard body, and Kate realised that she had learned to give with as much passion as she received. When he eased into her, slowly, achingly slowly, she realised that it was the exchange about their feelings that had given them this extra awareness of each other, of what they could be together.

There was no hurry, no rush to climax. Grant would stop moving and simply lie there, his heart beating over hers, his gaze locked with hers, his body filling and completing her. Then he would dip his head to take her lips and move again until Kate was lost in a spell of sensual, swirling pleasure. They were close, so close.

I love you, she thought and it was as though it was enough to tip them over into bliss, into a place where they were no longer two people, but one whole being, just as she had dreamed.

They made love again in the morning when they woke, a passionate tussle of urgency and need that left them panting and laughing. Grant ducked a flying pillow and pounced on Kate, tickling mercilessly, then subsided, pulling her against his side.

'I needed to laugh with you, Kate.'

Yes, I needed to laugh, too. I'll talk to him after breakfast, she thought as they subsided, breathless. 'Grant—'

'Hell, is that the time?' He rolled off the bed and made for the door to his room. 'I'm due at a meeting at the Lords at ten. Ungodly hour, I know, but I promised Pilkington. I think I will be supporting his group over several important pieces of legislation and we must discuss tactics.' He turned back, looked at her, shook his head. 'Incredible, I don't deserve to be so happy.' Then he was gone.

Kate was left staring at the door. It gave her no comfort, nor any inspiration. Finally she tugged the bell pull for Wilson. She couldn't sit in bed all day, her mind a blank. Perhaps a complete confession was not the answer. What if telling Grant about the blackmail made him an accessory unless he reported it to the magistrates immediately? He was loyal and she could imagine he would struggle with his conscience before incriminating her in such a shameful scandal, but he was also honourable.

He could not connive at extortion, so he would have to take action.

Perhaps she could establish Lord Baybrook's situation first. If he was safely married, that was one thing—he would probably go to great lengths to avoid her. But if he were not, he would probably still be smarting from Henry's demands, leaving aside the question of whether he would think her a loose woman on whom he could take revenge of a non-legal kind.

Once she knew the facts, then she could truthfully tell Grant that she had fallen foolishly for Jonathan Arnold, Lord Baybrook, but that, when Henry had approached him to tell him he must do the decent thing and marry her, Baybrook had revealed that he was already betrothed.

But then could she admit to Grant that Henry had known all along about Baybrook's impending betrothal, had set up a trap from the start? That he had demanded money, not as a settlement on the child, but as hush money so that its existence was never revealed to Baybrook's future father-in-law, the famously puritanical, and staggeringly wealthy, Lord Harlington?

Henry had sent her away to Scotland, not to hide her pregnancy, but to hide her from Baybrook and, when the child was born, to keep her out of his reach, to hold as a future threat against payments. When she had protested, told Henry that he should wait, not press demands beyond a decent competence to raise the child once Baybrook was safely married and in funds, he had threatened to take the baby as soon as it was born to make certain he had control and that Kate could not do anything *foolish*, as he put it. *Or honest,* she had thrown at him and he had laughed in her face.

She realised that she did not know what Jonathan's

reaction had been to Henry's demands for money. He was a rake, but not a fundamentally wicked man, she was certain. Surely he would have made a reasonable settlement on his love child, as soon as he could afford it. But Henry had no intention of settling for *reasonable*, not with Lord Harlington's fortune shimmering before his eyes. Jonathan might be paying up, being bled, or he might have told Henry to go to the devil.

And if he was paying, then she could not, in all conscience, let the blackmail continue.

Wilson came in, followed by Jeannie, Anna in her arms. 'She's fretting over her little tooth, my lady. Such a grizzle, she is, aren't you, my pet?' Jeannie handed her to Kate, who tried to soothe her and think clearly at the same time. One thing was certain, she thought as she gently massaged the sore gums, it was a recipe for disaster to sit passively waiting for disaster to strike, or to confess all to Grant when she did not know the facts.

After breakfast she checked the *Peerage* and a London directory in Grant's study, then rang for Jeannie. 'I would like you to go to this address in Hill Street and see if it is occupied.' She handed over the direction of what had been Baybrook's town house before his marriage. 'I need to know the name of the owner, whether he is in residence and whether he is married. And I need you to find this out without revealing why you are asking.'

Jeannie knew, she was certain, that Anna was not Grant's child, although it had never been spoken of between them. She met Kate's gaze and bit her lip. 'You'll be looking for a…relative, my lady?'

'Yes, that's it. A discreet enquiry.' She knew she could be putting a strain on Jeannie's loyalty. 'It is something about which I need to have all the facts clear before I speak to his lordship.'

The unease faded from the nursemaid's face. 'Aye, I can see that. Can I leave Lady Anna with you directly after breakfast, then, my lady? I could be walking past on an errand, sprain my ankle and have to hobble down to the area door to beg help from their cook. All kitchen staff gossip if they get half a chance.'

Jeannie came back mid-morning, rather pink in the face and inclined to giggle. 'I've made a conquest, I think, my lady. A Scottish footman at the Hill Street house. I managed to trip on a paving stone outside, right into his arms, and when he heard my accent he carried me down to the kitchen and then back up again after I sat awhile. And he insisted on calling me a hackney.' She sobered instantly when she saw Kate's face. 'I'm sorry, my lady, I'm blathering on. It is Lord Baybrook's house and he's in residence with his wife and they've just come back to London after their honeymoon tour.'

'Thank you, Jeannie. That will be all. I appreciate your assistance.'

So now what? The bad news was that Jonathan was in London, but the very good news was that Henry had not managed to do something so dreadful that the marriage had been called off. Although it still might mean that he was extorting money from the viscount, and if that was the case, then she had to stop it. It seemed, more and more, that she was going to have to approach Jonathan directly, assure him of her good intentions and discover just what her brother had done. The thought of Grant getting in the middle of this unholy mess didn't bear thinking about. He would be furious, he would call Jonathan out—and then someone might end up a widow.

It was a plan of sorts, but it did not make her feel any better. Hiding the truth from Grant had been bad enough, but now she knew the extent of his affection and trust, it felt like the worst of betrayals. But there was Anna, an innocent child to consider. And the equally innocent Lady Baybrook, and her own sister-in-law, unwittingly married to a blackmailer.

Now all she had to do was engineer a meeting with Jonathan and trust to his good nature and discretion. It seemed an awfully big risk.

Chapter Twenty

Grant did not come home for luncheon, which was not unusual. What was out of the ordinary was the note that arrived from him on Brooks's Club notepaper.

> Today, of all days, when I want to be with you, they ask me to meet the Home Secretary! Goodness knows when I'll get away, but I'll tell you all about it at dinner, I promise.
> Yours,
> G.

Kate rang for Jeannie and for Grimswade. 'I feel like taking the air with Anna. Lord Brooke is going for a walk with his tutor, I believe. Have the carriage sent round, Grimswade, if you please.'

When the butler had gone she turned to the nursemaid. 'I hardly know what I hope to achieve by this, but if I see Lord Baybrook, I will try to snatch the opportunity to speak with him. But I do not want him to see Anna, so you must stay in the carriage.' Jeannie seemed about to say something, but Kate forestalled her. 'I can't go out without a maid or a footman, his lordship would be furious. And there is no one else I can trust. But I probably won't encounter Lord Baybrook.'

'It's a nice afternoon,' Jeannie observed. 'A gentleman might take a stroll to his club.'

'Yes.' *And at least it will get me out of the house. I feel like a turnspit dog on a treadmill.*

Kate gave the coachman a circuitous route that took in a number of shops that she might plausibly want to visit and which brought them via Hill Street to Grosvenor Street. There was no sign of Jonathan's tall and elegant figure sauntering along, nor when they turned down Berkeley Street towards Piccadilly. 'It was ridiculous to think I would see him,' she observed to Jeannie. 'The number of places a gentleman can be in even the small compass of Mayfair must be countless.'

And then, as the carriage slowed to a crawl in the Piccadilly traffic, she glanced up Dover Street and saw him. 'He's there!'

Jeannie tugged on the check string, the carriage pulled over to the kerb and they stared at each other. 'I cannot accost him in the street.' Kate watched as he reached the road junction, a polished wooden box under his arm. 'He's been to Manton's, the gunsmiths, I think. Jeannie, look, he's crossing over to Green Park.'

'Hurry, my lady.' Jeannie opened the door and kicked down the step. 'You can speak to him in the park, there aren't many people around. I'll follow along behind, as if I'm not with you.'

Jonathan was held up by a brewer's dray while Kate, catching the attention of a crossing sweeper, was over the road before him. He went through the gate and into the park, not apparently in any hurry, for he strolled past the reservoir and cut across the grass towards the Queen's Walk. Kate walked briskly, came alongside him when there was no one close and realised she had no idea what to say.

He must have seen her out of the corner of his eye, for he stopped and raised his hat slightly. And then stared. 'Madam, do I know you?' The dawning recognition on his face would have been comical if things were not so serious. *'Catherine?'*

'Yes. Jonathan—Lord Baybrook, I need to speak with you.'

He had his composure back. His voice was icy, but perfectly controlled. 'I am sure you do.' His eyes ran up and down the fashionable outfit she wore. 'I see you have acquired some expensive tastes on my money.'

'No, I have not. Is Henry demanding payments from you? It is not with my agreement, believe me.'

'Believe you? My dear Miss Harding, why should I believe a word you say? The last true thing you told me was that you were innocent of a man and *that* I did not need telling, for you were a most uninteresting tumble,' he drawled. 'Your rat of a brother informed me you were with child. My child. Is that true or have I been paying out every month for nothing?' The mask of unconcern was slipping to reveal the fury beneath.

Anna. I can't let him find Anna. 'Yes, I was pregnant. I thought Henry was going to insist that you marry me.' She felt the heat rise in her face as Baybrook gave a bark of laughter. 'I did not think you would. But I thought you would make me a small allowance so I could bring the child up decently. That was all I wanted, all I expected. I had no idea that Henry was…'

'A blackmailer? Oh, really, my dear. Doing it rather too brown if you expect me to believe you knew nothing of this.' His anger was beginning to ride him now, overcome his habitual elegant indifference. 'Well, make your demands, and then I will tell you how I intend to deal with you.'

'I have no demands. I needed to know what Henry was doing—I haven't seen him for a year. I'll stop him, I swear. I'll do everything I can to stop him.'

'Do you take me for a fool, my dear?' He turned to face her fully, his voice a snarl of frustrated fury now. 'Do you think because I sampled your very rustic charms that I can be cock-led into another compromising situation? Have you any idea what life is like lived at the toleration of a Bible-thumping old bigot who doles out his money like drops of his own blood, always alert for any moral lapse that can be the excuse for a sermon or for withholding funds?'

'No, but—'

He caught her wrist, jerked her towards him. 'There are many reasons why I do not drag you down to the nearest magistrate's office this minute, but there are equally many, many reasons why you should be very afraid of me, my dear. Very afraid indeed.'

Over his shoulder she could see Jeannie, her face a picture of anxiety and indecision. *Stay there, do not try to help. Stay there,* she tried to signal.

Then he was jerked away from her. The wooden box fell to the ground and burst open, two duelling pistols fell out on to the grass, exquisite death glinting in the winter sunshine.

'Take your hands off my wife before I break all your fingers,' Grant said pleasantly, his own hands fisted in the lapels of Lord Baybrook's elegant coat. 'You'll need them to fire one of those pretty toys you've just dropped.'

For a long moment they stared into each other's eyes, almost nose to nose, two male stags in their prime locking antlers over a female. Then, when Kate thought she would burst with the tension, Jonathan stepped back, hands raised in the fencer's signal of yielding.

'Your *wife*? Allundale, is it not? I am Baybrook. My apologies, I had no idea. In fact, I had misread the situation totally. The lady asked me something and I thought—forgive me, madam—that she was…well, not to beat about the bush, I completely misunderstood her status. I could see no one with her. I was deep in thought and most unfortunately leapt to the conclusion that she was…er…importuning me.'

'Lady Allundale?' Grant's rigid formality failed utterly to veil the fury in his eyes.

He'll kill him, Kate thought. *If he has the slightest idea what is happening…* Jeannie, thank heavens, was keeping her distance, had turned away from the three of them so the child in her arms was not visible.

'It was, as the gentleman says, a misunderstanding. I was cutting across to the path, stumbled and caught at his arm and must have blurted out some words of apology. When he spoke to me I was confused, I did not realise what he thought and then when I did I was agitated, which made things worse… Jeannie had fallen behind, so I appeared to be unescorted.' She managed a tight social smile for Jonathan. 'Sir, it was entirely my fault. I am quite unused to London.'

He was a quick thinker, she had to hand it to him. And a brilliant actor. He was all contrition, all elegant apologies, and Grant was left with no option but to accept them.

He bowed, the merest inclination of his head, and offered Kate his arm. Jonathan bowed in his turn, picked up the pistols and strode off towards the Queen's Walk.

'Did he hurt you?' Grant demanded the moment they were alone. She shook her head and saw him relax a little. 'And what the devil was Jeannie playing at? Well?' he demanded as the maid hurried up to them. 'When you escort your mistress your duty is to stay with her, not stroll about like a moonling.'

'Anna has been very fretful,' Kate said hastily. 'I expect that is what held you up, Jeannie.'

'Yes, my lady, and then when I saw the gentleman, I didn't know what to do. Not when I had Lady Anna, because I thought he would frighten her.'

'Very well. Where is the carriage?'

'Waiting near the palace, my lord, at the end of the Queen's Walk.' Jeannie gave Kate the tiniest of nods.

'I'll go back with you in that case. I was walking back from the Palace of Westminster across the parks. Fortunately.'

'Yes, wasn't it.' Kate clung to his arm and hoped he would attribute her shakiness to the after-effects of the encounter with Jonathan and not shock at his own appearance combined with a hideously guilty conscience. 'That gentleman was not a friend of yours, then?'

'The Viscount of Baybrook? No. I've hardly ever seen him that close to. The man was a gazetted rake, and a wild one at that, before his marriage. I never ran in those circles, even when I was sowing my own wild oats—the gambling was too deep for me, for one thing, and I dislike being sodden with drink half the time. Now his father-in-law holds the purse strings so tight that Baybrook hardly dares sneeze without permission, by all accounts.' They walked on in silence until they were almost at the gravelled walk bordering the high walls of the fine houses that overlooked Green Park. Grant's fingers stroked reassuringly over hers and gradually her breathing calmed.

'It is strange, though, there was something so familiar about him.' Grant shrugged. 'Perhaps I've come across one of his relatives. Society is so interbred, I may know a cousin of his and not even realise it. Now, where is the carriage?'

It was waiting at the end of Milkmaid's Passage, where a footpath led from the park to the front of St James's Palace. 'Why did you not take the groom with you?' Grant demanded as they settled themselves inside.

'Um…idiocy?' Kate ventured and was rewarded with a smile.

'I shouldn't be cross with you. I forget what an innocent you are in London. This is not the moorlands where you may stretch your legs accosted by nothing worse than a flock of sheep.'

'No, my lord,' Kate said meekly and saw, from the smile in Grant's eyes, that she was forgiven. 'Sheep can be very dangerous, you know.' *I don't deserve him. How am I going to get out of this mire without someone getting hurt?* 'How did your meeting go, my lord? It was satisfactory, I hope?'

'Most. I suspect I have landed myself with a great deal of work, but I am interested in social issues.'

She would get the details out of him when they were alone and, perhaps, convince him that she read the newspapers, too, that she had views on social policy and could discuss the problems he was going to be tackling. *If he is still prepared to talk to me.*

Kate stared blankly out at the passing clubs and shops as the carriage climbed the slope of St James's Street. *What am I going to do about Jonathan and Henry now?*

Grant stood in front of his dressing mirror, tying his neckcloth and attempting to pin down the niggling sense of unease at the back of his mind. He had swept Kate upstairs and made love to her so thoroughly that she seemed to be entirely satisfied that he was not blaming her for the Green Park incident. It also served to satisfy his own primitive male feelings of ownership. He grimaced at himself as he acknowledged the response. Still, it could have turned nasty if he had not come across them. The behaviour was typical of Baybrook, by all accounts. The man might no longer be able to carry on his dissolute lifestyle, but he obviously could not resist accosting an attractive woman when one crossed his path.

What was unsettling was that the strange incident had reawakened all his niggling doubts about Kate. He had been trying to suppress them, tell himself that they were simply leftovers from his experiences with Madeleine, and that now he was so happy in his marriage they would vanish. But they had not. Perhaps the lack was in him and he had lost the ability to trust completely.

'Move the candles up, would you, Griffin?' The valet shifted a branch of candles to the left-hand side of Grant to balance those on the right, and he leaned close to the glass to slide in his tiepin. *Just so.* He met his own gaze in the mirror and grimaced. He was turning into a damn dandy, peacocking about for his Kate.

The thought lifted his spirits. Amused green eyes smiled back and he went still. *That* was what had been nagging away—Baybrook's eyes. For a few tense seconds they had stared at each other, almost nose to nose. And Baybrook's eyes were green, an unusual clear colour with golden flecks and a black rim to the pupil. The colour he had seen when he had compared Anna's eyes to his own. It was too much of a coincidence, that bizarre encounter between the earl and Kate and the colour of the man's eyes. *He is Anna's father.*

'My lord?' Griffin murmured, the equivalent from him of a nudge in the ribs.

'What?'

'Are you quite well, my lord? A migraine, perhaps?'

'No, I'm fine, just distracted by business.' He had to think about this, try to work out just what the other man knew. It was interesting that, although Jeannie had been with her, Kate had obviously not shown Anna to her lover. *Her ex-lover,* he told himself, exerting all his willpower to steady his breathing, his instinctive reactions. *Don't get into a jealous rage over this. There is no way he and Kate have been together since we married. Although what she was plotting now with apparently chance meetings in the park...*

The thought of Kate getting up to something underhand was like a stab. Was this what he had sensed was wrong all along?

He turned away and stood while Griffin eased him into his evening coat. A sliver of doubt seemed to have slid into his heart. She had lied, he realised, told him Anna's father was dead. So what else had she not told him? The cold fist closing around his gut was all too familiar from years of dealing with Madeleine's lies and evasions. *But not Kate. I need to trust her!*

Hell, he would be whimpering next that it wasn't fair, that she had told him she was happy with him. He was a man and he'd show some backbone over this, but he was not going to confront Kate with it, not yet. He examined that decision for cowardly motives and decided it was only right, and fair, to investigate first. If he was wrong about her, then a direct accusation would shatter that miraculous happiness between them for ever.

The place to start was her family. He should have insisted on contacting her brother before now. 'Griffin, fetch Mr Bolton to me at once. He is in, I assume?'

'Yes, my lord. He remarked he had some notes to transcribe. I believe he is in his room.'

When his secretary entered, tugging his sleeves down with one hand and running the other ink-stained hand through his hair, he looked harassed. 'My lord, I'm still working on your notes for this morning. I should have them finished—'

Grant waved a dismissive hand. 'My handwriting is execrable, I know. Some time tomorrow evening will be fine, for goodness' sake. Have your dinner in peace. Thank you, Griffin, that will be all for now.' As the door closed behind the valet, he added, 'In the morning I need to speak to a discreet enquiry agent.'

Bolton's eyebrows shot up. 'My lord? What sort of enquires, might I ask? I will enquire at your solicitor's office, but such men may come with, er, different specialisms.'

'I wish to trace someone, a connection of Lady Allundale's with whom she has lost touch.' He made himself smile. 'A bit of a black sheep, if you get my meaning. I would like to reunite them, but I will need to be satisfied of his character before I do so.'

'Of course, my lord. One cannot be too careful. I assume this will be a surprise for her ladyship?'

'Precisely,' Grant agreed. If she had deceived him

about her lover, then had she told him the truth about her brother—the man she was so very reluctant to get in touch with, despite her new position? If Kate was in trouble, he would do whatever it took to get her out of it, but the deceit wrenched at him. And now he was deceiving her and telling himself it was for her own good. Somehow he was going to have to go downstairs, face his wife over the dinner table and put on a mask, pretend nothing at all was wrong.

Caring is the very devil, Grant thought as he walked downstairs, schooling his face to reveal nothing whatsoever. Certainly not fear.

Chapter Twenty-One

'Allow me to summarise and make certain I have this correct, sir.' Mr Martin, the highly respectable and discreet enquiry agent Grant's solicitors had recommended, glanced down at his notes.

Grant, or Mr Whyte as he had introduced himself, sat in the comfortable client's chair in Mr Martin's elegantly simple office off Ludgate Hill and made himself sit still and apparently relaxed as Martin recapped.

'There is a gentleman, probably by the name of Henry Harding, resident, possibly in Suffolk, who entertained Lord Baybrook in the spring of last year. The gentleman is married, has a sister named, probably, Catherine, and is of a somewhat profligate nature. You wish to identify him.'

'That is correct.' Grant was fairly certain that Catherine had given him her correct name, because she surely would not risk the marriage being invalidated by her using a false one. 'How long will it take you?'

'If he is in Suffolk, and he is a gentleman, then not long. But if the information you have been given is incorrect, then I will need to attack this from the direction of

Lord Baybrook's movements and that may require some, shall we say, excavation.'

Grant remembered Kate's hesitation in answering his questions. At the time he had attributed that to exhaustion. Now he wondered. 'I would not be surprised if the county is incorrect.'

'Let us say a week, Mr Whyte.'

'So fast?'

The enquiry agent smirked modestly. 'I have many sources, sir. And Lord Baybrook is, or was, a colourful character. I will send to your solicitor as soon as I have news.'

Grant took his leave and hailed a hackney carriage to take him to Brooks's Club. He was avoiding going home, he knew that. He knew he could not make love to Kate and hide from her that something was wrong and so he pretended to have far more work with his Parliamentary colleagues than he was actually undertaking and retired to his study every night after dinner until he thought she would be asleep.

If this went on for more than a week, he was going to be desperate with the need to hold her, he knew that. Kate had shown him happiness, taught him how to trust his heart to someone else. Now he struggled not to flinch back from that trust, like a man who has already been grievously burned and who expects the same pain again when he reaches out. Something was wrong and he would make it right for her, trust that her reasons for pretending that Baybrook had not been her lover were good.

Grant had expected Kate to comment on his absence from her bed, perhaps to fuss that he was overworking, but she did neither. It was as though she was holding herself back from him, but he could not decide whether it was because she was frightened, or ashamed or simply could not trust him with her secret. In the small hours of the night he had lain awake, alone in his big bed, and fought back the suspicion that she did not care for him after all, that seeing Baybrook had rekindled her feelings for the other man.

Now he looked down the length of the breakfast table and felt all his affection for her welling up, forcing back the suspicion and the anger. She was not Madeleine. He should try to trust her and he would not question her, let her see his doubts and how his faith had been shaken.

'My lord.'

He looked up from the sirloin that he was mangling and could not help but smile at the dignified way she addressed him whenever the staff were present. She did not call him *my lord* when she was screaming his name in the throes of passion, her limbs tangled with his, her nails raking his back.

'My lady?'

'I think I would like to take a small trip, have a day or two away from London. I am not feeling quite myself and the weather is so fine, I thought the sea air would do me good.'

'Brighton?' Grant suggested. 'It should not be difficult to get good lodgings at this time of year, but it will be devilishly cold.'

'I really wanted to go now. To Southend-on-Sea, I thought. So much closer.'

'Southend? It is certainly respectable, but isn't it a trifle...dull?'

'I only want the fresh air and it will do the children good, don't you think? We could go on the steamer easily in the day.'

'I doubt I can get away immediately.'

'If Charlie comes, then Mr Gough can provide a male escort and I'll have Jeannie and Wilson. I could even take one of the footmen.' Kate looked anxious, not like someone planning a short holiday.

'Very well, if that would please you.' He looked directly at her. 'I'll miss you. I know I haven't been very good company these past few days, but even so, the house will seem empty without you.'

Kate was colouring up. Where had this sudden urge to go into Essex come from? Did she just want to get away from him, or was there some more sinister reason? He felt suspicion flare.

'Thank you.' She managed a very creditable impression of pleasure tinged with concern. 'If you are sure? Well, then, I'll speak to everyone and organise it. If I write to the Ship Inn for rooms, I should hear tomorrow and we can set out the day after. We had accepted very few invitations for the next few days. London is becoming very quiet now.'

The Ship Inn? Did she know the town or had she been doing some research? he wondered. 'Certainly, and do use Bolton to book the steamer tickets and so forth. He can send your regrets for the various engagements and I'll see which I want to go to by myself.'

'The first post, my lord.' Grimswade proffered a salver.

'If you'll excuse me, I'll take these off to the study and deal with them.' He stood as he spoke, the letters in one hand, one with the distinctive handwriting of his solicitor's head clerk on the top.

He broke the seal as soon as the door was closed behind him and drew out the letter from Martin enclosed in the wrapper.

Lord Baybrook spent a week as the guest of Sir Henry Harding, baronet, at his estate, Belchamps Hall, in the parish of Hawkwell, Essex, in the period specified. I am unable, as yet, to provide you with details of Sir Henry's character and means, but I am able to confirm that he is a married man with a sister named Catherine Jane Penelope.

I have sent my assistant by this evening's mail coach to Rayleigh, the nearest town, with instructions to discover as much as possible of Sir Henry's situation within the day.

Grant reached for Cary's road book from the shelves beside the desk and opened it on the map of southern England. Hawkwell was apparently too small to be shown, but if it was close to Rayleigh, it was also close to Southend. Not more than five or so miles, he estimated by eye. If Kate was going to Southend, then he was going to Rayleigh.

The steamer was an adventure, at least for Charlie, who was so thrilled that he was rendered speechless, although not still. Mr Gough got Kate, Jeannie, Wilson and the baby settled in the warm shelter of the first-class saloon with Giles the footman to watch over them and was then towed from one end of the vessel to the other by his charge. Kate knew this because, with great regularity, Charlie would erupt into the saloon, compose himself with an effort and inform her of some riveting fact concerning the engines or the weight of coal consumed or the potential speed of the ship, then rush out again to interrogate some unfortunate seaman.

'It is very comfortable compared to a coach,' Kate

remarked to Wilson, who was sitting bolt upright clutching her mistress's dressing case on her knees and eyeing their fellow travellers with suspicion.

'Indeed, my lady, although what it would be like on the open sea may be another matter.'

'Yes, I am not sure about venturing to Margate,' Kate admitted. 'I have no idea whether I would be seasick or not.'

But the saloon was comfortable, the company, if rather varied, was respectable enough and the speed was astonishing. Kate looked out of the nearest porthole at the passing river scene and told herself that everything was going to be all right. Henry would be at home and he would see reason about stopping his extortion. He might even be persuaded to pay the money back, although Kate was far less confident about that. But the main thing was to make him stop his criminal activity and write assuring Jonathan that he would hear no more from him.

Then, when there was no longer a crime involved, she could confess everything to Grant and just hope and pray that he would understand. In broad daylight when she was feeling strong, she was confident, but in the small hours, as she lay awake fretting about everything from him working too hard to the loss of his faith in her, she could not help but recall his words.

I am just saying, for the record, that I will call out any man who lays a finger on you—and do my damnedest to kill him. And if your Jonathan had abandoned you and not drowned, then I would go after him and kill him, too. What if he called Jonathan out for failing to marry her? But, heartbroken as she had been at the time, if he *had* married her they would surely be in an unhappy marriage

now, she would never have met Grant—and it was Grant
she loved. And Grant who, one day, might love her.

It was only when the hired chaise was bowling across
the flat farmlands around Hawkwell that Kate began to
think uneasily about Henry's reaction. What, exactly,
would her brother do with a sister who turned up, exceedingly inconveniently, and threatened to crack the golden
egg he was relying on? She had nothing to threaten him
with to make him do the right thing and she would not
put it past him to lock her in the attic while he thought
out his tactics. It was not as though he had ever expressed
any affection for her after all.

She had left Charlie and Anna with Jeannie and Mr
Gough at the Ship Inn, but she had not told either of them
where she was going, which, in retrospect, was not sensible. She had said nothing last night as they settled into
the accommodation—now she knew she should at least
have taken Jeannie into her confidence. The low-lying
pastureland looked sodden and depressing as she stared
out of the window, biting her lower lip as she thought.

'Giles, when I go into the house I am visiting, I will
take Wilson with me, of course. I would like you to remain in the carriage. Let the window down a crack and
then you will hear the church clock. It strikes the quar-
ters. If I am not out within an hour, or if I do not send
you a note with my name underlined, then I want you
to go to Mr Gough with all speed and ask him to come
here and demand to see me. He is to take no excuses, do
you understand?'

Giles looked appalled. 'My lady, my lord would have
my hide if he thought I had let you walk into somewhere
dangerous!'

'It is not dangerous, exactly. I certainly would not take Wilson with me if it were, but the owner may want me to stay against my will.'

'I've got a hatpin,' the maid said darkly. 'And I'll use it. No one will hurt my lady if I have anything to do with it. You do as you're told, Giles.'

'Yes, Miss Wilson.' The personal maid to the lady of the house easily outranked a mere footman. It seemed that Giles was more in awe of her than he was of his mistress. 'I'll listen, like you say, my lady, never fear.'

Kate felt easier with some precautions in place, even though she was probably being completely melodramatic and the worst that might happen was that Henry would laugh in her face and throw her out. *And if that happens,* she resolved as the chaise drew into the courtyard in front of Belchamps Hall, *then I am telling Grant everything.*

Leaving Giles anxiously listening for the clock, Kate marched up to the front door and beat a tattoo with the knocker. The heavy oak door creaked open and she found herself face-to-face with Claridge, the butler.

He said stolidly. 'Yes, ma'am?'

'Claridge, do you not recognise me? Miss Catherine.' She took a step forward as he gaped at her. 'Where is Sir Henry?'

The butler gave way before her, but he still looked utterly taken aback. 'In...in his study, Miss Catherine. But—'

'You were not expecting me, quite. And it is Lady Allundale now, Claridge. There is no need to announce me, I know my way.' Strangely she felt confidence flooding back as she smiled at the butler. She was here to fight dragons, defeat them for the sake of her love and her happiness. She lifted her chin, set back her shoulders, lifted her imaginary sword.

'Yes, miss. I mean, my lady.'

He stepped aside, jaw working as though he was searching for words, and went along the familiar panelled hallway, past the foot of the stairs and the great carved banister rail she used to slide down on her tummy when she was a child. They passed the door into the sunny front parlour, where she would sit and sew with her sister-in-law, and up to the door to Henry's study, not a place in which the women of the household were welcome.

'Make Miss Wilson comfortable if you please, Claridge.'

She entered on her knock and almost stopped dead in surprise. The old gloomy study Henry had inherited from their father had been swept away. Now it was freshly painted and boasted a handsome mahogany desk and chairs in the latest style, new bookcases and an array of books in fine leather bindings. The window had been converted into French doors leading out on to the rear terrace, and as she came in, she saw Henry standing there, the door ajar, apparently letting some chill fresh air into the stuffy room.

'Madam?' He blinked at her and she realised that for a moment he did not recognise her with her smart clothes and the gemstones winking in her earlobes. *'Catherine?'*

'Good afternoon, Henry.' She sat down in the chair opposite the desk, laid her reticule and tightly rolled umbrella on the glossy new leather surface and smiled warmly at him. 'What a handsome study, it must have cost you a pretty penny.'

'What are you doing here?' He stalked from the window

and stood clutching the back of his chair. 'Where in Hades have you been?'

'Oh, living my life.' Kate pulled off her gloves, slowly, finger by finger, as she looked around. 'While you have been accumulating the pretty pennies, it seems. What else have you been spending the money on, Henry? Oh, and I would love a cup of tea. And perhaps one of those delicious scones Mrs Hobhouse always used to make.'

He was so taken aback that he yanked the bell pull without arguing. Claridge must have been standing right outside the door. 'Sir?'

'Tea. Scones.' Henry flapped a hand at him and sat down. 'What are you doing here? And where did you get those clothes and those jewels?' He flung himself back in the chair and laughed. 'Oh, I see. You've found your-self a cosy little niche as some man's ladybird, have you? You're cleverer than I thought if you've fallen on your feet that way. Or should I say, on your back?'

'Don't be coarse, Henry.' Kate took the little silver case from her reticule and tossed a card across the desk to him. 'My husband would not appreciate it.'

He picked up the card and stared at it, the pasteboard creasing in his grip. 'Lady Allundale? *Lady Allundale?* How the devil? He knows about the brat?'

'What brat would that be, Henry? My husband's daughter?'

He stared at her. 'You couldn't have convinced him it was his, you were too far gone when you ran off.'

Claridge came in, placed a tray on the desk in front of Kate. 'Thank you, Claridge, that will be all. Tea, Henry?' she asked sweetly as the door closed.

'Damn the tea.' He watched, drumming his fingers on the arm of his chair, while she poured herself a cup, taking her time. She pretended to hesitate over a choice of scones until he demanded, 'What do you want?'

'I've come about the blackmail, Henry. It has to stop.'

'What blackmail?' He tried to look haughty and affronted.

'Don't pretend, Henry. You have been extorting money from Lord Baybrook. It is immoral, illegal and probably dangerous. His father-in-law won't live for ever and when he dies Baybrook is going to be a very rich man.' She took a sip of tea and was proud that her hand was rock-steady. 'Rich enough to take revenge on you in any way he chooses. Legal or illegal.' Was it her imagination, or had Henry gone pale?

'What do you want?'

His immediate move to negotiation made her wary. She had expected counter-threats, or, at the least, bluster. 'For you to stop demanding money. Write to Baybrook, tell him that no more will be asked.'

'Is that all?'

Of course it was not *all*. He was still being too accommodating, too calm. 'And you will return all the money you extorted.' Henry's jaw dropped. 'Just how much did you receive, Henry? How much did you demand from Baybrook every month?'

'Two hundred,' he snapped.

'Two hundred pounds? Two thousand four hundred a year. My goodness, that was ambitious, Henry.'

'He can afford it. And it is guineas, not pounds.' He smirked, obviously counting the golden treasure in his mind.

'Two thousand five hundred and twenty pounds,' she amended. 'A mistake to gloat about the guineas. That's an additional one hundred and twenty you are going to give me.' Could she convince him his only hope was to give her the money, or would he call her bluff?

'Give you the money? Are you insane? Why should I do a damn fool thing like that?'

'Because I'll see you in gaol if you don't, brother dear. My child, my fear and danger, my near disgrace. I think I have earned it, don't you?'

Chapter Twenty-Two

Grant held the hired hack to a controlled canter as he entered the village of Hawkwell. He had made good time, leaving London by post-chaise for Rayleigh as soon as Martin's assistant returned. Kate might have had a fast passage by the steamer, but he would be close on her heels.

'I couldn't do as much as I'd like, sir,' the man had explained, passing the notes across. 'But there's the address. In Rayleigh he's run up a fair amount of debt and they say he's a spendthrift on his own pleasures. His wife doesn't spend much at the local dressmaker or milliner, though. They think he keeps her on a pretty tight string and there are rumours he's not above knocking her around when he's in his cups. He also has a bit of a reputation for gambling—cock fights, the local card school, that sort of thing. The merchants I spoke to didn't have much of an opinion of him as a landowner. They say he leaves it all to his bailiff and he doesn't pay enough to get a man of the right calibre to do that wisely. I've made a note of the major debtors, sir.'

Now Grant drew rein in front of the church lychgate

as a thin man in a clerical collar and bands came out and closed it with care behind him.

'Good day, Reverend.'

'Good day, sir.' He smiled up at Grant. 'Have to take care or we get straying sheep in the churchyard and the silly creatures poison themselves on the yew. One could wish the Good Lord had given such useful animals more intelligence, but one cannot question His ways. May I assist you in any way, sir?'

'I am looking for Sir Henry Harding's house. Belchamps Hall, I believe.'

'Yes, indeed.' Was it his imagination or did the vicar's smile become less genuine? 'You have the right road. Just continue through past the green, take the second on the left and it is rather under a mile.'

'Thank you.' Grant touched his whip to his hat brim and urged the hack into a trot. So, debts, a reputation for gambling and not the vicar's favourite member of his flock. If Sir Henry was a churchgoer at all.

The clergyman's directions were accurate. Grant came alongside a high brick wall at about three-quarters of a mile from the village and then slowed as he saw a hired vehicle standing on the driveway. A postilion was perched on a low wall smoking a clay pipe and, clearly visible through the window of the vehicle, was the face of his own footman.

'Giles.'

'My lord!' The footman threw the carriage door open.

'Is her ladyship inside?'

'Yes, my lord. She went in three-quarters of an hour ago. My lord—'

Grant swung down from the horse, tossed Giles the

reins and strode up to the front door, leaving the footman mid-sentence. He had his hand raised to the knocker when instinct stopped him. Better to scout the ground before blundering in. Something strange was going on with Kate and her brother and he would rather discover what it was without it being filtered through whatever barriers they chose to erect.

The house was very quiet. Grant glanced into windows as he trod softly around the moss-covered path that skirted the walls. In one room a lady sat, head bent over some sewing, but she was no one he recognised. He rounded the corner to find himself on a flagstone terrace overlooking a bleak, level garden. Halfway along a glazed door stood ajar and, feeling a touch melodramatic, he walked cautiously up to it. Voices came clearly from the room inside.

'Just how much did you receive, Henry?' That was Kate's voice. Grant edged closer. She sounded very calm, very cool and strangely dangerous. He was grappling with that when she added, 'How much did you demand from Baybrook every month?'

Blackmail? That had to be what they were discussing.

'Two hundred,' a man snapped. And that must be her brother, Henry.

'Two hundred pounds? Two thousand four hundred a year. My goodness, that was ambitious, Henry.'

Kate sounded not at all shocked. In fact, from her question, she had obviously expected to hear that money was being extorted. A faint hope that she was talking about money for the support of her child faded. That sum was way in excess of what might be expected to provide for a by-blow. Not that he'd ever had to do the sums himself… Grant jerked his attention back to the voices in the room.

'And it is guineas, not pounds.'

'Two thousand five hundred and twenty pounds. A mistake to gloat about the guineas. That's an additional one hundred and twenty you are going to give me.'

Nausea gripped his gut. Kate wanted the blackmail money, was demanding it in a hard, cold voice that belonged to another woman, not the one he'd married. Not his Kate.

'Give you the money?' her brother protested. 'Are you insane? Why should I do a damn fool thing like that?'

'Because I'll see you in gaol if you don't, brother dear. My child, my fear and danger, my near disgrace. I think I have earned it, don't you?'

Grant reached for the door handle, his vision blurred by a haze of anger and betrayal. Kate, his Kate. He would never have believed that the woman he trusted with his life and his honour would turn into this hard-voiced, grasping witch.

Never have believed it. He jerked his hand back so hard his knuckles hit the rough surface of the brick, the pain like a dash of icy water in the face. *Trust.* If he abandoned her at this first test of his feelings, what did that make of their marriage but a hollow sham? This was Kate. Yes, she had not told him that Baybrook was Anna's father. Yes, she had not told him why she had come to Essex. But there could well be reasons as painful and as difficult to talk about as his feelings about Madeleine had been. He owed Kate his faith and, if things really were bad, his understanding and forgiveness. He had to get her to trust him to give her that and he could begin by not leaving her to fight this dragon alone.

* * *

Henry was spluttering now. 'Where the devil do you think I am going to get that money from? I have spent most of it.'

'Well, unspend it, Henry. Sell things, borrow, pawn. I want a banker's draft for every shilling.'

'Or what? All right, I agree that I'll write to Baybrook, tell him his debt's paid. But you can't get the money out of me, and if you utter any more threats, I'll just have to keep you here until you see reason.'

So, she had been right to leave Giles with instructions. 'My man is outside in the carriage. He knows what to do if I do not come out, or if I send him a note without a certain code word in it. I really am not as foolish as you always thought me, Henry. And as for how I intend to extract that money from you, why, I will simply confess all to my husband. Grant Rivers is a law-abiding, honest man and—'

The door behind her opened. 'I am flattered that you think so, my dear,' said a deep, calm voice.

'Grant.' Kate found she was on her feet, facing the door where her husband stood surveying the room with a chilly hauteur that sent a dangerous wave of sheer desire through her. Behind the broad shoulders in the caped greatcoat she could glimpse the butler, bobbing about in agitation.

'Sir? My lord?'

Grant half turned and handed Claridge his hat and gloves. He kept hold of his riding crop. 'Thank you. That will be all.' He shut the door in the butler's face. 'Sir Henry Harding, I assume? My brother-in-law.' He stayed on his feet, looming over the seated man at the desk. 'I wish I could say it is a pleasure, but I doubt it will be, for either of us.'

'Grant, please sit down.' He might be intimidating Henry, which was a good thing, but he was terrifying her.

'If you wish, my dear.' He picked up one of the heavy carved chairs that sat against the wall and spun it across, one-handed, to thud in front of the desk next to Kate, then he sat down, crossed one booted leg across the other and began, very softly, to tap the riding crop against the polished leather. 'So, allow me to summarise the situation as I see it, Harding. Your sister is with child by Baybrook. You send her away where he cannot marry her even if he wishes to, and then you extort money from him under threat of informing his immensely wealthy and very, very moral prospective father-in-law. Am I correct so far?'

Henry stared like a mesmerised rabbit in front of a stoat until Grant slapped the crop harder against his boot and Henry twitched. 'Yes, well…'

'And you put her in the way of a confirmed rake in the first place? Yes, I assume so. And not content with ensuring that he pays a suitable sum to your sister to raise her child decently you decide to keep it all yourself—and to ask for as much money as you think you can possibly extract. Yes?' There was another slap of whip on leather.

'Yes. But now she wants it all! She threatened me!'

'With me. Very wisely. I am trying to recall what the judicial penalty for blackmail is.' Grant rocked the heavy chair back and studied the ceiling, deep in thought. 'So few people come forward with a complaint, that is the problem. Most seem to deal with it by other methods. Direct methods.' He brought all four chair legs back to the floor with a thud and Henry cringed back in his own seat.

'You mean *murder*? Catherine said you were an honourable man!'

'And she is correct, I hope. Let me think now. The navy is always short of men. That would give you a healthy outdoor life with plenty of fresh air and exercise, and we are not at war at the moment, so there are only falls from the mainmast, shipwreck and over-amorous shipmates to worry about. Oh, and the food, of course. Or there's the East India Company—always on the lookout for men, I understand. A pity India is such an unhealthy country, but we can't have everything. I am making new acquaintances all the time these days. Men of influence in the navy and the East India Company for example.'

'You wouldn't.' Henry was pale now—in fact, Kate thought he might vomit on his shiny new desk. 'I'm a married man.'

'From what I hear Lady Harding would be quite relieved by your absence. Of course, your loving sister would support her in remaining here, make sure she had a good bailiff and not the useless one you inflict on your tenants now.'

'I'll pay! I'll find the money somehow, although I don't know how…'

'We'll work it out, never fear, Harding.' Grant stood up and nodded to Kate. 'Ready, Lady Allundale? I'll be back tomorrow, Harding. Oh, and don't try to make a run for it. I know far too much about you.'

Kate was confused, anxious and deeply relieved to have Grant there, all at the same time. The mixed emotions might be uncomfortable, but at least he now knew the truth about her. But how did he feel? There was no way of telling, not when she could not ask him, could not take his hand and look into his eyes. He was in control of himself, of Henry and of the situation, but whether he was furiously angry, disgusted or merely resigned to her betrayal she had no idea, and a chaise containing a lady's maid and a footman was not the place to find out.

She thanked Giles for his attentiveness and Wilson for her patience and then sat, hands folded in her lap, her mind utterly blank of any kind of meaningless small talk while Grant surveyed the flat farmland on either side of the road back to Southend. He had tied the hired hack on behind the carriage, so she had not even had the time to sit and think without looking at him and having that steady green gaze look straight back at her.

Perhaps this was how a prisoner in the dock felt as she watched the faces of the jurors. Guilty or not guilty? Condemned or pardoned?

Somehow she kept control of herself on the interminable drive back. Kept her chin up, her back straight, her expression composed. One did not show weakness in front of the servants. Besides, pride would not let her give way.

When they reached the Ship Inn and Grant issued orders for the hired horse's return she dismissed Wilson and Giles and climbed the stairs to the large suite of rooms she had taken. Jeannie and Anna were bright-eyed and pink-faced from a chilly walk along the beach. Charlie and Mr Gough were still out there, swathed in scarves, skimming pebbles, prodding driftwood and doing whatever men and boys did by the seaside.

'His lordship has returned with me. Please let everyone know that we are not to be disturbed until dinner time. His lordship has a great deal of business to attend to.' *Such as dealing with his deceitful wife.*

'Which is our room, my lady?' Grant had come up the stairs while she stood on the landing, steeling herself.

'Through here. I took virtually the entire floor.' He was addressing her formally and the chill of it was like the touch of a cold finger on the nape of her neck, unpleasant yet bracing. She walked in through the door he opened for her and took the chair by the window, let the light fall on her face. There was no hiding anything now.

Grant sat down facing her and leaned forward, his forearms on his knees. 'Are you all right, Kate?'

It was the last thing she expected him to say, this expression of concern for her, and it almost undid her.

'Don't cry,' he said, firmly and without reaching for her. *The prosecuting counsel...*

'I am not and I will not.' Easier to promise than to keep, she suspected. 'You seem to know a great deal, but I expect you would like me to tell you myself why I have lied to you.'

Grant moved, an involuntary gesture that she read as acknowledgment of her betrayal. So be it. 'Henry likes to gamble and he met Jonathan in some hell or another and invited him to stay. I think he had made up a plan on the spur of the moment when he realised that Baybrook needed to escape his creditors and get out of London for a while before news of his debts reached Lord Harlington, his future father-in-law. I did wonder whether it was some deep-laid plot or whether Henry simply had a flash of inspiration, but it was probably the latter. He brought him home, made much of him, invited all his cronies round for card play, let him shoot our coverts. And did nothing when Jonathan began to flirt with me. I thought Jonathan was serious, that Henry's unconcern meant approval. I was inexperienced, lonely—ripe for the plucking, I suppose.

'I told myself I was in love, that he was an honourable man who intended marriage. I was not the first naive girl to fall for it and I will not be the last. When Jonathan had gone, his pockets lined with enough winnings from the local squirearchy to keep his tailors happy, I realised he had made me no promises, not even to write. And then I found I was expecting and Jane told Henry and he went off to London.'

'To tell Baybrook he must marry you.' Grant leaned back in his chair and steepled his fingers. *The judge listening to the evidence, weighing it up...*

'That's what he told me, but I realise now he knew perfectly well that Jonathan was in no position to do that. He was contracted to the daughter of a powerful and wealthy man and he could not afford to risk that alliance. Henry told me about it when he got home. *He'll pay,* he promised. And like an idiot I asked if that meant there would be enough for me to have a little cottage somewhere, raise the child in modest respectability. He laughed and said that we did not need money for that, he would find a home for the baby easily enough. And then he explained it all, how he could extort money from Baybrook for years, how he needed to get me out of the way so Jonathan could not find me, how a foundlings' home would take my baby.'

'I think I would like to see your brother through the sights of a duelling pistol on the nearest common at dawn,' Grant remarked. 'What did you do then?'

'I did as I was told and I went up to the lodge in Scotland.' Now they were coming to it. The story so far had been one of her own foolish innocence in allowing Jonathan to seduce her. But what followed was not innocent. 'I should have written to Jonathan, told him that I was not in league with Henry, promised him I would support a statement to a magistrate. But I didn't. I allowed myself to be used. And then it was too late, I was on my way north and all I could think about was how to get away, how to keep my baby.'

'You left it very late.' Grant's voice was dispassionate. She found she could not look at him, so she watched Charlie running along the road towards the inn, laughing and calling back to Mr Gough. *My son. I could lose him, too.*

'I wasn't well at first, and then I had no money. It took me a long time to get it together, stealing the odd shilling from the housekeeper's purse over weeks so no one would notice and suspect. They were all paid by Henry. I had nothing to offer them to win their loyalty.' Charlie had vanished, but she could hear his voice faintly from the hallway below, happy, laughing. She shrugged. 'You know the rest.'

'Why did you tell me that Anna's father was dead?'

'At first, just instinct to hide, to cover up. That was why I told you I came from Suffolk and didn't tell you about Henry's baronetcy. And then, later, you were so protective, so possessive. I was afraid you would confront Baybrook, call him out. If I told you about the blackmail, then that made you an accessory after the fact, didn't it? So you would have no option but to expose Henry, and I know he deserves it, but it could have ruined Jonathan if his father-in-law found out and cut him off financially.'

'You have a high opinion of my sense of honour and of how law-abiding I am,' Grant said drily. 'It did not occur to you to tell me this whole story and let me set it right?'

'Of course not. I had deceived you, allowed you to marry me, save Anna and myself, embroiled you in this. How could I turn around and dump the whole mess at your feet?'

'It was why you were so reluctant to come to London, I suppose. Kate—' He broke off. His lower lip caught between his teeth, then, as though he was making himself ask, he said, 'Did you meet Baybrook in Green Park by appointment?'

'No! When you told me how you felt about me, saw for myself that you were happy in our marriage, saw how much you trusted me, I knew I had to stop pretending everything was all right. I went looking for Jonathan to find out exactly what Henry had been demanding, promised him I would put it right somehow. I saw him in the park that day and followed him.'

'Anna has his eyes, that unusual clear green with gold flecks.'

'She got that from him?' Kate shook her head, bemused by the detail. 'I can't remember what colour his eyes are. Anyway, I knew I had to go to Henry, make him stop, get the money and pay it back.'

'All two thousand five hundred and twenty pounds,' Grant said.

'How did you know it was that much?'

'I arrived outside the window just as you were discussing it, demanding that he give it to you.'

Kate thought back on what she had said, when she had said it, when Grant had walked in the door. So that was how he knew so much. 'You must think I am as bad as he was, that I wanted the money for myself?'

Chapter Twenty-Three

'I had a bad moment.' Grant held up his hand and she saw the raw graze across his knuckles. 'I hit the wall, which was foolish. But you are my wife, Kate. I owe you my loyalty. I owe you my trust.'

He meant it, she could tell. For a moment the happiness bubbled up, almost painful in its intensity. Then she realised that he was making himself trust by an effort of will, against the evidence. The happiness wavered and went out like a candle flame in the wind.

He has to trust me because he is loyal to me. Not because he knows I wouldn't do such a thing, not because he loves me. Grant is honourable and Madeleine rejected him and Charlie. Now he has the courage to risk his heart and his happiness all over again on a woman who has been deceiving him since the moment we met. What if I let him down, slip up, fail to have the nerve to always be truthful?

Grant needed to believe in her, she realised. He needed that faith that she would be true to him.

I am on a shaky pedestal where I have no right to be.

'Thank you.' She could feel the pedestal rock beneath her feet as she groped for balance, the right words. 'I was optimistic in thinking Henry would actually give me the money, but I had to try. I would have given it all back to Jonathan somehow.'

'Will you let me deal with this if I promise not to call Baybrook out? I will repay him, assure him of our silence, of the end of Henry's extortion, provided he forgets he ever met you.' When she opened her mouth to protest he smiled thinly. 'And Henry can repay me.'

'It may take some time.' It seemed she could breathe again. Grant believed her.

'I will put some of my own people in. That will sort him out. He may come to think longingly of a nice sea voyage to India after all, by the time I have finished with him.'

'I am glad you are on my side and not against me,' Kate ventured, daring a feeble joke. Grant's smile was still tight. 'I should not speak lightly. And I should not expect you to deal with Baybrook. It was my fault. I will—'

'You will do no such thing.' With the suddenness of a pistol firing Grant lost his temper. He was on his feet, his fist thudding into the wall, his voice a barely contained shout. Kate stared horrified at the smear of blood from his unhealed knuckles, the mark of violence across the neatly papered wall. Grant never lost his temper, never shouted. He swung round, towering over her. 'I deal with threats to my family, my wife, my daughter. Is that clear?'

Kate nodded, unable to drag her gaze from his face. 'I am so sorry.'

He swore, crudely, harshly. 'And don't apologise!' It was a shout now. Grant slammed away across the room, turned and glared at her from ten feet away, six feet of infuriated male pride and muscle. 'Your brother, who should protect you with his life, uses you, an innocent, to bait a honey trap, makes you party to a criminal act, puts you in fear for your child. You could have died in that hovel. You probably would have done if I had not come past by the merest chance. You have the guts to fight for your daughter, take risks for her. You have given my son the mother he deserves, made my house a home, driven away my demons.'

Grant lifted his hands, scrubbed them across his face. 'Don't you dare apologise to me, Kate.' He stared at her as though he had forgotten who she was, what they were doing there. Stared as if he was having a revelation and not a very happy one at that. Then he moved. Ten long strides took him past her to the door. 'Get back to London first thing tomorrow, let me sort this out. I don't know when I will be back.'

He stopped, turned on the threshold and came back to her, pulled her into his arms and took her mouth. The kiss was hard, possessive, almost punitive. Through her confusion she could taste his anger and his desire and, beneath it all, a sort of desperation.

And then he was gone, booted heels clattering down the steps.

'Lady Allundale?'

Kate blinked and the room came back into focus. Mr Gough was standing in the doorway, regarding her warily. 'Yes?'

'His lordship has…er…left?'

'Yes,' she repeated and somehow managed to think of something other than Grant's mouth on hers, kissing with the sort of desperation a condemned man might use if he were to be hanged the next day. 'We are going back to London tomorrow morning, first thing. Please can you arrange that, Mr Gough?'

'Certainly, Lady Allundale.'

'Was that Papa? I didn't know he was coming here. I heard him shouting.' Charlie appeared from his bed-chamber door, a clean shirt half on. 'Papa never shouts like that.'

'He has had a very trying day, dear.' *Possibly almost as trying as I have had.* Kate forced back the hysterical laughter that was threatening. 'We will be going back to Grosvenor Street tomorrow, first thing.'

'Oh, good.' Charlie's anxious expression turned to a broad grin. 'It is interesting here. I like the sea. But it's not long until Christmas and we've got to get ready.'

'Yes, of course.' Kate hoped she looked less fraught than she felt. Christmas had completely slipped her mind. There was the anniversary of the old earl's death to deal with and the challenge of creating a perfect new set of Christmas memories for Charlie and presents to buy and… *And a husband who I thought I understood and now…*

'Run along and finish getting changed, Charlie. And try not to bother Mr Gough. He has lots of things to do.'

She went back and sank down into the chair, considered indulging in hysterics and concluded, rather wildly, that they would have to wait. 'Wilson!'

'Yes, my lady?' The maid had a pile of folded underwear in her hands. Gough must have lost no time in telling her the news.

'What is the date?'

'The fifteenth, my lady.'

The old earl had died on Christmas Eve. They would travel back to London tomorrow and she must decide the best way to handle the anniversary for Charlie. Then there was Christmas to prepare for, which was also Anna's birthday. When would Grant be back—and in what mood? No, this was definitely no time to have the vapours. Kate blew her nose briskly and found some paper and a pen. Lists were what she needed now. *And my husband.*

The clock struck midnight as Kate reached for the last sheet of paper and began to wrap up the pretty dress length and ribbons she had bought for Jeannie. All the presents had been bought in exhausting expeditions around the shops in the days after they got back from Southend.

All that was left was to worry about Grant. The note had arrived this morning from, of all places, Newport Pagnell. What he was doing there she could not imagine, nor could she gauge his mood, for it had simply read:

I will be there on the twenty-fourth. G.

Something had been written beneath that scrawled initial, then crossed out. She had squinted at it, held it up to the light, to a candle flame, and all she could make out was a small circle. Or perhaps a heart.

Now it was Christmas Eve. She had not dared hope, had hardly dared think about Grant and instead had plunged into planning, shopping and endless decision-making. The staff were not used to the family spending Christmas in London and seemed incapable of making the slightest decision without her. So footmen had been dispatched to enquire when evergreens would be available in Shepherd's Market, Cook had been given guidance on two weeks' worth of menus, decisions had been made on when the staff would have their Christmas meal, which carriages would be required for what

church services and when a holly wreath should be hung
on the front door.

Now Kate just wanted to sleep and not be plagued by
dreams about Grant vanishing into the mist. She gathered up the scissors and ribbon, brushed paper scraps
off the bed and took off her robe. As she reached for the
snuffer, there was a noise from Grant's bedchamber, then
another. Muffled, cautious sounds. Sounds of someone
who did not want to be heard.

When she snuffed the candle a thin line of light
showed beneath his door. He was home.

Kate reached for the wisp of negligee that lay at the
end of the bed, then, with a shake of her head, fetched
the old flannel wrapper. This was no time for seduction.
Either this marriage would hold because of what was in
their hearts and in their minds, or it would not.

She made no effort to be quiet as she opened the connecting door. Grant was sitting on the side of the bed in
the position she knew meant that he was contemplating
pulling off his boots and was really too tired to bother,
or to ring for Griffin. He looked up as she entered and
she stopped, thinking wryly that when she had been rejecting thoughts of seduction she had not counted on the
physical effect that her husband had on her. He looked
saddle-weary, travel-stained and beyond tired. And he
also looked magnificently male, strong and determined.

'I am so glad you are home,' she said simply. 'Let me.'
And as she had once done before, when she had first
come to Abbeywell, she straddled first one leg, then the
other, and pulled off his boots.

'Thank you.' He waited until she turned and then
reached out, put one hand on either side of her waist and
drew her in to stand between his spread thighs. 'I went

to see Charlie first, woke him up. I wanted him to know I kept my promise to be back.' He looked up at her, serious, watchful.

'Of course.' She resisted the urge to smooth his wind-tangled hair. Goodness knew what had happened to his hat. 'Has he gone back to sleep or did he tell you the plans for tomorrow?'

'He told me and went back to sleep. I had to promise to inspect all the decorations, right down to the very miniature yule log in the drawing room. You've done a magnificent job between the pair of you.' He put his head slightly to one side as he studied her face. 'Don't you want to know where I've been?'

'I don't care, so long as you are back here.' It was the truth. She trusted him to deal fairly with Henry and she knew he had not called Baybrook out. He would not risk killing Anna's father. She gave in to the urge then and lifted her hands to cup his face. 'I missed you.'

'I lost my temper back there in the inn.'

'I noticed.' Was that the faintest curve of his lips? 'You lose it so rarely that it is most impressive when you do.'

'I swore.' *Yes, that is most definitely the beginning of a smile.*

'But not at me.' He had her tight against him now and the old flannel wrapper seemed to be having no effect on his body's responses.

'No. At me.' The ghost of the smile flickered and was gone. 'Kate, you have a very short-sighted husband who could not see what was under his nose, nor read what his heart was telling him.'

It was suddenly very hard to breathe, let alone speak, so she leaned forward and kissed him lightly on the lips until the gentle returning pressure gave her courage. 'You can read it now?'

'Yes. And I love you, Kate. I think I have loved you for a long time and had no idea what it was. I should have realised in that moment in the receiving line at the Larminster reception that what I was feeling was something far more than happiness.' His voice was harsh, but the green eyes locked with hers were tender and vulnerable and full of promises. 'I puzzled over why I trusted you despite your deceptions, despite what I heard with my own ears, and then it hit me in the Ship Inn. And I had been cold and grudging. I made you tell me your secrets as though I was forcing a confession out of you, when I should have taken you in my arms and held you and protected you and trusted you without reservation, without you having to explain a thing.'

'Oh, my love. You aren't a saint.' She tugged at his arms and he came to his feet, held her by the shoulders as he stared down into her face. 'We could both have trusted more, risked more—if we were perfect, but we aren't. We are human and we had both learned the pain of love betrayed.'

'You called me… Kate, you can't…' How could the fact that this strong, articulate man was having trouble getting a simple question out make her so happy?

'I can. And I do. I love you, Grant. I have loved you for months and I did not dare tell you.'

'Did not dare?'

'You would have been kind to me, wouldn't you? You would have felt sorry for me. I could live with loving you without hope of that being returned, but I could not bear your pity.'

'Oh, Kate. That must be the only thing you would not

dare.' Grant pulled her in close so that she was against the hard strength of him, safe and surrounded by love. By impossible, wonderful love. It didn't matter that Grant smelt of leather and sweat and horse. It simply made this moment more real, more certain that it was not a dream. 'I love you so very much.'

'Come to bed,' she said into the crumpled folds of his neckcloth. 'Show me.'

'I'm filthy,' he protested half-heartedly, his fingers already on the buttons of his waistcoat.

'Most of it is your clothes.' Her fingers were as urgent, pushing the coat back from his shoulders, tearing a ribbon on her old robe as she threw it aside. 'I don't care. I just want you. Now, always.'

There was no finesse left in either of them. They fell on to the bed in a tangle of limbs, of kisses, of desperate fingers, all impeded by Grant's breeches, which he kicked off with a final heave before he rolled Kate over, covered her with his body and slid into her in one movement.

Then he stilled, propped on his elbows, his hips cradled by her thighs, his forehead resting against her brow. 'Home. Home at last.'

His heart thudded over hers, his breathing was ragged, his fingers, always so sure, so controlled, shook as they sifted through her hair. The lack of control touched her as no skilled caresses could ever have done and she tipped her head to capture his lips, curled her legs around the slim hips and rocked him deeper.

It became a blur, a mixture of passion and love, of relief and joy and urgent need. Kate knew she was talking, broken phrases, words, his name. 'I love you. I love you. Grant…'

He stretched up above her on his hands, tightening

the junction between their bodies so she could no longer tell where his pleasure ended and hers began. She looked up and saw he was watching her, even as he lost control and let the wave crash over him. 'I love you. Kate. Now. Always. *Kate.*'

Chapter Twenty-Four

They went to church in the morning with Charlie and sat and thought about the old earl and then came home and spent the day talking about him. Grant told them tales about his own childhood and had Charlie alternately gasping and giggling about the tricks he used to play and the trouble he would get into.

'Truly? You let all the hounds into the house while Great-Grandmama was having the Ladies' Church Social and they ate all the cakes and peed on the Chinese rug? And you climbed all the way to the top of the great oak on the front lawn?'

Kate rolled her eyes at Grant, who grinned and shrugged. 'And fell out and broke my arm and spent a month learning to write left-handed so I could do all the lines my tutor set me as punishment.'

'Tell me again about Great-Grandpapa and the bishop and the bull at the church fête.'

Kate curled up in her armchair and indulged herself by watching Grant, relaxed and happy, sprawled on the hearthrug with his son. The day that could have been so sad, the anniversary of a loss where they could not be together, was turning into a happy time and, she suspected, the beginning of a family tradition. She and Charlie had planned it together, both of them, she was certain, convinced that this time Grant would be home in time.

After luncheon Charlie announced that he was going to write down the stories in case he forgot any. 'And I'll add my stories, too,' he added, marching off to the desk by the window.

Grant put his arm around Kate and pulled her down beside him on the sofa at the other end of the room. 'I must tell you where I have been these past days.'

'I confess I am consumed with curiosity about Newport Pagnell.' She curled into the crook of his arm and played with the curling ends of hair around his ears. It was bliss to be able to touch Grant without wariness, without being afraid that her gestures would be read, quite correctly, as signs of love.

'I took your sister-in-law there. When I left you I went back to Belchamps Hall, riding a positive tidal wave of anger with your brother. She overheard our discussion and delivered a bombshell to dear Henry by announcing that if he was paying off his debt to Baybrook, he could pay her an allowance and she was going to live with her sister.'

'So Henry is going to repay the money? I would have thought that was like wringing blood out of a stone.'

'Apparently I look forbidding enough for him to believe my threats about the navy or India. One of the brightest clerks in my banker's office is going down there to do a complete audit and Henry's about to acquire a new bailiff in the form of Grimswade's nephew, who is as tough as his uncle and has been cutting his teeth as my farm manager.'

'You are brilliant, Grant.' She kissed his ear.

He broke off in an attempt to capture her lips. 'Temptress.'

'Grant! Not in front of the children.'

'Anna's fast asleep and Charlie's lost in composition. Oh, very well, I'll behave, but that gown is devilishly provoking.' When she escaped to the other end of the sofa he growled, but carried on with his story. 'I made arrangements with Henry, sent off all the necessary letters, conveyed Lady Harding, bag and baggage, to Newport Pagnell and got back to town late yesterday afternoon. Then I tracked Baybrook down—'

'You didn't hit him or call him out or anything dreadful?'

'No. I managed to convince him that I intended to give him money, not demand it, and we ended up having a very civilised dinner at his club. He's not the scoundrel I thought him to be. Or perhaps I should say that he isn't now. He seems to be genuinely fond of his little heiress and he doesn't want to hurt her, at least as much as he doesn't want her father finding out about his sins. He's more than grateful about the return of the money and he accepts that it was not your doing.' He looked at her quizzically. 'What is it?'

'Men are so strange. You were breathing fire and brimstone, you were ready to call him out just for insulting me in the park and now there you are dining with him.'

Grant shrugged. 'He gave us Anna, didn't he?'

'Yes, so he did. And Madeleine gave us Charlie.'

He pulled her close again and they sat in silence,

watching the children as the winter daylight ebbed into darkness and the candlelight glowed off holly berries and swags of evergreens and the fire burned bright in the grate.

Kate had thought of the same night one year before as she'd carried Anna up to her cot and Grant and Charlie went to change for the grown-up dinner they had promised the boy so that he could make the toast to his great-grandfather's memory. A year ago she had been cold, desperate and in pain with no hope for the future, only a desperate will to make it through somehow.

I wonder if I can be any happier than this? she thought, watching Grant bend to kiss Anna goodnight. *Perhaps, when I tell Grant the final secret I am keeping.*

Christmas morning dawned bright and, to Charlie's huge delight, snowy. 'May we make a snowman?' he asked at breakfast. 'There's all that snow in the back garden. Or...' His eyes grew wide. 'The park! We could build dozens of snowmen, an army of snowmen!'

'This afternoon,' Grant promised. 'Presents first. Anna's birthday, then the staff, then our Christmas presents.'

Anna was predictably more enchanted by the silver paper, the flicker of candlelight and the trailing scarlet ribbons than she was by her presents, but, as Kate pointed out to Grant, he was going to get far more fun out of her presents than she was.

'I know. I want to spoil her, to make up for that first birthday, that first Christmas,' he said, smiling at the dolls, the pretty dresses, the stuffed rabbit and the little horse on wheels.

'You gave her that first Christmas,' Kate whispered

in his ear and then found she had to blow her nose very inelegantly.

They lit the yule log together, played with Anna, listened to the sounds of fiddle music, singing and laughter wafting up from below stairs. It seemed the staff were having a good time getting ready for their Christmas meal. Charlie, bursting with pride, led Kate and Grant, with Anna fast asleep in Grant's arms, downstairs to deliver the family's Christmas good wishes and thanks for all their hard work during the year.

'He is growing up so fast,' Kate whispered as Cook gathered Charlie to her capacious bosom and gave him a hug that turned his ears scarlet. Then they trooped back upstairs, collecting Mr Gough as they went, and shared out Christmas presents.

My family, Kate thought as she watched them, the love filling her heart as softly as the snowflakes swirling down outside the window. Charlie was thrilled with a new saddle and a pair of ice skates. Grant peacocked around the room in the heavy silk robe Kate had found for him and winked at her to show he knew exactly how she imagined him wearing it, with nothing underneath. The tutor was delighted with a subscription to a circulating library and Charlie presented his parents with two pairs of handsome, and only slightly lopsided, bookends that, he confided, he had made with the assistance of the estate carpenter.

Kate was trying not to crane her neck and see if there was anything left in the litter of paper for her when Grant announced, 'We are going out for a walk.'

'We are?' Kate almost protested that it was too cold, too snowy, and that she wanted to spend as much time as possible with Anna on her first birthday. But there was something about Grant's expression that was both serious and yet happy. He had a surprise for her and she was not going to spoil it for him.

'Yes, and I have a new bonnet for you to wear.' He lifted a hatbox, white with bright red ribbons, from beside his chair.

Kate took the box and opened it. The bonnet nestled in tissue paper, a confection of white velvet with a wide brim to frame her face and a delicate pale blue gauze veil with deeper blue silk ribbons, the colour of her eyes. 'Grant, it is lovely. It is almost—' *Bridal.*

'You did not have anything pretty a year ago,' he said. 'Shall we go out now? We'll be back in time to build a small snowman, Charlie.'

Kate took Grant's arm and allowed herself to be led through the snowy streets, along narrow ways she had not known existed, up to the door of one of the little chapels of ease that had been built to serve the expanding neighbourhood north of Oxford Street. It was not one they had ever used and, when they entered, it was obvious from its plain furnishings and lack of memorials that it was not a fashionable church.

Grant had been carrying something in a straw basket, the kind that a goose would be brought home from market in, and Kate had been vastly curious to see what it held. He set it down on the porch and took out a posy. Trailing ivy, the red of holly berries, the pearl glow of mistletoe, crimson ribbons.

'It was rather a plain wedding, was it not?' Grant said and handed her the bouquet. 'One sprig of holly, if I remember rightly. I think we should do it again, don't you?'

'It made me very happy, that first ceremony,' Kate said, wondering how it was possible to want to cry, even as she smiled. 'But I would like very much to marry the man I love, all over again.'

'Shall we?' He crooked his arm for her and together they walked down the aisle. She saw a clergyman waiting in a side chapel, two chairs set before him.

'Welcome.' He came forward, shook hands, ushered them to the seats. 'I have never blessed a marriage on Christmas morning before,' he confessed. 'Weddings, yes. So many working people take advantage of the holiday. But this is rather special, is it not?'

So special. 'Grant, thank you,' she whispered and did not realise she was crying until he took off his gloves and gently wiped away the tears with his thumb. He was giving her the one thing their marriage lacked, the one thing she had not thought important until that moment— a romantic wedding day.

The clergyman handed them a battered prayer book to share. 'I thought we would read it through,' he said. 'And then I will do the blessing.'

They sat, following the familiar words read in the old man's steady, gentle voice. Grant slipped the ring he had given her from her finger and then, as he made his vows, slid it gently back.

'With this ring I thee wed, with my body I thee worship...'

Kate knew she was crying again, happy tears that slid down her cheeks and moistened her smiling lips and, when they rose from their knees, made their kiss salty and sweet.

She thanked the clergyman with Grant, linked her arm through his again and went out into the brilliant sunshine of the snowy noonday. 'That was the most perfect Christmas gift, thank you.' He simply squeezed her hand against his side, but she could tell from his face that he had been deeply moved by the little ceremony. 'When you came, that Christmas Eve, I thought you were my Christmas miracle. And now we have another, our love.'

'We have two very different Christmases we will never forget.' Grant's voice was husky. Neither of them spoke for a while as they crunched through the snow.

'I have a gift for you that might make this one even more memorable,' Kate confessed as they came into Berkeley Square. 'I did think I ought to wait another few weeks, just to be certain, but I can't bear to keep the secret.'

'Oh, my love.' Grant stopped dead, right outside Gunter's tea shop. 'I did wonder whether you were simply blooming because you were happy or whether there was another reason.'

'Both,' Kate said. 'I'm in love, I'm blissfully happy and I think we are going to be a family of five for next Christmas!'

* * * * *

THE MISTRESS OF
HANOVER SQUARE

ANNE HERRIES

Chapter One

Amelia stood for a moment on the steps of her house in Hanover Square, gazing across to the Earl of Ravenshead's London home, which was at the far side. She knew that he was not in residence and supposed that he was at his estate in the country. It was only because she had wanted to do some shopping for Christmas and deliver some gifts that she and her companion had themselves come to town for a few days. She had hoped that she might perhaps meet the earl, at the theatre or at some other affair, but it had not happened.

'Is something wrong?' Emily Barton asked.

Amelia looked at her in surprise and then realised that she had sighed. Her companion was a sensitive girl and always seemed to know when Amelia was out of sorts.

'No, I was merely wondering if I had forgotten anything. I should not wish to arrive at Pendleton and then remember something I had left behind.'

'I am sure you will not.' Emily smiled at her. 'I helped Martha pack your trunks and I am certain nothing was left out.'

'Thank you, my love. I know I can always rely on your good sense.'

'You are not upset by your brother's visit, I hope?'

For a moment Amelia's eyes clouded. Her brother, Sir Michael Royston, had paid her a brief but intensely unpleasant visit to complain. He always seemed to be in a temper these days and Amelia had come to dread his visits.

'No, dearest. As you know, my brother is…difficult. However, I am not upset.' She took Emily's arm. 'Come, we must not keep the horses standing. I want to make good time, for the sky has all the appearance of bad weather and I would like to get to Pendleton before it turns to snow.'

'I am looking forward to spending Christmas with our friends,' Emily said and smiled as she glanced across the carriage. They had been travelling for some time now and the streets of London had given way to pleasant countryside. 'Before I came to you, Amelia, Christmas was always a time of regret.'

'Was it, my love?' Amelia Royston looked at Emily in concern. She was aware of her companion's secret sorrow, but it was something Emily hardly ever spoke of. 'Are you happier now that you have been living with me for more than a year?'

'Oh yes, much. If only—' Emily broke off and shook her head. 'No, we shall not think of things that make us sad. Do you think that the Earl of Ravenshead will be at Pendleton this year?'

'Susannah said nothing of it when she wrote to invite us,' Amelia said, and a faint colour stained her cheeks. It almost seemed that Emily was reading her thoughts. 'Why do you ask, Emily?'

'Forgive me, perhaps I ought not to have spoken, but I thought…in the Season and at Helene's wedding earlier this year…I did think that perhaps there might be something—' Emily broke off and shook her head. 'It was not my place to ask…'

'Have I not told you that you may say anything to me, Emily? We are friends and have no secrets from each other. Since you ask, I shall tell you that I did think Gerard might speak some eighteen months ago, but he was called to France on family business. When we met him in London this year he paid me some attention, but…' Amelia sighed. 'I think now it was merely friendship he had in mind for us. There was a time when we might have married, but my brother sent him away. He married another woman some months later, which must mean that he did not suffer from our parting as I did.'

'You cannot be sure of that, Amelia. The earl may have married for various reasons. Perhaps it was on the rebound?' Emily frowned. 'I think you told me his wife has since died?'

'Gerard told me she was ill after the birth of their daughter and never recovered. I think that perhaps he is still grieving for her.'

'He will surely wish to marry again, if only for the sake of his daughter.'

'Yes, perhaps—though I am not sure I should wish to be married for such a reason.'

'I did not mean…please do not think I meant that he would marry you for the sake of his child,' Emily apologised and looked upset. 'I believe he likes you very well, Amelia.'

'Yes, I believe we are good friends,' Amelia agreed.

She leaned her head back against the squabs, closing her eyes. It would be very foolish of her to give way to emotion. She had cried too many tears when Gerard went away the first time. He had vowed that he loved her with all his heart, asked her to be his wife and then simply disappeared. When she was told he had joined the army, she had suffered a broken heart. She had not understood then that her brother had forced him to walk away from her—and threatened him and used violence. His desertion had left her feeling abandoned and distraught. When she first saw him again in company some four years later, she had been overwhelmed, and it had taken all her self-control not to show her feelings.

Gerard had been polite and friendly, but then, when someone had attempted to abduct Amelia when she was staying at Pendleton the summer before last, Gerard had been so concerned for her. She had believed then that he still cared, had begun to hope that he might speak, but he had been called away to France.

They had met again this summer. Gerard had been as generous, polite and kind as ever, but still he had not spoken of marriage. Of course there was no reason why he should. Too much time had passed, more than five years. If he had ever felt anything for her it had gone, or at least faded to a gentle affection. It was foolish of her to hope that he might feel more than mere friendship.

She opened her eyes and saw that Emily was looking upset.

'You have not distressed me, dearest.' Amelia smiled at her. 'We are almost there. I am so looking forward to seeing Susannah and Harry again.'

'I should never wish to distress you, Amelia. You have done so much for me, taking me in when many would have turned me from their door, because of my shame...'

'Do not look like that, Emily. You have more than repaid me for any kindness I have shown you. As for your shame—I will not have you speak of yourself in such a way. Come, smile and look forward to spending Christmas at Pendleton.'

'Amelia dearest,' Susannah exclaimed and kissed her on both cheeks. 'You look wonderful. That colour green always becomes you so well—and Emily, how pretty you look!'

'Oh, no...' Emily shook her head and blushed. 'It is this bonnet. I admired it in a milliner's window and Amelia bought it for me without my knowing. She said it was the very thing to brighten my winter wardrobe and of course she was right. She has such excellent taste.'

'Yes, she does.' Susannah looked fondly at Amelia. 'I may be biased, but I think Amelia is everything that is perfect and good.'

'Between the two of you, you will turn my head.

I shall become impossible and start expecting to be treated like a duchess.'

Susannah trilled with laughter. 'You deserve to be a duchess,' she said. 'You must both come up to the nursery and see my little Harry. He is such a darling. His father thinks he is the most wonderful child ever born. I cannot begin to tell you all the plans he is making for when he can walk and go to school.'

'I always knew Harry Pendleton would be a doting father,' Amelia said, much amused.

'He spoils me dreadfully,' Susanna confessed as she led her friends up to their chambers. 'I've given you the apartments we had when I first stayed here, Amelia. I was so terrified of Harry's relatives and this vast house. I could not imagine how I should cope with it, but everything runs like clockwork. I hardly have to do a thing—just as Harry's mama told me it would be. And we always have guests so it is never too big or lonely, because people love to stay here. We shall have some twenty or thirty invited guests this Christmas, but it is quite possible that as many more will simply arrive on our doorstep. I tell Harry it is because he is such a generous host, but he thinks it is because they are all in love with me.'

'I dare say it is a mixture of both,' Amelia told her and smiled. She was delighted that her friend had not changed one bit since she became Lady Pendleton. She might not be quite as impulsive as when she had first visited town as Amelia's guest, but if anything her confidence had grown.

Susannah took them to the nursery, where the young heir was being prepared for bed by his nurse. After some twenty minutes or so admiring the admittedly beautiful child, Amelia and Emily were taken to the apartment they were to share during the Christmas period. It had three bedrooms and a sitting room, which was pleasant if one wished to escape from the rest of the company at times, and was quite a privilege.

Amelia allowed Emily to choose the bedchamber she liked best, and was pleased when her friend chose the one Susannah had used during that first visit. It meant she could take the room she preferred, and felt perfectly at home in.

After Susannah left them to settle in, Amelia walked to the window and looked out. Her view was of the lake and park, and, as she watched for a moment, she saw three horsemen canter to a halt and dismount. They had obviously been out riding together for pleasure and were in high good humour. Her breath caught in her throat as she heard laughter and caught sight of one familiar face. So Gerard *was* to be one of the guests this Christmas!

Amelia realised that she had been hoping for it, her heart beginning to thump with excitement. Oh, how foolish she was! Just because Gerard was here did not mean that he would speak of marriage. Why should he indeed? Had he wished to, he had had ample opportunity to do so before this.

She turned away to glance in the mirror. She was still attractive, but she was no longer a young girl. It was quite ridiculous to fancy herself in love; the time for such things had passed her by. The most she could hope for now would be a marriage of convenience, as Emily had suggested on the way to Pendleton. If perhaps Gerard were looking for a mother for his daughter, he might consider Amelia a suitable choice.

Amelia shook her head, dismissing her thoughts as a flight of fancy. There were a dozen young and beautiful girls Gerard might think of taking as his wife. Why should he look at a woman of her age? She had just turned eight and twenty. Besides, he was probably still grieving for the wife he had lost. Why had he married only a few months after their parting? Her brother Michael had behaved disgracefully to Gerard, of course, but why had he not told Amelia at the time the real reason behind his sudden departure? She would have run away with him had he asked her then.

No, if he had ever loved her, his love had faded and died.

She must not spend her time dreaming of something that would never happen!

Her thoughts turned to her companion. She knew that this time of year was often sad for Emily, because of her secret sorrow. None of their friends knew of Emily's secret, but she had told Amelia the truth when they first met. In doing so she had risked losing the chance of a good position, for many would have turned her away. Amelia had admired her honesty. She had done everything she could to make Emily forget the past, but nothing could take away the ache Emily carried inside.

Amelia was thoughtful as she prepared to go downstairs. She was almost sure that Mr Toby Sinclair would be a guest at Pendleton that Christmas. He had paid Emily some attention earlier in the year, but nothing had come of it. If he were to offer for her…but nothing was certain. Amelia would not put the idea into her companion's mind, but if it happened she would be delighted.

If it did not, perhaps there was something she might be able to do to help the girl she had come to love almost as a sister.

Amelia was glad that she had seen Gerard from her window; the knowledge that he was here at Pendleton made it possible for her to meet him without that element of surprise she might otherwise have felt. She was able to greet him in the drawing room later that evening with perfect serenity.

'How nice to see you here, sir,' she said, offering her hand and giving no sign that her heart was beating rather too fast. 'People are arriving all the time. I think Susannah will have a great many guests this Christmas.'

'Yes, I imagine she will,' Gerard agreed. He held her hand briefly. 'How are you, Miss Royston? I trust you have had no further trouble since I last saw you?'

'None at all, sir—except for a raid by some foxes on our hen houses. But I know you did not mean that.' Amelia laughed softly. 'You are referring to the abduction attempt made the summer before last when we were all here together, I imagine?'

'Yes, I was. I am glad nothing more has happened to disturb your peace.' He looked at her thoughtfully. 'I am glad that you are here this Christmas. I was hoping that I might have a private conversation with you concerning my daughter? I would rather like your advice.'

'I should be delighted to help you if I am able.' As he smiled, Amelia's heart stopped for one moment, and then raced on madly. 'Of course, my experience with children is limited to my orphans and the children of friends—but I am fond of them.'

'It is your feeling as a woman of compassion that I need,' Gerard assured her. One of the other guests was headed towards them; from her manner and gestures she was clearly intent on speaking with Amelia. 'This is not the time, however—perhaps tomorrow we might take a walk in the gardens?'

'Yes, certainly,' Amelia agreed. Her smile and quiet manner continued undisturbed. Gerard had asked for help with his daughter and she was quite willing to give it if she could, even if she could not help wishing that his request to walk with her had stemmed from a very different desire. Seeing him, being close to him, had aroused feelings that were not appropriate for a woman who was unlikely to marry. She closed her mind to the tantalising visions of herself in his arms…his bed. That way lay disaster and heartbreak! She must remember her dignity at all times. As a young woman she had not hesitated to confess her love, but things were different now. 'I am available to you at any time, my lord.'

'Do you not think we could be Gerard and Amelia?' he asked. 'We are friends of some long standing, I think?'

'Yes, indeed we are,' Amelia agreed. For a moment the look in his eyes was so intense that she could not breathe. He should not look at her so if he wanted nothing more than friendship.

Their conversation was ended as they were drawn into the company. Susannah's guests were of all ages and included some young people, who had been allowed to come down to dinner because it was nearly Christmas. The eclectic mix of young and old, Harry's relatives and friends of the couple, made for a lively evening. The younger members were sent to bed after their meal, but the older guests continued in their merry way until long past midnight.

It was not until the moment that she had decided to retire that Gerard approached Amelia once more.

'Shall we say ten o'clock for our walk?' he asked. 'If that is not too early for you?'

'I am always an early riser.'

'You must wrap up well, for I think it may be a cold morning.'

'I enjoy walking in any kind of weather, except a downpour,' Amelia assured him.

Their arrangements made, Amelia went upstairs to the apartment she shared with Emily. She saw that Emily was looking thoughtful and asked her if she had enjoyed the evening.

'You did not find the young company too much, dearest?'

'It was a delightful evening,' Emily assured her. 'Mr Sinclair and I joined in a guessing game with some of the young people at the dinner table. I do not know when I have had such fun.' A wistful expression came to her eyes. 'I was an only child and I doubt I shall have…' She blinked hard, as if to stop herself crying. 'I am certain Mr Sinclair means to make me an offer, Amelia. What shall I do?'

'I believe you should tell him the truth. He will keep your confidence—Toby Sinclair is a true gentleman. If he still wishes for the marriage, he will make it clear to you.'

'And if he does not?' Emily lifted her head as if to seek guidance and then nodded as she answered her own question. 'I must bear it. You are quite right, Amelia. I cannot be less than truthful, though it may make things awkward for the rest of our stay here.'

'Perhaps if you could prevent him speaking for a few days, and then tell him just before we leave. If he needs time to consider his feelings, he would have his chance before following us to Coleridge.'

'You are so wise and sensible,' Emily said and looked relieved. 'I shall do my best to avoid being alone with him until the day before we leave.'

'Try not to brood on the outcome.' Amelia kissed her cheek. 'I believe it may all turn out better than you imagine, dearest.'

Having done her best to reassure her friend, Amelia went to her own room. She dismissed her maid as soon as the girl had undone the little hooks at the back of her gown, preferring to be alone with her thoughts. It was easier to settle Emily's doubts than her own, for she had no doubt that Toby Sinclair was deeply in love. It was more difficult to understand Gerard Ravenshead's feelings.

Sometimes his look seemed to indicate that he felt a strong emotion for her, but at others his expression was brooding and remote. They were friends, but *was* that all? These days it seemed that Gerard thought of her as a mature lady in whom he might confide his worries concerning his daughter. He could have no idea of the passionate and improper thoughts his nearness aroused in her. She must be careful to conceal her feelings, otherwise there might be some embarrassment.

'No! No, Lisette...I beg you...do not do it...forgive me...' Gerard Ravenshead's arm twitched, his head moving from side to side as he sat in the deep wing chair in the library at Pendleton. He was dreaming...a dream he had had too many times before. *'No, I say! Stop...the blood...the blood...'* He screamed out and woke to find himself in a room where the fire had gone cold and the candles burned out.

Unable to sleep, he had dressed and come down to read for a while and fallen into a fitful sleep. He hoped that his nightmare had woken no one. Having gone for some months without one, he had thought they were finished, but something had brought it all back to him.

Gerard rose from the chair and walked over to the window, gazing out as the light strengthened. It was dawn and another night had gone.

The library was an impressive, long room with glass-fronted bookcases on three walls, a magnificent desk, occasional tables and comfortable chairs, and three sets of French windows to let in maximum light. Gerard was an avid reader and, when at home in his house in Hanover Square, often sat late into the night reading rather than retiring to his bedchamber, where he found it impossible to sleep. Indeed, he could hardly remember a night when he had slept through until morning.

Gerard was a handsome man, tall, broad in the shoulder with strong legs that looked particularly well in the riding breeches he most often wore. His coats had never needed excessive padding at the shoulder. His hair was very dark but not black, his eyes grey and sometimes flinty. His expression was often brooding, stern, perhaps because his thoughts caused him regret. At this moment he wore a pair of buff-coloured breeches and topboots and his fine linen shirt was opened to the waist. A glass of wine was to hand, but he had scarcely touched it. Gerard had long ago discovered that there was no forgetfulness in a wine bottle.

Before falling into a restless sleep, he had spent the night wrestling with his problem. His daughter was in need of feminine company, and not just that of nursemaids or a governess. He too was in need of a female companion: a woman with whom he could share his hopes and dreams, a woman he could admire and respect. In short, he needed a wife. Having made one mistake with the young French girl he had married out of pity, he did not wish to make another. Easy enough to find a mistress or even a young woman willing to become Countess Ravenshead, but there was only one woman Gerard wanted as his wife—the woman he had been denied when he was a young man and head over heels in love.

He touched the scar at his right temple, the only blemish on a strong and handsome face, his eyes darkening at the memory it aroused. Amelia's brother had instructed his servants to beat him when he dared to ask for her hand as a young man; he had not been wealthy enough to please the proud Sir Michael Royston! However, it was not fear of Sir Michael's displeasure that made Gerard hesitate to ask Amelia Royston if she would be his wife now. Guilt weighed heavily on his conscience, because he had not told anyone the whole truth concerning his wife's death. It was the reason for his nightmares.

'Damn you, Lisette. Let me be...' His eyes were dark with memories as he relived the dream. *'So much blood...so much blood...'*

She *had* been ill for a long time after the birth of her child, but it was not that illness that had caused her death. Lisette had died by her own hand.

He found her with her wrists cut in a bath of warm water. She was still alive when he dragged her from the bath, but barely breathing. He had tried frantically to save her, sending his servant for the doctor, but his efforts were in vain and she was dead when the doctor arrived. Lisette had been buried and Gerard mourned the loss of a young life.

He had not loved her, but she haunted his dreams because he blamed himself for her death. He had married her out of pity, because she was young, alone and with child, abandoned by her lover in a country that was not her own. He knew that the father of her child was an English officer, but Lisette had never named him. His own dreams turned to dust, Gerard had done what he believed was the right thing—a good thing—but he had been unable to love her; when Lisette finally understood that, she had taken her own life.

'I am so sorry...so very sorry...'

Gerard had never been able to confess the truth to another living soul. He carried it inside, where it continued to fester. If he allowed his guilt to haunt him, it would ruin his life. Gerard had no idea whether or not Amelia would marry him if he asked her. What would she think if she knew the truth concerning his wife's death?

He had been on the point of asking her to be his wife once, but an urgent message had sent him hurrying to his daughter's side in France. Little Lisa was a demanding child and she did not like her papa to leave her for long periods. Realising she needed more than her nurses, Gerard had brought her to England and placed her in the charge of an English nanny, but neither Lisa nor her papa was truly content.

Gerard had reached the conclusion that he would never know true happiness unless he asked Amelia Royston to be his wife. He could not marry her without confessing his secret, which was one of the reasons why he had hesitated so long, for he feared that she would turn from him in disgust. He had wanted to die on the battlefield the first time he lost Amelia; to let himself hope and then lose her a second time would destroy him.

This was ridiculous! He was a man of six and thirty and should be able to face up to the truth without fear of rejection. It might be better if he forgot about marriage altogether. He had broken Lisette's heart, causing her to commit suicide. Perhaps he would do better to remain unwed.

Amelia saw Gerard waiting for her the next morning as she went down to the hall. He was wearing a long coat with several capes, a warm muffler bound about his throat and a fur hat in the Russian style. He smiled his approval as he saw that she too was wearing a thick cloak and muffler, her gloved hands tucked inside a fur muff that hung suspended from a chain about her neck.

'I see you are prepared for the weather, Amelia. There is a fine frost this morning.'

'As there should be for Christmas Eve,' she replied. 'I think it will be just right for a brisk walk about the gardens, sir.'

'My daughter would not agree with you.' Gerard looked rueful. 'I believe I was wrong to leave her so long in France. She finds our English weather cold and damp and asks constantly when do we return to Paris.'

'Do you think of leaving England permanently?' Amelia asked, doing her best to conceal her feeling of acute disappointment.

'I considered it for a while,' Gerard confessed. 'However, I have decided that I should prefer to live in England where I have friends rather than mere acquaintances. Lisa must come to terms with the situation. I believe she will be happier once the summer comes.'

'I think you may have been in the habit of giving her her own way?' Amelia tipped her head to one side, her eyebrows slightly raised.

'Yes, I have spoiled her,' Gerard admitted and laughed. 'She is a little charmer and I fear that I may have given in too often to her whims—which may be why she is giving poor Nanny such a difficult time. I hear complaints that she is sometimes sulky and unresponsive, though with me she is very different.'

Amelia was thoughtful. 'Is the nanny well recommended?'

'Her references were good. She came from a family with whom she had served for more than six years.

However, I have wondered if she is a little too strict with the child. I may have been too lenient, but I would not have Lisa's life made a misery. It is not easy for a man alone…' Gerard glanced at Amelia, a rueful look in his eyes. 'I feel in need of a lady's advice. Some ladies take little interest in their children. They feel their duty is done once the heir is produced, but you make it your business to care for unfortunate children. You might be able to tell me what to do for the best as far as my daughter is concerned.'

Amelia kept her smile in place despite her disappointment. It was as she had feared—he wanted only to discuss his daughter. 'I would need to see Lisa and her nanny together. It would be best if it happened casually. If Nanny knows she is being observed, I should learn nothing.'

'You understand at once, as I knew you would,' Gerard said, looking pleased. 'I brought Lisa to Pendleton with me, though I did not allow her to come down to dinner last evening for she is not ready yet. However, she will be present at the children's party this afternoon. Susannah has lots of small presents and prizes for the young ones. I shall be there. Perhaps…if it is not too much trouble?' He arched his brows at her.

'I had intended to be there anyway. I enjoy these things and Susannah will need a little help to organise the games and present giving. It will be no trouble to observe your daughter and her nanny.'

'How generous you are…' He paused as Amelia gave an impatient shake of her head. 'It will be good to have a lady's opinion in this matter. I have no female relations that I may call upon.'

'Does your late wife not have a family?'

'I have no idea. I met Lisette after a bloody battle between the French and the Spanish troops. She had been ill used and I took pity on her. I married her to protect her and to give her unborn child my name. She never spoke of her family. I imagine they were killed during the conflict…' Gerard was looking straight ahead, a nerve flicking at his temple. 'I knew nothing about her, except that she was French and clearly of gentle birth.'

'You love the child very much, do you not?'

'I fell in love with her when she was born. I was present and helped bring her into the world for there were few doctors available to us—and so she became mine.' Gerard glanced towards her. 'After I left England, I was a disappointed man, Amelia. At one time I had nothing to live for. Indeed, I might have welcomed death on the battlefield. I married Lisette because it seemed the best way to protect her and I had abandoned all hope of happiness…but when her child was born I loved the child from the first moment of seeing her.'

'Yes, you mentioned something of this once before.' Amelia looked thoughtful. 'You said that your wife was ill for a long time after the child's birth?'

'She took no interest in the babe at all. I was able to secure the services of a wet-nurse. Often I cared for the child myself, changing her and feeding her as she began to take solid foods. Lisette had no interest in anything for a long time. When she recovered a little…' He shook his head, as she would have questioned him. 'After she died, I engaged the services of a nurse, and when the war was over I made the decision to keep Lisa in France with me. At that time I was not sure what to do for the best.'

'You thought you might live there because your child's mother was French?'

'I must confess that for a while I considered leaving the child in France with a nurse,' he admitted. 'I was a soldier, a single man—and my estate was in some trouble. I have rectified that now, though I am not as rich as Pendleton or Coleridge.' He gave Amelia a rueful look. 'When we first met I had hardly any fortune at all. I dare say that was the reason Sir Michael did not consider me a worthy husband for his sister.'

'He had no right to send you away.' Amelia hesitated, then lifted her gaze to meet his because she needed to ask. 'Why did you not send me word of what happened? Surely you knew that I would have gone with you had you asked? I would not have allowed Michael to prevent our marriage if I had known. I suspected that he had had a hand in it, but when you told me what he did to you—' She broke off and sighed. 'It was a wicked thing that Michael did to you—to us...'

'I ought to have known you would elope with me, despite what your brother said when he had me beaten,' Gerard admitted. 'I suppose I was humiliated and angry—even bitter. I was not certain that you loved me enough to defy him. At that time I did not expect to be my uncle's heir. He had a son who should have inherited. Had my cousin not died of a putrid chill, I must have made my living as a soldier. Perhaps your brother had some right on his side, Amelia.'

'No, he did not,' she contradicted at once. 'Your lack of fortune meant nothing to me, Gerard.'

'I am no longer a pauper. I have worked hard and my business ventures prosper. However, your own fortune surpasses mine these days. I well remember that you had nothing when I asked you to be my wife.'

'I did not expect that to change. It was a surprise when my great-aunt asked me to live with her—and when she left everything to me. She had told me that I would have something when she died, but I had no idea that she was so wealthy.'

'It was a stroke of luck for you, I suppose.'

'Yes…though it has its drawbacks. My brother and sister-in-law are resentful of the fact that I inherited a fortune they believe should have gone to them. Michael has been unpleasant to me on more than one occasion since my aunt died.'

'They had no right to expect it. Lady Agatha might have left her money anywhere.'

'Indeed, she might,' Amelia said. 'I believe her deceased husband also had relatives who might have hoped for something—but they at least have not approached me on the matter.'

'And your brother has?' His brows arched, eyes narrowed and intent.

'Several times,' Amelia said. 'It has been the subject of endless arguments between us. Michael thinks I should make most of the money over to him. I have no intention of doing what he demands, but it has made for bad blood between us.' She hesitated, then, 'I have not spoken of this to anyone but Emily—but his last visit was almost threatening. I was a little disturbed by it, I admit.'

'Sir Michael is of a violent temperament…'

Amelia was silent for a moment, then, 'You are thinking it might have been he who tried to have me abducted at Pendleton the summer before last? I believe you thought it then?'

'It is possible, but I may have been mistaken. My own encounter with him may have coloured my thinking. If it was him, why has he not carried the threat further? Why stop at one attempt?'

'I do not know. For a long time I thought that there might be another attempt, but nothing happened.'

'It is puzzling. The likely explanation seems that it was actually Susannah who was the intended victim and you were mistaken for her. As you know, there was some awkwardness between the Marquis of Northaven and Harry Pendleton at that time.'

'That is one possibility, and yet I cannot think that we are alike. Emily is convinced that my brother means me harm. She overheard something he said to me some months ago and she suggested that he would benefit if I died.'

'Would he?'

'At the moment he is the largest, though not the only, beneficiary.'

Gerard nodded. 'It might be wise to change that and let it be known that you have done so, Amelia.'

Amelia's expression was thoughtful. 'I cannot think that Michael would wish to see me dead—even for a fortune. My brother is bad tempered and arrogant, but I would not have thought him a murderer.'

'It would not hurt to take some precautions. I could arrange for you to be watched over—as I did once before. And changes to your will might help if you would consider making them.'

'Yes, I may do so after the New Year. We are to attend Helene and Max's ball at Coleridge. Shall you be there?'

'Yes, I believe so,' Gerard said. 'As you know, both Harry and Max are particular friends of mine.'

'And their wives are good friends of mine,' Amelia said. 'I should be grateful if you could arrange some kind of protection, for Emily as well as me. I have no idea how it may be done and it may not truly be necessary. I shall, of course, pay the men myself.'

'As you wish,' Gerard said. 'The breeze is very cold. I think we may have some snow. Should we return to the house before we freeze to death?'

'Yes, perhaps we should,' Amelia replied.

She had the oddest feeling that he had been on the verge of saying something very different, but at the last he had changed his mind. Nothing more of note was said between them, and they parted after returning to the house. She pondered on what might have been in Gerard's mind as she went in search of her hostess.

It was good of him to say that he would find suitable men to protect her if he thought her in danger from her brother's spite. If, of course, it was her brother she needed protecting from…but who else could it be?

'What made you think I would be interested in such an outrageous proposition?' The Marquis of Northaven looked at the person sitting opposite him in the private parlour of the posting inn to which he had been summoned that evening. He had considered ignoring the note sent to his lodgings in town, but curiosity and a certain intuition had brought him here. However, to the best of his knowledge he had never met the gentleman before. 'Kidnapping is a hanging offence...'

'I had heard that you have a score to settle with a certain gentleman.'

'Where did you hear that?' Northaven was alert, suspicious. The other man's features were barely visible in the shadows, his face half-covered by the muffler he wore to keep out the cold.

'One hears these things...of course there would be money once the ransom was paid.'

'Money...' Northaven's mouth curved in a sneer, a flash of hauteur in his manner. 'I have not yet run through the inheritance my uncle left me.'

'Then forget I asked you. I had thought you might care to see Ravenshead brought down, but if you do not have the stomach for it there are others willing, nay, eager to do my bidding.'

'How would this bring Ravenshead down?' Northaven asked, eyes narrowed, menacing.

'He imagines he will marry Amelia Royston. I do not wish to see that happen. Once I have finished with her, she will marry no one!'

The Marquis of Northaven shivered, feeling icy cold. He had done much in his life that he was not proud of, but something in the tone of the person who was asking him to arrange Amelia Royston's downfall was disturbing. Northaven had seduced more than one young woman, but contrary to what was said and thought of him, he had taken none against their will. Indeed, they usually threw themselves into his arms—

and why should he say no? Handsome beyond what many thought decent, he had an air of unavailability that made him irresistible to many ladies. He was by no means a white knight, but neither was he the traitor some thought him. He might cheat at cards when desperate; he might lie if it suited him and would not deny that he had sailed close to the edge a few times, but a cold-blooded murderer he was not.

Northaven had been angry with the men who had once been his friends. He had hated the holy trilogy, as he was wont to call Harry Pendleton, Max Coleridge and Gerard Ravenshead. He hated them because they despised him, believed him worse than he truly was, but with the turn in his fortunes of late much of his resentment had cooled. He would have dismissed the proposition being made to him out of hand, but he was curious to hear more.

'Supposing I were interested in bringing down Ravenshead,' he said. 'What would you be willing to pay—and what do you plan for Miss Royston?'

'I was thinking of ten thousand guineas. Her fate is not your affair. All you need to do is to deliver her to me.'

The words were delivered with such malice that Northaven's stomach turned. He imagined that Miss Royston's fate might be worse than death and it sickened him. He was well aware that Amelia Royston had once thought him guilty of the callous seduction and desertion of her friend; he had allowed her to believe it, but it was not true. A few months previously he might have left her to her fate. He had then been a bitter, angry man, but something had happened to him the day he watched a young girl marry the man she loved—the man she had risked everything to save when she thought he was about to die.

No woman had ever loved Northaven enough to take a ball in the shoulder for him. Susannah Hampton had been reckless and could easily have died had his aim been slightly to the left. The moment his ball had struck her shoulder, Northaven had felt remorse. He had been relieved when Susannah made a full recovery. Something drove him to mingle with the crowd on her wedding day. When her eyes met his as she left the church on her husband's arm, they had seemed to ask a question. He had answered it with a nod of his head and he believed she understood. His feud with her husband was over.

He had not fallen in love with her. Yet she had touched him in a way he had never expected. He had suddenly realised where he was headed if he continued on his reckless path: he would end a lonely, bitter man. For a while the resentment against his one-time friends had continued to burn inside him, but of late he had felt more at peace with himself.

Perhaps at last he had found the way to redeem himself.

'Let me think about it,' he said. 'Ten thousand guineas is a fair sum—and I have no love for Ravenshead. Give me a few days and I shall decide.'

'Meet me here again in two days and I will tell you more. We can do nothing over Christmas. Miss Royston goes to Coleridge in the New Year—and that will be our chance...'

Chapter Two

Gerard cursed himself for a fool as he parted from Amelia. He had let yet another chance slip, but after discussing his daughter and her brother the time had not seemed right. If he had asked Amelia to marry him in the same breath as telling her that she ought to think of changing her will, she might have thought he was asking her for reasons of convenience to himself. He had made his circumstances clear so that when he did speak there would be no misunderstanding. He was not in need of a rich wife, though Amelia was extremely wealthy. Her fortune was yet another reason why he hesitated—but the burning problem besetting him was whether her opinion of him would suffer when he told her the truth of Lisette's death.

To conceal the details from her would not be honest. If they were to come out at some time in the future, she might feel that he had deceived her and there would be a loss of trust. All in all, Gerard considered that he had done what he could to prepare the ground for a future proposal. He felt they were good friends, but he could not be sure that anything of their former love was left on Amelia's part, though every time he saw her he was more convinced that she was the only woman for him. She was beautiful, charming and the scent of her always seemed to linger, making him aware of a deep hunger within. He wanted her more than he had ever wanted anything in his life. Without her...

'My lord...' The footman's voice broke through Gerard's reverie. He turned as the man approached him. 'This was delivered for you early this morning, sir.'

'For me?' Gerard stared at the parcel wrapped in strong brown paper and tied with string. 'Was there a card? Do you know who delivered it?'

'It was a gentleman's man, sir. I do not know his name, but he said his gentleman had bid him deliver this to you here.'

'I see...thank you.' Gerard frowned as he took the parcel. He had left gifts at the homes of some friends in London; however, he had told no one but Toby Sinclair that he was coming here for Christmas. The gift might have come from one of the other guests, but it was more normal to exchange them after dinner on Christmas Eve. He shook the parcel gently and discovered that it rattled. Intrigued, he took it into a small parlour to the right of the hall and untied the strings, folding back the paper.

There was no card, but inside the paper was a wooden box. He lifted the lid and stared at the contents. At first he thought that the doll must be a present for

Lisa. However, the head was lying at an odd angle, and, as he lifted it out, he saw that the porcelain head had been wrenched from the stuffed body. It was broken across the face and the body had been slit down the middle with a knife or something similar.

Gerard felt cold all over. There was something disturbing about the wanton destruction to what had been a pretty fashion doll, the kind that was often used to show off the wares of expensive couturiers rather than a child's toy.

It could hardly have been broken accidentally. No, this had been done deliberately. He could not imagine who had sent such a thing to him or why. However, he felt that the broken doll was a symbol of something—a threat. The implication was sinister for it must be a warning, though he could not think what he was being warned about or why it had been sent to him at such a time.

Gerard realised that he must have an enemy. His first thought was that he had only one enemy of any note that he knew of and that was the Marquis of Northaven. Northaven had been bitter because Gerard, along with Harry and Max, had ostracised him after that débâcle in Spain, blaming him for the fact that the French troop had been expecting an attack. Northaven had engineered a duel with Harry, which had almost ended in tragedy, but since then none of them had heard much from him. It was as if he had dropped out of sight.

Somehow, it seemed unlikely that the doll had come from Northaven. The man had always denied betraying his friends to the Spanish; he had been prepared to fight any of them in a duel to clear his name—but this doll was something very different. It was meant to disturb, to sow confusion and anxiety—though its message was obscure. Was the sender threatening his daughter?

Gerard felt sick inside as he pictured his daughter being mutilated as the doll had been. Surely the sender could not be threatening Lisa? She was an innocent child who had harmed no one. Besides, what had he done that would cause anyone to hate him to this extent?

'Gerard...' Harry entered the room behind him. 'I thought I saw you come in here.'

'Yes. I wanted to open this...' Gerard held the box out to him. 'One of your footmen gave it to me a moment ago. Apparently, it was delivered earlier this morning.'

Harry looked at the doll, his eyes narrowing as he saw what had been done to it. 'Good grief! What on earth is that about?'

'I have no idea. I wish I did.'

'A threat, do you think?' Harry's mouth was a grim white line. 'To your daughter—or a warning?'

'Perhaps both...'

'There was no message?'

'None that I could find.'

Harry picked up the box and looked inside. Then he saw a small card lying in the discarded paper and string and held it out to Gerard.

'If you value her, stay away from her. This is your one and only warning and sent in good faith. Ignore it and the one you love may end like this.' Gerard frowned as he read the words aloud. 'What can that mean—how can I stay away from my own daughter?'

'Are you sure the doll is meant to represent your daughter?' Harry asked. 'Only a few of us even know she exists, Gerard. Perhaps the person who sent this does not know you have a child.'

Gerard stared at him and then nodded. 'You are right. Only a handful of my friends know about Lisa. So if the doll isn't her...' His gaze narrowed. 'You don't think—Amelia...?'

'It makes more sense,' Harry said. 'Whoever sent this used a fashion doll, not a child's toy. Amelia is an extremely elegant woman and it is more likely that the doll represents her. We suspect an attempt to kidnap her was made that summer at Pendleton. Max had an idea that the reason no further attempts were made to kidnap her was because you were no longer around.'

'Yes, he mentioned something of the kind some months ago, but I did not think it possible. Good grief!' Gerard was horrified. 'You think they tried to abduct Amelia because they thought I might be about to ask her to marry me—and then I returned to France. Nothing happened while I was away, but now I am back...'

'And you receive this warning.' Harry looked concerned. 'If that is the case, Amelia could be in grave danger.'

Gerard frowned. 'She told me this morning that Miss Barton had asked her if her brother would benefit from her death. Apparently, he has been demanding that she hand over most of the fortune her great-aunt left her.'

'Is Royston such a brute?' Harry pondered the question. 'I do not know him well, but I would not have thought it. He might bully her into giving him money, but murder?'

'Northaven?'

'I am not sure that the murder of a woman is his style. He would be more likely to force a duel on you if he wished to pursue a quarrel.'

'My thoughts entirely. It must be Royston—I can think of no one else who would be affected if she were to marry me.'

'You cannot think of anyone who has cause to hate you?'

'None that I know of,' Gerard replied, but looked thoughtful. 'Everyone makes enemies, but I cannot think of anyone who would wish to harm me or mine. Royston does not like me. He had me beaten when I asked for Amelia's hand as a young man—but surely he has not harboured a grudge all this time? Besides, why harm his sister? If his quarrel is with me, why not have me shot? There are assassins enough to put a ball between my shoulders on a dark street.'

'Royston had you beaten when you asked for Amelia?' Harry's brows shot up as Gerard nodded. 'The scar at your temple! I knew something had happened but you never spoke of it… You have never sought retribution?'

'How could I? Whatever happened, Royston is Amelia's brother. I love her, Harry. I would do nothing to harm her. He has no reason to hate me that I know of—I swear it.'

'Then this threat must have been made in order to gain control of her fortune,' Harry said grimly. 'If you marry her, he loses all chance of inheriting if she dies.'

'Good grief! If I ask her to marry me, I could be signing her death warrant.'

'And if you do not, she remains vulnerable,' Harry pointed out. 'You cannot allow this threat to alter your plans.'

'I am damned whichever way I go!' Gerard cursed. 'I must arrange protection for her. She must be watched around the clock.'

'And for yourself,' Harry warned. 'Do not shake your head, Gerard. You need someone to watch your back, my friend. I am not certain that we have reached the heart of this business. You need to investigate this affair immediately. I shall question my servants. Perhaps one of them may know something of the man who delivered that thing.'

Gerard had replaced the broken doll and closed the box. 'The footman knew nothing, but someone else may have seen the messenger who delivered this thing. Any clue would be welcome, for at the moment I have little to go on.'

'You know you may call on me for assistance?'

'Yes, of course. Please say nothing of this to your wife or Amelia for the moment. I do not wish to throw a cloud over the celebrations this Christmas. Besides, I believe Amelia must be safe enough here for we are aware of the danger…' He frowned. 'Does it not strike you as odd that I was warned? If the rogue wants Amelia dead—why warn me of the possibility?'

'Perhaps he simply wants to prevent you speaking to her?'

'Perhaps…' Gerard looked thoughtful. 'Or someone else sent it to alert me to danger. Something puzzles me, Harry. I think there is more to this than we yet know, but I confess I have no idea what it may be.'

* * *

Amelia was thoughtful as she went upstairs to change. Speaking to Gerard confidentially had made her think about her situation. It was hard to think that her brother could mean her harm, but she could not deny that he had several times spoken to her in a manner that might be thought threatening.

Perhaps it would be sensible to take some precautions, though she would hate to think her life might be in danger. Of course, if she were married, her brother would have no hope of her fortune—which might be why he had several times made it plain that he would never agree to her marrying Gerard. She was her own mistress, of course. Michael must know that he could not stop her marrying whomsoever she wished.

Amelia looked out of her bedchamber and watched her companion walking towards the house. Emily Barton's head was down and her manner one of thoughtfulness. She was quite alone.

Emily had a gentle beauty with her dark honey-blonde hair and blue eyes that were startling in a pale face. However, because of her modest manner and way of dressing, she was often thought unremarkable until she smiled, when she could look stunning. Amelia frowned, because of late Emily had seemed quieter than usual. She was clearly brooding.

Amelia suspected she knew what was troubling her. Emily had been scrupulous in confessing her shame when she applied for the position as Amelia's companion.

'I must tell you that I have a secret, Miss Royston.' Emily had looked at her steadily. 'Only my parents and a few servants knew, for my father did his best to hide my shame.'

'Your shame—are you telling me that you have borne a child out of wedlock?' Amelia had sensed it instinctively.

'I…was forced,' Emily told her, cheeks pale, eyes dark with remembered horror. 'He was not my lover— but he held me down as he raped me, and, later, I knew that I would bear his child.'

'My dear,' Amelia cried. 'It is shocking that men can be so vile. Please tell me what happened then.'

'My father never believed that it was not my fault, but I swear to you that I am innocent of duplicity in this.' Emily's eyes brimmed with tears, though she did not weep. 'If this makes me unacceptable as your companion…'

'No, do not think it.' Amelia smiled at her. 'What you have told me makes me more determined to give you a home. You will live with me, meet my friends and learn to be happy again, my dear.'

'You are so very kind…'

'I know what it is to have a broken heart, Emily.' She shook her head as the young woman raised her brows. 'Put your shame behind you, my dear. I absolve you of blame.'

If only Emily had been able to put her shame and unhappiness behind her! Amelia knew that she still had days when she was deeply unhappy.

She must do something to help her companion. For some time now Amelia had been considering the idea of trying to find Emily's child. The babe had been taken from her at birth and she did not even know where her daughter was. If she could be told that the little girl was well and healthy, living happily with her foster parents, perhaps this deep ache inside her might ease.

Amelia had hesitated because she did not wish to cause her companion more pain, but to see Emily unhappy even when she was in company was hard to bear.

Instead of brooding on her own problems, she would think about Emily. Surely there must be a way of finding the child?

Having changed into a fresh gown, Amelia prepared to go down and join Emily. She would say nothing to her for the moment, but after Christmas she would see what could be done.

Alone in his bedchamber, Gerard paced the floor. It seemed he was caught between a rock and a hard place—if he spoke to Amelia and she accepted his offer of marriage, it might place her in danger. Yet if her brother did plan her death in order to inherit her fortune, she needed protection. If she married, she would no longer be at the mercy of her grasping relatives.

He was aware of a burning need to protect her. Amelia was his, the love of his life. He could not give her up because of an obscure threat. He would make every effort to keep her safe. It would probably be best to let her know he believed she might be in some danger, but he was sure that she was safe enough for the moment. Harry would alert his servants to be on the lookout for strangers, and by the time she was ready to leave Pendleton he would have measures in place for her protection. He would summon the men he had used once before.

He could at least do this for the woman he loved, though he was still undecided whether to speak to her of marriage. Did he have the right? Amelia was still beautiful, a woman of fortune and charm and she must be much sought after. He had heard whispers, her name linked with various gentlemen, but nothing seemed to come of the rumours. Gerard had no idea whether she had received offers. If she had, she had turned them down—why? Was she suspicious of the motives behind every proposal that came her way? Did she imagine that no one could love her for herself? Surely not! And yet if her brother had been browbeating her because of her fortune, it would not be surprising if she thought others interested only in her wealth.

Gerard decided that he would tell no one else of his suspicions until Christmas was over, because he wanted it to be a happy time for Amelia and his daughter. He certainly did not wish to cast a shadow over the festivities for Susannah and her guests.

'Susannah asked me to help with the younger children,' Emily said to Amelia as they went downstairs together that afternoon. 'She thinks that they will need help to unwrap their presents and Nanny has been given time off.'

Amelia saw the happy smile on her face. Emily loved children and the knowledge that her own daughter was living with another family must be torture for her. She wondered if Emily had ever tried to discover the whereabouts of her child, but supposed it was unlikely. She had devoted her life to her ailing mother until that lady died and had then been forced to look for work. Perhaps Amelia might mention the possibility to Emily another day, but now was not the time.

'I think Susannah is very brave to have the children's party without her nanny, for I am certain that some of the ladies have no idea of looking after their own children.'

'I think it will be great fun. I always wished that I had brothers and sisters, and envied those who did.' The wistful expression had come back to Emily's face.

Amelia saw it and made up her mind that she would ask someone to make enquiries concerning the lost child for her. However, it would be better to say nothing to Emily for the moment in case the child could not be found.

'I am certain that we shall enjoy ourselves this afternoon,' Amelia said. 'I am eager to meet Gerard's daughter. She has been brought up in France until the past few months, and I dare say she may not understand English as well as she needs to if she is to communicate with the other children. I know that Gerard's nanny will be present, so we shall have help.'

The two ladies smiled at each other as they approached the large salon where the celebrations for the younger guests were taking place. Entering, they saw that the room had been decorated with silver and gold stars; there was also a crib with wooden animals and a doll representing the Baby Jesus and two of the servants were dressed as Joseph and Mary. Some of the other servants were dressed as the three kings, and they had big sacks of gifts. These would be distributed to the children at the end of the entertainment.

All kinds of delicious foods that might appeal to children had been set out on a table: sweet jellies, bottled fruits, cakes and tiny biscuits, also fingers of bread and butter with the crusts cut off and spread with honey.

'Amelia…Miss Barton.' Gerard approached them with a smile. 'May I have the pleasure of introducing my daughter, Lisa, to you? Lisa—this is Miss Amelia Royston—and Miss Emily Barton. Greet them nicely, my love.'

'*Bonjour*, Mademoiselle Royston, *bonjour*, Mademoiselle Barton,' Lisa said and dipped a curtsy. 'I am pleased to meet you.' She tipped her head and looked at Gerard. 'Was that correct, Papa?'

Her manner was that of a little coquette. She was pretty, an enchanting little doll dressed in satin and frills, her dark eyes bright and mischievous; ringlets the colour of hazelnuts covered her head and were tied with a pink ribbon. Amelia adored her at once, completely understanding why Gerard had fallen in love with his daughter. For although Lisa did not carry his blood, she was undoubtedly his in every other way and the affection between them was a joy to see.

'It was charming, Mademoiselle Ravenshead.' Amelia smiled at her and held out her hand. 'Your English is very good. I see that you have been attending your lessons. Shall we go and see what Lady Pendleton has given us for tea?'

'Papa always speaks to me in English.' Lisa hesitated, then placed her tiny hand in Amelia's. She looked at her in a confiding manner. 'I am hungry, but Nanny said that I was not to eat anything. She says that the food is not suitable for me.'

'Oh, I think it would be a shame if you were not to have any of it,' Amelia replied. 'Perhaps not too much chocolate cake, but I think a small piece and some bread and honey could not hurt anyone.'

'We always had honey for tea in France,' Lisa told her with a happy smile. 'Nanny says a boiled egg is better, but I like honey for tea.'

'Well, do you know, so do I. Shall we have some?'

'Yes, please. Can I have a piece of cake? Nanny doesn't allow me cake.' Lisa looked sorrowful and then a smile peeped out. 'I have cake sometimes with Papa.'

'I think Christmas is an exception, don't you? Besides, Lady Pendleton would be very upset if all this lovely food went to waste—do you not think so?'

'Yes, I should think so,' Lisa said, giving her a naughty look. 'Could I have some of that red jelly, please?'

'I think perhaps that would be acceptable,' Amelia said. 'We shall have bread and honey and a jelly each— and then a piece of cake. How does that sound?'

'I beg your pardon, Miss Royston, but I do not allow my charge to eat such rich food as a rule.'

Amelia turned her head to look at the woman who had spoken. The child's nanny was a severe-looking woman with iron-grey hair and a thin mouth. She was perhaps fifty years of age and had doubtless ruled more than one nursery with a rod of iron. Amelia took an instant dislike to her, but hid it behind a polite smile.

'I believe we should relax the rules a little, Nanny,' she said pleasantly. 'This is Christmas, after all, and the earl asked me especially to make sure that his daughter enjoys herself. Lisa will not eat too much.'

'It is just that I do not wish her to be sick all night, ma'am.'

'I do not think it likely,' Amelia said. 'Please do what you can to help with the other children, Nanny. Lisa will be quite safe with me.'

The woman nodded and moved away. From the set of her shoulders, Amelia guessed that she was angry. She hoped that her refusal to accept Nanny's authority would not lead to some form of punishment for Lisa later.

'Do you like to play games?' she asked Lisa, making up her mind that she would speak to Gerard on the subject of his daughter's nanny later.

'I do not know, mademoiselle. I have never played any—except that Papa takes me up on his horse with him sometime. We run and chase each other in the garden when Nanny cannot see us. Is that a game?'

'Yes, one kind of a game but there are many others. Do you not have puzzles or a hoop to play with?'

'Papa gave me things when we came to England, but Nanny says I should study my books. She says playing with toys is a waste of time.'

'Does she indeed?' Amelia kept her voice light and without criticism. 'Lady Pendleton has several games for us to play today—musical chairs and pass the parcel, and I have seen some spilikins. I think that you and I might play these games together. It is Christmas, after all—and there are prizes to be won.'

Amelia smiled as she saw the little girl's face light up. Gerard was right to be concerned about his daughter's nanny. Lisa was clearly a high-spirited child and needed discipline, but not to the extent that she was forbidden time to play or the food that she enjoyed.

Two hours later, Amelia had fallen totally in love with her new friend. Lisa had blossomed, becoming a natural, happy little girl, as they joined in noisy games of pass the parcel and musical chairs. Susannah had been in charge of the music and saw to it that every child managed to win a small gift, which was most often sweetmeats or a trinket of some kind. Lisa won a little silver cross on a pink ribbon, and as a gift she was given a doll with a porcelain head and a stuffed body. It was wearing a pink satin dress that matched hers and, when the party ended, she ran to show it to her father.

'Beautiful,' he said and kissed her, gazing at Amelia over the child's head. 'Has this scamp of mine been good, Amelia?'

'Oh, I think so,' Amelia said. 'We have enjoyed ourselves, have we not, Lisa?'

'Oui, merci, mademoiselle,' Lisa said and curtsied to her. 'Will you come and see me again, please? I would like you to be my friend.' There was something a little desperate in the child's look as she saw her nurse coming to claim her. 'Please…'

'Yes, certainly. I shall come in the morning,' Amelia said. 'I have a gift for you, Lisa—and I think we could go for a walk together in the park or even a ride in the carriage since it is cold. You, your papa and me—how would that be?'

'I should like it above all things, *mademoiselle*.' Lisa threw herself at Amelia and hugged her.

'Come along, Miss Ravenshead,' Nanny said. 'You are over-excited. You will never sleep and I shall be up all night with you.' The woman shot a look of dislike at Amelia.

Mindful that it would take time to replace her, Amelia made no reply. However, she turned urgently to Gerard as Nanny led the child away.

'I must speak to you privately. I have made certain observations and I think you should consider replacing that woman.'

'You do not like her either?' Gerard looked relieved. 'I am so glad that I asked you to take note, Amelia. She was recommended to me, but I have thought her too sour. I was not sure if I was being unfair—and I know that children need discipline...'

'Not to the extent that all the joy of life is squeezed out of them,' Amelia said as they walked from the room into a smaller parlour where they were alone. 'Lisa is high-spirited, but she is a delightful child and has good manners. I think Nanny is too strict with her. She is not allowed to play or to have honey for tea—and that I must tell you is a terrible deprivation.'

'And entirely unnecessary,' Gerard said and laughed. 'I knew I might rely on you, my very dear Amelia. I was afraid that my partiality for Lisa made me too lenient. I have a nursemaid. I shall put her in charge and dismiss Nanny. Oh, I will give her a year's wages and a reference, but she shall not have charge of my daughter again.'

'Oh dear, the poor woman. I feel terrible now for

she has lost her employment, and at Christmas—but I confess that I did not like her. I once employed a woman of that sort at the orphanage and had to dismiss her soon after, because she ill treated her charges. I do not understand why some people feel it is necessary to treat children as if they were criminals.'

'Some can be little monsters. I remember that I used to put frogs in the bed of my nanny.'

'Did you? I did that once and she went to my father. He sent me to bed and I was given nothing but bread and water for two days—and I had to apologise.'

'My father thrashed me. It did me the world of good, for as he said—think what a shock it was for the poor frog.'

'The frog…' Amelia went into a peal of delighted laughter. 'Oh, no! That is a great deal too bad of you, sir. You have a wicked sense of humour.'

'Yes, I have at times,' Gerard admitted. 'Though I have not laughed so very much of late. Amelia…may I tell you something?'

'Yes, of course.'

He led her towards a little sofa. 'Please sit down. This is not easy for me. I have wished to tell you something that almost no one else knows, but I fear it may give you a bad opinion of me.'

'Have you done something wicked?' she asked with a smile.

'I have not told you the whole truth about something.'

Amelia's smile faded. This was clearly serious. 'Please explain. I do not understand.'

'I told you that my wife died after a long illness?'

Amelia nodded. 'It was not quite the truth. She had been ill, but she had recovered in her physical health at least, though I know now that she must still have been suffering in her mind.'

'Gerard! Please explain. I do not understand.'

'Lisette seemed happy enough while she was carrying the child, but afterwards…she complained that I did not love her—that I thought more of the child…'

'Surely any father would love their child? Perhaps she was pulled down by the birth? I have heard that some women are deeply affected by childbirth.'

'Yes, it may have been that…' Gerard hesitated. Now was his chance to tell her the whole truth, but he was reluctant. 'I may have neglected her. I tried to be good to her, to give her my protection and all that she needed, but perhaps it was not enough for her. I am not the man I was when we first met, Amelia. I have become harder, I think, less caring of others.'

'Oh, Gerard! I cannot think that you deliberately mistreated your wife?'

He stroked the little scar at his temple. 'No, not deliberately, but I may have been careless perhaps. Lisette was vulnerable, easily hurt. I should have been kinder.' He paused, then, 'It may not be possible for me to love anyone completely. Something died in me the night your brother had me thrashed. At first I believed that you knew—that you felt insulted by my love. I suppose that I became afraid to show love, and Lisette suffered because of my lack.'

Gerard hesitated. He wanted to tell her that Lisette's death was his fault, to tell her of the night when Lisette had crept into his bed and offered herself to him—of the way he had turned from his wife, because she was not the woman he had loved so deeply. It would be right and fair to make Amelia aware of what he had done, but he could not bear to see her turn from him in disgust. He knew that Lisette had been terribly hurt—that it had driven her to a desperate act.

'What happened—how did she die?'

'One day when I was out she ordered a bath and then…' He paused, almost choking on the words. 'When I returned I found her. She had slashed her wrists and bled to death. I pulled her from the water and did what I could for her. She died in my arms…' His face twisted with pain. 'I did not mean to hurt her. She must have been desperately unhappy and I was not there for her. Something in me must be lacking. How could I not know that my own wife was so desperate that she would take her own life? I have blamed myself for her death ever since.'

He had told her the truth, leaving out only a few details that he felt unable to communicate.

'Gerard…' Amelia was on her feet. She held out her hands to him, her expression understanding and sympathetic. 'My dear—how terrible for you! It was a tragedy for a life was lost—but it was not your fault. Lisette could not have recovered completely from the birth. How could you have known she was unhappy if she did not tell you?'

'She may have been unwell, but I was not aware of it. I should have known.'

'You rescued her when she was alone. You married her, were kind to her so she turned to you, gave you her heart. If she felt unsure of your love, it may have made her desperately unhappy, but the blame is not all yours.'

'You see things so clearly...' Gerard moved closer, his eyes searching her face. 'So you do not hate me? You will not turn away in disgust? You understand that I am not as I once was?'

'I could never hate you. Surely you know...'

'I know that you are a wonderful, wise and lovely woman,' Gerard said passionately. 'I would be honoured if you would become my wife, Amelia. You were prepared to marry me all those years ago. Dare I hope that you still find the idea agreeable?'

'Gerard...' Amelia gasped. 'Yes...'

She meant to say more, but he lowered his head to kiss her on the lips. Amelia responded with all the love that was in her, her arms going about his neck as her body melded with his. This was what she had longed for, dreamed of so many lonely nights! She had never expected to be so fortunate.

'My beautiful Amelia,' Gerard said. 'I am a fool! You are such a sensible woman. You understand everything. You would not do something stupid because of a foolish quarrel. I should have asked long ago. You are exactly the woman I need in my life. You will not expect more than I am able to give.'

Amelia withdrew a little. She waited for him to say the words she needed to hear, but he did not speak of love and she was conscious of a slight disappointment.

She looked at him uncertainly. 'I had thought you meant to ask me before, but then you seemed to withdraw and I was not sure you cared for me.'

'I have always admired and cared for you,' Gerard

replied. 'We should have married years ago had your brother not had me beaten for having the temerity to approach you.' He paused, then, 'I fear Sir Michael will not take the news kindly, Amelia.'

'Michael may be pleased for me or stay away from my home. I am not obliged to him and he may not deny me this time. However, *you* should take care, for I know he can be a spiteful man, Gerard.'

'I shall take care for myself and for you. I do not forget that someone made an attempt to abduct you, Amelia. It will be my first duty to protect you, my dearest.'

'Thank you. I feel it unlikely that Michael would do more than vent his displeasure on me verbally—but it is always best to be careful.' She looked at him, her doubt writ plain on her face. 'Do you wish to announce our engagement at once?'

'That is entirely up to you, Amelia. If you wish for more time to consider...'

'No, I think not,' Amelia told him. 'I have given you my answer and I shall not change my mind.'

'Then you have made me the happiest man alive,' Gerard said. 'I have a Christmas gift for you, Amelia—but it is not a ring. I was afraid to tempt fate. However, I did commission a ring. I shall send to my jeweller and have it delivered at Coleridge.'

'Perhaps we should announce our engagement at the ball there,' Amelia suggested. 'We shall consider ourselves pledged, Gerard—but tell only our best friends until the ball.'

'As usual you have solved the thing,' he said and leaned forwards to kiss her softly on the lips. 'I look forward to our wedding, Amelia. You are a good friend and you will be a wonderful wife. Lisa already adores you and this is the best thing I can do for her. You will have the comfort and security of marriage and I shall have a beautiful gracious wife…we shall all get on famously.'

Amelia allowed him to kiss her, but she did not cling to him as she had the first time. At the back of her mind a tiny doubt had formed. She did not want to think it, but she was afraid that Gerard had proposed to her because he needed a suitable wife and a mother for his delightful daughter! Much as she knew she would love Lisa, she could not help thinking that if things had been different she might have been the child's mother. She would be a good mother to Lisa, but her heart ached when she thought of what might have been.

Did Gerard imagine that she had remained single because she had not received another offer? Amelia frowned as she went up to change for the evening. She might have been married soon after Gerard disappeared, but she had refused every man her brother brought for her to meet. Michael had tried to push her into marrying a marquis, but she had not allowed him to bully her.

Since she came into her fortune, she had received six offers of marriage. Not one of the gentlemen had made her feel that she wished to be married, even though she believed that at least one had been in love with her. Despite the hurt Gerard's apparent desertion had inflicted, she had never ceased to love him. No other man could ever replace him in her heart.

Amelia's feelings now were mixed. Gerard had proposed and she had accepted, but the doubts had begun to creep in. Was he truly in love with her—or did he simply wish for a convenient arrangement? He needed a mother for Lisa, and he wanted a wife who would not make too many demands.

She tried to remember his exact words, but had only a vague memory for his proposal had swept all else from her mind. She thought he had told her that he cared for his wife, but he could never love with all his heart, because something had died in him the night Michael sent him away. Lisette had wanted more and because of that she had become desperately unhappy. Amelia imagined that she had still been low after the birth of her child, for more than one young one woman had been known to suffer a deep melancholy after giving birth.

Amelia frowned. Gerard's words as he proposed seemed to indicate that he was looking for a comfortable marriage that would not make too many demands on his emotions. Was he saying that *she* must not expect too much—that he simply needed a complaisant woman to care for his child and his home?

Did he care for her at all?

What nonsense was this? She was such a fool! Amelia's thoughts were confused as she changed for dinner that evening. For years she had regretted the love she had lost. She had felt the years slipping away, her youth lost. There were times when she believed she would die an old maid, unfulfilled and unloved.

Recently, after meeting Gerard again, she had begun to long for him to speak. Now he had proposed and she had accepted, and yet she was beset by doubts. A tiny voice in her head was telling her she should not hope for a love match. Gerard was older and he had undoubtedly changed from the young man who had declared his love so passionately. He had spoken of caring for Amelia and of looking forward to her becoming his wife—not the words of a man desperately in love. Not the passionate declaration she had hoped to hear!

Gerard *had* asked her to marry him because it was a convenient arrangement. He wanted a wife—a mother for his beautiful daughter. Had he not asked her to give him her opinion of Lisa's nanny? She had done so and her thoughts coincided with his, which had made him feel she would make an ideal wife and mother. In her first rush of delight that he had spoken, Amelia had imagined that he was proposing because he loved her as she loved him. However, she was certain that he respected and liked her—and was that not a perfectly sound basis for marriage?

She took a turn about the room, her thoughts tumbling in confusion as she came to terms with her situation. Was a marriage of convenience acceptable? Could she be happy as Gerard's wife, knowing that he cared for her but was not in love with her?

Of course she could! Amelia scolded herself for the feeling of disappointment she had been experiencing since leaving Gerard. She was no longer a green girl. She ought not to expect romance at her age. Her heart told her that Gerard was the only man she would ever love. If she behaved foolishly and changed her mind, because his proposal was not the declaration of love she desired, she would be cutting off her nose to spite her face—and that would be ridiculous.

Amelia was faced with the choice of remaining unwed for the rest of her life or marrying the man she loved, understanding that he did not feel romantic love for her. Had she been that young girl of so many years ago, she would have demanded an equal partnership where both partners loved, but the years had taught her some hard lessons and she was a woman of sense. The prospect of remaining single all her life was one she had faced, because there seemed no alternative. However, she now had a chance of some happiness. She would have a husband who cared for her in his own way and she would have a family; she was still young enough to give Gerard an heir. In her mind she saw pictures of their sons growing through childhood to manhood, hearing their laughter as an echo in her head and seeing their smiling faces. If she did not marry, she would never have a child of her own to love. She might not have the passionate love she had longed for, but she would have a family, children and companionship.

It was enough, she decided. She would make it enough, and perhaps Gerard would recapture some of the feeling he'd once had for her. His kiss had told her that he was not indifferent in a physical sense. He found her desirable. Perhaps in time true love would blossom once more.

A marriage where the feeling was stronger on one side than the other was not unusual. People married for many reasons, quite often for money or position. She acquitted Gerard of wanting her fortune—he had made it plain to her at an earlier time that he had enough for his needs. He wanted a companion, a sensible woman who would love his daughter and not make too many demands. Could she be that woman? Amelia decided that she could. She had had years of learning to hide her emotions; it should not be too difficult to give Gerard the kind of wife he desired. It would be a convenient arrangement for them both.

Amelia picked up her long evening gloves and pulled them on, smoothing the fingers in place. She glanced in the mirror and smiled at the picture she presented. She looked serene, untroubled. No one would ever guess at the ache in her heart.

She was about to open her door when someone knocked and Emily walked in. It was obvious that she was distressed and Amelia forgot her own problems instantly.

'Something is wrong! I can see it in your face, Emily.'

'Mr Sinclair…I could not prevent him from speaking,' Emily said, her voice catching. 'I told him that I must have time to consider…and I think he was angry with me for his face went white. He inclined his head and walked away from me without another word. I should have called him back, but I could not speak.'

'Oh, my poor Emily,' Amelia said. 'Could you not find the words to tell him the truth?'

'I was afraid of what I might see in his eyes,' Emily confessed. 'We must somehow manage to speak to each other while we are both guests here…' She gave a little sob. 'I am in such distress for I would not hurt him for the world and I am sure he was hurt by my hesitation. Yet how could I tell him the truth?'

'Do not distress yourself, my love,' Amelia said. 'You have done nothing wrong. Many other ladies ask for time when first asked that question. When next it happens, you will be ready to make your confession.'

'Yes, I shall. I intend to seek Mr Sinclair out tomorrow evening after the celebrations. One of us may leave the following day—I could go home if he did not wish to leave.'

'Do not be so pessimistic, Emily.' Amelia was encouraging. 'I still believe that Mr Sinclair will be more understanding than you imagine—and now, my love, you must wish me happy. The Earl of Ravenshead has asked me to be his wife and I have accepted him. We shall not announce our engagement until the ball at Coleridge, but I wanted you to know.'

'Amelia!' Emily's face reflected surprise and then pleasure. 'I am so very happy for you, dearest. I have thought that perhaps you liked him and he liked you, but I was not sure what your intentions were regarding marriage.'

'It will be…a convenient arrangement for us both, for my brother will have to accept that he is no longer my heir. Especially if I should have a child, which I hope will be the case.'

'A convenient arrangement?' Emily looked puzzled. 'It is not my business to pry, but are you sure that is all it is? I am sure the earl has a deep regard for you, Amelia.'

'Ah, yes, we are comfortable together—good friends,' Amelia said, avoiding Emily's probing gaze. She was doing her best to appear dispassionate, but Emily knew her too well. 'Shall we go down, my love? We do not wish to keep Susannah and her guests waiting.' She saw a doubtful look in her companion's eyes.

'You must not think that I would wish to dispense with your company, Emily. While I should be happy to see you marry a gentleman of your choice, I should be sad to lose you. Be assured that your home is with me until you decide to leave.'

'You are always so generous,' Emily replied. 'Thank you for making that plain to me. Like you, I have met only one man I would care to marry, but you know my thoughts and I shall say no more, for this is Christmas Eve.'

Amelia noticed how thoughtful her companion was as they went downstairs and joined the other guests. She smiled and nodded to the company, but was quiet and merely nodded her head when Toby offered her his arm to take her into dinner. Obviously, he had controlled his hurt feelings and was determined to remain Emily's friend. Amelia had always thought him a likeable young man and now found she approved of his manners—he was everything he ought to be as a gentleman.

Gerard took Amelia in to dinner. He told her in a whisper that he had confided their secret to Harry and Susannah, also to Toby Sinclair.

'For the moment I have asked that they keep the news to themselves,' he said. 'We shall make our announcement at Coleridge, as we planned.'

'I have told Emily, for it would have seemed secretive and unkind had I excluded her. She would have been worried that her position might not be secure had she heard something from another person.'

'I doubt that Miss Barton will need to work as a companion for long,' Gerard said. 'You must have observed that a certain gentleman has a distinct partiality for her company?'

'Yes, I know that Mr Sinclair has made Emily an offer, but she is a little nervous of her situation in life and asked for more time.'

Gerard raised his brows. 'She feels that she may not suit the ambitions of his family, because she is employed as a companion?'

'I believe she does feel something of the kind, but I hope the matter will be resolved satisfactorily.'

'Toby will inherit a decent estate when his father dies, but I am certain he will make his own fortune. Although he is close to his family, I do not think he would allow them to dictate to him in such a matter—and I see no reason why Emily should not be acceptable to them. Toby is of good family, but he is not the heir to an illustrious title, merely his father's baronetcy. I see no cause for anyone to object to his choice.'

Amelia nodded. She had wondered if she might ask for Gerard for help in trying to find Emily's child, but she had hoped to find a way of concealing the mother's identity. Even if that was impracticable, now was not the time or place to reveal it.

'Well, we must hope for a happy outcome,' she said. 'I was wondering when you thought would be a suitable moment for us to marry? Do you wish for some time to make your arrangements or would you prefer the wedding to be held quite soon?'

'Personally, I believe the sooner we marry the better for all concerned,' Gerard said. 'I know that my daughter would be happy to have a new mama—and I am certainly looking forward to our wedding. Do you wish for a longer engagement or shall we settle it for a month after the ball?'

'I think a month after the ball should be adequate time,' Amelia replied. 'It will give me a chance to make necessary changes. Will you wish to live at Ravenshead on a permanent basis?'

'Are you thinking that you would like to spend a part of the year at your estate, Amelia?'

'I like to spend some part of the summer in Bath and I must visit London several times a year to oversee my children's home, but I dare say I shall like Ravenshead very well.'

'There will be time enough to decide once you have visited,' Gerard told her. 'We must have the lawyers draw up the settlements, Amelia. I should not wish to control your fortune, though I will help you to manage it if you so wish. It might be a sensible idea to put a part at least in trust for your children.'

'That is an excellent notion,' Amelia agreed, a faint blush in her cheeks. 'I have a great deal of property—mostly houses. Great-Aunt Agatha acquired a considerable portfolio during her lifetime. I have wondered whether it might be better to sell most of them and re-invest the money. I should greatly appreciate your opinion, Gerard. I have my man of business, naturally, and my lawyers—but there has been no one I could turn to with my problems. No one I could truly trust. I have good friends, of course, but one does not like to ask advice in these matters.'

'I am sure Harry would have been happy to help you, Amelia. He has an excellent head for business. However, you have me now, my dearest. Any concern—the slightest worry—you may address to me, and I will do my best to take it from you.'

'Thank you, Gerard. You are most kind...' Amelia spoke carefully. He seemed so considerate, but was it merely the kindness he would offer to any friend?

Gerard looked at her oddly. She thought he was about to speak once more, but they had reached the dining room and Amelia found that she was sitting between Gerard on her left side and an elderly gentleman she knew slightly on the other. The time for confidences had passed, and though she made polite conversation with both gentlemen throughout dinner there was no chance of talking privately to Gerard.

Amelia glanced round the dinner table. Everyone was smiling and looking pleased. Susannah was a generous hostess and her cooks had excelled themselves. Course after course of delicious food was served to the guests and it was late before Susannah rose to take the ladies through to the drawing room. The gentlemen remained to drink port and smoke their cigars, while the ladies took tea in the drawing room.

It was nearly eleven o'clock when the gentlemen joined them at last, and then the present-giving ceremony took place. Susannah and Harry had bought gifts for all their guests. The footmen took these round on silver trays and there was a great deal of exclaiming and cries of pleasure as the small gifts were unwrapped to reveal things like Bristol-blue scent bottles for the ladies and enamelled snuffboxes for the gentlemen.

Amelia had already exchanged personal gifts with Susannah and Harry and would open those she had received in privacy. She had purchased a silver-gilt card case for Gerard, which she planned to give him the next morning after breakfast.

Chapter Three

It was five and twenty minutes to twelve when the guests separated. The older members of the family said goodnight and went up to their rooms, whilst the younger guests donned cloaks and greatcoats and went out to the waiting carriages. They were driven to Pendleton church, where they joined villagers for the midnight mass. This was a special part of Christmas as far as Amelia was concerned. She felt that this year it was even more so, because she was sharing it with her fiancé. Now that she had made up her mind, the thought warmed her and she felt a little thrill of happiness. How much better life would be in the future, even if her husband were not desperately in love with her.

Amelia left the church on Gerard's arm, feeling happy. The bells had begun to ring and it was almost a forerunner of their wedding day. As they paused for a moment for the carriages to come forwards to pick them up, their breath made patterns on the frosty air.

'Gerard…' Amelia began, but was shocked when he suddenly pushed her to one side so that she stumbled and fell against a prickly holly bush. 'What…?' Before she could finish her sentence, a shot rang out, passing so close to her that she felt a puff of air. She was struggling to recover her balance, as Gerard took out a pistol and fired at something in the shadows.

Almost at once, Amelia found that Harry and Susannah were at her side, assisting her. Everything else was confusion as people shouted and rushed about, some of the men setting off in pursuit of the would-be assassin.

'Amelia dearest,' Susannah cried, looking at her anxiously. 'Are you hurt? I do not know what happened…'

'The earl saw him just in time,' Emily said, for she too had rushed to Amelia's side. 'I noticed someone lurking over there in those trees. However, I did not realise what he meant to do until I saw him lift his arm.'

'Did you see his face, Miss Barton?' Harry asked. 'I'm dashed if I noticed anything until I heard the shot.'

'He was wearing a dark hat and a muffler,' Emily told him. 'I am sorry. I know that is of little use to you, but it was all I saw.'

Harry nodded and looked grim. 'Forgive us, Amelia. We expected something might happen, but not like this…on such a night. What kind of a man would attempt murder on Christmas Eve?'

'What do you mean?' Amelia stared at him. Her wrist stung where a thorn had penetrated her glove and she was feeling a little sick inside. 'Why did you expect something to happen?'

'Come, get inside the carriage, ladies,' Harry said. 'We must take you home. Gerard will explain later. He is coming now…' He glanced at the earl, who had gone after the assassin. 'Any luck?' Gerard shook his head and Harry swore.

'Amelia, forgive me for pushing you into the holly,' Gerard apologised. 'I knew I must act quickly—but have you been hurt?'

'A mere scratch,' Amelia told him. 'Had that ball found its mark, I might be dead.'

'I think it was meant more as a warning to me,' Gerard said. He climbed into the carriage with her and Emily. Susannah had gone with some of the other ladies and Harry. 'I received a threat this morning, when I returned from our walk, Amelia. It was somewhat obscure and I was not truly certain of its meaning, though I had an idea that I was being warned to stay away from you.'

'To stay away from me?' Amelia stared at him in dismay. 'What can you mean?'

'I think someone had guessed that I meant to ask you to marry me—and whoever that person is he has decided that he does not wish for the marriage to go ahead.'

'He would rather see me dead than as your wife?' Amelia's hand shook and she felt cold all over. 'Who could be so evil? I do not understand who would do such a thing.'

'Your brother threatened you,' Emily reminded her. 'He warned you against renewing your acquaintance with the earl.'

'Is this true?'

Amelia met Gerard's concerned look. 'Yes. Michael has warned me that you are interested only in my fortune many times. I told him that I did not believe you to be so mercenary—and he did tell me that I would be sorry if—' She broke off and shook her head. 'I cannot believe that my brother would try to shoot me like that.'

'He knows that if you marry me he would no longer have a chance of claiming your fortune for himself. I am sorry to say that there are some men who would stop at nothing where a large amount of money is concerned.'

'Michael is a bully—but I am not certain he would murder for gain.'

'At the moment he is our most likely suspect.' Gerard reached for her hand and held it. 'Do not fear, Amelia. You will be protected. I have already set measures in hand to have you watched all the time. I had not thought it necessary while we stayed at Pendleton. I imagined that you might be at risk once we announce our engagement, but my men will be in place by then.' His expression was grave. 'Unless you wish to withdraw in the circumstances?'

'I refuse to let anyone dictate to me!' Amelia lifted her head proudly. 'Whoever this person is, the threat would not go away if we postponed the announcement of our engagement, Gerard.'

'You are as brave as I imagined.' Gerard squeezed her hand comfortingly. 'I had planned to tell you all this after Christmas. I did not want to spoil the celebrations for Susannah and her guests—but I am afraid that this unpleasant incident will cast a shadow over things.'

'Can you not let people think it was merely a poacher or some such thing?'

'At half an hour past midnight?' Gerard smiled. 'I

could try, Amelia, but I doubt I should be believed. We might tell everyone that it was an attempted robbery.'

'That would be much better—and it may even be the truth,' Amelia said. 'You say that you were warned, Gerard—how exactly were you warned?'

'I was sent a doll that had been mutilated. A note in the wrappings said that if I cared for her I must stay away from her.'

'Could that not have meant Lisa?'

'Very few people even knew that I had a daughter until today,' Gerard said. 'Besides, why should I stay away from my own daughter—who could that benefit? She does not have a fortune…'

'No one could benefit from her death. It would in any case seem that I am the target after what happened this evening.' Amelia looked at him steadily. 'It is most unpleasant, Gerard… that someone should wish to kill me for money.'

'It is wicked!' Emily burst out, obviously upset. 'I think he should be ashamed of himself! Oh, do not look at me so, Amelia. It must be Sir Michael behind this monstrous plot. Who else could it be?'

'I do not know—yet I am loath to think my brother would stoop so low.'

'You think well of most people,' Gerard said as the carriage began to slow down. 'Forgive me for allowing that evil man to get near enough to take a shot at you this night, Amelia. I promise it will not happen again.'

He jumped out as soon as the carriage drew to a halt, helped Amelia down and sheltered her with his body as he hurried her into the house. Once inside, he saw how pale she looked and took her into his arms for a moment, holding her close. Amelia wanted to cling to him and weep, but controlled her feelings. Gerard would not care for a clinging wife. She stood unmoving within his arms and he let her go as they heard the other guests, who had attended mass with them, arriving.

'Perhaps you would prefer to go straight up?'

'Yes, I should. I do not wish to discuss the matter further at the moment. Excuse me, I shall see you in the morning.'

Amelia went quickly up the stairs, followed immediately by Emily. She was conscious of an irritation of the nerves. When Emily tried to follow her into her bedroom, she turned to her with a hasty dismissal.

'Please excuse me, Emily. I would prefer to be alone.'

'Yes, of course.'

Emily looked a little hurt at her tone, but Amelia was in too much distress to notice. It was bad enough that someone should try to shoot her, but to know that they all thought it was her brother who was behind the plot to murder her was lowering. Amelia had suffered much at the hands of her brother and sister-in-law—but murder was too terrible to comprehend.

She took off her bonnet and shawl, feeling glad that she had put on a gown that fastened at the front and told her maid not to wait up for her. At the moment her mind was in such turmoil that she could not speak to anyone.

Amelia slept fitfully and was awake long before the maids brought breakfast to her room. However, she had recovered from her irritation of the nerves and asked that the breakfast be laid in the sitting room. Wearing a pretty new lace peignoir, she went through to the little parlour and found that Emily was already there.

'Good morning, my love. May I wish you a Happy Christmas?'

'Thank you—Happy Christmas to you, Amelia. I hope you will like my gift. It is not much, but was chosen with care.'

'I am sure I shall.' Amelia presented her with an exquisitely wrapped parcel and smiled as Emily gave a cry of pleasure on opening it. Inside was an evening purse made of delicate links of gold, which fastened with a crossover clasp set with diamonds. It was a very expensive gift and reflected Amelia's true regard for her companion.

'This is so beautiful…you are always so generous to me…' Emily's lashes were wet with tears. 'To think that anyone could wish—' She broke off and wiped her hand across her cheek. 'I know you will not wish me to mention it, but I have not slept for thinking of what happened. Had the earl not been so alert you might not be here this morning…'

'You must not let a silly incident upset you. It will not happen again,' Amelia said and opened her parcel. Discovering a scarf she had admired some weeks before Christmas, she went to embrace her friend. 'This is exactly what I wished for, Emily. How sweet of you to remember it.'

'I bought it the day after we saw it,' Emily said and helped herself to some toast and honey. 'Lady Pendleton gave me a lovely scent flask with silver ends last evening, but this purse…it is the most beautiful thing I have ever owned.'

'I am glad you are pleased with it, my love. Has Mr Sinclair given you a gift?'

'No—but I think he has one for me. I believe he intended it to be a ring…' She fiddled with her toast. 'I bought a horn-and-ivory card case inlaid with gold for him, but I am undecided as to whether I should give it to him or not.'

'I am certain that you should exchange gifts with Mr Sinclair, Emily. He is a close friend and I also have a gift for him. You may deliver mine at the same time if it makes you feel better, my love.'

'Yes, I think it would. I should not feel so particular. May I ask what you have bought for Mr Sinclair?'

'I purchased a rather fine diamond stickpin. It has the shape of four hands linking and I thought it might appeal to him.'

'It will be the very thing for him,' Emily said and laughed delightedly. 'He was so very desperate to become a member of the Four-in-Hand Club and he delights in wearing the special waistcoat.'

'I am very fond of that gentleman,' Amelia said with a smile. 'He played his part in the fortunes of both of my protégées. Susannah and Helene have both been lucky. I should be happy to see you settled as well, Emily my love.'

A delicate blush appeared in her companion's cheeks. 'I think I may say without fear of boasting that Mr Sinclair does care for me—but whether he could accept my shame…'

'Emily, that is enough! The shame belongs to the man who forced you, my love. I will not have you hang your head. I was thinking that I would ask you to be my bridesmaid—and, of course, Susannah and Helene will be matrons of honour if they can spare the time from their busy lives—and Lisa must be a bridesmaid also, of course.'

'I should be honoured,' Emily told her and finished eating her toast. 'Mr Sinclair asked me if I would be paying my usual morning visit to the nursery and I said yes. I have a gift for Susannah's son—and also a little ring that I had as a girl, which I mean to give to Lisa.'

'How thoughtful of you, my love,' Amelia approved. 'I bought a doll for Lisa…just in case she was staying here with her father this Christmas. I think I shall come with you this morning—if you would not mind waiting until I dress?'

'I should be delighted. I usually go for a walk after I visit the children, but it snowed early this morning. Not enough to make walking impossible, but I felt…' She floundered to a halt.

'Yes, I understand.' Amelia nodded. 'I too shall be very careful when and where I walk until Gerard has his men in place. It may be as well to remain indoors for the moment—and we may blame the weather for it is inclement.'

'You wish to keep last night's incident as private as possible? I doubt that it will be possible, Amelia. Not everyone will keep it to himself or herself. I dare say the incident will be whispered of, if not openly admitted.'

'Yes, I fear that it may.' Amelia sighed. 'We, however, shall make light of it—there was a rogue near the church who sought to rob us. It is a weak excuse but it will suffice. Excuse me while I dress.'

'There is no hurry. I have something to do first—besides, you have not yet opened all your letters.'

'I have rather a lot of them, but I shall open one or two before I dress.' She looked with pleasure at the pile of letters waiting for her.

One of Amelia's chief pleasures in life was in writing to her friends. It was a good way of keeping in touch with many acquaintances she hardly ever saw. Amongst the cards and greetings she had received that Christmas morning was one from a lady for whom she had profound sympathy. The lady was very much in the position Amelia had been for years, at the mercy of her family. Except that Marguerite had no chance of marriage at all and Amelia might have married if she had wished.

Something must be done for her friend, Amelia thought. A Season in town would not solve Marguerite's problem, but perhaps she could think of some way of getting her away from her family for a while. She wrote a long and cheerful letter and sealed it. It had occurred to her that she would need someone she trusted to help her care for Lisa. Marguerite adored children and she might enjoy helping with Lisa's education.

Glancing at the clock, Amelia realised that it was time she paid her visit to the nursery. Lisa would have had her breakfast and she would be waiting for the gift Amelia had promised her. She hoped the child would be pleased with the doll she had chosen.

Amelia spent a pleasant half an hour in the nursery, playing with Lisa, who had been given several pres-

ents, including a pretty doll from her father. Lisa was
delighted to have two dolls, especially as Amelia's had
curly hair.

'She is like me,' she said and put the doll up against
her face. 'Thank you, Mademoiselle Royston.'

'You may call me Amelia. We are going to be
friends, Lisa.'

'Papa says you are to be my mama.' Lisa's eyes were
large and apprehensive. 'Will you live with us, Melia?'

'Yes, I shall live with you and your papa,' Amelia
replied. 'That is why I want us to be friends, dearest.
As you grow up, it will be I who buys your dresses and
teaches you to be a young lady. You will have a governess, but she will be kind and I shall make certain that
your studies include games as well as the dull things.'

Lisa's face lit up, then a shy expression came into
her eyes. 'Will you love me, *mademoiselle*?'

'I already love you,' Amelia said and took her into
her arms, hugging and kissing her. 'You are a delight to
me, Lisa—and perhaps one day you may have brothers
or sisters to play with you.'

'I should like that but…Papa will not send me away
when you are married?'

'No, of course not. Why should you think that?'

'Nanny told me it would happen if I did not do
everything she told me.'

'That lady has been dismissed. I shall choose another
nurse to help look after you, and I assure you that she
will be kind.'

'I love you,' Lisa said as she climbed on Amelia's
knee and put her arms about her neck. 'Nanny hasn't
left yet, Melia. I saw her in the garden as I looked from

my window. She was talking to someone—a man. I have seen her talk to him before, but she said that if I told Papa she would whip me.'

'She was very wicked to threaten you like that.' Amelia controlled her anger. 'Your papa has dismissed her. If she has not already left this house, she will do so within a few hours. I dare say your papa thought it would be unfair to make her leave at Christmas-tide. However, she will not be allowed near you again.' Amelia touched her hair. 'You must always tell Papa or me these things, Lisa, if someone hurts or fright-ens you—or if you see someone who makes you feel uncomfortable.'

'I will tell you. Papa might think I was telling tales—and gentlemen do not approve of such things.'

'There are times when telling a grown-up the truth is important. If someone frightens you, Lisa—or threat-ens you—you must tell us. Please promise me you will?'

'I promise.' Lisa slid from her lap as some of the other children came running into the nursery school-room. They were all clutching new toys of some kind. 'I must not keep you, *mademoiselle*. Nanny said that mothers only spend a few minutes with children; they are too busy to waste their time with us.'

Amelia smothered a sigh. Gerard had not dismissed that woman a moment too soon!

'When we are all living together, you will spend a part of your day with your papa and me when he has the time. It is true that gentlemen have their business to keep them busy, but I assure you that I shall take you for walks and I think your papa might teach you to ride a pony.'

'Ride a pony?' Lisa's face lit up. 'Truly? Would Papa truly teach me to ride himself?'

'I am sure that he will, as soon as he considers you are ready.' Amelia kissed her cheek. 'I must go now, my love, but I shall ask your papa if he will take us both for a little carriage ride after dinner.'

Amelia received an enthusiastic hug. She was smiling as she went downstairs. As she turned towards the large drawing room where she knew many of the other guests had gathered, she was unaware that she was being watched from the gallery above.

Turning away to return to the room she would have to leave in the morning, Lisa's former nanny, Alice Horton, gave a spiteful smile. The Royston woman was riding for a fall. She had not hesitated to use her position and influence to have Alice dismissed from her position, but she would not see herself installed as the Earl of Ravenshead's wife. There were plans afoot that would prevent their marriage. When *he* had first approached her, Alice had been reluctant to give him any information about her employer or his daughter. However, she had no such scruples now.

He had paid her well for the news that Lisa was to have a new mama very soon. Alice had enough money to see her through the next few months without having to apply for a new position—and if she did what *he* asked, she might never have to work again...

Amelia saw Gerard standing near the window in the large salon. He had been in conversation with Harry, but as soon as he noticed her, he said something to his friend and came to greet her.

'Have you been to see Lisa? Toby told me that he saw you with Miss Barton on your way there.'

'I took her my gift. I had bought her a doll. She received several dolls, but mine had curly hair like hers and that pleased her.' Amelia lifted her hand to her own neat, dark locks. She had allowed her maid to dress it in a softer style and believed it suited her. 'I have made Lisa a promise on your behalf, Gerard. She seemed to think that she must not expect us to visit her for more than half an hour in the mornings. I told her that when we were married I should take her for walks—and that you would teach her to ride a pony. I hope I have not spoken out of turn?'

'Of course you have not,' Gerard assured her instantly. 'I had intended to buy the child a pony quite soon—and I shall certainly teach her to ride it myself. Since we shall be spending much of our lives in the country there will be plenty of time for such pleasures. You must feel free to do as you think best, Amelia. I am confident that your sure judgement will bring many benefits to both Lisa's life and my own.'

'I shall do my best to be the mother she lacks.'

'You will be the best mother she could have—the only one she has known.'

'I am glad you feel as I do,' Amelia said. 'I know that in many families the children are confined to the nursery until they are old enough to come out—but I do not approve of such rigid rules. Naturally, they must study and there are times when they might be a

nuisance to guests, but when it is just the family I hope
we shall often be together.'

He gave her a look of warm approval. 'You are a
constant delight to me. I knew you would be generous
towards my daughter—but this is more than I could
have expected.'

'I love her. She is a delightful child, Gerard.'

A tiny pinprick of hurt entered her heart, because
it was so obvious that he wanted and needed a mother
for Lisa. Would any woman have done—or did he feel
something stronger toward her?

'Yes, she is.' He smiled and took a small box from
inside his coat. 'This is my gift to you for today,
Amelia. I shall be sending for the family jewels and
you may make your choice of them—though I warn
you that they will need to be refurbished for they are
heavy and old-fashioned. This is something I thought
might please you.'

Amelia unwrapped the box and took out the beautiful diamond brooch inside. It was shaped like a delicate
bouquet of flowers and the heads trembled as she took
it from its box.

'This is beautiful,' she said and pinned it to her
gown. She reached into the pocket of her gown. 'I
have a small gift for you, Gerard—it is a mere trinket…' In value, it was a similar gift to the one she had
given Toby Sinclair, something she might have given to
any member of her close friends and family. Not what
she might have chosen had she known they would be
engaged by Christmas Day.

He took the box and dispensed with the wrappings,

revealing the silver-gilt card case. 'More than a trinket, Amelia. Thank you.'

Amelia shook her head, changing the subject. 'Emily was saying that she would not walk alone, because of what happened last night. I too think it would be best to take care for the moment. I wondered if we might take Lisa for a little ride in your carriage after dinner?'

'I see no reason why we should not go for a drive,' Gerard said. 'As for what happened last night, the matter is in hand. Any strangers seen on the estate will be stopped and questioned.'

Amelia recalled what Lisa had told her about the nanny speaking to a man in the gardens—a man the woman had spoken to before. However, she had no reason to suppose that the man could have anything to do with the incident outside the church. As unlikely as it seemed, Nanny probably had a follower.

Dismissing the nanny from her mind, she smiled as Susannah came up to them. She was wearing the pearl-and-diamond pendant that Amelia had given her as a Christmas gift and the next few minutes were taken up with her delight and her gratitude. By the time Amelia and Gerard spoke again, the nanny had been forgotten.

It was a pleasant morning. Amelia exchanged gifts with several friends, enjoying some music before nuncheon. After they had eaten, Gerard sent for his carriage. Lisa's nurse brought her downstairs. She was wearing a pretty pink coat and hat and had a fur muff that her papa had given her. She was excited to be going for a drive, chattering about the many gifts that she had received that morning.

'I had four dolls altogether, Papa—was I not fortunate?' she said as they went out to the carriage. 'One was broken.'

Gerard's attention was caught. 'A broken doll—who gave you that, my love?'

'I do not know, Papa. I asked Nurse Mary. She said there was no card.'

'I shall have a look at the doll later,' Gerard said. 'It was a shame the doll was broken.' His eyes met Amelia's over Lisa's head.

'I did not mind,' Lisa said. 'I had so many pretty things. I did not expect so many presents. Nanny said it was obscene for one small child to have so many expensive clothes as I have. What does obscene mean, Papa?'

'I think it means that I spoil you,' Gerard said, but his mouth had pulled into a grim line.

Amelia touched his hand. He glanced at her but his expression remained grim.

'I have been spoiled too,' Amelia said and smiled at the child as she touched the brooch she was wearing. She had fastened it to the scarf Emily had given her, and she was wearing a new black velvet cloak she had purchased in London; it had a fur lining and was very warm. 'I was given this lovely scarf and this brooch— do you see how it trembles as I move?'

'Did Papa give it to you?' Amelia nodded. 'It is very beautiful—but you are *très ravissante*, Melia. Papa will be lucky when you marry him.'

'We shall all be lucky to have each other,' Amelia said. 'Look, Lisa—can you see the deer over there? I think they have come closer to the house than usual.

I know that Susannah has food put out for them when the weather is inclement.'

'They are lovely...' Lisa said, pressing her face to the carriage window. 'Papa, do we have deer at Ravenshead?'

'I believe not,' he said. 'We might have some brought into the park if you would like that, Lisa.' His face had relaxed. He smiled as he met Amelia's eyes. She nodded slightly, understanding his feelings. The broken doll was worrying, but might simply be a coincidence.

'Oh, yes, please. I should love that, Papa—and could I please have a puppy...?'

'Is there anything else, miss?' he asked, brows rising indulgently.

'Oh, no, Papa,' Lisa said and put her hand into Amelia's. 'But Melia did say I should tell you anything I wanted.'

'Did she, indeed?' Gerard laughed. 'I can see that I am to be petticoat-led now that I have two beautiful ladies in my life.'

Amelia was pleased that he had managed to put his worries to one side, and yet she sensed a shadow hanging over them.

She glanced out of the carriage window. A light dusting of snow clung to the trees and shrubs, but it was beginning to melt. A pale sun had brightened the day. Shadows might gather in the distance, but for today Amelia would try to forget them and think only of pleasant things.

Lisa was singing a little French song when Amelia took her up to the nursery and handed her back to Mary.

The little girl turned to her, hugging her as she took her leave.

'Thank you for my lovely afternoon, Melia.'

'You are very welcome, Lisa. It was a pleasure for me.'

Amelia smiled and left the child with her nurse. The future was looking so much brighter. Children were a blessing and already the ache she had carried deep inside her was easing. She was a mother to Gerard's daughter and in time they would have others of their own.

She hastened to the apartments she shared with Emily, because the hour was late and she would have to hurry if she were to change and be ready in time for dinner. As she entered the little parlour, the sound of sobbing met her. The sight of Emily weeping desperately brought her to a halt.

She went to her at once. 'Emily, dearest—what is wrong?'

'Oh…Amelia…' Emily lifted her head to look at her. 'Forgive me. I did not mean you to see me like this…' She wiped her hand across her face. 'I should have gone to my bedchamber.'

'Do not be foolish. You should not hide your tears from me, Emily. Can you not tell me what is wrong?'

'I spoke to Mr Sinclair when we exchanged gifts,' Emily said, her body shaken by a deep, hurtful sob. 'He gave me a beautiful sapphire-and-diamond ring and I… told him that I could not marry him. He asked me why and I told him that I had given birth to a child…' She bent her head, the tears falling once more.

'Emily, my love.' Amelia knelt down beside her and

took her hand. 'Did you explain that you were forced?' Emily shook her head and Amelia gave her fingers a gentle squeeze. 'You should have made that plain. He did not understand the circumstances.'

'He did not give me a chance,' Emily said. She took a kerchief from her sleeve and wiped her face. 'He looked so stunned, Amelia. It was as if I had thrown a jug of cold water over him. He drew back, shaking his head and looked…as if he could not bear the sight of me. I think he must hate me now.'

'Emily! I am certain it was merely shock. He did not understand the circumstances. Mr Sinclair is a gentleman. I do not believe he would have done that to you deliberately.'

'I begged him not to look at me that way. I pleaded for a chance to explain, but he said that he must have time—and then he walked away and left me. It is over. He has a disgust of me now.'

'He was shocked, that is all. I am sure that when he has recovered from his…' Amelia paused, searching for the right word.

'Disappointment?' Emily lifted her head. 'I saw it in his eyes, Amelia. He was stunned, disappointed, even revolted—I think he could not bear the idea that I had been with another man.'

'It must have been upsetting for him, but he may have thought you had a love child, Emily. You must try to understand that he had put you on a pedestal. He may have misunderstood you. He may think that you took a lover. You must tell him the truth.'

'I could not! I do not think I could bear to face him again.'

'Emily dearest,' Amelia said, 'I understand that it would be too difficult for you to tell him everything— but I could speak to him. I could explain how badly your family treated you. I am hopeful that once he has had time to think about things he will still wish to marry you.'

'No! Please do not,' Emily begged, a sob in her voice. 'I cannot bear to speak of it.' She jumped to her feet and ran into her own bedroom, shutting the door and locking it behind her. Amelia knocked at the door.

'Emily. Please listen to me. You must not let this destroy you. If Mr Sinclair truly loves you it will all come right. Do not throw away your chance of happiness too soon.'

'Please do not ask me to see him. I shall not come down this evening.'

'Emily…'

Amelia sighed as she heard a renewal of wild sobbing from her companion. In the hall downstairs the longcase clock was chiming the hour. She realised with a start that she would be late for dinner. She must hurry and change her clothes. Emily would come to her senses when she had cried herself to sleep. In the morning they would talk about things calmly—and she would have a few words with Mr Sinclair. If he had behaved as badly as Emily claimed, he was not the gentleman she had thought him!

Amelia apologised to the company when she joined them in the drawing room. She spoke to Susannah, telling her that Emily had a headache and would not be joining them that evening.

'I am so sorry.' Susannah was concerned. 'I hope it is nothing serious. Should we send for the doctor?'

'No, I am sure that will not be necessary,' Amelia told her. 'I am sorry if Emily's absence has unbalanced your dining table.'

'As it happens she is not the only guest missing,' Susannah replied. 'Toby Sinclair received a message from home and left us two hours ago. His parents had not joined us for Christmas because Mr Sinclair was feeling a little unwell. He had insisted that his son join his friends, but perhaps he has taken a turn for the worse. Toby seemed in a strange mood. He was abrupt—distant—and that is not like him…not like him at all. Harry thinks that his brother-in-law must be quite ill to send for his son.'

'I am sorry to hear it. Illness in the family is distressing, especially at this time of the year.'

'Had it been at any other time Harry would have gone to his sister immediately, but we cannot desert our guests. Lady Elizabeth is staying with her daughter this Christmas, so Harry's sister will not be completely alone should anything happen.'

'We must hope that it is not serious.' Amelia was thoughtful as she joined the guests moving into the long dining room. If Toby Sinclair had received bad news, it was understandable that he had left—but he ought to have left a note for Emily.

Gerard came to offer her his arm. 'You look serious, Amelia. Is something wrong?'

'Emily has a headache. I am sure she will be better in the morning.'

'I am sorry she is unwell. I understand that Toby

has taken himself off in a hurry—there wouldn't be a connection?'

'Perhaps—but I cannot tell you, for it is not my secret.'

'Then you must keep it.' He paused, then, 'I have spoken to Lisa's nurse and looked at the doll. It is not the same as the one I had sent to me. I believe it may just be a coincidence—I must hope so, otherwise it would be serious. If I believed the child was threatened, I should take her back to France.'

'I think we must talk about this matter. I know your opinion—but I am not sure.' Amelia shook her head as his brows lifted. 'We shall not discuss this tonight. The morning will be soon enough, but I must tell you that I believe your theory about my brother may be wrong.'

'Yes, you may be correct. We shall talk tomorrow, Amelia. We must make arrangements for the future and discuss this other business.'

'Yes, the morning will be time enough. We shall enjoy this evening, for Susannah has gone to so much trouble for us all.'

Chapter Four

Throughout dinner Gerard was very aware of the woman sitting beside him. She was lovely, but more than that she had an air of serenity, a presence that was lacking in so many other ladies. He was not certain why she had accepted his proposal of marriage. Was it only that she wished to be married and felt comfortable in his presence? They were good friends and shared an interest in many things. Marriage to Amelia would, he had no doubt, be pleasant and comfortable whatever the case, but he was not looking for someone to place his slippers by the fire and arrange for his favourite meals to be served. He wanted so much more! He wanted a woman who would welcome him to her bed with open arms.

The scent of her perfume was intoxicating. She seemed to smell of flowers and yet there was a subtle fragrance that was all her own. The sight of her, the way she turned her head, the way she moved, her voice... her smile...all these things set him on fire with longing. He wanted to take her in his arms and make love to her that very night, but was not sure that she would welcome a show of passion.

Amelia's manner gave little away. Her first reaction to his proposal had seemed positive, but since then she had become more reserved. He was not sure why. The incident at the church had been upsetting, of course—but he did not think Amelia would allow that to upset her. She had insisted that she wished to go on with the engagement.

Was it something in Gerard himself that had caused her to withdraw? He knew that his rejection of Lisette the night she had crept into his bed had been the reason for her desperate unhappiness. He had not been able to tell Amelia that he had rejected Lisette's attempt to ask for his love. After her death he had regretted his curt manner that night. He had married her on a whim, indulging his sense of honour and pity—and he had still been angry with Amelia and her brother. Later, when he began to realise that there was only one woman he wanted despite what had happened, he had regretted the impulse that had urged him to wed a woman he did not know or love. However, he had meant to honour his promise, but, in rejecting Lisette when she tried to give herself to him, he had hurt her. He believed it was his rejection that had driven her to take her own life. Perhaps there was more, perhaps he was incapable of making a woman happy…

'Susannah is a wonderful hostess, is she not?' Amelia remarked, breaking into his thoughts. 'When I recall how anxious she was the first time she stayed here, I cannot believe how much she has matured.'

'Harry seems very content with his family,' Gerard replied. He smiled inwardly, wondering if Amelia guessed how aroused he was when she turned to him and made some intimate remark. It was fortunate that the table hid the evidence of his intense need at that moment. He must think of other things!

Several times since the incident outside the church he had wondered if he had placed Amelia's life in danger by proposing. Harry was aware of his anxious thoughts and had been forthright in his opinion.

'I have no idea who this enemy of yours is, Gerard—but to give in to him would be more dangerous, believe me. If it is Royston, Amelia would be at his mercy, and if it is not...' He shook his head and frowned. 'She would never truly be safe—and nor, my friend, would you.'

'Then we are working in the dark. I have searched my memory for someone I have offended, but I can think of no one—at least, no one who would think it worthwhile to kill Amelia simply to spite me. I am still of the opinion that the plotter is Royston.'

'You may well be right, but Susannah is very close to Amelia. She thinks that Amelia is doubtful about her brother being the culprit.'

'It would be hard for any woman to accept such an idea,' Gerard said. 'I have not tried to impress my feelings on her, but for the moment I can see no other reason for the attempt on her life.'

Gerard felt Amelia's loss keenly when the ladies retired to the drawing room to take tea. He wished that he could follow at once, but custom dictated that he remain with the gentlemen to drink port and discuss politics and sport. When the gentlemen at last made their move towards the drawing room, Harry invited him to play a game of billiards. Not wanting to offend his friend, he agreed.

They had been playing for half an hour or so when he caught the smell of the perfume he always associated with Amelia and turned to see her watching them. The wistful expression he surprised in her eyes set him wondering. Was she wishing that they might be alone? Did she burn to be in his arms? He realised that despite their long friendship he hardly knew her. Gerard well remembered the passionate girl who would have given herself to him one never-forgotten night—but who was she now? Beautiful, serene, sophisticated, she was surrounded by friends, loved by those who knew her best, envied by many—but who was the woman behind the mask? How did she really feel about their marriage? He wished he knew.

'I came to say goodnight,' she said. 'I must see if Emily is feeling better. I shall speak to you in the morning, Gerard—shall we say at nine?'

'If that is not too early for you.' He inclined his head, then went to her, taking her hand and turning it to drop a kiss into the palm. 'Sleep well, my dearest. I hope you find Miss Barton much recovered.'

'Thank you.' Amelia smiled as she bid both men goodnight and then walked from the room.

'You know that I shall be happy to stand up with you at your wedding,' Harry said and lined up a coloured ball, striking it with the white so that it rolled into the pocket. 'Have you agreed the day yet?'

'We are thinking of a month after the ball at Coleridge,' Gerard said. 'I hope that I am doing the right thing…if I thought I was putting Amelia's life in danger by marrying her…'

'If you have an enemy, we shall find him out,' Harry said and potted another ball. 'I have told my men to be on the lookout for strangers, but I doubt that whoever it was the other night will try anything more just yet. I have been wondering if that shot was just another warning.'

'We cannot even be certain that the target is Amelia…' Gerard frowned, missing his ball. His heart was not in the game. All he could think about was Amelia. He wanted her so badly. He would be a fool to let whoever was threatening her have his way.

Amelia sighed as she went into the private sitting room she shared with Emily. She wished that she might have had more time alone with Gerard that evening, but it was not possible. There were so many guests staying and she was acquainted with all of them; mere politeness decreed that she must spend a little time with as many as she could.

She saw that her blue cloak with the fur lining was lying on one of the chairs. She had told Emily that she might wear it that morning, because the weather had turned so cold and she had her new black one, which was even more sumptuously lined. Emily must have left it lying there. That was unusual, for she was by habit a tidy girl. Amelia's maid knew that she had loaned the cloak to her companion and had left it where it was instead of putting it away as she normally would.

Amelia went to her companion's door and knocked softly. 'Are you awake, dearest? Is your headache still bad? Would you like to talk to me about anything?'

There was no reply. Amelia did not persist; she did not wish to wake Emily if she was sleeping. She knew that it was Emily's heart that ached rather than her head, and she felt annoyed with Toby Sinclair. Really, she had thought better of him! Surely he could have accepted that Emily had had a child? It was shocking, but not the crime some thought it, in Amelia's opinion, especially since Emily had been forced. Toby might at least have asked her about the circumstances. Obviously, he had wanted to get home quickly after the news that his father's health had taken a turn for the worse, but he could have left a note for Emily. To leave her without a word—to run away like a disappointed schoolboy—was not what Amelia would have expected from him.

If he really could not face the fact that Emily had given birth to a child, even though she was forced and not willing, he could have found a way of telling her. To simply abandon her like this was so hurtful. It was no wonder that Emily had taken to her bed this evening. She was suffering from a broken heart.

Amelia went to her own bedchamber. She allowed her maid to undo the hooks at the back of her gown and then dismissed her. She sat down at her dressing table, picked up her brush, but then just stared at her mirror.

She was anxious about Emily. The girl was assured of a position with her for as long as she needed it, but there was very little she could do to help with the pain of a disappointment in love. Amelia had once suffered much as her companion was suffering now. She had not even known why Gerard had gone away without speaking to her or telling her he was leaving. For years she had alternated between distress and disappointment at his desertion, but then she had finally understood that her brother was to blame. Michael had acted in a high-handed, ruthless manner, not caring who he hurt!

He had not been a good brother to her. Indeed, there were times when she had come close to hating him. His last letter had been a hateful tirade about her selfishness towards her family that had left her in tears—but would he truly wish her dead so that he could get his hands on her fortune?

Amelia shuddered at the thought. They had quarrelled so many times, but although she had sensed violence in him he had never actually harmed her—except by sending Gerard away.

Her thoughts turned to the man she had never ceased to love. She had thought there was something of the man she had known when she was young in him that evening…a simmering passion that had made her catch her breath.

She longed for him to want her, to love her—need her, as she loved and desired him. Was she a fool to believe that their marriage could work? If all he truly wanted was a complaisant wife who would care for his child, he might feel cheated when he realised that she was in love with him.

It must not matter! She knew that a marriage that was not equal in love might lead to hurt in the years to come, but perhaps if she were careful to hide her feelings he need never know. He wanted a companion rather than a wife so that was what she would be. Besides, it would break her to leave him now. If she waited, gave him time to know her, he might begin to feel the passion he had once had for her.

Smiling a trifle ruefully, Amelia went to bed. She might be foolish, but she thought that she had seen passion in Gerard's eyes that evening…

Amelia slept a little later than usual. She was woken by her maid pulling back the curtains and yawned, sitting up and blinking at the bright light.

Glancing at the clock, she saw that it was half past eight. 'Has it been snowing again, Martha?'

'Yes, Miss Royston. It has stopped now, but I believe there was a heavy fall last night.'

'What have you brought me this morning?'

'I thought you might like a light repast in bed instead of going down to the breakfast room. Since you slept in, Miss Royston—'

'How thoughtful you are,' Amelia said. 'I shall need some warm water at once for I have an appointment at nine this morning.'

'I should have woken you sooner, miss—but you were so peaceful.'

'I have half an hour; it is plenty of time if I hurry.'

'I will fetch the water now, miss.'

'Oh…' Amelia said as the girl turned away. 'Have you seen Miss Barton this morning?'

'No, miss. I went into her room to ask if she wished

for breakfast in bed, but she was not there. Her bed had been made, but Miss Barton often makes her bed.'

'Yes, she does, because she is a thoughtful girl,' Amelia said. She broke a piece of the soft roll, buttered it and ate a piece as she poured a cup of the dark, slightly bitter chocolate she liked to drink when she indulged in breakfast in bed. It was not often she did so and wished she might linger longer this morning, but she did not want to be late for her meeting with Gerard.

By the time Martha returned with her hot water, Amelia had finished her roll and her cup of chocolate. She washed hastily and dressed in a simple morning gown that she could fasten herself. For once she left her hair hanging loose on her shoulders, merely brushing it back from her face and securing it with a comb at either side. Since she scarcely glanced at herself, she had no idea that she looked much younger and more like the girl she had been when she first met Gerard.

The beautiful mahogany longcase clock in the hall had just finished striking when Amelia went downstairs. She found that Gerard was waiting for her. He looked handsome, elegant in his coat with three layers of capes across the shoulders, his topboots so glossy that you might see your reflection in them. He was frowning, but as she called to him he turned and smiled. Amelia's heart did a somersault, leaving her breathless for one moment. She truly thought that he had the most compelling eyes of any gentleman of her acquaintance and they seemed very intent as he looked at her.

'Forgive me if I have kept you. I slept later than usual and did not think to ask my maid to wake me. I am normally up much earlier.'

'We have all been keeping late hours at Pendleton. I should have suggested ten rather than nine, but I thought we should be sure of being alone. I have the carriage waiting…'

'We have not been much alone,' Amelia said as they went outside together. 'I have been thinking about what happened the other night outside the church, Gerard.'

'I have thought of it constantly.' His eyes dwelled on her face for some moments. 'We shall talk in the carriage. I would not care to be overheard.'

'Surely here there is no one that would wish us harm?'

'Our friends would not,' Gerard agreed, taking her arm and leading her out to the carriage. He helped her inside and she found that a warm brick had been brought so that she might place her feet on it, and a thick rug provided for her knees. 'I hope you will be comfortable, Amelia. It is a bitterly cold day.'

'I dare say your coachman will feel it, but we shall not be out long.'

'Coachman has his comforts, a warm coat and a blanket, I am sure,' Gerard told her. 'You say that you are safe here with friends and to a certain degree I concur, but servants talk—and sometimes they pass on information for money without realising what harm they may do.'

'Yes, I am sure that is so,' Amelia said. 'I believe someone may have mentioned the fact that we had been talking together—for no one but our close friends know that we are engaged.' She frowned. 'Of course, Lisa knows. When did you tell her you were thinking of marrying me—before or after you dismissed Nanny?'

'I believe it was before...' He stared at her. 'You think Nanny may have heard something and passed on the information?'

'Lisa told me yesterday that Nanny did not leave Pendleton immediately. She saw her talking to a man in the gardens—a man that she had seen Nanny speak to before.'

'Why did you not tell me that yesterday?'

'I did not think it important at first. I imagined Miss Horton might have a follower, but when you said just now that servants talk, I realised that she could have been selling information—perhaps because she had been dismissed.'

'Yes, you are right. I should have forced her to leave the house instantly.'

'It would not have changed anything. If she already had the information...'

Gerard swore angrily and then apologised. 'Forgive me. I should not use such language in your presence, Amelia. I have been careless. I did not imagine that my servants would gossip to strangers.'

'It makes little difference. Our enemy would have heard as soon as our engagement was announced.'

Gerard looked concerned. 'I have wondered if I was wrong to ask you. If I have put your life at risk...'

'If my marriage to you renders me liable to be murdered, then it is best that I am aware of it. This threat will not go away if we deny it, Gerard. We must discover who wishes me ill. There is some mystery here and it needs to be solved.'

'You do not accept that it is your brother?'

'I am loath to do so. I know that Michael resents the fact that Great-Aunt Agatha did not leave him anything. He has tried to bully me into giving him at least half of my fortune. We have quarrelled because I refuse to do as he wishes. Had my aunt wished him to share in her fortune, she would have left him money. I might have done something for him before this had he behaved in a civilised manner. Perhaps—if you believe it is Michael…' She shook her head. 'No! I shall not be blackmailed into giving him my aunt's money. She would not have wished me to do so.'

'I do not think he would be content with a part of it. If he is willing to murder you, then he wants it all.'

'Well, he shall not have it.' Amelia lifted her head proudly. 'I have my own plans for part of the money— though some must be put in trust for our children.'

'You are thinking of your charity?'

'That and other things. I have helped two young ladies find happiness. I know of at least two more deserving cases…' She halted as Gerard raised his brows. 'You do not approve?'

'I am happy with whatever you choose to do, Amelia. I told you that I did not wish to control your fortune and I meant it.'

'It will be *our* money. I should not dream of giving large sums away without first consulting you.'

'I am not your brother, Amelia. Your fortune is not my first concern.'

'Have I made you angry, Gerard? I beg your pardon. I did not mean to.' She looked at him uncertainly.

'I am not angry, but I would not have you think I asked you to marry me for your fortune.'

'I did not.' She hesitated, then, wishing to change the subject, 'Shall we travel to Coleridge together?'

'Yes, certainly.' He was silent for a moment. 'I have made arrangements for you to be protected—Lisa too. If you feel that my theory is wrong I must think carefully. Sir Michael seemed the most obvious since he would inherit.'

'Have you considered that this person may have something other than money on his mind—or her mind? I suppose it could be a woman...'

'A scorned mistress?' Gerard looked amused. 'I have none to my credit, Amelia. When I first returned from the wars there was a lady in France, but we parted as friends when I returned to England the first time. There has been no one since.'

'Oh...' Amelia digested his statement in silence. Most gentlemen had mistresses before they married. She found no cause for distress in an old affair. 'Then we are at least certain it is a man. My sister-in-law has no love for me, but she would think murder most vulgar.'

'Vulgar?' Laughter gleamed in his eyes.

'You do not know Louisa. She is very strict—rude when she chooses, but *never* vulgar.'

Gerard laughed. 'She sounds formidable?'

'She would consider murder beneath her—and she would not approve of her husband being involved with anything of the kind. Indeed, if she suspected something untoward she would have a deal to say on the subject.'

'Then perhaps I should look elsewhere for a motive.'

'I cannot think of anyone I have offended other than my brother.' Amelia sighed and looked distressed. 'Perhaps you are right—there is no other explanation.'

'Unless I have an enemy…'

'Gerard?' Amelia's eyes widened. 'Have you thought of someone?'

'Unfortunately, no. I dare say I have enemies, though none I would have thought…there is Northaven, of course. He may hate me enough to threaten, but to kill you…' He shook his head. 'I cannot think it, Amelia. He might wound me in a duel if he could or knock me down, but truth to tell I do not see him as a murderer.'

'I do not see my brother in that light. A bully—yes.'

'It is difficult. All we can do is wait until *he* shows himself—whoever he is. I have agents who may discover something, but…it might be best to delay the announcement of our engagement.'

'You would give in to him? Surely that way he wins? And if my fortune is his object…' Amelia waved her hand in distress. 'As you say, it is difficult. If you wish to withdraw—'

'Damn it, no! You cannot think it, Amelia?'

'No…forgive me. I hardly know what I am thinking.'

'All I want is to make you happy.'

'Then we shall not allow this person to dictate to us. I dare say there is some risk if we go ahead and announce the engagement but there is risk in any case. At the moment our enemy is merely a shadow. Perhaps when he sees he cannot bully us he will step out into the light.'

'You are both wise and brave,' Gerard murmured, taking her gloved hand to kiss it. 'Now we shall talk of happier things? How many guests shall we invite to our wedding—and do you think we should hold an engagement ball?'

'Oh, I think we shall give a ball on the eve of the wedding. I believe that will be sufficient. Shall we all go down to Ravenshead after the Coleridge ball? I think I should like to see your home, Gerard—and we must discuss what I ought to do with Aunt Agatha's estate. I told you that I thought we should sell some of the property, but she loved that house and I am very fond of the garden...'

Amelia was feeling more settled in her mind when they returned to the house an hour or so after they left it. They had discussed most aspects of the wedding and settled that they would keep Amelia's home and also the house in Bath and Gerard's London house, which was larger than her own. Most of the other property would be sold or let to tenants, and the money invested in some form of trust for their children. However, the identity of the person who was trying to prevent their marriage remained a mystery. She knew that Gerard still felt her brother the most likely culprit, though he intended to set his agents the task of discovering if either of them was being watched. There was nothing more they could do for the moment except be vigilant.

Amelia parted from Gerard and went upstairs to her own apartments to change into a more suitable gown.

She noticed that the blue velvet cloak she had loaned Emily was not lying on a chair in the sitting room. She could not recall if it had been there when she left earlier that morning, because she had been in too much hurry. Either Emily had taken it and gone out or she had tidied it away. Perhaps she was in her room now.

Amelia knocked at the door. Receiving no answer, she opened it and went in. As the maid had said earlier, the bed had been made and the room was tidy, as always. The gold purse Amelia had given Emily for Christmas was lying on the dressing table, as were one or two other gifts. It was a little odd that Emily should leave them lying there; she would normally have put them in her dressing case for safety. Amelia had an odd sensation, a feeling that Emily might have done something foolish. Surely she had not run away? Or something more desperate! Chills ran down Amelia's spine as she recalled her childhood friend Lucinda's terrible fate. A few years ago, Lucinda had taken her own life in her desperation—but Emily would surely not be so foolish.

Going to the armoire, she looked inside, feeling relieved as she saw the leather dressing case and Emily's clothes. At least she had not run away. Amelia was certain that her companion would not have left without at least taking some of her clothes and the dressing case. Besides, the girl was too conscientious to go off without at least leaving a letter—and, she believed, too sensible to take her own life.

A little reassured, Amelia went to change her clothes. Shortly after, she paid a visit to the nursery, where she talked to Lisa and some of the other children. She was asked to read a story from a book that one of the children had received as a Christmas gift. She read aloud, taking Lisa and one of the others on to her lap. The others crowded about her, clutching at her clothes and staring up into her face adoringly as she acted out the story for them.

She was unaware that Gerard came to the door and watched for a few minutes before leaving.

It was almost nuncheon before Amelia was able to break away from her audience and go downstairs to join the others.

She was at the buffet table, helping herself to cold chicken, a dish of potatoes and turnips and some green vegetables when Gerard came up to her.

'I saw you just now,' he said. 'It is good of you to give so much of your time to the children, Amelia.'

'I enjoy it. Lisa asked if I would read to her and the others wanted to listen. I believe they enjoyed themselves—and, after all, Christmas is for the little ones, do you not think so? Our Lord was born at this time and it is for his sake that we hold these celebrations.'

'You deserve a large family of your own, Amelia.'

'I hope to have several children—if God wills it.'

She looked up into his face and her heart began to race wildly. The way he was looking at her set her on fire and she wished that they were somewhere else—anywhere that they might be alone. She wanted so desperately to be in his arms, to feel his mouth on hers—but most of all she wanted his love. She felt what was becoming a familiar ache about her heart. Gerard had loved her once, but he had told her that something had died inside him when her brother sent him away and he believed that she had merely been toying with his heart. Would he ever be able to love her as she loved him?

'Gerard—' she began and broke off as a footman came up to them, offering a silver salver to him.

'This was delivered for you a few moments ago, sir.'

'For me?' Gerard frowned and opened the sealed note. He swore softly and then looked at Amelia in some bewilderment. 'I do not understand—this note implies that you are a prisoner. I am to pay the sum of forty thousand pounds or you will die…but you are here…'

'Yes…' Amelia shivered as a trickle of ice slithered down her spine. 'But Emily is not…' She glanced round the room, which was filling up with guests. 'I believe she went out early this morning and, as far as I know, she has not returned.'

'Would she stay out so long in this weather?'

'I cannot think it. She was feeling unhappy. I wondered if she had run away, but her things were all in her room.'

'Who would snatch Miss Barton and demand such a huge ransom?'

'Someone who did not know me well,' Amelia said. 'On Christmas Eve I was wearing a dark blue cloak with fur lining. I had bought myself a new black one for Christmas, and because the weather was so very cold I loaned the blue one to Emily. If she was wearing it when she went out, she could have been mistaken for me.'

'Good grief!' Gerard was astounded. 'We must send at once and make certain she is not in her room.'

'I shall go up myself,' Amelia said. 'She was not in her room when we returned from our drive. I thought she wished to be alone and did not search for her. I should have alerted you before this, but I did not imagine that she was in danger. Excuse me…'

Amelia left her food untouched as she went immediately in search of her companion. She ran up the stairs. The sitting room was empty and so was Emily's room. Nothing had been moved since Amelia's last visit.

Her maid came from the other bedchamber, carrying an evening dress. Amelia asked her if she had seen Emily.

'No, Miss Royston. I came up to fetch this dress. I was going to iron it for you for this evening. Is something wrong?'

'Emily appears to be missing,' Amelia said. 'Please continue with your work, Martha—but make inquiries as you go. I am worried about Miss Barton.'

'Yes, miss. Of course. I'll ask if anyone has seen her this morning.'

Amelia went back down the stairs. Gerard and Harry were talking together in the hall. They turned to look at her. Amelia shook her head.

'Martha hasn't seen her. Her room is just as it was when I was last there.'

'I have alerted my butler,' Harry told her. 'He will make sure that all the servants are asked for their last sighting of her. If we know what time she left, we may discover how long she has been missing.'

'What can we do?' Amelia asked. 'How long have we

been given to find the ransom, Gerard? I do not have that kind of money available, but I will sell some investments—anything I can to recover my poor Emily.'

'We will all contribute,' Harry assured her. 'However, it may be possible to recover her without giving this rogue a penny.'

'I cannot risk Emily's life. She was taken because they thought she was me...' Amelia could not prevent a sob of despair. 'If only we knew who had taken her. I shall never forgive myself if anything happens to her.'

'You cannot blame yourself,' Gerard said and frowned. 'I must confess that I should have been devastated had they managed to get their hands on you, Amelia.'

Amelia's eyes flashed with anger. 'Are you saying that Emily's life is less important than mine? That is unfair, Gerard. She is a lovely person and I am very fond of her.'

'I did not mean to imply that she was less worth saving.' Gerard ran fingers through his hair. 'Of course we shall do what we can, but once they know they have the wrong person...'

'Are you saying that they will kill her?' Amelia was rapidly becoming distraught. 'No! How do we let them know that I will pay?' She looked at him wildly. 'This is all my fault. If I had given my brother what he wanted... Oh, no! It is too much.'

At that moment there was a disturbance at the door and then two people entered, their clothes sprinkled with a dusting of snow.

Amelia looked towards the door and saw her companion. She gave a scream and ran to her. 'Emily, my love! I have been out of my mind with worry! Where have you been?'

'I went for a walk…' Emily sobbed and threw herself into Amelia's arms. 'I was snatched from behind and thrust into a carriage. I had a blanket over my head and I did not know what was happening. After some time, perhaps half an hour or so, the carriage stopped and I was carried into a house. I was left alone in a bedroom. It was a very cold house. I screamed and tried to get out but both the window and door were locked. As they carried me in, I heard one of them say that if the money did not come through I was to be killed…'

'Emily…' Amelia drew back in shock to look at her face. 'How terrifying for you, my love. What happened? How did you escape?'

Behind her, at that moment, she heard what seemed to be a quarrel break out. Turning her head, she saw that the man who had entered the house with Emily was the Marquis of Northaven. From the look of it, both Harry and Gerard were threatening him.

'Please, you must not be angry with the marquis,' Emily cried. 'It was he who saved me and brought me back. Had he not come, I should still have been in that room.'

'Is this true?' Gerard demanded. 'Explain yourself if you please, sir.'

'I think we should speak privately,' Northaven said. He took a few steps towards Emily. 'I am sorry that you were subjected to such an ordeal, Miss Barton. I tried to warn the earl that he must be careful, but I did not expect that they would take you. I understood Miss Ravenshead was their quarry.'

'You tried to warn me...' Gerard frowned as something clicked into place. 'Was it you that sent the doll?'

'Yes. A clumsy trick, I think, but I was not sure how else to do it. I wanted to alert you to the fact that Miss Royston might be in danger.'

'Why did you not say so plainly?' Gerard glared at him.

'Would you have believed me if I had signed my name? Would you have received me had I tried to warn you in person?' Northaven lifted his head proudly. 'I do not pretend to be without vice. I have done many things that I might wish undone—but I am not a murderer, though you persist in thinking me one. If I caused the death of comrades by loose talk, I regret it—but it *was* careless talk, no more.'

'I think you need to do more explaining,' Gerard said. 'Amelia, please take Miss Barton upstairs and see that she is cared for. You might wish to send for the doctor?'

Emily shook her head in alarm. 'I am not harmed. I was frightened, but I am well enough now.'

'I shall take you upstairs, my love.' Amelia put a protective arm about her. 'You are cold and trembling. You shall go to bed with a warming pan and a tisane. I shall sit with you and you may tell me all about it.'

Amelia drew her companion from the room. She would have liked to listen to all the marquis had to say, but she knew that Gerard did not wish either her or Emily to hear all the details lest it frighten them more. They had both had a terrible shock and it was only thanks to the Marquis of Northaven that things were not much worse. Amelia could hardly bear to think of what might have happened.

'Were you far from the house when they took you?' she asked Emily as they walked upstairs together.

'Only in the knot gardens,' Emily told her. 'It must have been within sight of the house, but of course it was very early. I dare say even the servants had not risen.' She gave a little sob. 'I lay awake all night. I was tossing and turning and thought that a walk might clear my head. I had forgot what we said—besides, I did not imagine anyone would try to snatch me. It was you I believed in danger.'

'My poor Emily.' Amelia squeezed her hand. 'You were taken because they thought you were me. A huge ransom was demanded, but I should have paid it, my love. We were trying to think how it could be done when you came in. I could not have borne it had anything happened to you.'

'Amelia! I am so glad you did not have to pay—and I am sorry if you were worried. I did not dream that anyone would try to kidnap me.'

'I dare say they would not had you not been wearing my blue cloak,' Amelia said. 'You must not wear it to walk in again until this rogue has been caught and dealt with, Emily.'

'Have you any idea of who it could be?'

'No, not truly. I suppose you heard nothing?'

'They spoke of someone of whom they were afraid,' Emily told her. 'However, they did not name him.'

'I know everyone thinks it must be my brother and I fear it may be so, though I do not wish to believe it.'

'It is so wicked. I do not know who could do such

things.' Emily shivered. 'I was to have been strangled had the money not been forthcoming—but that was after I told them who I was. I believe they realised their mistake too late. They spoke of a ransom note and said that if the money was not paid they would amuse themselves before disposing of me.'

'My love! How awful for you. I am so sorry that you were exposed to such wickedness.'

'It was fortunate for me that the marquis came to get me.'

'How did he know that you had been taken—and where to find you?'

'I have no idea. I did not think to ask. I was simply grateful that he got me out of that house before...' A fit of shuddering overtook Emily. 'I have never been as frightened in my life.'

'I am certain that Gerard and Harry will wish to know where the marquis got his information,' Amelia said. 'Come, dearest, let me help you undress. Martha will bring you a pan filled with hot coals and a tisane. Tomorrow I shall take you home.'

'No, please do not. I want to go to the ball as we planned,' Emily said. 'I shall not let this frighten me— nor shall I dwell on what happened with Mr Sinclair. At one time last night I considered taking my own life, but what happened made me see that I want to live. It will be hard to meet Mr Sinclair again, but I shall bear it.'

'My poor love.' Amelia kissed her brow. 'You are a very brave girl. You must forget Mr Sinclair; if he could not behave in a proper manner, he is not worth breaking your heart over.'

Chapter Five

'Well, I am waiting,' Gerard said. 'I am grateful to have Miss Barton back, but this begs an explanation. How did you know that there was a plot to kidnap Miss Royston and how did you know where to find Miss Barton?'

The marquis made a wry face. 'I thought they had Miss Royston until I got there and realised that they had snatched the wrong lady. I persuaded them to drink some rum to keep out the cold and laced it with laudanum. As soon as they became groggy I snatched Miss Barton and brought her here. *He* will know that I tricked them and I dare say my life may be at risk, but I do not value it so highly that I shall lose sleep over it.'

'You have still not told us how you knew what was going on,' Harry objected. 'And who is behind this business?'

'Don't look at me like that, Pendleton,' the marquis said. 'If you must know, I was offered money to help capture Miss Royston. However, I believe he sensed that I was not going to do his bidding and so he moved ahead of time. I was told the abduction was planned for when she journeyed to Coleridge.'

'You were offered money—how much?'

'Ten thousand pounds.' Northaven laughed ruefully. 'A pittance, I dare say, when you consider her fortune. A few months ago I might have taken his money. I was in debt and the bitterness inside me was much stronger than it is now. You may thank a lady for that—and, no, I shall not name her.'

'Why did you not come to us—tell us who we have to deal with?' Gerard demanded.

'If I knew his name, I would have told you. He keeps to the shadows and hides his face—though I have seen it since our first meeting. I let him believe that I would help him, learning what I could of his intentions. I have tried to follow him, and I think he spotted me, which may be why he did not trust me in the end. However, I knew where they meant to hold Miss Royston for the first few hours—and I was on my way here early this morning. I had decided that I could not handle this alone and meant to ask you to listen to my story. As I walked towards the house, I saw what I thought was Miss Royston being snatched. There was no time to warn you so I followed them. They had not changed the rendezvous—and, thankfully, his rogues still trusted me.'

'You have no idea of his identity?'

'I know that he calls himself Lieutenant Gordon, but I doubt it is his name—though I believe him to have been an officer, for he has the manner of a military man. However, I do not recall that he ever served with us.'

'It was not Sir Michael Royston?'

'Miss Royston's brother? Good lord, no! I would have known his voice. I played cards with him quite recently.'

'Could he not be in league with this rogue?'

'He could, but not to my knowledge.'

'Why were you approached?'

'He believed that I might want to bring you down, Gerard. He must have heard of our quarrel, which is known well enough in certain circles. His plans for Miss Royston were not simply to ransom her, believe me. Had you paid what he asked, he would have taken the money—and then I believe he meant to despoil her and kill you.'

'My God!' Gerard turned pale. 'He must hate me.' He took a turn about the room, then returned to where Harry and the marquis stood. 'What have I done to him that he should hate me so?'

'Only you can answer that,' Northaven said. 'Have you ruined a man at the tables or taken his woman?'

'No...unless...Lisette—' Gerard broke off and smote his forehead with the palm of his hand, a look of disbelief in his eyes. 'I do not know. My wife...was carrying the child of her lover when I married her. She was honest with me. Lisette told me that he had died and that she was alone in the world. I married her to protect her, but if her lover were severely wounded and then recovered...to discover that she had married me...he may blame me for her death.'

'That may be your answer,' Northaven said, eyes

narrowed in thought. 'If Gordon believes that you took her from him, he may wish to take what you love in revenge. Since Miss Royston is wealthy and you have your own fortune, he thinks that he may also have some financial gain from it.'

'But I did not take her from him…' Gerard shook his head. 'When I found her she was close to death. She was lying at the side of the road, bruised and beaten. She told me that some French soldiers had raped her—more than one, I believe. I nursed her back to life and then I married her to keep her safe. She was very ill after the birth, but then she recovered…' He paused, a nerve flicking in his cheek. 'Lisette took her own life. I believe because she wanted more from me than I could give her.'

'Good grief!' Harry cried, shocked. 'I had no idea… My dear fellow. I am so sorry.'

Gerard shrugged off his sympathy. 'I told no one until recently. Miss Royston knows some of it, but not all—and I ask you both to keep my secret. I believe Lisette took her own life because I did not love her.'

'*He* blames you for her death,' Northaven said grimly. 'It is as plain as the nose on your face! This Lieutenant Gordon—whoever he is—*he* blames you for the death of the woman he loves.'

'In a way I am guilty, though I never meant to hurt her. I thought Lisette understood that I had married her simply to offer my protection, but she wanted me to love her. I failed her…and her death has haunted me ever since.'

'I believe you have established a motive, Ravenshead—now you need to know who he really is. She did not give you the name of her lover?'

'No. I never asked; I believed him dead and it did not matter.'

'Does he know the child is his?' Harry asked. 'If so, he may feel that you have stolen her as well.'

'I doubt he knows it,' Gerard said. 'She had not seen him since he rode away to battle some weeks earlier— one of his friends told her he had been killed. She was trying to discover more when she was set upon by those rogues who raped her and left her for dead.'

'Then it is best that Gordon never knows the truth,' Harry said. 'Until you can discover the identity of your enemy, Gerard, you must be very careful.'

'Yes, you are right,' Gerard agreed. He looked at Northaven. 'Are you willing to help us?'

'Of course. You had only to *ask*.' Northaven's eyes gleamed. 'Tell me what I may do for you and I shall do my best to oblige.'

Amelia sat with Emily until she drifted off into sleep. After some tears and a fit of the shudders, she had finally settled. Leaving her to rest, Amelia decided to change for the evening. She was thoughtful as she sat for her maid to dress her hair into the new softer style, caught up in an intricate swirl at the nape of her neck. During one of her crying bouts, Emily's deep sadness at the loss of her child had come tumbling out.

Amelia had comforted her as best she could. She had made up her mind that she would definitely speak to someone soon about employing an agent to make inquiries. It might not be possible to trace the child, and even if Emily's child could be found they might not be able to recover her. She would have a family, perhaps a mother and father who loved her—but perhaps it would be enough for Emily to have news of her daughter.

Amelia would do what she could to find the child, but she would say nothing until she knew whether or not it was possible. Having settled that much in her mind, she went down to the parlour where guests had begun to gather for drinks before dinner. She saw Susannah and several of the other guests but there was no sign of Gerard or Harry.

'They went out earlier and have not yet come in,' Susannah said when Amelia asked. 'Harry told me what Northaven had done. I could hardly believe that he had acted so heroically. He was not always courteous to me in the past—and yet I am not sure that he is black as he is often painted.'

'I owe the marquis a debt of deep gratitude,' Amelia said. 'I do not forget that he once fought a duel with Harry and that you were wounded, my love. However, I do not believe he meant to injure you—and perhaps he has gone some way to redeeming himself by bringing Emily back to us.'

'Oh, I forgave him for that long ago.' Susannah smiled. 'He watched us when we walked from church after our wedding, you know. There was something in his eyes…I think he meant me to know that Harry was safe from him, as he has been.' Susannah looked thoughtful. 'He is undoubtedly a rake and has almost certainly done things that would shock us if we knew the whole—but everyone is entitled to a second chance.'

'Yes, I am sure you are right.' Amelia frowned. 'I wanted to speak to Harry, but it will keep.'

'Is there something I can help you with, Amelia?'

'No, Susannah. I need a man's advice about something, my dear. I had thought to ask Harry, for I believe that Gerard has enough on his mind at the moment—but another day will do.'

'Well, I dare say they will not be long, though Harry told me not to hold dinner.'

'I expect they have some business.'

'I dare say they do. It seems very odd that the Marquis of Northaven is involved; Harry was much against him at one time.'

'Gentlemen are contrary creatures,' Amelia teased. 'They can be at odds one minute and the best of friends another.'

'Do you think we can trust him?' Harry asked as they entered the house, shaking a light dusting of snow from their coats. 'I must admit I should not have given him a chance to speak had he not brought Miss Barton back to us. I should probably have told the footmen to throw him out.'

He went over to the magnificent mahogany sideboard in his library and poured brandy for them both, giving one to Gerard and holding the other to warm it in his hands before sipping.

'At the moment I do not have much choice,' Gerard confessed. 'His tale of a Lieutenant Gordon might be a falsehood, but I am inclined to believe him. Lisette had a lover. She believed he had been killed, but it is possible that he still lives. Men fall in battle and are reported dead and then turn up somewhere...' He sighed with frustration. 'If he went looking for her and heard tales of her death, it would explain why he hates me. He probably thinks I am a monster and that I treated her ill. I gave her everything I could, but she needed so much more.'

'If you could speak to him, tell him what happened...'

Gerard shook his head, dismissing the idea. 'I doubt he would listen. In his place I would want revenge.' He groaned his frustration. 'What am I to do, Harry? How can I marry Amelia, knowing that by doing so I am endangering her life? When I thought she was in danger from her brother it was one thing, but now...'

'You cannot be sure of anything. This tale of Northaven's may be a ruse. He could still be in league with the rogues. Besides, you cannot wish to withdraw? You do not wish to jilt Amelia Royston? Think how it would look? Susannah would never speak to you again.'

'Of course I do not wish to jilt her! Good God! It is the last thing I want—but if the marriage is rendering her the target of a madman...'

'I can only advise you to wait. We shall see that she is protected, of course. Northaven says that he will try to discover the true identity of this man...get as close to him as he can and then bring you news of his whereabouts. We must hope that he will keep his word.'

'Yes, though, if he drugged the rogues who snatched Miss Barton, Northaven's life could be at risk. Lieutenant Gordon will have him shot on sight.'

'He knew that was possible when he agreed. This may be his way of atoning, Gerard. Even if he did not betray us that time in Spain, it was his loose talk while drunk that led to the deaths of several men. The French knew we were coming. Our mission was secret. Only the four of us knew, for we did not tell the troopers where we were going. They followed us blindly to their deaths—and Northaven did not turn up that morning. He says that he woke too late after a night of heavy drinking and gambling, but I am still not certain I believe him.'

'We sent him to Coventry and branded him a coward and a traitor,' Gerard observed grimly. 'He always swore that he was innocent, but in his heart he knew that his loose tongue was to blame. He provoked you into a duel and would have killed any of us in anger— but I believe he has changed, though I have no idea why.'

'He said it was a woman.'

'If rumour does not lie, he has ruined more than one in his time. *She* must be remarkable if she has reformed him. I am not certain that his story is the true one, but I have no other clues. So far this Lieutenant Gordon has managed to cover his tracks. I have set my agents to looking for him, and I am having Northaven watched too. I do not trust him entirely even yet.'

'Then you must carry on as if nothing has happened. If you change your plans, Gordon will become suspicious. There is no guarantee that he will leave Miss Royston in peace, even if you give her up. If I were in your shoes, I would double the number of men watching over her and Miss Barton and go ahead with your plans.'

'I must make Amelia aware of the danger—but I

think you are right. We did not tell many people, but these things get out. To draw back now would look as if we had quarrelled. I shall just have to be vigilant.'

'It is all you can do for the moment. I shall come to Coleridge a few days after you, Gerard. In the meantime I will send some of my grooms with you. I know you have your own men, but they will do better in the shadows. My grooms will be armed and ride with you.'

'Thank you, but I hardly like to involve you in this business, Harry. You have a wife and child to think of and this may be a nasty affair before it is ended.'

'We swore to help each other that day in Spain,' Harry reminded him grimly. 'We survived that day because the three of us defended each other's backs. You were there for me when I needed you—I shall not desert you in your time of need.'

'You believe that all this may be because of Lisette's lover? Someone she knew before you married her?' Amelia stared at Gerard in the moonlight. He had come to her as she was about to go up to bed, requesting that she stroll with him in the gallery. The candles had burned low in their sockets, but the moonlight filtered through the long windows, giving them light enough to see each other's faces. Had it not been for the subject under discussion, it might have been romantic. She did not think that he had mentioned that Lisette had had a lover before this, though perhaps she had not perfectly heard him. 'Gerard—how can that be? I am at a loss to understand. Why should this man blame you for what happened?'

'I do not know. Northaven said that Gordon hates me

and I can only think he must be bitter because Lisette died. I told you that she took her own life some months after the birth of her child. If he went looking for her in the Spanish village where we lived and was told that she slashed her wrists, he would be horrified, angry. In his shoes I might want revenge.'

'Why did she marry you if she had a lover?'

'She believed he was dead. She was alone and in desperate need.'

'Lisette died four years ago, Gerard. Why has this man never tried to kill you in all those years? Why now?'

'I have no idea. I cannot even be sure that Northaven is telling me the truth. He could have planned the whole thing to gain some advantage for himself.'

'Surely he would not?' Amelia looked thoughtful. 'There must be some other reason that has kept this man from moving against you, Gerard. Something must have changed. Perhaps he did not know how Lisette died and then discovered it.'

'I wish I knew...' Gerard hesitated. 'You know in what danger you stand. Would you prefer it if I went away? I should still try to discover my enemy, but you would be safer. And in time I could return. It would be merely a postponement.'

'You know my answer. I refuse to hide in the shadows. Besides, he would not be fooled. If this man knows so much about us, he would soon learn the truth. If we let him part us, it would be for ever. Do you want that?'

'No! Damn it, no.'

'Then we have no alternative but to go ahead with our plans.'

'It is odd that he knows where we are. I told only a few people I was coming here this Christmas.'

'Most of my acquaintances knew I would be here,' Amelia said. 'However, I told no one that I expected to see you for I did not know if I should.'

'It is a mystery,' Gerard said. 'I may have been followed, of course. I feel like a blind man stumbling about in the dark. As Harry says, we cannot be certain even now for it is all merely theory.'

'I believe the only way is to carry on as normal and hope that he will make a mistake.'

'You are very brave.' Gerard looked at her gravely. 'I would rather give you up than have your death on my conscience, Amelia—but, as you say, if we give way now it does not follow that you will be safe. I think it is better than we go ahead with the wedding as soon as possible so that I am in a position to take care of you.'

Amelia felt as if her heart had been squeezed. Gerard would rather give her up than have her death on his conscience. How could he say such a thing to her? She would rather die than give him up, but it seemed he did not feel the same way.

Lisette had been desperately unhappy because he did not love her. Amelia could not help but wonder if she were laying up pain for herself in the future. She loved him so very much. Would she one day feel desperate because Gerard was unable to love her? Would she ever feel so alone that she would be driven to take her own life?

No, she had known heartbreak and lived through it. She was stronger than Lisette.

'I am certain there is more to this mystery than you

yet realise,' she told him. 'Your enemy knows where we are and what we are doing. He knows all about me. How can that be? We must have a mutual acquaintance. Someone close to us who knows where we intend to be.'

'Yes, that would seem to be the case. I am damned if I know who it is, though!'

'We must both think hard. Since I was the target, you cannot be certain that he is your enemy, Gerard. He might very well be mine.'

'You are sure she means to go to Coleridge?' Lieutenant Gordon asked of the woman he had met late at night in the shadows of a summerhouse. 'If I have men waiting on the road and she goes to another location, I may miss my last chance of surprising them.'

The woman's mouth curled in a sneer. 'Your fools bungled it once. Do you imagine that you still have the element of surprise? No, you lost that when you involved Northaven in your plans. Why did you not ask me? I should have told you that he would not do it. I know he spoke of hating them, but he hated only that they distrusted him—thought him a traitor. He is no angel, but neither is he a murderer. I could have told you had you asked my advice.'

'How do you know so much about him?' Gordon asked, looking at her jealously. She was his second cousin. When they were children they had played together in the meadows. She had given herself to him when she was thirteen. Wild and enchanting, she had had the power to command him, making him her slave, but when he joined the army as a young man he had broken free of her. He had fallen in love, but Lisette had betrayed him. He had searched for her when his wounds healed, and when he discovered the truth of her death he had been devastated. On his return to England some months ago, he had sought his childhood love out, discovering that her power to enslave him had become stronger. 'Is Northaven your lover?'

She laughed mockingly. 'I may once have indulged myself with the gentleman for an hour or so one summer, but I never loved him. You have no need to be jealous.' She laid her hand on his arm, giving him a seductive smile. 'Have I not helped you by telling you where you could find Miss Royston? Have I not helped you to plan your revenge on the man who stole your lover?'

'Lisette was a silly little fool. I was angry when I discovered that he had married her and made her unhappy—but I never loved her in the way I love you. I have always adored you. You are the one who hates him. Or is it Miss Royston you hate?'

'She is nothing to me. I care not whether she lives or dies, but he loves her and so her fate is sealed. You want Gerard Ravenshead dead and so do I—we are agreed on this, are we not?' He nodded, though it was she who had demanded Ravenshead's death as her price—the price he must pay to have her. 'Then there is nothing else you need to know.'

He moved towards her, reaching out to pull her hard against him. His mouth was demanding on hers, bruising and possessive. 'You know I love you. I have hated him for what he did to Lisette, but—'

'You would have let him live?' Her eyes snapped

with scorn. 'She cut her wrists…bled to death…and you would let him live? You snivelling coward! I thought you had more courage. Perhaps I should find another to help me.'

'No!' Gordon caught her wrist as she would have turned away from him. 'I will see her dead and he shall witness her death, as I promised you.'

'She must be ravished and he must see it! I want him to suffer. His death is not punishment enough.'

'Why do you hate him so much? What did he do to you?'

'That is my affair,' *she* told him and her eyes blazed with bitter anger. 'I want revenge and I know how to get it. Forget your ideas of ambushing them on the road. They will have outriders and grooms and all will be armed. The rogues you employ will turn tail and flee at the first shot fired at them. No, I have a much better idea. Listen well, because this is what we shall do…'

'I wish that we were coming with you.' Susannah hugged Amelia as they parted. Christmas was over and the snow had cleared, but the overnight frost had turned the ground hard. 'I know that we shall see you at Coleridge, but I am concerned for you on the journey.'

'You must not be, dearest.' Amelia kissed her cheek. 'Thank you for giving us such a wonderful Christmas. Perhaps another year you may come to us.'

'I doubt if the relatives would give up the Christmas visit. It is tradition, you know—but I shall be very glad to stay with you at other times. The *Old Crusties*, as Toby Sinclair calls them, enjoy their stay. I shall be fortunate to get to Coleridge before the day of the ball.'

'You make them too comfortable.' Amelia laughed. 'Well, I must not keep Gerard waiting; I know he is anxious that we should make good time.'

'I shall see you soon. You must write to me as soon as you arrive.'

Amelia laughed. 'You sound like Marguerite. She is always anxious to hear my news. I must write to her again soon.'

Susannah frowned. 'Marguerite? I do not think I know her.'

'No, perhaps I did not mention her to you. We did not communicate for some years following a family tragedy, but then she wrote to me and I learned how miserable her life has become. Since then I have written to her at least twice a month and sometimes more.'

'Is she another of your lame ducks, Amelia?' Susannah laughed teasingly.

'Marguerite's situation is more difficult. Her parents are not poor. Indeed, they have money enough to give her a Season in town if they wish—but they refuse to allow it. Marguerite never goes into company without her mama. She is kept very strictly at home.'

'That is such a shame. Poor girl! What has she done to deserve such a fate?'

'She is hardly a girl. I believe we are of a similar age. She may be a year or so older. Marguerite has done nothing to merit her fate, which is why I feel for her so strongly. Her parents blame her for something that happened to her sister and that is unfair.'

'You must ask her to stay with you,' Susannah said. 'Perhaps you could find her a husband. After all, she is old enough to marry without permission, is she not?'

'Yes, but her father is a bully. I think she is afraid of him. However, I do have something in mind, though I am not sure she would wish to accept. I did invite her to stay with me in Bath, but her father would not allow it at that time.'

'That is so unfair, especially if she has done nothing wrong,' Susannah said and hugged her again. 'She is lucky to have you as a friend, Amelia. I am sure you will do something to help her if you can.'

'I have written to Marguerite with my suggestion. I wrote as soon as I knew Lisa would need a new nanny. Marguerite's parents will not allow her to have a Season in London or Bath, but they may allow her to stay with me in the country to help to care for a motherless child. If Lisa were in her care, I should feel that we could safely leave her sometimes.'

'And you entertain a great deal so she would have company and make friends.' Susannah clapped her hands. 'How clever you are, Amelia! It is exactly the thing. I do not see how her parents could object to such a suggestion for their daughter.'

'Well, we shall see. Marguerite may not like the idea of becoming a child's nanny—but she will live as one of the family and have the opportunity to meet all my friends. In time she might meet someone suitable that she might marry.'

'I do hope it all works out for her,' Susannah said. 'And now you really must go, because I can see Gerard in the hall and he looks impatient.'

'Farewell for now, dearest Susannah. I shall write to you and you will join us at Coleridge within the week.'

Amelia parted from her friend and went into the hall

where Gerard was in close conversation with Harry. He turned as soon as she came up to him, looking relieved.

'We must go, Amelia. I am sorry to hurry you, but I wish to reach Coleridge before dark. We shall change the horses, but we shall not stop for refreshments. Harry's chef has put up a picnic for us and we may eat on the road.'

'Yes, of course. I understand perfectly.' Amelia glanced at Harry. 'You will not forget what I asked of you, sir?'

'The matter is already in hand. I have the details and my agent will deal with it as a matter of urgency.'

'Thank you. I am in your debt.'

Harry bowed over her hand. 'No, no, Amelia. You brought Susannah to me. I shall forever be in your debt.'

Amelia shook her head and smiled as she followed Gerard outside. He looked at her oddly.

'What was that about, Amelia? If you need the services of an agent, I could have arranged it for you.'

'I know and I would have asked, but you have enough worries as it is—and it is a matter for someone else, Gerard. It is not personal and need not concern you.'

'Very well,' he said but there was a jut to his chin, as if it had not pleased him that she had asked Harry to execute her commission.

Amelia was prevented from saying more because Emily was standing by the carriage. She could not tell Gerard that she had asked Harry to see if he could find Emily's daughter at that moment. Besides, though she had been forced to confide the details to Harry, she had done so in confidence and would not speak of it more than she need, even to Gerard.

He looked a little serious as he handed both ladies into the carriage. Amelia wondered if she had offended him and regretted it. She did not wish anything to overshadow their wedding. Gerard's careless words had given her a restless night, but eventually she had told herself that she was being foolish. Gerard cared for her safety, which meant she was important to him. It was foolish to wish for the romantic love of their youth. Had she not already decided that a marriage of convenience would do very well?

She was impatient for their wedding so that they could begin their new life together. This threat hanging over them was unpleasant, but she had perfect faith in Gerard and his ability to protect her. She could not help feeling relieved that he no longer believed her brother had been trying to murder her. Michael would not be pleased when she wrote to him to tell him that she intended to marry the man he had expressly forbidden her to wed. She frowned as she wondered just why her brother was so much against the marriage. He had gone to great lengths to prevent it when she was younger, but Gerard had inherited an estate he had not expected to inherit. He was not as wealthy as Harry Pendleton or Max Coleridge, but he was certainly not a pauper and his estate was free of encumbrances. It was unreasonable for Michael to be so against the marriage now.

Amelia turned to her companion as they settled in their seats. Gerard had chosen to ride behind the carriage for the first part of the journey and the ladies were alone, Amelia's maids following in the second coach with Lisa's nurse and the child.

'Nurse insisted that Lisa ride with them for a while,

but I think when we stop I shall tell her to come in with us—you will not mind that, Emily?'

'Of course not. She is a delightful child, intelligent, and seems older than her years, though she is almost five now...' The shadows were in Emily's eyes, though she was no longer weepy and was clearly making an effort to be cheerful.

'Are you sure you wish to come to Coleridge? If you would prefer to go to Bath until I am settled at Ravenshead, I would understand.'

'Of course I wish to come. I am looking forward to seeing Helene.'

'You know that Toby Sinclair may be there for the ball?'

'We are bound to meet in company,' Emily said. She lifted her head; her face was proud though her mouth trembled a little. 'I have accepted that he has rejected me. I am in control of my feelings now, Amelia. I shall not break down again.'

Amelia reached for her hand and squeezed it. It was Emily's hurt that had prompted her to have a search made for her child. If she could arrange for Emily to visit her little girl now and then, it would be something.

'I think you have behaved with dignity, my love. It is natural that you should weep for your lost hopes. I must tell you that Mr Sinclair is not the man I thought him.'

'I cannot blame him. I should have told him the truth when I first knew he was becoming interested. It was my own fault for allowing him to think me something I am not.'

'You must not think of yourself as a fallen woman,

Emily. The fault was not yours.' Amelia saw that her companion was unconvinced. 'I told you of my friend Lucinda, did I not?' Emily nodded. 'Lucinda took her life because she was too ashamed to have her baby. You were braver. I am proud of you, my love.' She touched her hand. 'Now, I have a request to make of you...'

'Anything. You know I am always happy to oblige you, Amelia.'

'Lucinda had a sister. She was a year older than Lucinda and not as pretty. When Lucinda took her life and her parents understood that she had been seduced, they became much stricter with Marguerite. They refused to let her go to dances or anything where she might be alone with gentlemen. She is taken out only when her mother goes into company with her friends, which is, as you can imagine, a tedious life for a young woman.'

'Poor Marguerite.' Emily smiled. 'I can guess what you mean to ask me, Amelia. You are going to invite her to live with us.'

'I have written to her parents and asked if she may be allowed to live at Ravenshead to help care for Lisa. I am not sure Marguerite will wish to come, but if she does I hope you will make her feel at home with us.'

'Naturally I shall. It is most unfair that she should be denied the pleasures of society just because her sister was seduced...I know just how she feels.' Emily's voice quivered with passion. 'She has been treated most unfairly!'

'Of course you know, dearest,' Amelia said and smiled at her. 'I thought you could help Marguerite to find her way in society again. She may find it a little frightening after so many years of being almost a prisoner in her parents' home.'

'I shall do all I can to help her,' Emily said and looked thoughtful.

Amelia felt a warm satisfaction. Emily would find some ease for her own pain in thinking of others—and perhaps soon both of her friends would find happiness.

In the meantime, she could only hope that their journey would be accomplished peacefully. She could not help but be aware that they were surrounded by grooms, far more than she would normally dream of travelling with—and all of them armed. Gerard and Harry were taking no chances and she could only be grateful for their care of her.

They stopped briefly to change the horses, and, in the case of the ladies, to relieve themselves in private at a good posting inn. Lisa transferred to the main carriage and was as good as gold, perhaps because Amelia had thought to bring along a book filled with bright pictures. The ladies ate a picnic in the carriage and fortunately did not need to get out again at any point. In consequence, they were able to make good time and it was not yet dark when they arrived at Coleridge.

Helene came to greet them eagerly, kissing Amelia and then Emily. She looked radiant and very happy, as she told her friends that she was increasing.

'I believe Max thinks it is a little soon, but he is merely concerned for me,' she said as she led the way upstairs. 'Your rooms are adjacent and there is a connecting door should you wish to use it. I hope you will both be very comfortable with us. I have been looking forward to your visit so much. Did you enjoy yourselves at Pendleton?'

'Susannah made us very welcome, as always,' Amelia said. 'I am delighted at your news, my love. I must tell you that I have a little news myself. I am to be married.'

'Amelia! I am so pleased. You must be promised to the Earl of Ravenshead?'

'Yes. Gerard asked me to wed him at Pendleton and I agreed. However, I fear there is someone who does not wish us to marry and has already tried to prevent us.'

'Amelia?' Helene looked at her in alarm. 'Are you speaking of your brother?'

'Michael does not wish for it. Indeed, he forbade me—but this is someone else: someone who would prefer to see us dead rather than happy. As yet we are not certain of his identity, though we believe he may use the name of Lieutenant Gordon.'

'How can that be? Who would wish to see you dead?' Helene looked shocked.

'We are not certain.' Amelia frowned. 'I do not wish you to worry, Helene—especially in your condition. If you would prefer that we leave…'

'Certainly not. How could you think it? After all you have done for me, Amelia, I would never close my door to you—and I am sure that Max will wish to help Gerard in whatever way he can.'

'Thank you, dearest.' Amelia smiled her gratitude. 'I was sure you would feel that way. We have decided to announce our engagement at the ball.'

'I am so happy for you. I must admit that I thought

you might never marry, but now you are to wed the earl and I know you will be content—he is a good man.' Helene turned to look at Emily. 'How are you, dearest? I have thought that you might also have some news for me.'

'No, I fear I have not,' Emily replied, avoiding Helene's bright gaze. 'Besides, I should not dream of leaving Amelia while she had need of me.'

'I could not bear to part with you,' Amelia told her, guessing how much it was costing her to keep her smile in place. Helene would never deliberately hurt Emily and she could have no idea how much her care-less remark had wounded her. 'I expect you will have many guests for the ball, Helene—but I hope you will find room for one more. I mentioned Marguerite to you in my last letter, did I not?'

'Yes—and I sent her an invitation, Amelia. I have had no reply.'

'I dare say her father would not permit it. However, I have appealed to her mama to let her come to help me with my stepdaughter. You have not yet met Lisa, Helene. Her nurse took her straight upstairs, as you may have noticed. She is lovely and also a little charmer.'

'I shall look forward to meeting her,' Helene said. 'You know that I once wished to find a position as a teacher in your orphanage, Amelia. Lisa is so much luckier than the children you help, because she has you and Gerard.'

'She will also have Emily and possibly Marguerite to make a fuss of her.' Amelia laughed softly. 'It will be a wonder if she is not utterly spoiled—but she lost her mama when she was a small child and the nanny

Gerard employed when he brought her to England was not kind to her. I want her to be content and I think it will be a happy release for Marguerite to come to us. I told her we should be here until a day after the ball and then we shall go down to Ravenshead. If I find the house acceptable, and Gerard assures me I shall, we shall spend most of our time there. We shall visit Bath and London in the Season, naturally, but our home will be at Ravenshead.'

'Will you not miss your home?'

'Perhaps at first—at least the garden. However, I shall make a garden of my own at Ravenshead. We shall keep my aunt's estate for our second child.'

They had reached the upper floor, which housed the bedchambers. Having seen Emily installed in hers, Amelia looked at her own with pleasure.

'This has been freshly refurbished in the colours I love, Helene.'

'Yes, it has. It was done especially for you—for the best friend that I could ever have.' Helene reached forwards and kissed her cheek. 'You are such a generous person, Amelia. I cannot imagine that anyone would wish to harm you.'

'Well, it may be all a storm in a teacup,' Amelia said and laughed in a dismissive manner. 'Gerard and Harry took great precautions to safeguard us on the way here, but nothing happened. I dare say having made a blunder once the rogue has decided it is not worth the effort to try anything of the sort again.'

Helene was clearly puzzled. Amelia told her about Emily being kidnapped and then restored to them by the Marquis of Northaven.

'He told you that Emily was taken in mistake for you?' Helene was amazed. 'Oh, Amelia—it is almost like when attempts were made on Max's life and we thought it might be his cousin, but in the end it turned out to be his cousin's physician. When someone wishes you harm, it is difficult to know who they are.'

Amelia nodded but looked thoughtful. 'I hope this will not distress you, my love. I wonder if perhaps it would be better if we did not stay for the ball...'

'I should be most distressed then.' Helene lifted her head proudly. 'I was not frightened when that awful man threatened to kill me in order to get to Max...at least only a little and not until it was over. I do not want you to leave, Amelia. Max will help Gerard discover who this wicked rogue is. Gerard helped us—as did Mr Sinclair...' She frowned. 'I had thought that Toby Sinclair might propose to Emily.'

Amelia hesitated, then, 'In actual fact he did at Christmas, but she turned him down.'

'Emily turned down Mr Sinclair? Why? He is perfect for her.'

'She has her reasons, I dare say. It would be best if you did not speak of him to her, Helene—unless she takes you into her confidence, which she may. I know you were good friends.'

'We still are. Emily writes to me once in a while.' Helene looked thoughtful. 'I know she has a secret. I shall not ask you or her to reveal it, but I have seen the sadness in her eyes.'

'I shall tell you only that she had had an unhappy life before she came to me. I too had hopes of Mr Sinclair for her, but it seems that it was not to be. He left the same night and we have not heard from him since.'

'Then you do not know that his father died?'

'Oh, no! That is sad news indeed. I had wondered why he went so suddenly. Susannah told me he had an urgent summons to return, but I had no idea it was so serious.'

'Extremely serious. I know Max had a letter only this morning. Toby gave us the news and said that he was not sure if he could attend the ball. His mother and sister are in great distress. I dare say he cannot leave them immediately, especially for a ball. I am sure Toby will have written to Harry and Susannah, but perhaps the letter had not reached him before you left.'

'No, I dare say it had not, for he would have mentioned it,' Amelia replied. 'It is a sad time for the family and I do not expect that Toby will feel able to attend your ball. Indeed, it would look wrong if he did. I think too that Harry's sister will need him at her side at this difficult time.'

Helene chattered on for a while, but Amelia was thoughtful. She might have misjudged Mr Sinclair somewhat. She had thought him cruel and rude to abandon Emily so abruptly, but if he had received terrible news and then arrived home only in time to see his father on his deathbed, it was not to be expected that he would write immediately to Emily.

'His mother and sister must come first—and of course there will be business to be done. He must be very distressed, I imagine.'

'Yes, very sad. I am sorry that Emily refused him— but perhaps she will reconsider.'

'I should be happy to think she might. However, at the moment I do not think it possible.'

Left to herself, Amelia took off her pelisse and fur-trimmed bonnet. The news about Mr Sinclair's father was shocking. She did not know if his family had expected it, but even so it would have devastated them. Susannah had certainly not expected it. The very fact that Toby Sinclair had intimated that he might come to Coleridge even now made Amelia think that he had not completely given up the idea of wedding Emily. She would tell her companion the sad news, but she would not speculate about Toby Sinclair's intentions.

If he had any he would make them clear himself in time. Amelia's thoughts turned once more to Marguerite. She fully intended to make sure that Marguerite had every chance to meet a decent gentleman—and to help persuade her parents if the chance of a marriage presented itself.

Chapter Six

'Mr Sinclair's father has died?' Emily was shocked and distressed when Amelia told her the news the next morning. 'How terribly sad! I had no idea that he was so ill.'

'I do not believe anyone realised quite how precarious his health was—at least no one outside the family.'

'I thought…how selfish of me to be so upset about my own concerns.' Emily blushed. 'If Toby has been caught up in family problems—' She broke off and shook her head. 'No, I must not allow myself to hope. If he wished to communicate with me he could have sent me a letter.'

'I dare say he may have had too much on his mind.'

'You said he wrote to Helene to tell her the news—could he not have written to us?'

'He could…but perhaps he felt a letter inappropriate. What he has to say to you must be said face to face.'

'You are trying to make me feel better, but you did

not see his expression when I told him about my child.'
Emily raised her head. 'It would be foolish to imagine
that this changes anything. If Mr Sinclair comes to
the ball, I shall greet him as if nothing has happened
between us, but I dare say his mama will need him with
them for some time.'

'Yes, I think you may be right,' Amelia agreed.
'However, you should not give up hope entirely, dearest.'

'It was foolish of me to think that I might marry. My
father told me that no decent man would want me and
he is right.' The sheen of tears was in Emily's eyes, but
she held them back. 'Perhaps we should go down now,
Amelia. We do not wish to keep everyone waiting.'

Amelia did not answer. She knew that Emily was
suffering, but there was no cure for a broken heart, as
she had discovered to her cost when she was younger.
Time alone would soften the hurt. She could only hope
that Toby Sinclair would not visit Coleridge unless he
was prepared to say something of importance to Emily.

'Now that I understand the circumstances I am prepared to make allowances for Toby,' Amelia told Gerard
when they walked together in the long gallery later
that day. 'However, I think that he might have made
an effort to write to Emily—if only to tell her of his
father's death.'

'Letters are sometimes too difficult to write,' Gerard
said. He stopped walking and looked at her. 'Think of
the wasted years, Amelia. Had I written to you at the
time, we might have saved ourselves so much unhappiness.' He reached out to touch her face, remembered

sorrow in his eyes. 'If you knew of all the tortured nights I spent thinking of you…longing for you. I should never have let your brother poison my mind against you. I should have known that he lied when he said that you had asked him to send me a message.'

'Is that what he said to you? How dared he? You must know that I would never have done something like that.'

'Afterwards, when I had time to think it over, I began to see that I had been a fool to believe him, but at first I was too bitter. I married Lisette while still resenting both you and Michael, Amelia. And then it was too late…'

Amelia took a step towards him. Her body throbbed with a deep and urgent desire, making her discard her usual reserve. 'You were not alone in your despair, Gerard. I thought that I should never know the happiness of loving…never feel the touch of a lover's hand… because I could not forget you even though others asked for me.'

'That would have been a sin.' He smiled, his eyes warm with laughter. 'I know there is passion in you.' He reached forwards, bending his head to kiss her. Amelia did not hold back, clinging to him, giving herself to him without reserve. 'I can hardly wait for our wedding night.'

'Nor I.'

'Perhaps we need not wait…' Gerard was about to kiss her again when they both heard something. He looked beyond her at a woman who stood watching them from the other end of the gallery. 'We are not alone.'

'Forgive me,' the woman said and came forwards. She was a tall woman, slim with silky blonde hair that was caught back from her face in a severe style, and her gown was a dull grey that did nothing for her complexion. 'Lady Coleridge thought I might find you here. I wanted to let you know I had arrived, Amelia—but I did not mean to intrude.'

'Marguerite!' Amelia exclaimed in surprise. 'My dear friend. I am so pleased that you came. I hoped your parents would permit it, but I was not sure. I have had no word that you were coming.'

'I have not been well. Nothing serious, merely a chill. However, Mama thought it would do me good to have a change of air—and of course she is always willing to oblige you, Amelia.'

'How is your dear mama?'

'Very well, thank you.'

'Gerard—this is Miss Marguerite Ross.' Amelia turned to him. 'I am not sure if you know each other? Marguerite's family lived near my father's home when I was a girl. You may have met her when you visited the area. You stayed with friends for some weeks one summer—Max and one other were also visiting in the district... Marguerite, this gentleman is the Earl of Ravenshead. We are engaged and it is his daughter that I have asked you to come and meet.'

Gerard extended his hand. 'I do not think we can have met. I am certain I should have remembered. It is a pleasure to meet any friend of Amelia's, Miss Ross.'

Amelia realised he was puzzled and explained, 'Marguerite's parents do not go out much in society. I asked her to come and stay with us. I believe she might enjoy helping me with Lisa. I do not think we need another nanny. Lisa has her nurse and Marguerite has often told me that she adores children—is that not so, my love?'

'Yes, indeed that is true, Amelia.' Marguerite did not take Gerard's hand. Instead she dipped a curtsy, her head bowed. 'I am sure we have not met, sir. I am delighted to be here and I hope I may be of service to Amelia and you.'

'I am certain you will.' Amelia smiled. 'You are not to think you are a servant, Marguerite, though I shall of course make you an allowance. It will be a pleasure to me to have you live with us—and I shall always be certain that Lisa is safe in your care.'

'I promise you that the child will be cared for as if she were my own,' Marguerite said. 'I shall not intrude on you longer, Amelia. I merely wanted you to know that I was here.' She turned to leave, but Amelia put out a hand to stop her, giving Gerard an apologetic glance. 'Forgive me, Gerard. I want to make sure that Marguerite is settled in—and to introduce her to Lisa…'

'Yes, of course. I must speak to Max about something. I shall see you this evening.'

'You will excuse us?'

'Yes. Please go with Miss Ross.'

Amelia held out her hand to Marguerite, who smiled and took it. She felt a little regretful as she glanced back at Gerard and saw him staring after them. They had reached a new stage of their relationship and it was a pity they had been interrupted. However, they had a whole lifetime ahead of them and she did want to make sure that Marguerite was comfortable.

* * *

Gerard stared after them as they left. He had said that he did not recognise Miss Ross; indeed, he could not recall having met her—and yet there was something at the back of his mind. She had looked at him oddly when he said that they had not met, a flicker of annoyance or resentment in her eyes.

Was it possible that they had met at some time in the past? He knew that any woman might feel offended if a gentleman they remembered claimed not to recall their meeting. The name Ross seemed to ring a chord in his subconscious, but he could not immediately find a reason for it.

He must be mistaken. Had they met before he would surely have remembered. Miss Ross was not beautiful, but she was not unattractive. Indeed, she might look very well dressed in a different style. She reminded him of someone, but he could not place the memory.

It would come to him in time. He gave it up and went in search of Max. He had hoped to spend an hour or so with Amelia, but since she was otherwise engaged, he would seek out his friend.

'You look thoughtful.' Max, Lord Coleridge, raised his brows as Gerard entered the library. 'Has something happened to trouble you? You have not received another threat?'

'No. Though the broken doll was, according to Northaven, a warning and not a threat. As you know, I expected there might be an attempt to hold up the carriage on the way here. It would have been easy enough to make it appear the work of a highwayman. However, we were strong enough to fight off a gang of ruffians and perhaps they knew it…which begs the question: how do they know where we go and what we do?'

'A spy in our midst, you think?' Max Coleridge frowned. 'A servant, perhaps—the nanny you dismissed?'

'She could certainly have passed on information after I asked Amelia to marry me, but I doubt she knew anything of her until then.'

'Do you trust Northaven?' Max asked. 'You told me that he brought Miss Barton back to you after she was abducted—but could that not have been arranged to gain your confidence? A ruse to get close to you?'

'Harry and I thought of that, but we believed him genuine in his desire to make amends. I believe we may have misjudged him. He is by no means a knight in shining armour, but may not be the traitor we thought him in Spain.'

'You say he believed he knew where he might find this Lieutenant Gordon—if that is the rogue's real name?' Max picked a speck of fluff from his otherwise immaculate coat. 'I suppose you have heard nothing from him?'

'Not as yet,' Gerard said. 'Perhaps Gordon will give up his attempts now that he knows we are aware of him.'

'Do you really believe that? If he hates you, as seems to be the case, can you see him just giving up and walking away?'

Gerard sighed. 'If I speak truly, no. I suppose I hoped that he might have decided we are too well protected, but I dare say he will simply become more devious.'

'Exactly. We must remain alert at all times, Gerard. Helene has invited so many guests to the ball that it would be an ideal moment to strike. I shall have the grounds patrolled all night, every night—but I think we should have a man on guard outside Amelia's door at night too, just in case.'

'As long as the ladies are not aware of it. We must dress the guard as a footman or we may alarm the guests.'

'Certainly. I am sure we have enough livery to accommodate your men, Gerard.'

'Would you rather we went home and saved you the bother? It is a lot to ask of you, Max. I should not have brought this trouble to your house.'

'Damn you, Gerard! We swore to be true friends in Spain, to help each other in time of need. If it had not been for you, Helene might have died last summer. You stood by me then and I shall stand by you now.'

'Thank you. Both you and Harry have been the best friends a man could have,' Gerard said. 'I do not know why I am so uneasy. I have a feeling that the danger is closer than we imagine—but I have no idea why…'

'Emily, my love. This lady is Marguerite Ross—I mentioned to you that she was coming to live with us.'

'Miss Ross.' Emily dipped a curtsy. 'I am so happy to meet you. I am Emily Barton—Amelia's companion. I hope you will be happy with us. Indeed, I know you must be. Amelia is the most generous of friends.'

'Miss Barton—may I call you Emily?' Marguerite gave her a nervous smile. 'I am so fortunate that Amelia wrote to Mama. My life has been…less than happy since…' She sighed and shook her head. 'No, I shall not dwell on the past. I am here now and I am looking forward to my duties and helping Amelia where I can.'

'You will not find your duties onerous,' Amelia said. 'Lisa has her nurse. Nurse Mary will continue to care for her clothes and to give Lisa her meals. All I ask of you is that you will read to Lisa, play with her—and perhaps help her to study books I shall provide for her pleasure. She is too young for a governess as yet, but she needs friends. I want you to be her friend, Marguerite.'

'She is an adorable child. It will be no hardship to be Lisa's friend,' Marguerite said. 'She is a fortunate child to have a stepmother like you, Amelia. Most women in your place would not wish to take on the daughter of their husband's first wife. They would employ a strict nanny and stay away from the nursery.'

'The earl has just dismissed one nanny for being too strict,' Emily said with a little frown.

Marguerite turned her gaze on her. 'Has he, indeed? I remember our nanny was very strict. Papa told her she must make sure we behaved ourselves. I dare say it did us no harm.'

'I am sure it did not,' Amelia said, 'but I love Lisa as if she were my own. I intend to spend some time with her myself most days. However, there will be times when I cannot and then I shall be able to relax in the knowledge that you are caring for her. I know my dear Emily would care for her, but she may have other concerns. Emily does so much for me.'

Amelia smiled at her companion. Had it not been

for Emily's hopes of marriage she would probably not have thought of bringing Marguerite here, but she was pleased that she had done so. The young woman had been living a terrible life, because her parents had made her suffer for her sister's shame and it was not fair.

'However, you must not think that I asked you here simply to be Lisa's friend, Marguerite. You will live as one of the family and accompany us when we go visiting. Lady Coleridge is holding a ball this weekend. I hope you have a suitable gown?'

'I have not had a new ballgown for years.' Marguerite looked distressed. 'I have nothing suitable. I did not realise that I should need one and brought only a few things with me.'

'We are of a similar size.' Amelia's eyes went over her. 'I think that my clothes may fit you, though you may need to adjust the hems slightly. I have a new green gown that I have not worn. I think it will suit you well, Marguerite.' She glanced at her feet. 'I do not think my shoes will fit, for I have smaller feet than you do. Emily—do you have a pair of dancing slippers that might fit Marguerite?'

'Yes, I think I have a pair I have worn only once. You can try them on and see,' Emily said. 'I shall be very happy to give them to you, for I have several pairs to choose from.'

'You are both very kind.' Marguerite's eyes held a glimmer of tears. 'I do not know how to thank you.'

'When we go down to Ravenshead I will commission a seamstress and a shoemaker. I shall need a trousseau and you may as well be fitted out at the same time,' Amelia said. 'No, do not thank me, Marguerite. I have been very fortunate and it is my pleasure to help others less so. All I truly want is for us to live comfortably together.'

Marguerite dabbed at her eyes with a lace kerchief that smelled of rose water. 'I do not know what I have done to deserve such kindness from you.'

'I was distressed when Lucinda took her own life,' Amelia replied. 'She was my friend. I did not know you as well, Marguerite, but I have often thought of you. Had I realised sooner how your life had changed, I should have done more to help you. I know your mama refused to allow you to stay with me, but had I appealed to her personally, she might have done so. I shall write and thank her for allowing you to come to me.'

'Mama admires you, Amelia. I am sure she needs no thanks for agreeing to something that costs her so little.'

'Nevertheless, I shall write to her.' Amelia smiled. 'It will be so pleasant to have your company, Marguerite.' She turned to Emily, missing the odd look in Marguerite's eyes. 'Will you help Marguerite settle in, dearest? I am going to sort out a few gowns that I do not need. I shall bring them to your room later, Marguerite. You would look well in green or blue—colours will suit you so much better than that grey gown.'

'Come with me, Marguerite,' Emily invited. 'I shall show you the rooms we mostly use here—and then you may try on those dancing slippers.'

Amelia found six gowns that she thought might appeal to Marguerite. She chose a green ball gown that she had never worn, a blue evening dress, a silver-

grey evening dress, two afternoon dresses and a striped
green morning gown. She added a spangled shawl, two
pairs of evening gloves and a velvet evening purse.

She judged that the gowns would be enough to see
Marguerite through their short stay at Coleridge. Once
they were at Ravenshead, she would order new gowns
for all of them.

'Martha, would you take these to Miss Ross's room,
please?' Amelia said when she had finished laying out
the clothes. 'You may take the silver-grey gown first
and the others can follow later. I am not sure whether
Miss Ross has a gown pressed for this evening, but this
one is ready to wear.'

'Yes, Miss Royston. Are you sure you meant to give
this ball gown away, miss? It is new and your favourite
colour.'

'It becomes me well, but I have many others. My
friend was unable to bring much with her and she will
need these gowns until new ones can be ordered.'

'Yes, miss. I just wanted to be sure.'

Amelia smiled to herself as the maid took the gown
away. She was dressed ready for the evening and she
wanted to go down early. She had sensed that Gerard
was surprised by Marguerite's arrival and she ought to
explain that she had said nothing to him only because
she had not been sure her friend would come. She had
not expected Marguerite to simply arrive, imagining
that she would receive a letter from Mrs Ross in the
first instance.

Now that she had a moment to herself, she was at
last at liberty to think about the scene in the library
with Gerard. He had kissed her and she had not held

back. What might have happened had Marguerite not come in at that moment?

Gerard had told her more of his feelings when Michael had him thrashed and sent him away. He had spoken of his bitterness, his longing for her and lonely nights. For the first time Amelia understood how he had felt, realising that his pain had been as deep as hers, if not deeper. He had been hurt and humiliated—her brother's bullies had been too many and too strong for him to fight back.

He had married Lisette while still feeling resentful. She had thought he must care for her but it seemed he hadn't loved her. When he spoke of her he seemed deeply disturbed. He had spoken of Lisette's terrible unhappiness, which drove her to take her own life. He said that he could not give her what she needed…would it be the same when they married? Or had Gerard been unable to love his wife because in his heart he still wanted Amelia?

His kiss had been passionate and hungry. She had felt that he truly wanted her. Perhaps he did love her in his way…

'I trust your judgement completely,' Gerard said after Amelia had explained why she had asked Marguerite to come to them. They had met once again in the library so that they could be alone for a few moments before dinner. A fire had been lit and the candles burned brightly, giving the room a warm, intimate feeling. 'It is a sad thing that Miss Ross should have been treated so badly. I did not remember her when we spoke earlier, but I have been thinking and I seem to recall a

young woman with a similar name.' He frowned, an
odd, slightly uneasy expression in his eyes. 'Was not
Lucinda Ross Marguerite's sister? I think Lucinda Ross
was the young woman who killed herself some years
ago?'

'Yes, that is correct. Lucinda was in some trouble. It
happened during that summer. I thought at one time—'
She broke off and shook her head. 'Northaven... I know
that he had been to the house a few times. I once saw
him flirting with Lucinda in the gardens.'

'Both Harry and I were also invited to some func-
tions at the home of Mr and Mrs Ross—but Harry
would never dream of seducing a young woman of good
family. Nor would I, come to that, but at the time I
could think only of you. It was you I loved, Amelia.'
He frowned, hesitated, then, 'I do recall the name, but
not Lucinda's face, though I remember meeting her. I
might have liked her sister more for I believe I danced
with her a few times, but there was nothing more than
politeness between us. Indeed, I could not recall her
when we met, but she may have changed. That gown
and hairstyle are not becoming to a young woman.'

'You do not mind that I have invited her to stay with
us for a while? She is not beautiful, but I think she
would be attractive wearing the right clothes. I hope
that she may meet someone she likes who will offer for
her.'

'Playing matchmaker again?' Gerard teased.

'No, for I have no one in mind for Marguerite. I
merely wish to give her the chance she has been denied
so long. Besides, she loves children and she will be a
big help to me.'

'Then I am delighted she has come,' Gerard said and smiled. 'Are you looking forward to the ball, my love?'

'Yes, of course.' Amelia moved towards him, her breath catching as she gazed up at him. 'We shall be able to dance together as often as we wish. Once our engagement is announced no one could lift a brow if we danced all night—though I suppose it might be thought rude to ignore one's friends altogether.'

'I think it would be pistols at dawn if I dared to monopolise you completely,' Gerard said teasingly. He turned his head and frowned, then strode towards the door and threw it open.

'Is something the matter?' Amelia asked.

He turned to Amelia, frowning. 'I thought someone was eavesdropping outside the door. If someone was listening to our conversation, he or she fled before I could discover who it was.'

'Listening to our conversation?' Amelia stared at him. 'Surely not? In this house...who would spy on us, Gerard?'

'I wish I knew.' Gerard's eyes darkened. 'It is foolish, but since we came here I have grown more uneasy.'

'You expected an attack on the road, did you not?'

He nodded. 'We were prepared for it, but it did not happen. Therefore our enemy has something else planned—something more devious and perhaps more dangerous. I have men watching the grounds, Amelia. I can shoot a man who tries to abduct you, but I have a feeling that something more sinister is going on.'

'What are your reasons? What has changed?'

'I do not know, but I trust my instincts. They served me well in Spain and at other times.'

A shudder caught Amelia and for a moment she was afraid of something she could not understand. 'I must confess that frightens me...'

'Won't you withdraw before it is too late? I could go away—take the danger with me, for I feel it is directed at me. However, you may be hurt, because this person will use you to get to me.'

'No! I have already told you nothing will keep me from you. Would you go away and condemn me to a life of solitude?' Amelia demanded. She moved towards him, clutching at the lapels of his immaculate coat. 'Will you let me die a maiden—unfulfilled and regretful?' Her eyes were fearful, desperate. 'Have you no idea of the feelings I have for you—the longings I know must seem immodest in an unmarried lady?'

'My dearest one! You cannot believe me indifferent? You are beautiful. Any man would be grateful to have such a woman as his wife.' Gerard caught her to him, kissing her with a fierce hunger that set her pulses racing. She clung to him, her body melting into his as the raging desire swept through her. 'I would leave you only to protect you, believe me.'

'If you do, I may as well die.'

'Never!' Gerard gazed down into her wild face, a thrill of laughter and triumph sweeping over him as he saw the passion he had always believed was in her. 'I shall not give you up, Amelia—and nothing shall part us for a second time.'

'Do you swear it?'

'I swear it with my life. Only my death will part us.'

Amelia pressed herself against him, lifting her face for his kiss. As he took her mouth, she parted her lips for him, meeting his tongue in a delightful dance of sweet desire. Her body flamed, tingled with the need to know him, to lie with him.

'Gerard, I want to be truly yours.'

'I burn for you, my love.' He smiled ruefully. 'I would we were at Ravenshead. I could come to you there without ruining your reputation, Amelia. Here, I hesitate to abuse our hosts' hospitality.'

'Once we are at Ravenshead we shall not wait,' Amelia said. 'Nothing must part us now, for I could not bear it.'

Gerard kissed her, but this time softly. 'We must wait for the moment, but I agree that nothing shall part us, my dearest.'

Hidden behind a heavy curtain, the eavesdropper sat curled up on a deep window ledge and listened. For a moment it had seemed that Ravenshead had discovered the presence of a third person, but he had gone to the slightly open door, thinking the listener was outside. Seeing no one, he had believed himself mistaken. He was mistaken only in the location. What good luck that quick thinking had prevented discovery the instant they entered the room!

A smile touched the lips of the hidden one. Gerard Ravenshead thought himself so clever, but revenge was close. It was like the taste of honey on the tongue of the person who hated him. A smile hovered. Soon now. Soon the debt would be paid...

Amelia went to bed feeling happier than she had been for years. She could no longer doubt that Gerard felt a strong passion for her. He might not love her as he once had, but he was certainly not indifferent. They would not lack for passion in their marriage. She longed for the time when they would be at Ravenshead...when she could at last become one with him.

She had lingered downstairs for as long as she could, but Gerard had been caught up in a discussion about politics with some of the other gentlemen. He had thrown her an apologetic glance, telling her by means of a look that he longed for some time alone with her, but it was impossible. She knew that they must be patient; in a few days they would leave Coleridge and then...

A smile on her lips, Amelia sat down at her desk and took out her writing box. She opened it and took out some sheets of vellum, then dipped her pen in the ink and began to write a letter. She was not yet ready to sleep and she wished to tell several friends her news, for she knew it would please them.

After she had been writing for some half an hour or so she sanded and sealed her letters, four in all, leaving the one addressed to Marguerite's mother on the top of the pile. In the morning she would take them down to the hall and place them with others to be franked by Max and taken to the receiving office with any other letters his guests wished sent.

Amelia brushed her hair, washed her face and hands and then went to bed. She blew out the candle and settled down to sleep, but her mind was busy and it was a while before she settled. She was resting, but not sleeping, when the sound of her door opening startled her. For a moment she lay listening, thinking that she must be mistaken. She had not locked the door to her dressing room for it was that way the maid entered in the morning, but her maid would not creep unannounced into her darkened bedchamber at this hour.

'Who is there?' she called and sat up in bed, her hand reaching for the candle by her bed. It was a moment or two before she secured it and some seconds more before she could strike the tinder. 'Who are you?' she cried as a dark shadow fled through the dressing-room door.

Amelia lit her candle and got out of bed. She went through the door to the dressing room. The intruder had left it open in his haste and she saw that the door that led from the dressing room to the servants' stairs was also open. Whoever had been in her room must have come and left by that means.

Amelia knew that her own maid would not have reacted in such a way. No other servant ought to have been there at this late hour and would not be on their lawful business. Yet someone had come to her room— why? What were they searching for? Amelia's jewellery was locked away in her dressing case, which she kept by the bed as she slept. A brief glance told her that it was still there and untouched. So what had the intruder been doing?

Amelia felt chilled, because this was something she had not expected. What might have happened had she been asleep? She wondered if she had been meant to die—or was it merely an attempt to rob her? She shivered, feeling uneasy and anxious. Ought she to send for someone? Amelia hesitated, but it was past midnight and she did not wish to make a fuss at this hour. How-

ever, in future she would make sure that the dressing-
room door was locked—at least until they were safe
at Ravenshead. Her maid could knock if Amelia were
still asleep when she came, but it was more likely that
she would be wide awake!

Amelia returned to bed. She was not unduly frightened now that the door was locked. She would not be
disturbed again this night, but the incident had shocked
her more than she liked. She would have to tell Gerard
about the intruder in the morning—and of course Max
would have to know. He would wish to make enquiries
amongst his servants. It did not seem that anything had
been taken, but it could quite easily have been simply
a bungled robbery. He would have to warn his people
to be vigilant.

'You are certain that the door to the hall was locked?'
Max asked the next morning when Gerard asked him
to meet in private. 'Whoever it was came from the
servants' stairs?'

'Amelia tried the door leading into the hall and it
was locked. She is positive that the intruder came and
went by means of the servants' stairs. Indeed, she saw
the shadow escape that way, though it was too dark to
be certain whether it was a man or a woman.'

'It would be easy enough for anyone to come that
way once the servants have retired for the night.
However, I gave strict instructions that all the outer
doors and windows were to be secured at night.' Max
frowned. 'I am loath to think that any of my people
would do such a thing, Gerard—but of course our
guests have brought their own servants.'

'It is difficult to point the finger at anyone,' Gerard agreed. 'We had a guard outside Amelia's room and Miss Barton's room. Nothing untoward was seen.'

'And we have men patrolling the grounds...' Max swore softly. 'Are you thinking...?'

'That the intruder must have come from inside the house.' Gerard nodded. 'Amelia suggested that it could have been an attempt to steal her jewels, but I am not so sure.'

'I dare say she does not wish to think it anything more. It is fortunate that she was not asleep.'

'Very.' Gerard looked grim. 'I have been aware that something had changed, but I cannot put my finger on it, Max. I know only that I am uneasy.'

'What does Amelia feel?'

'She says that her maid must knock if she is not awake. She will lock her dressing-room door at night.'

'She is very composed about this, Gerard.'

'Perhaps too much so for her own good. Amelia trusts everyone.'

'What do you mean?' Max's gaze narrowed. 'Has something occurred to you?'

'Yes...at least it is just a little seed of doubt. Something I cannot quite place...' He shook his head as Max lifted his brows. 'I am not certain therefore I shall lay no blame, but my instincts are telling me I am right.'

'You do not wish to tell me?'

'Yes, of course. You have the right to know—but you will not tell Helene or anyone else except Harry when he arrives, for I may be wrong.'

Amelia wandered around her bedchamber. She was looking for something, but she was not sure what it was. Her dressing case was there and the contents were intact. Her silver evening purse was lying on the dressing table where she had put it last night before she undressed. What else had she done before she went to bed? Ah, yes, she had written some letters.

The letters were missing. She had left a small pile on the desk. They had gone and she had not taken them downstairs herself when she went down to speak to Gerard earlier, for she'd had other things on her mind. She frowned as the door opened and her maid entered carrying a gown she had pressed.

'Martha—did you by chance take my letters down to be franked this morning?'

'No, Miss Royston. I saw them lying on the desk when I woke you first thing, but I was not certain you wished for them to be sent yet. You would have asked had you intended me to do it for you.'

'Yes, I should,' Amelia agreed. 'It is most odd, for I did not do it myself. I wonder if Emily…'

'Miss Barton did come to your room earlier, miss. I saw her leaving as I came to collect your gown for this evening. It needed pressing and I had taken some other things to be laundered earlier so I returned to fetch the gown and Miss Barton was leaving. She asked if I knew where you were.'

'Perhaps she took them down. I shall ask her later.'

Amelia picked up a book she wished to offer Lisa as more interesting reading than those Nanny Horton had considered suitable and left the room. As she went into the nursery, she saw that both Emily and Marguerite were before her. They were playing a game of Blind

Man's Buff with Lisa and another child and the children were screaming with laughter.

Amelia watched, smiling as Marguerite allowed herself to be caught by Lisa and accepted the blindfold from her hand. She stopped suddenly, as if becoming aware of Amelia.

'Oh, we are playing a game. I hope you approve?'

'Melia…' Lisa cried and came running to hug her. 'Marguerite has been teaching me games and Emily has been playing with us. Have you come to join us?'

'I came to bring you this book. It is a bestiary and there are lots of pictures of animals and birds. I thought you would like to have it—but you may look at it another day. Go on with your game, my love.'

'I would rather look at the book with you,' Lisa said and took hold of her arm, pulling her towards a sofa. 'It is just a silly game and the book is beautiful.'

Glancing at Marguerite, Amelia saw her flush and smiled, shaking her head. 'Now that is unkind, Lisa—and Marguerite was very good to play with you.'

'Thank you, Mademoiselle Ross—and Emily…' Lisa tilted her head, a beguiling smile in her eyes. 'I like to play, but I like books with pictures best.'

'Well, you have run us ragged and we must rest,' Emily said, laughing. 'Next time I shall bring a picture book, miss.'

Lisa giggled and shot a look of mischief at her. 'I like to play sometimes.'

'You won't get round me that way,' Emily teased. 'Is there anything you need, Amelia?'

'No—oh, yes, one thing. Did you by chance take my letters down to the hall this morning?'

'No. I would not without asking you first. You might not have finished them.'

'But your letters were downstairs earlier,' Marguerite said and looked at Emily oddly. 'I wrote a letter to my mother and placed it in the hall for franking, as Lady Coleridge said I might. I saw a letter from you to Mama, Amelia—and some others. If Emily did not put them there, your maid must have done so. Was there something you wished to alter?'

'No. They were ready to go, but Martha says she did not take them and I did not for I had other things on my mind…' Amelia was about to mention the intruder, but changed her mind. Emily had already suffered a bad experience and she did not wish to make her nervous. 'Someone else must have done so. Perhaps one of the other maids went in to clean and saw them there. Well, it does not matter.' She smiled at Lisa. 'When I was young I used to look at this book with my nanny. I believe you will like it.'

'Let me see…' Lisa pulled at her hand. 'Let me see.'

Amelia smiled and sat down, taking the child on to her lap. The small boy who had also been playing with them looked on shyly until Amelia beckoned to him. He came and leaned against her shoulder, his eyes fixing hungrily on the pictures she was showing to Lisa. After a few moments, both children fired questions at her and she was so engrossed with them that she did not look up for some time. She saw that Emily had gone, but Marguerite was still there, watching, a strange, half-envious expression in her eyes.

Thinking that she understood, Amelia handed the

book to Lisa and allowed the children to look through it alone.

'Children are such a blessing,' she said to Marguerite and went to stand next to her by the window. 'I thought once that I should never have my own, but now I have hopes for the future—and already I have a daughter to love.'

'Yes, I dare say the care of a motherless child is as good a reason for marriage as any.'

'It is certainly one reason,' Amelia said. 'Lisa is a delightful child and Gerard did need someone to help with the care of her, but we are good friends.'

'Friendship is more than most find in marriage. Men are always so faithless…though I do not imply that the earl will be faithless to you, Amelia. After all, you will bring him a fortune when you marry.'

'Yes, that is true. I expect to be very happy in my marriage. You should not think that all men are faithless, Marguerite, though I know you think of Lucinda.'

'Lucinda was foolish to trust the man who betrayed her.'

'Perhaps she loved him and did not think further.'

'Perhaps. Can you love the child of another woman?' Marguerite's eyes were watchful. 'Will you not think of her, of his wife…?' She shook her head. 'Forgive me. I should not have spoken to you so, Amelia. It was not my place.'

'Emily knows that she may say anything to me—and so may you, Marguerite. If something is on your mind?'

'No.' She hesitated, then, 'I just wondered if the shadow of…the manner of his wife's death might hang over you.'

'I am sorry for the way she died,' Amelia replied, glancing at Lisa, who was happily absorbed in the book. She wondered how Marguerite knew of Lisette's suicide, because not even Emily knew more than that Gerard's wife had died in Spain. 'It is sad when someone dies tragically but I know that Gerard did all he could for her.'

Marguerite looked as if she would speak, gave a little shake of her head and walked to where the children were still entranced by the pictures of animals and birds. She pointed to some words beneath one of the pictures.

'Do you know what this says, Lisa?'

'It is funny writing. I cannot read it.'

'That is because it is in Latin. It says that the picture is of a parrot…'

Amelia watched for a moment as Marguerite continued to explain what the words meant. She thought that she had chosen well, for Marguerite was obviously good with children. She was surprised that Marguerite should have mentioned Gerard's first wife. It almost seemed that she knew exactly how Lisette had died, and yet Amelia was sure he had not spoken of it to many people. How could a woman he had never met know anything about Lisette's suicide?

Amelia was thoughtful as she went downstairs, but then she realised that Marguerite had not actually said anything directly about the suicide. She must, of course, have imagined that Lisette had died from the fever she'd caught after her child was born. So many women died that way that it would be easy to assume it was so. Satisfied that she had misunderstood, Amelia dismissed

Marguerite's words. The look in her eyes was harder to dismiss, for it had seemed to carry a warning.

Amelia dressed that evening in a ball gown of blue satin overlaid with swathes of silver lace. It had a deep scooped neckline that revealed a tantalising glimpse of her soft breasts, and little puffed sleeves. Around her neck she had fastened a collar of lustrous pearls with a diamond clasp that had a large baroque pearl as a drop. On her wrists she wore gold-and-pearl bangles and she had a magnificent sapphire-and-diamond ring on her left hand. Gerard had given it to her after tea that afternoon, slipping it on her finger himself.

'It fits. I am relieved,' he told her, lifting her hand to kiss the palm. 'I hope you like it, my love. It was commissioned for us. In time I shall send for the family jewels and you may take your pick of them, though I know you have jewels enough of your own.'

'Most of Aunt's jewellery was not to my taste and remains in the bank. She was extremely fond of amethysts, but I prefer pearls—and of course sapphires and diamonds.' She looked at the deep blue of the sapphire oval ring surrounded by fine white diamonds. 'This is lovely, Gerard—perfect. Thank you.'

'I am glad you are pleased.' He reached out to touch her cheek. 'I care for you so very much.'

Amelia admired her beautiful ring as she went down to the ballroom. It was a long gallery that normally housed musical instruments and several sofas as well as music stands. This evening it had been cleared of furniture and the rooms connecting on either side had their double doors thrown wide so that the effect was of one very large room.

In the first room, Lord and Lady Coleridge stood waiting to receive their guests and footmen were circulating with trays bearing glasses of the best champagne. Amelia accepted a glass and went to stand with Helene. She was one of the first to appear, but she could already hear the strains of music coming from the gallery.

'May I see your ring?' Helene asked and exclaimed over it. 'How lovely, Amelia. Three stones is a shape that suits your hands very well—and I believe you already have a small sapphire-and-diamond cluster that was your mama's?'

'Yes, I do, though the shank is wearing a little thin and I did not bring it with me—for I must have it repaired.'

'That sapphire is such a deep colour,' Helene said. 'I am so happy for you, Amelia. If it had not been for you, I should never have met and married Max. I wanted you to be happy too, and now you are.'

'Yes, I am,' Amelia said and kissed her. She moved away as Emily and Marguerite entered the room, wandering into the far room where flowers from a hot house had been arranged. There were some exotic blooms and the perfume was quite heavy, making her want to sneeze.

'Are you all right, Amelia?'

Amelia heard the voice and turned as Marguerite came up to her.

'Yes, perfectly, thank you. I was feeling a little nauseous for a moment, but I think it may have been these flowers—they have a strong smell, not unpleasant but a little overpowering.'

'You looked pale,' Marguerite said. 'Are you sure you feel quite well?'

'I shall be perfectly well, but I must not linger near these flowers; they are giving me a headache.'

'Why do you not go out for a breath of air?'

'It is too cold. Besides, I am looking forward to the ball. Excuse me.' Amelia saw Gerard coming and walked to greet him. She smiled and held out her hands to him. 'You look very handsome tonight, sir.'

'And you look beautiful, Miss Royston.' Gerard's eyes went over her hungrily. 'I see some people are beginning to dance—shall we?'

'Yes, please.' Amelia took his hand. 'I have been longing to dance with you again.'

The slight feeling of nausea she had experienced earlier vanished as he took her into his arms. The dancing had begun with a waltz and Amelia felt that she was floating on air as he whirled her along the gallery and back. She felt such sweet sensation, like being carried on a wave of sparkling sea to the stars, lost to everything, but the touch of his hand against her back and the faint masculine scent of him in her nostrils. She wanted to go on and on for ever.

Too soon the dance ended and almost immediately the guests came up to them to congratulate Gerard and wish Amelia happiness. Everyone wanted to know when the wedding would be and all their best friends demanded to be invited, which Amelia assured them would be the case.

A few of her friends told her that they had gifts for

her, but the engagement was a surprise to most and they exclaimed over it again and again. Some of their closest friends teased Gerard and said that he had stolen a march on them and she was swept away to dance with several of the gentlemen. It was some time before they danced together again, but she noticed that Gerard danced once with Emily, Marguerite and Helene.

'I am glad to see you have been dancing,' she told him when they danced the final waltz before supper. 'It was good of you to ask Marguerite.'

'I asked Miss Barton because she was looking sad and had hardly danced at all,' Gerard told her. 'I could not avoid asking Miss Ross because it would have seemed rude. She said that she had remembered me and reminded me of the night we met. Apparently, we danced twice that evening and I fetched her some champagne.'

'Did she remember so clearly?' Amelia frowned. She would have liked to ask Gerard if there was any way that Marguerite could have known that Lisette had taken her own life, but the evening of their engagement was not the moment. 'She has not spoken to me of knowing you—though you told me you knew her sister, Lucinda, better.'

'Lucinda was an odd girl...'

Amelia saw his expression. Something in his look made her spine prickle. 'What do you mean? I always thought her a sweet and gentle girl.'

'Did you, my love?' Gerard's forehead creased. 'I thought something different, but keep your memories, Amelia. I hardly knew her after all.'

Amelia was intrigued, vaguely disturbed. He was

hiding something from her. She sensed a mystery, but again this was not the time to inquire further. A niggling doubt teased at the back of her mind, but she dismissed it almost at once. Earlier, Marguerite had almost seemed to imply that Gerard was marrying her for her fortune and that he would be faithless once they were married. Did she know something that Amelia did not? She felt cold for a moment and shivered, then squashed the unworthy doubts.

She raised her head and smiled. Nothing should be allowed to spoil her special evening.

'Are you happy, Gerard?'

His gaze seared her. 'Can you doubt it? I cannot wait until we are at Ravenshead…to be alone with you…'

Amelia felt reassured. He felt something more than friendship for her. She would be a fool to doubt it, to let her thoughts be poisoned by a casual remark.

Turning her head at that moment, she suddenly saw Marguerite looking at them. The look on her face was so strange that it sent a shiver down Amelia's spine. Marguerite looked…angry…resentful.

Why should she look as if she hated to see others happy? Amelia had an uneasy feeling that something was very wrong, and yet a moment later, as Marguerite saw her glance she smiled and the shadows were banished from her face.

Amelia decided that she had been mistaken. Marguerite's expression must have been wistful, not resentful. She was thinking of all the dances and happy times she had missed. After all, why should she resent the people who had given her this chance to enjoy herself? Of course she would not. She had several times expressed her gratitude. It would be foolish to imagine resentment where there was none.

Chapter Seven

Emily came to Amelia as she was standing by the buffet looking at a bewildering array of dishes. Her complexion was pale and there were shadows beneath her eyes.

'Are you not feeling well?' Amelia asked in concern.

'I have a headache,' Emily confessed. 'Would you mind if I left after supper and went to bed? Is there anything I can do for you before I retire?'

'I have all I want. Are you truly ill, my love—or is it because…?'

'I truly have a throbbing headache. I do not know why, for I scarcely ever have them, Amelia. I think it must be something to do with the soap that the maids used for laundering my kerchiefs. I came to ask if I might borrow one of yours this morning, because mine all had a strong perfume clinging to them, which seemed to bring on my headache. The pain has been lingering all day and is worse this evening.'

'I am so sorry. Yes, of course you must go to bed, Emily. If you are still unwell in the morning, I shall have the doctor to you—and I will have Martha launder your kerchiefs with the soap she uses for mine.'

'Thank you…' Emily hesitated. 'I did not touch your letters this morning, Amelia. I just went into your room, saw you were not there and then left—you do believe me?'

'Of course. Why should I not? You have always been honest with me.'

'Someone suggested to me that I had taken the letters and lied to you.'

'Someone…' Amelia's gaze narrowed. 'Do you mean Marguerite?'

'I do not wish to say—but I should be distressed if I thought you believed I would lie to you.'

'Well, you may rest easy, Emily. I know you too well to ever think you would lie to me.'

'Thank you.' Emily's eyes carried the sheen of tears. 'I thought…but I shall forget it. My foolish head hurts so. Excuse me, I must go. Goodnight, Amelia.'

'Goodnight, my love. Ask Martha for a tisane if you wish. I hope you feel better soon.'

Amelia frowned as she watched Emily leave the supper room. She was sorry that her friend was feeling unwell for she had enough to bear. The scent clinging to her kerchiefs was odd, for Amelia had experienced a similar thing in the room where all the exotic flowers had been displayed; overpowering perfumes could bring on headaches, especially if one were in close contact through a piece of personal lingerie.

She would ask Martha to wash all of Emily's things

as well as Amelia's for the next few days. Helene's maids must be using something that was quite unsuitable.

Amelia was thoughtful as she ate a little supper. She had hoped that Emily might have something to celebrate this evening, but Toby Sinclair had not been able to tear himself away from his family at this sad time. She supposed that he could not decently attend a ball so close to his father's funeral. He was perfectly correct not to come. Perhaps he would write to Emily— or seek her out when they went down to Ravenshead in two days' time. She put her thoughts to one side as Marguerite came to sit with her and eat a syllabub.

'Are you enjoying yourself, Marguerite?'

'How could I not when everyone has been so kind?' Marguerite's mouth curved in a smile. 'Is Emily unwell? She told me she was going to bed...'

'She has a little headache. I dare say it will pass by the morning.'

'She was pale. I would have made her an infusion to help her had she mentioned her headache.'

'Oh, I dare say she will ask Martha. It is a pity that it should come this evening, for Emily seldom has headaches.'

'Perhaps she has been feeling out of sorts. Someone mentioned that she had suffered a disappointment recently. Heartache sometimes manifests itself as illness, do you not agree?'

'You should not listen to gossip,' Amelia said. 'Besides, I am sure Emily will be better soon.'

Gerard watched the woman from across the room. Why did he have the feeling that she was not all that she appeared? Her smiles made him uneasy—for she seemed to be saying that she knew something he did not. He was pleased when he saw her leave the room. He wished it was as easy to send her packing altogether, but knew that Amelia trusted her, was fond of her. To voice his suspicions would only bring a cloud to their time of happiness—and perhaps he was wrong.

For the moment all he could do was to watch and wait. He turned as Max joined him, understanding that there was something he needed to tell him.

'A few moments of your time, Gerard—in private?'

'Of course,' Gerard agreed. 'I am promised to Amelia for the next dance, but she is otherwise occupied for the moment.' His eyebrows arched. 'You have discovered something?'

'Yes. It means nothing and yet it might…' Max said. 'One of my footmen was up with a toothache early this morning and he saw something that might interest you.'

Amelia saw Gerard leave the supper room with Max. She frowned, because she had wanted a few moments alone with him. However, on further reflection she decided that what she had to say would keep for another day. She turned as Helene came up to her.

'Emily was looking pale earlier,' Helene observed. 'Has she by chance taken a chill?'

'She says that the perfumed soap your maids used for washing her kerchiefs gave her a headache. I shall ask Martha to use my soap for her in future since it seems that she is sensitive to strong perfumes, as I am myself.'

'I was not aware we were using strongly perfumed

soap.' Helene looked puzzled. 'I shall ask my house-keeper and it shall be changed, Amelia. Some of the lilies used this evening had a very strong scent. I had one pot taken out this morning because it was over-powering.'

'Yes, I noticed the lilies,' Amelia said. 'I should have developed a headache had I stayed near them for long.'

'I shall not use that particular variety in the house again,' Helene said. 'I am sorry Emily was made unwell. I had thought it might be something else.'

'You mean because Toby Sinclair did not come this evening?'

'No...' Helene hesitated, looking slightly conscious. 'Forgive me, Amelia—but I am not sure that Emily likes Miss Ross. I think they may have had words... but I may be mistaken.'

'Emily is always so thoughtful,' Amelia said. 'I cannot think she would take a girl like Marguerite, who has suffered much at the hands of her parents, as she did herself, in dislike. They hardly know one another, after all.'

'As I said, I may be mistaken—' Helene broke off as Marguerite came up to them. 'Miss Ross—have you enjoyed yourself this evening?'

'Thank you. It has been a lovely evening. Amelia was so kind as to give me this dress...' Marguerite held out the skirt of the green gown. 'It is beautiful.'

'It becomes you well,' Helene said. 'I have seen you dancing several times. I think you have made friends and admirers, Miss Ross.'

'Thank you,' Marguerite said, but did not smile. 'I passed Emily as I went to my room just now, Amelia.

I believe she had been to yours. She said that she has a terrible headache. I offered to make her a tisane myself, but she refused me.'

'Emily had no doubt been in search of Martha to ask *her* to make her a tisane, as I advised,' Amelia said. 'Ah, here comes Gerard—I am promised to him for the next dance.'

Amelia said goodnight to Gerard. He had escorted her to her door, seeming reluctant to let her go inside. He kissed the palm of her hand, closing her fingers over the kiss.

'Keep that until we can be alone,' he said. 'Sleep well, my dearest. I trust that nothing will disturb your sleep this evening.'

'I dare say it will not. Martha has instructions to lock the dressing-room door when she leaves the room. Max provided her with a key and I also have one so I do not think anyone will intrude on me again.'

'Max has his footmen on duty all night so you should be quite safe,' Gerard told her. 'I shall see you in the morning, but you will sleep in and I have things to do—so you need not look for me before noon.'

Amelia nodded and went into her room. Martha came when she rang the bell and unfastened her gown at the back, helping her off with it.

'What is that smell, Miss Royston?' she asked, wrinkling her nose. 'You do not have a new perfume?'

'No...' Amelia glanced around her. 'I had just noticed it myself—it smells like lilies...the exotic ones they grow in hot houses that have strong perfume.' She took a step towards the bed, halting as the smell became overpowering. 'I think…behind the chair…is that a pot of lilies? It is not easy to see, but I believe it must be the source of that smell.'

Martha went quickly to look. 'Now how did that get here? I swear it wasn't here when I came in earlier to turn down the bed. The nasty thing!' She picked it up and went to the door, speaking to someone outside for a moment. 'I've given it to the footman to get rid of. I wonder who could have put that in here.'

'I cannot imagine for one moment,' Amelia said. 'Have a look around the room to make sure nothing else has been hidden and then you may go to bed. I am sure you have become tired waiting up for me.'

'I like to see you when you come back from a ball, miss. Have you enjoyed yourself?'

'Yes, very much,' Amelia said, watching as Martha went round the room, looking behind chests and under tables. 'I am sure you will find nothing else. Remember to lock the dressing-room door when you go out, Martha.'

'Yes, of course, miss. I have kept it locked since you told me. If someone entered your room, they must have a key or they came from the hall. You do not lock it when you leave.'

'Whoever it was must have entered from the hall. Lord Coleridge assured me that we have both keys to the dressing room. I have not been accustomed to locking my doors during the day. I have never needed to before, but I shall consider it in future.'

Before retiring, Amelia checked the door to the hall and the one to the dressing room. Both were locked. She was pensive as she pulled back the top covers on her bed and looked to see if anything unpleasant had been placed between the sheets. They were fresh and sweet smelling, just as Martha had prepared them for her.

The lilies were further evidence that someone was stirring up trouble for her. She had not dreamed up the intruder of the previous night—and there were the letters that no one would admit to having taken down to the hall. She had not bothered to ask Max if he had franked them for her, but she might do so in the morning.

She knew that if she spoke to the footman outside the door, Gerard would come to her, but she did not consider the pot of lilies reason enough to disturb him. Their perfume still lingered and she found it strong so she opened her a window a little to let in some fresh air. It seemed odd that Emily should complain of a strong soap used for washing her kerchiefs and now the lilies…

Amelia's thoughts were confused. Emily would not lie to her, but Marguerite had implied that she had taken the letters—and that she had seen her coming from Amelia's room this very evening. If she had not trusted Emily implicitly, she might have wondered if her companion had played a trick on her.

Why would anyone take some letters? Why would they hide a pot of lilies in her room? Supposing it was all part of a clever plot to make her believe that Emily was lying to her… Amelia dismissed the idea immediately. Someone was trying to unnerve her. Why? Was it to make her so distressed that she called off her wedding?

She thought it must be the most likely explanation. Yet why should anyone want to prevent her happiness? The only person she could think of who refused to accept her marriage was her brother. However, he had not been invited to Coleridge for the ball, because Helene did not like him.

Michael could certainly not be behind the odd things that had happened this past few days—though he might have paid someone to do it, of course. A servant, perhaps?

In another moment she would be thinking that Martha had placed the lilies in her room herself! This was so foolish and she would not think of it any more.

Martha had left a jug of lemon barley by her bed. She poured some into a glass and drank most of it. It was a little stronger than usual, but not unpleasant. She snuffed out the candles and closed her eyes. No one would disturb her sleep that night!

Martha awoke her by pulling back the curtains the next morning. Amelia yawned as she sat up, feeling that she could have slept a little longer, but as she looked at the pretty enamelled carriage clock she kept by her bed, she saw that it was almost noon.

'I am late this morning,' she said as she sat up and threw back the covers. 'Please pour me a cup of chocolate while I dress. Lisa will think I have deserted her.'

'I looked in twice, miss,' Martha said. 'You were sleeping so soundly that I thought it best not to wake you.'

'I must have been tired. I do not usually sleep this late even after a ball.'

Amelia went behind the dressing screen, washed and dressed in the green-striped linen gown that Martha brought her. She drank her chocolate at the dressing table, while Martha brushed her hair and wound it into a shining twist at the back of her head, securing it with pins.

'Thank you. I shall not eat, because it will be nuncheon very soon. I must hurry to spend a few minutes with Lisa before we are summoned.'

Amelia went up to the nursery. Nurse Mary was folding clothes as the children played with puzzles and books at the table.

'I am sorry to visit so late. I overslept this morning.'

'Miss Ross has been to play with the children,' Mary said. 'Miss Barton usually comes, but she hasn't been this morning. It is the first time she has missed since before Christmas.'

'She had a headache last night. Perhaps she still has it.'

Amelia spent a little time with the children. She promised Lisa that she would return later that day.

'We are going to Ravenshead tomorrow,' she said. 'I shall have more time to take you for walks then, my love.'

'Will you be my mama then? Must I call you Mama?'

'I shall always be your friend,' Amelia said. 'If you wish to call me Mama, you may, but if you would rather call me Melia, you can, Lisa.'

'Nanny said I would have to call you Mama—even though you are not my mother...' Lisa frowned. 'My mother died, didn't she?'

'Oh, darling, yes, she did, soon after you were born. Why do you ask?'

'How did my mama die? Did it hurt her?' Lisa's eyes were dark and a little fearful.

'No, she wasn't in pain. She had been ill for a long time—and she just went to sleep. You shouldn't think about it, Lisa. Your mama loved you and she would want you to be happy.'

'You won't die, will you, Melia?'

'No, my love. Not for a long time.'

Lisa clung to her hand. 'Promise me you won't go away and leave me and never come back.'

'I promise. I may go somewhere for a visit with your papa sometimes, but we shall both come back to you. We love you very much and we shall all be together as much as possible.'

'Thank you for telling me.' Lisa's eyes fixed on her intently. 'I love you, Melia.'

'I love you too, my darling.' Amelia embraced her, then looked into her face. 'Who told you that your mama died?'

'I asked Emily, because *she* said—' Lisa broke off as Marguerite entered the room. 'I want to read my book…' She ran to pick up the picture book, her head bent over the beautiful illustrations.

'Emily is unwell,' Marguerite said. 'She has vomited this morning and I think she has a fever. I believe she may be sickening for something. Perhaps we should ask for the doctor to call?'

'Yes, perhaps we should,' Amelia said. 'I must go, Lisa. I shall come again later.'

Amelia hurried from the room. She felt anxious about Emily. It must be something more than strong perfume on her kerchiefs if she had been vomiting. She would visit her and then make a decision about sending for the doctor.

'I am sorry to be so much trouble,' Emily said, looking pale and wan as she lay with her head against a pile of pillows. 'I do not know what is wrong with me. I was awake most of the night and vomited three times.'

'I am so sorry you are ill,' Amelia said. 'I shall send for the doctor. He will give you something to help with the pain.'

'I never have headaches. I thought it was the perfume on my kerchiefs, but it throbs so and I feel terrible...' Emily put a hand to her head. 'I am sorry to cause all this bother, Amelia.'

'You are not causing a bother. I shall call the doctor and hope that you are well enough to travel in the morning, Emily. However, if you are still unwell, we shall put off our journey for a few days. I have no intention of leaving you behind, my love.'

Leaving Emily to rest, Amelia went downstairs. She was late entering the dining parlour and apologised to the assembled company.

'I am sorry to keep you waiting, but Emily is most unwell—and I slept late.'

'I am so sorry Emily is unwell,' Helene said. 'Have you sent for the doctor?'

'Yes, I spoke to one of your servants, Helene. Emily is too sick to keep food down. I have asked Martha to make her a tisane and I shall go up to her as soon as I have eaten.'

'I could help nurse her,' Marguerite offered.

'It would be better if you stayed away from Miss Barton,' Gerard said from across the table. 'If she *is* sickening for something infectious, I would not wish it passed on to Lisa. Your first duty is to the child, Miss Ross.'

Marguerite's face remained impassive, but, happening to look at her, Amelia noticed that a little nerve flickered at the corner of her eye. She was not sure if Marguerite were angry or distressed.

Amelia frowned. 'I promised to visit Lisa this afternoon, Gerard. Perhaps I should not—unless Emily is merely suffering from an excess of nerves?'

Gerard stared at her for a moment in silence, then inclined his head. 'I shall bow to your good judgement, Amelia. However, it might be best if you left the nursing of Emily to Martha or one of the other maids.'

She gave him a reproving look. 'Emily is my friend. She needs me.'

'You are Lisa's mother now. She should be more important to you. I hope you will not let her down, Amelia.'

Gerard's expression was hard to read, but she thought that he was angry. Amelia was puzzled and a little hurt. How could Gerard think that she would desert Emily when she was so ill? Lisa had her nurse and Marguerite, and if Gerard was afraid of cross-infection then she would simply have to stay away from the nursery until Emily was better.

She did not like his tone or the way his words seemed to imply that Amelia's own wishes must come second to the child's. Of course she would never intentionally let Lisa down, but neither could she abandon Emily when she was so ill.

Gerard had been acting a little oddly recently. Amelia was not certain what some of his remarks were supposed to mean. She would ask him to explain, but for the moment it did not look as if she would have time to speak with him alone.

The doctor visited Emily. After examining her, he shook his head and looked grave, but said nothing until Amelia followed him into the small sitting room.

'She has no physical signs of illness other than the vomiting and the headache. There is no fever and I cannot see any sign of a rash—nor does she have any lumps in her stomach that might indicate an internal problem.' He polished his little round spectacles on a white kerchief. 'Could she be suffering from an excess of feeling, perhaps? Has she suffered a disappointment?'

'Yes, I believe she may have.' Amelia frowned. 'That happened some days ago and she was well enough then, distressed but not unwell. Are you sure there is nothing wrong with her?'

'It is my opinion that she is of a delicate constitution and, as you may know, some ladies go into a decline after suffering a severe setback.'

'I would not have thought that Emily had a delicate constitution.' Amelia wanted to say more, but held the words back. 'Thank you for your time, sir. You may send me the bill.'

'I shall send something that may help with the head-ache—but I believe she needs a tonic to lift her spirits. Perhaps she should go to Bath and take the waters there.'

'Yes, perhaps. I shall suggest it to her.'

Amelia returned to Emily's bedchamber after he left.

'He will send something for the headache, but I believe one of Martha's tisanes would do as well, Emily.'

'I am not sure, but I think it was the tisane that made me sick,' Emily said. 'Martha brought it to me and I left it beside my bed. I was sleepy and did not drink it then, but later…something woke me. I got up to relieve myself and then drank the tisane. Some minutes later I started to vomit.'

'Martha's tisane could not have caused you to be sick,' Amelia said. 'She has made them for me many times when I have felt a little unwell and they always do me good. It is very strange.'

'Well, perhaps it was not the tisane,' Emily said. 'I feel a little better now, but I shall not get up. I want to be well enough to come with you tomorrow, Amelia.'

'If you are not, we shall delay our departure. I shall not leave you behind, dearest. If you are not completely better once we are at Ravenshead, I shall call another doctor. I would send you to my own doctor in Bath, whom you know and like, but I cannot come with you.' Amelia was thoughtful. 'Unless you would like to go alone?'

'No, I should not. I do not want to leave you. Especially at the moment…while you may be in danger.' Emily's fingers moved nervously on the covers. 'I have not forgotten that it was you those rogues meant to

snatch when I was kidnapped—the things they said...'
She gave a little shiver. 'You must be careful, Amelia—
even when you think there is no reason.'

'I know you care for me, Emily. We must just hope
that you are soon feeling well again, my love.'

Amelia came upon Gerard as she was on her way
back from the nursery. She had spent a pleasant hour
reading to Lisa. The child seemed much happier than
she had at Christmas, though she had clung to Amelia
and was clearly reluctant to see her leave.

'You have been to visit Lisa?'

She met Gerard's questioning gaze, looking directly
into his eyes.

'The doctor says that Emily may be suffering an
excess of the nerves. I am not sure that he is correct,
but he says there is no fever. She is not infectious. I
have visited Lisa as I promised her. Had Emily been
infectious, I should not have visited the nursery until
it was safe.'

'Are you annoyed with me for suggesting it?'

'You have every right to protect your child. I know
she is important to you.'

'It was not simply that...' Gerard frowned. 'Something odd is going on, Amelia. I am not sure what it is,
but I have sensed it for a while.'

'I am not sure that I understand you, Gerard. I know
Emily was abducted at Pendleton, but nothing else has
happened since then. Unless you know something I do
not?'

'There was the matter of the intruder in your bedchamber.' Gerard hesitated. 'A footman saw a woman

leaving the back stairs that evening. She went into the hall and up the main staircase. He did not see her face clearly for it was dark and she had no candle, but he thought she wore a grey gown. He thought it odd that she did not carry a candle and reported it to Max.'

'Perhaps there was sufficient light from the stars.'

'But why not take a candle—unless she did not wish to be seen?'

'You think a woman came to my room—a woman who was not a servant?'

'I think perhaps she might have been your intruder.'

'I was not harmed and nothing was taken.'

'But someone was there and must have had a reason.' He frowned. 'The footman thought it might have been your companion.'

'You cannot think it was Emily?'

Amelia had said nothing to Gerard of the letters taken from her desk or the pot of lilies in her room, because the incidents were merely annoying and not of consequence.

'We only have Miss Barton's word—and Northaven's, of course—that she was abducted.'

'Gerard! How could you?' Amelia raised her brows. 'What are you implying? You do not think that Emily would lie about a thing like that? Why would she pretend to be abducted?'

'At the moment I hardly know what I think. Yet something is nagging at the back of my mind.'

'You must tell me later.' Amelia smiled. 'Here comes Marguerite.' She went forwards to meet her. 'Are you on your way to the nursery? We have good news, Marguerite. Emily is not infectious, but she is far from well. I have told her that we shall not travel to Ravenshead until she is better. Indeed, if she does not recover I may have to take her to Bath to visit my own doctor. However, in that event, you would accompany Lisa to Ravenshead—she needs the comforts of her home about her.'

'I am sad to hear that Emily is ill. Is there anything I can do for her, as she is not infectious?' Marguerite's gaze flicked towards Gerard and for a moment her eyes seemed to spark with an emotion that might have been resentment.

'She would rather be left to rest. The vomiting has passed, but she still has a headache. Besides, as Gerard said, you came to us to help with Lisa, did you not?'

'Yes, of course. I just wish to be of as much help to you as I can, Amelia.' Marguerite glanced at Gerard and for a moment her eyes were hard with dislike. 'I shall not hurt or abandon you.'

'I am sure you would not.' Amelia smiled and kissed her cheek. 'I do not know when Emily will be able to resume her duties. In the meantime, I shall need your help, Marguerite.'

'You know that I am always willing to be of service to you, Amelia.'

Amelia glanced at Gerard. 'I shall see you later, sir. I have a little errand for Marguerite and I must explain what I need.' She turned to the other woman. 'Emily usually helps Martha to pack my clothes, but she is not well enough. Indeed, I believe she may need help herself if we are to leave in the morning as planned.'

She took Marguerite's arm and walked away with her, leaving Gerard to stare after them, a puzzled look in his eyes.

Amelia left Marguerite after giving her the task of helping Martha with their packing. She went to visit Emily, but found her sleeping and, after some thought, made her way downstairs to the parlour where she found some of the ladies sitting taking tea. When the ladies began to disperse, going to their rooms to change for the evening, Amelia had a few minutes alone with Helene.

It was almost six when she went up to change for dinner. Meeting Gerard on the stairs, she begged him not to delay her.

'Martha has had all the packing to do. I asked Marguerite to help her, but I must make sure everything has been done that needs to be done—and if I do not hurry I shall be late for dinner.'

'What are you playing at, Amelia?' Gerard's dark eyes narrowed, intent on her face.

'I do not know what you mean, sir.'

'When did I become sir again? I thought everything was settled between us?'

'Of course it is, Gerard,' Amelia said. 'It is true that I have something on my mind, but...' She shook her head. 'Tell me—have you made any discoveries about this Lieutenant Gordon? Has the marquis been in touch since we left Pendleton?'

'Unfortunately I am no nearer solving the mystery than I was then.' He frowned. 'As you said, nothing of significance has happened and yet my instincts tell me that the danger is very close.'

'We must all continue to be on our guard,' Amelia said. 'I admit that I should feel more comfortable if this horrid business was over, but until we know who wishes to prevent our marriage, there is nothing we can do—is there?'

'Very little except be alert. If anything puzzles you…any little incident seems odd—you must tell me, Amelia.'

'Yes…' Amelia was thoughtful. 'Tomorrow we shall be at Ravenshead if Emily is feeling well enough to travel. Things may be easier to control then, Gerard. For a while, at least, there will be only the four of us, the servants—and Lisa, of course.'

'What are you thinking?' Gerard tipped her chin with his finger, looking into her face. 'Is there anything I should know?'

'Like you, I have an odd feeling…' Amelia shook her head. 'There is nothing I can put into words. Believe me, I would tell you if I knew what to say. Tell me, if you had an enemy, Gerard, would you wish him to be in the shadows where you could not see him, or under your nose?'

'I suppose it would be best to keep him close. You cannot fight an enemy you cannot see.'

'I imagined you would say that.' Amelia nodded in agreement. 'I think I should prefer that too—but do not ask me to explain.' She looked up at him. 'If I thought I knew the answers to your questions, I would tell you.'

'Then I suppose I must be content to wait.' He

reached for her hand and kissed it. 'You are not regretting anything?'

'Certainly not. I am looking forward to our wedding,' Amelia told him. 'Besides, Lisa would be hurt if I changed my mind at this late stage, would she not? And now, if you will excuse me, I must go up for I shall almost certainly be late otherwise.'

She smiled and ran up the stairs, leaving him to continue on his way. Gerard thought she was hiding something from him, but it was not so. There were a few things that made no sense—and a feeling that had been growing on her that someone was lying to her.

The problem was that, for the moment, she could not be certain who had lied and who had spoken truly. She might know more once Helene had spoken to Max.

Gerard was thoughtful after he left Amelia. She had put up the barriers again, shutting him out. He had thought when they kissed that she was truly able to put the past behind them, believing that she still felt much of the passion she had when they were first engaged. Now he had begun to wonder.

Amelia had been giving him some odd looks. She had changed in the last day or so, as if she were no longer sure of her feelings for him.

When she entered the bedroom, Martha was folding some clothes and packing them into a large trunk. She looked a little put out and Amelia guessed the cause, but the maid did not complain, merely coming to assist her as Amelia began to change for the evening.

'The tisane you made for Emily last evening—was it the same as you make for me?'

'Yes, Miss Royston. Just an infusion of herbs and a little honey to sweeten it.' Martha gave her a direct stare. 'There was nothing in it to make her sick. I know my herbs, miss, and I would not make a mistake.'

'Did someone imply there might be a mistake?'

'It was suggested that I might have made the infusion of herbs too strong. There was no mistake, Miss Royston.' The maid frowned. 'But I shan't tell tales so don't ask me.'

'No, I am certain that you did not make a mistake, for you never do.' Amelia smiled at her. 'Tell me, Martha—what do you think of Miss Barton?'

'She is a pleasant young lady and always helpful...' Martha set her mouth. 'And if you are going to ask what I think of Miss Ross...I would rather not say.'

'Oh dear.' Amelia smothered the urge to laugh. 'Was she not helpful, Martha? I thought she would save you having so much work to do since Emily is not well enough to do her own packing.'

'The intention was there, miss—but I've had to unpack and start again or we should never find everything again. I have an order to my work, Miss Royston. Pushing things in anywhere will not do for me.'

'Then I shall go down and leave you to work in peace. I am very sorry, Martha, but Miss Ross wanted to be of use and I thought it would be something for her to do.'

Chapter Eight

'I wish I were coming with you,' Helene said as she kissed Amelia's cheek the next morning. They were in the hall and Amelia was about to leave. 'Please promise me to take care of yourself.'

'Of course I shall,' Amelia said and embraced her. 'Was Max able to answer the question I asked?'

'He said to tell you it was three.' Helene looked puzzled. 'I do not see how that helps you, Amelia.'

'I assure you that it does. It is exactly as I suspected and the answer to a small mystery. Thank you, my love. You are not to worry about me.'

'I shall try not to—though I would be happier if I knew what was going on.'

'Nothing that need concern you, my dearest,' Amelia said and squeezed her hand. 'Truly, it is a mere trifle. I shall write and tell you everything when I can. I must go now. Gerard is impatient to be off.'

'You haven't quarrelled with him? He seems…a little odd. I thought he might be angry about something.'

'I dare say he is merely anxious. I fear we are a little at odds, but that may be my fault. He thinks I am keeping something from him—and, truthfully, I am.'

'Amelia! What are you about?'

'Believe me, there is nothing to worry you, Helene.'

Amelia pressed her hand and went out to the waiting carriage. Marguerite was already inside, clearly ready to leave. Emily was sitting in one corner, looking pale, dark shadows beneath her eyes and clutching a kerchief soaked with healing lavender water. The scent of it wafted through the carriage, but was quite pleasant. Amelia had asked earlier if she would like to stay on at Coleridge for a while, but she had refused, insisting that she was well enough to make the journey.

Gerard gave Amelia his hand to help her inside, but said nothing, his mouth set in a grim line. He moved away as the groom put up the steps and turned to mount his horse. Lisa was travelling in the second coach with her nurse and Martha.

'I fear the earl grows angry, Amelia. He seems impatient to get away.' Marguerite's words broke Amelia's reverie.

'Yes. I believe he wishes to be home by this evening.'

'I wonder that you can bear his ill humour…' Marguerite clapped a gloved hand to her mouth. 'Forgive me. I should not have said that…I am sure it is simply a natural impatience to be home. Yet it is not pleasant to live with a man of uncertain temper. My father is such a man and I have suffered from his rages.'

'I am sorry for that, my dear.'

'I have learned to accept it, but I should not wish you to be unhappy, Amelia. Many ladies are unhappy in their marriages, I think. Men are so faithless—at least many are.'

'Yes, I believe so.' Amelia was silent for a moment. 'Gerard can seem harsh at times, I know, though he is usually good natured.'

'Yes, of course. I did not mean to imply…' Marguerite looked as if she wanted to say more, but was apprehensive. 'You will bring so much to the marriage; he must surely be grateful. Of course he would never do anything to harm you.'

'No, he would not. Why should he?'

'I meant nothing. My words were ill considered and foolish.' Marguerite fiddled with her gloves, twisting them nervously in her hands and then putting them on. 'I hope I have not offended.'

'I told you when you came that you might say anything to me. If you have something to say about the earl, please do so now.'

'Oh, no…' Marguerite shook her head. 'One hears rumours, of course—but I would never repeat anything I did not know for sure.'

'It is always best not to do so. Perhaps I know the rumour you speak of—concerning his wife?'

'Well, yes, I did hear something about the way she died.' She glanced at Emily, who was holding her kerchief to her nose. 'I am not sure who told me.'

'You ought not listen to gossip,' Amelia said and frowned. 'I hope you will forget it—the earl did nothing to harm Lisette.'

'No? Then it was a malicious lie and I am glad I did not repeat it to anyone.'

Marguerite sat back against the squabs, her expression subdued. Obviously, she felt that she had spoken out of turn. She ought not to have repeated gossip, of course. Amelia was glad that Gerard had told her how his wife died, otherwise she might have wondered.

Marguerite had hinted several times that Gerard might be marrying her because of her fortune. Amelia had not considered it, because he had told her that he was not interested in her money. She did not know why Marguerite seemed to dislike Gerard, but she was afraid there was some resentment on Marguerite's part. At the beginning neither one had been prepared to admit they had met before, though later both had remembered that they had known each other in the past.

What did Marguerite know that Amelia didn't? What was she hinting at when she suggested that men were unfaithful?

Amelia frowned. Gerard had left her without a word that summer. He said it was because her brother had warned him off, but could she be certain he had not left for another reason entirely? He had sworn he loved her that summer, but within a few months he had married Lisette.

Had he truly loved Amelia? Or was the truth that he had never—and could never—love anyone? Was he the kind of man who loved lightly and moved on?

No! It was wicked of her to think such things. She did not know why she had allowed the thoughts to creep in. She would put them from her mind at once.

It was late in the evening when they arrived at Ravenshead. However, lights blazed in all the front windows, for the candles had been lit in anticipation of their arrival. The butler and housekeeper came out to welcome them, and Gerard's servants were lined up inside the house to meet them. Amelia was introduced to them all and then the housekeeper took her, Emily and Marguerite up to their rooms.

'I've put Miss Ross in one of the guest rooms, as the earl instructed,' Mrs Mowbray said when they were alone. 'Miss Barton has a room nearer the nursery. I hope that is acceptable?'

'Yes, of course—though perhaps…' Amelia shook her head. If Gerard had asked for the rooms to be allocated that way, she would not interfere. She had hardly glanced at the hall downstairs, though she had received an impression of marble tiles on the floor and elegant mahogany furniture, but here she was aware that the décor was new and the colour variations of the pale aquamarine she liked so much. 'Have these rooms been recently refurbished?'

'The earl had them done in October, Miss Royston. I hope you will be comfortable here?'

'Yes, thank you—they are everything I could wish.'

Amelia sighed and took off her bonnet and pelisse. She had come straight up to her apartments so had not taken them off in the hall. It was obvious that Gerard had had the rooms done specially for her. She wished that she could thank him in the way she would like, but something warned her that she must be careful.

She was exploring the bedchamber, discovering the space in the large armoire, when she heard something behind her. Turning, she saw that Gerard had entered through the dressing-room door. For a moment she was surprised, then realised that these apartments had been planned for when they married. As long as the key was his side, he could come and go as he pleased.

'Gerard…you startled me. I was not aware that we had adjoining apartments.'

'You do not object? Should I have knocked at the hall door?'

'No, of course not. It will be convenient when we wish to talk.'

'And at other times…' Gerard moved closer. He reached out to touch her cheek. 'We spoke of being together in a special way when we came to Ravenshead? You have not changed your mind?'

'I think we should be careful for the moment.' Amelia saw his quick frown. 'I have good reason for what I do and say, Gerard—but please do not doubt my feelings for you.'

'I do not understand you…' Gerard began, but someone knocked at the door. Amelia gave him a little push towards the dressing room. He went through and closed the door.

'Just a moment,' Amelia called. 'Come in, please.'

The door opened and then Marguerite entered. She glanced round, her eyes absorbing the décor. 'What a beautiful room, Amelia. Did I hear voices? I am sorry if I interrupted something…'

'You did not,' Amelia replied. 'Did you need something, Marguerite?'

'Nothing. I have a very adequate room. I merely came to see if I might be of service to you?'

'Martha will see to my unpacking. I am ready to go down if you are, Marguerite. Mrs Mowbray will have a light supper prepared for us, I am sure. Emily told us that she requires no supper so we shall leave her to rest for the moment.'

'Well, if you are certain I can do nothing,' Marguerite said and turned to leave. 'Just remember that I am always ready to help you. Especially as Emily is not well enough to run errands for you. If ever you are unhappy or in distress, you may rely on me for help.'

'I am sure you will make yourself indispensable,' Amelia told her with a smile. 'I am very pleased you came to me, Marguerite—and I am sure Lisa adores you already.'

'She is a pretty little thing and she has good manners. I dare say she is very like her mother.'

'Yes, perhaps. I suppose you did not know her mama?'

Marguerite looked startled for a moment, then shook her head. 'She was French, was she not? I have few friends, Amelia. You know that it was almost impossible for me to meet anyone after Lucinda…' Her voice cracked on a little sob. 'Mama and Papa broke their hearts when she died. She was so foolish. She should have named her seducer and faced her shame. He might have been forced to marry her. His desertion broke her heart.' Marguerite's eyes flashed with sudden anger. 'If I could, I would make him pay for what he did to her.'

'She would not tell me his name. Did she never say anything to you, Marguerite?'

'She hinted once or twice…' Marguerite shook her head. 'I do not know his name, Amelia—just that it was a gentleman we all knew. Someone who ought to have known better than to seduce an innocent girl.'

'That is a wide field. I was so sorry when Lucinda took her own life.'

'If she did…' Marguerite's eyes flashed with sudden anger. 'How can we be sure that she did kill herself?'

'I thought there was no doubt?'

'I have sometimes thought…' Marguerite hesitated. 'Just before she died she was happy. She hinted that she might have something exciting to tell me soon… and then she disappeared and they dragged her body from the river. Her dress had been torn and…a ring she had been wearing had gone from her hand. I think her lover gave her the ring and…I suspect he took it from her before he…killed her…'

'Marguerite!' Amelia stared at her in horror. Prickles of ice danced along her spine. 'You think her lover killed her—but why?'

'I know he killed her! Even if she had taken her own life it would have been his fault. He would still have been her murderer,' Marguerite said bitterly. 'She was but a child and he took advantage. I think when she threatened to reveal his name, he pushed her into the river and watched her drown. She could not swim.'

'How can you know that? You do not even know his name.'

'I know most of what happened.' Marguerite lifted her head defiantly. Something flickered in her eyes. 'If I knew his name…I should not rest until he was punished.'

Amelia touched her arm. 'I understand your pain and distress, but hate will not bring her back, Marguerite. You cannot change the past.'

'I have suffered for her stupid lack of morality. If

she had behaved as she ought, none of this would have happened. Why did she give herself to a faithless rogue? She ruined her own life and mine.'

'You must try to forget it. You are here now, Marguerite. You will meet my friends and Gerard's. You have every opportunity to find happiness.'

'My parents would not allow me to marry.'

'I think they might if it was a good match,' Amelia said. 'I believe I might be able to persuade them if you found someone you thought you could love.'

'Men are not to be trusted,' Marguerite flashed at her. 'They seduce you with their smiles and sweet words and then they destroy your life. Be careful who you trust, Amelia. Even marriage does not mean you are guaranteed happiness.'

'Are you suggesting that the earl cannot be trusted?'

'His first wife was unhappy enough to take her own life...' Marguerite said and then put a hand to her mouth in horror. 'I should not have said that...now you will send me home. Yet it is true and you should be careful, Amelia. Be sure that he truly cares for you or you may be hurt too.'

'No, I shall not send you home,' Amelia said, looking at her steadily. 'Tell me, do you really believe that Lisette's death happened because Gerard made her unhappy? Are you saying that he was cruel to her?'

'I only know what someone told me.' Marguerite looked at her oddly. 'What do you think, Amelia? Why would she take her own life if she were happy?'

'I know the truth of it and I know it was not Gerard's fault,' Amelia said. 'But perhaps I shall ask him about it again.'

'You should.' Marguerite gripped her wrist. 'For your own sake, Amelia. I should be so sorry if something were to happen to you because of him.'

'You are hurting me.'

'Forgive me. I did not realise what I did...'

Amelia drew away and Marguerite let go of her wrist. Amelia rubbed at it. 'There is nothing to forgive. I know you are thinking of me—but we shall not speak of this again.'

'I am sorry. You have been so good to me. I had no right to speak but I care about you.'

'I know you do.' Amelia smiled at her. 'Do not look so anxious, Marguerite. I am not going to send you away.'

'You are too forgiving,' Marguerite said. 'People take advantage of you. Emily told me what you did for Lady Pendleton and Lady Coleridge.'

'Had I known how unhappy you were, I should have asked for your company before this,' Amelia told her. 'However, it is not too late for you to make a new life. Nothing that has happened so far should make it impossible for you to find happiness—if you can let go of the past.'

Marguerite stared at her in silence. Amelia nodded at her encouragingly, hoping she might respond to the invitation, but Marguerite turned her face away, going ahead of her down the stairs.

Amelia thought she understood why Marguerite thought so badly of Gerard. She was still grieving for her sister and did not trust any man. When she came to know him better, she would realise that she was wrong to distrust him.

* * *

Amelia was seated at her dressing table later that night when the door to the dressing room opened and Gerard entered. He went to the hall door and tried the handle, nodding his satisfaction when he discovered it was locked. Amelia stood up. Her hair had been taken down from its customary style and hung loosely on her shoulders, and she was wearing a pale blue lace peignoir over a matching silk nightgown. Her feet were bare. She picked up a perfume flask and dabbed a drop behind her ears.

'Why did you check the door?'

'Because I wanted to make certain we were not interrupted this time, Amelia.'

Amelia saw that he was still fully clothed, though he had taken off his boots. 'To what do I owe the pleasure of this visit, Gerard?'

'I have not been able to speak to you alone for days,' he said, looking frustrated. 'We need to talk.'

'Yes, I agree. I think you should tell me the whole truth about Lisette, Gerard. You told me something, but I do not believe it was all—was it?'

'What do you wish to know?' Gerard's gaze narrowed.

'You told me that you married her while still angry with my brother and me—but did you love her?'

'No. As I told you, she had been raped and was lying by the side of the road, beaten and close to death. I nursed her back to health and then she told me her lover was dead. She was having his child. I married her to protect her and the child—and because I thought I could never have you.'

She gazed up at him. 'I know you said something died in you the night Michael had you beaten, but do you think you can learn to love me?'

'Did I say that to you?' Gerard looked puzzled. 'I felt that way for a long time, but you cannot believe it now? You must know that I care for you, my dear one.'

'I hoped that you might in time…'

'Believe me, you are the only woman I want as my wife.'

'You truly mean that?'

'Yes, of course.'

'Why did you come to me tonight?'

'So that we could talk. Why?' His eyebrows arched.

'I thought you might have come for another reason,' she said and moved closer to him, the scent of her body inviting and tempting.

Gerard looked at her steadily. 'You told me you thought we should be careful—and I have noticed something odd in your manner of late. You asked me about Lisette and I have answered you truthfully. Will you tell me what is troubling you?'

'Yes, perhaps I should,' she agreed. 'But do not expect me to solve the mystery, Gerard. I am concerned because I think… Emily and Marguerite do not truly like one another. Helene noticed it and…Marguerite has hinted that Emily is lying to me.'

'Good grief!' Gerard frowned. 'What has she said exactly?'

'Some letters were taken from my room. I asked Martha, Emily and Marguerite if they had taken them. They all said no, but Marguerite told me she had seen letters in my hand on the salver in the hall. As you know, Max always franks his guests' letters to save their families the expense of some sixpences.'

'Letters...' Gerard wrinkled his brow. 'I can see nothing wrong in anyone taking them down for you. What is strange in this?'

'Nothing—except that one of them must have taken the letters, but none of them will admit it.'

'You have questioned your maid?'

'Yes. Martha would only take the letters if I told her. Marguerite told me that Emily had been to my room that morning. She still denied having taken them—and Max told Helene that he had franked three letters for me. I wrote four.'

'Four...you are certain?' Amelia inclined her head and Gerard pursed his lips. 'Was there anything of value in any of the letters? Were they important?'

'They were thank-you letters for Christmas gifts—and one to my brother to inform him of our marriage.'

'You do not know which one was taken?'

'I cannot know for certain. Max recalled the number, but he would not have remembered to whom they were addressed—but one was to Marguerite's mother, to thank her for allowing her daughter to come to us.'

'You think it may have been the letter that went astray?'

'I do not know...' Amelia hesitated. 'And there were the lilies...a pot of them in my room. Martha noticed the smell and took them away. If we had not noticed it, they might have given me a headache for they were very strong. It was a silly incident—but something Marguerite said has led me to believe that it might have been Emily. Unless...' She sighed. 'It is quite ridiculous. I have wondered if Marguerite wishes to take Emily's place in my affections…and if Emily feigned illness because she is perhaps a little jealous.'

'This is all trivial stuff,' Gerard said. He reached out to lift her chin with his finger. 'You are certain this is all, Amelia?'

'There have been other hints…things said that I felt not quite as I would like, but nothing that means anything. Someone spoke of Lisa's mother dying to her. She was upset until I told her that her mother died peacefully with no pain.' She saw him flinch. 'It would be wrong to tell her the truth, Gerard. I believe she was afraid that I might die or leave her. I told her it would not happen for a long time.'

She said nothing of Marguerite's hints that he might be unfaithful to her. He had told her the truth about Lisette and to question about the summer he had courted her would seem as if she distrusted him.

'Who told her? You should speak to whoever it was, Amelia. Make it clear that you will not tolerate this kind of thing.'

'Emily has been unwell. I shall speak to her when she is better.'

'You think it was Miss Barton?' Gerard's gaze narrowed, became intent. 'Did Miss Ross tell you it was Emily?'

'No. Lisa started to tell me something, but after I explained, she seemed content and wanted to look at her book. To question her would make more of an incident best forgotten. I shall talk to Emily once she has fully recovered from whatever ails her.'

'Perhaps you would do better to let them both go,'

Gerard suggested. 'We could find a governess for Lisa—'

'Gerard! They are my friends. I could not be so cruel as to dismiss either of them for such trivial things.'

'Are you sure they are trivial?'

'No more, Gerard.' Amelia reached up to touch his cheek. 'Now you know why I hesitated to tell you in the beginning. Someone has lied to me—and someone said things they should not—but at the moment I can make no sense of it all. Emily's abduction has turned everything upside down. It is easy to start at shadows, to imagine fault where there is none. Besides, if there was something…we need to know the truth, Gerard. To send the guilty person away might mean that we should never be free of this shadow.'

'If I thought either of them meant harm to you or Lisa…' A glint of anger leapt in his eyes.

Amelia placed her fingers to his lips. 'Lisa is safe, my dearest. Why should anyone wish to harm her? Besides, they both love her. I am sure they do.'

'Why should anyone wish to stop our marriage?'

'It could not benefit either Emily or Marguerite. No, I am certain this is just because of a little jealousy.'

'Then we are no nearer to discovering our enemy.'

'I think we may be,' Amelia said. 'I cannot give you a reason, but I feel that things have moved forwards, though why is not clear. Something is at the back of my mind, but I cannot tell you what it is.'

'You are not holding back from me?' Gerard's eyes seemed to look deep into her soul. Wordlessly, she shook her head. He smiled oddly and reached for her, drawing her close so that she felt the heat of his body and the urgency of his need. 'I should not be here. You are too tempting, my love. I want to sweep you up in my arms and carry you to that bed. I want to kiss and know every inch of your lovely body.'

Amelia's lips parted invitingly, her breath sweet and quick. 'You know how much I want to be with you, Gerard—to be yours. I should not deny you if you took me now.'

'I am tempted beyond bearing, but something is warning me that I ought not to take advantage—that I should wait…' His fingers traced the arch of her white throat. He bent his head to lick the little pulse spot at the base of her neck. Amelia quivered, pressing herself against him, her body surrendering to the need inside.

'Gerard…forget the shadows…forget caution. I want to be yours.'

'Supposing something happens to me…if there should be a child…' he warned as he caught her to him; his mouth pressed against her neck, warm and moist as he nibbled gently. She arched into him, melting in the heat of their mutual desire, lifting her face for his kiss. 'Amelia, my love. I want you so much…'

'If something happened to part us, I should have known your love,' she whispered passionately. 'I am not a green girl, Gerard. I am a woman, but I have never known a man's love—never felt the happiness of being one with you. Do not let me go to my grave never having known what it is to be loved, I beg you. If either of us should die before we wed, we should at least have had this night.'

Gerard's resolve melted as she pressed herself against him. There was a wild, wanton look in her eyes; the barriers were down and he could not resist their mutual need.

He moaned softly in his throat, bending to sweep her up in his arms and carry her to the bed. She smiled up at him trustingly as he lay her down amongst the soft sheets, her peignoir falling open to reveal the sweet swell of her breasts. His body throbbed with the need to have her and he began to strip away his shirt, ripping the fine material carelessly. Amelia undid her peignoir, pushing it back from her shoulders, slipping her arms out so that all she wore was the thin nightdress that did nothing to hide the contours of her shapely body.

Gerard stripped off the rest of his clothing. Amelia's eyes travelled over the lean length of him, his strong legs and arms, his smooth chest and the sprinkling of dark hair that arrowed to his aroused manhood. The sight of his beautiful naked body was shocking and breathtaking, making her quiver with anticipation as he raised her so that he could pull her nightgown over her head and dispose of it with his clothes.

Then he was lying beside her on the sheets. He faced her, his mouth close to hers. He could smell the sweetness of her breath, the light taste of wine on her lips, and the perfume of her hair was intoxicating. His hands stroked down her back, smoothing the arch, cupping her buttocks and pressing her against him. She moaned softly, lips parting for the invasion of his tongue. He sucked at her, tasting her, their tongues meeting in little experimental darts of sensation, seeking, finding pleasure beyond all expectation.

He caressed her back and her shoulders, stroking firmly until she quivered and moaned with pleasure.

Bending his head, he sucked at her nipples, taking first one and then the other into his mouth, the roughness of his tongue against them sending jolts of pleasure through her. His hand stroked her thigh. His tongue traced its way over her navel to her mound, and then his hand parted her legs. He stroked the sensitive inner thigh for some minutes, making her pant with endless, aching need to feel his fingers touching her inner citadel.

When he touched her there she gasped, her back arching as the sensation of fierce pleasure shot through her. She opened wide, allowing him to stroke and then to enter her moistness. His mouth returned to hers, kissing her as his body slid over hers, and then the hot, hard probing of his manhood entered her with gentle thrusts, deeper and deeper until he found what he was seeking.

Amelia cried out as he broke through her maidenhead. For one moment the pain was sharp, but then his kiss was taking it away, soothing her. His hands stroked and pleasured, bringing her back to a state of blissful desire so that the moisture ran and she opened, taking him deep inside her. Their bodies moved together in a sensuous rhythm, the almost unbearable sensation making Amelia's breath come in quick gasps and then all at once Gerard gave a shout and she felt his release. She clung to him as the powerful spasm took her, making her cry out and arch beneath him.

After the intense sensations had faded to a pleasant feeling of satisfaction, Amelia turned her face into his shoulder as he lay beside her, still stroking the silken arch of her back. Her cheeks were wet with tears for she had not expected to feel anything as wonderful…as fulfilling as this sweet certainty of belonging.

'I dreamed…' she whispered. 'I dreamed so many nights…but I could not guess at what it would be…so beautiful…'

'You made it beautiful,' Gerard told her. 'I have never loved anyone else…never known such completeness… such happiness.'

'Gerard…' she murmured against his shoulder. 'We are one, together. No one can part us now.'

'I shall not let them,' he vowed fiercely as he lifted himself on one elbow to gaze down into her face. 'You are mine. Nothing and no one can come between us now.'

They held each other, falling asleep wrapped in each other's arms.

Amelia had not drawn her curtains completely. The light of the candles clearly showed the outline of two people as they moved together and embraced.

The woman watched for a few moments. In the light of the moon, which had just moved out from behind some clouds, the anger and bitterness was stamped on her features. So intent on what was happening in that room was she that she did not hear the man approach and jumped as he touched her shoulder. She whirled round, fingers clawing at his face. He gave a shout of alarm, jerking back and grabbing her wrists.

'What do you think you are doing? It is me— Gordon.'

'You startled me. Creeping up on me like that! I thought I was being attacked.'

'Wild cat,' he said and grinned as he caught her to him. He kissed her hungrily, but she pushed him away with an angry cry.

'I told you! Not until I have what I want. Gerard Ravenshead must die.'

'What of her?' Lieutenant Gordon nodded his head at the window. 'You said she must be raped and he must watch. I'm not your man for that…I'll gladly put a ball into his black heart, but she has done me no harm. I've never killed a woman and the idea has bothered me.'

'I wanted her to suffer as someone else suffered, but that no longer matters. Now all I want is that he should see her dead. He must suffer—he must know what it feels like to lose everything.' Her eyes glittered with hatred. 'His death is not enough for what he has done. If you want me, you must take revenge for me—and for yourself.' She smiled at him, suddenly luring him with a look that took his breath. 'I know you want me…but first I need my revenge.'

'You shall have it. I'll kill him for you and willingly,' he vowed. 'I heard that they are to be married soon. Shall it be before or after the wedding?'

She glanced back towards the bedroom window. There was no sign of the couple embracing now. She imagined them lying together…making love. At that moment her anger was so intense that she shook, but she fought the rage, knowing she must not give way to one of her fits. She was so close now—so close to the revenge she craved.

'It must be soon,' she said. 'There is no reason to wait longer. I have been making plans. Where can I reach you if I need you quickly?'

'At the inn in the village. Send a letter—or find a stable lad to bring your message.'

'Meet me here again in one week and then I shall tell you what I plan.'

Amelia woke to find the bed cold beside her. She looked at the indentation in the pillow where his head had lain, touching it, inhaling the scent of him that still clung to the sheets. Gerard had left her before the servants were about, because he was still trying to protect her reputation. She smiled, stretching, aware of how good she felt. The night had been filled with pleasure as they explored each other's bodies, touching, kissing, reaching a place that Amelia had never been. Gerard had told her it was the same for him.

'No other woman has ever made me feel as you do, my love,' he'd told her just before she fell deeply asleep.

She had slept so soundly that she had not felt him leave their bed. Perhaps he had tried not to wake her. Amelia was a little amused at his gallantry for her maid would know when she changed the sheets. Amelia's blood had stained them, and the masculine smell of Gerard clung to them. Martha would know. She might keep the knowledge to herself, but it would not be long before it became common knowledge below stairs.

Once, Amelia might have worried that her good name might be soiled, but she was too much in love to care. She was engaged to the man she loved and in a few weeks she would be Gerard's wife. Nothing else really mattered…but life went on. She had obligations she must fulfil.

Amelia rose, washed in the water that remained

from the night before in the jug on the washstand and dressed in a serviceable gown, leaving her room before Martha arrived to open the curtains. She walked along the passage and up one short flight of stairs to the rooms nearer the nursery. When she reached Emily's door, she knocked and called softly, 'May I come in, my love?'

'The door is open,' Emily replied. 'Please enter, Amelia.'

Amelia went into the bedroom to discover that Emily was already up and dressed, her bed neatly made. However, she was still a little pale and it was obvious that she had not slept well.

'How are you feeling, my love?'

'I am about the same as yesterday. I have not been sick, but my head still aches a little.'

'I am so sorry.' Amelia looked at her anxiously. 'Shall I ask Gerard to send for the doctor, my love?'

'No, I do not wish to trouble him,' Emily said. 'I am sure it is nothing serious, Amelia. I shall be better soon.' She fiddled with the sash of her gown, pulling at a slight crease. 'I should wish to be of use to you. Is there anything I can do...help you with the wedding invitations? You will have much to do if the wedding is to be soon.'

'I should prefer that you rest as much as possible. I do not like to see you so low, Emily. Marguerite may help for the moment—and you may join me when you are feeling more the thing.'

'I am much recovered—and I would rather help you than stay in my room.'

'Very well. I have drawn up a list. You may look

through it with me and see if I have forgotten anyone. When it is complete, Gerard will have the invitations printed and I shall sign them. I dare say you will be well enough to address some envelopes for me. And there will be thank-you letters to friends, for I believe his notice to *The Times* should be inserted any day now.'

'You look so happy,' Emily said and smiled. 'Please do not worry about me, dearest Amelia. This should be a happy time for you—and I shall be well enough in a few days.'

'I hope so, my love. Meet me in the little parlour at the back of the house at eleven, Emily. I am going to visit the nursery first—and then I shall accompany Mrs Mowbray on a tour of the house, but I should be finished by eleven o'clock.'

As Amelia had expected, she found Lisa wide awake and ready to play. She spent a delightful hour reading to her and helping her to draw pictures on her slate. Lisa drew a credible picture of a dog and then looked at Amelia.

'Will Papa remember I wanted a puppy?'

'I should think he might, but if he doesn't I will remind him.'

'You are so good to me! *She* told me he would forget… *She* said that he did not truly love me, because he did not love my mama…' Lisa's eyes were dark with anxiety. 'Papa does love me…he says he does.'

'Who said that to you, Lisa? Was it Emily?' Amelia frowned. 'Was it Emily who told you that your mama was dead?'

Lisa shook her head. She shuffled her feet and glanced over her shoulder. '*She* said if I told you Nanny would come back and punish me.'

'Nanny will never come back. I promised you that, Lisa.'

'But I saw her…I saw her outside in the gardens last night. I saw her from the window. I like to look out at the moon, you see…'

'You saw Nanny? Miss Horton—you saw her here in the gardens last night?'

'Yes. Nanny was talking to a man—and then they both walked away.'

'I shall tell your papa about this,' Amelia said. 'Nanny has no right to be here and she will be sent away. Who told you that Nanny would come back, Lisa?'

Lisa opened her mouth and then shut it as someone entered the nursery, but her eyes flew to Amelia's face and something in them answered her question. Amelia held her hand and smiled at her reassuringly.

'Papa will not forget, my love,' she said, holding her close to whisper in her ear. 'Whatever anyone else tells you, I shall not let you be hurt or neglected.'

Lisa hugged her, clinging to her as if she did not want to let her go.

'Run to your nurse now, my love. I have other things to do this morning, but I shall return later and we will go for a little walk in the garden this afternoon.'

Amelia turned and greeted Marguerite with a smile. 'You are up early,' she said. 'Perhaps like me you like to be up with the lark?'

'I often rise early. It is the best part of the day. I like to walk before anyone else is about.'

'Excuse me, my dear. I have things I must do this morning…' Amelia said.

Chapter Nine

After completing a tour of the house with Mrs Mowbray, Amelia consulted with her on various things. She was asked if everything was to her satisfaction and if there were any changes to the routine that she would like to instigate.

'For the moment I think I am pleased with everything,' she said. 'However, I believe Nurse Mary needs more help in the nursery. She cannot do everything and I do not want Lisa to be left alone at any time.'

'I thought Miss Ross was to have charge of the nursery, Miss Royston?'

'Miss Ross is part-governess, part-friend,' Amelia said. 'She will spend time with Lisa—but I want another sensible girl to work with Mary. Someone who would know what to do in the event of an emergency. Do you have a suitable girl—or should we employ another?'

'There is Beattie...' Mrs Mowbray frowned. 'She is a good-hearted lass and has eight brothers and sisters younger than herself at home—but she isn't a clever girl. Beattie is very loyal, but she can't help with Miss Ravenshead's studies or anything of the sort.'

'I think Beattie may be just the girl I am looking for,' Amelia said. 'Will you send her to my room in a few minutes, please?'

'Yes, of course, miss. This will be a step up for the girl, Miss Royston. She will be pleased.'

'She must have a rise in her wages. I leave it to you to decide what would be appropriate, Mrs Mowbray.'

'Now that is generous.' The housekeeper beamed her approval. 'Beattie gives most of her money to her mother and this will be a help to them. I think five shillings a month would be fair.'

'Then we are agreed,' Amelia said. 'I am going up to change my gown now. Please send Beattie to me as soon as you can.'

Amelia left the housekeeper and went up to her room.

She had finished changing her gown and was struggling with a hook at the nape of her neck when a knock at the door announced Beattie's arrival.

'Ah, there you are,' Amelia said. 'Could you do this up for me, please?'

'Yes, miss, of course.'

Beattie fastened the hook and then stood before Amelia, her hands clasped in front of her.

'Do you like children, Beattie?'

'Oh, yes, miss. I love them. It's as well I do, miss. Ma has nine of us at home and I helped with the young ones until I came to work here.'

'Then you would enjoy looking after Lisa?'

'Yes, miss. She is a lovely little thing.' Beattie was beaming all over her face.

She was a plump, homely girl with curly hair and blue eyes, but there was something sturdy about her and Amelia could see why the housekeeper had recommended her.

'I am asking you to help Nurse Mary, because I do not wish Lisa to be left alone at any time. Either you or Nurse Mary will accompany her at all times—in the nursery or when she goes out. The only exception is when the earl or I take her out ourselves. Nurse Mary is in charge of the nursery, but if there is anything that worries you at any time, you may ask to speak to me.'

'Yes, miss. I understand,' Beattie said. 'You can trust me to keep an eye on her.'

'Yes,' Amelia said and nodded. 'That is exactly what I need, Beattie…'

Amelia was in a small parlour that overlooked the rose gardens when Gerard entered. She had been going through the list of guests for the wedding with Emily, but when he entered Emily stood up.

'If you will excuse me, Amelia. I shall go up to my room. I have a headache coming on and I think I shall lie down for half an hour before nuncheon.'

'You must not come down for the rest of the day if you are unwell, my love. Something can be brought to you on a tray.'

'Thank you. Martha will make me a tisane and I shall be better soon.'

Gerard frowned as Emily left the room. 'Do you

think Miss Barton is pining? I could write to Sinclair if you wish—ask him to explain himself.'

'No. He had his reasons for what he did,' Amelia said. 'I dare say he will come here when he feels ready. Besides, I am not sure that is the reason for Emily's headaches.'

'If she is really ill, we should have the doctor.'

'I shall send for one if she does not improve within a day or so.' Amelia smiled and got to her feet as he came to her. 'How are you this beautiful morning, Gerard?'

'It may have escaped your notice, but it is raining and there is a gale blowing.' Gerard laughed softly and held out his hands to her. 'Yes, it is a beautiful morning, my dearest one.' He took her hands, gazing down into her eyes. 'You have no regrets?'

'None. Have you?'

'You know the answer to that, Amelia.' He bent his head to kiss her softly on the mouth. 'I loved you before last night—but now I worship you, my lovely, passionate woman.'

Amelia blushed faintly. 'I dare say you think me wanton?'

'Deliciously so. I think myself the most fortunate man alive this morning, my love.'

'Oh, Gerard…it was so wonderful…all that I had dreamed of, longed for, for so many years.'

'And so many years wasted.' Gerard frowned. 'I was a damned fool to let your brother send me away. Nothing will stand between us now, Amelia. The only thing that can prevent our marriage is death.'

'And your men will patrol the grounds, Gerard. Are they in place?'

'Yes. I have given orders this morning. Why do you ask?'

'Because Lisa saw Nanny Horton and a man in the garden last night…'

Gerard swore. 'We must have been followed here. I had men riding behind us, some distance apart. None of them reported a shadow. I thought it would take a few days before anyone realised where we were.' His brow wrinkled. 'But why would Nanny Horton be here in the garden? I do not understand.'

'I think I begin to—' Amelia broke off as the door opened and someone entered. 'Good morning, Marguerite. Have you just come from the nursery?'

'Yes. I spent an hour reading to Lisa. She has a new maid. The girl refused to leave the room when I asked her to fetch something. I think she may prove insolent, Amelia. You may have to replace her.'

'Oh, I think not,' Amelia replied with a smile. 'Beattie has been told that Lisa is not to be left alone.' She glanced at Gerard, her eyes seeming to convey a message. 'I think I should reveal something to you, Marguerite. The earl received a warning—a broken doll. We believe this may constitute a threat against his daughter. Perhaps an abduction for a ransom? Therefore I have asked that one of the maids is always at hand. If an attempt at abduction were to be made, you might be overcome if you were alone, but if two of you are there I think she should be safe for one may raise the alarm—do you not agree?'

'A threat to abduct Lisa?' Marguerite was clearly shocked. 'That is terrible, Amelia. How upsetting for you! I understand why you have given orders that Lisa should never be left alone. I do not know how anyone can be wicked enough to threaten a child—and she is adorable!'

'Yes, she is,' Amelia said. 'I think I would prefer to be threatened myself. If anyone harmed Lisa, I would never forgive them.'

'Indeed, no,' Marguerite said. 'How could you?'

'Was there something you needed?' Amelia asked. 'You came in search of me—for a particular reason?'

'Oh… Emily told me that she is unwell again,' Marguerite said. 'She said that she would ask Martha for a tisane. I do not know what herbs your maid uses, Amelia—but some can cause headaches in certain people. However, I find camomile tea very soothing. Would you like me to make some for Emily?'

'Did you ask her?'

'She refused me, but perhaps if I took it to her room…'

'That would be very kind of you, Marguerite. Emily might find it soothing. I do myself.'

'Then I shall.' Marguerite inclined her head towards Gerard and went out, closing the door behind her.

'What was that about…?' Gerard began, but Amelia shook her head. She went to the door and opened it, looking out. Gerard watched her, brows raised in inquiry. 'What are you up to, Amelia? You did not tell me that you had arranged for another maid for Lisa.'

'I should have done so in a moment had we not been interrupted. It was a precaution after Lisa told me about Nanny Horton.'

'But the tale about the doll? We already know that it came from Northaven.'

'I know that—but I wish others to believe that we think it a threat to Lisa.'

'By "others" I take it you mean Marguerite Ross?' He stared at her hard. 'Something about her has been nagging at me, but I cannot think what…' He stopped, his gaze intent on her face. 'You know something—tell me.'

'I am not certain, but I believe that Alice Horton may once have been in the employ of Mr and Mrs Ross… as a nanny when the girls were young. I believe she was dismissed when they were older, but she may have kept in touch with Marguerite…' Amelia paused. 'Marguerite likes to write letters, as I do myself. I think it possible that they have never lost touch.' She looked at him. 'Tell me, how came you to employ Alice Horton?'

'I made inquiries at an agency…and she was one of those who applied for the post. She had letters of recommendation. I checked her last employer and they said she was reliable.'

'I dare say she is in many ways, but too strict for my liking.'

'I do not see the connection.' Gerard looked puzzled. 'You said Marguerite was a friend. You invited her here because you felt sympathy for her plight.'

'Her sister was my friend. After Lucinda died I wrote to console the family. Mrs Ross wrote to me a few times and I responded—then Marguerite wrote to me and told me of her plight. She begged me to say nothing to her mother, because Mrs Ross's health was precarious at that time.'

'None of this makes sense. Why did Miss Ross come here?'

'I believed she came to help us. I know that she has longed for a child, but did not expect to have one. She told me that she had no hope of marriage for she seldom mixed in society and the only gentlemen she met were her father's friends and too old.' Amelia frowned. 'When I invited her here I was not sure she would be allowed to come. As I told you, I wrote to her mother to thank her for allowing it, but now I am sure that letter was not sent.'

'So you think you've solved the mystery of the missing letters?' His brow arched.

'Precisely. I could not see why anyone would want to steal one of my letters. I wondered if perhaps one of them had been damaged and the ruse was to cover up carelessness on the part of someone. I was not sure if it was Emily, Martha—or Marguerite.'

'And now you think it was Marguerite? Why? Why would she wish to prevent your letter to her mother reaching her?'

'I wish I knew. I think Nanny Horton knew we were coming here and perhaps came on ahead. If Lisa is right, Nanny Horton spoke to a man last night in the gardens. I do not know who the man was, but...' She paused and gave him a significant look.

'You are wondering if it could have been Lieutenant Gordon?' Gerard pursed his lips as Amelia nodded. 'It would explain some of the mystery.'

'Yes, it would explain how they knew where we would be. I have been writing to Marguerite for more than a year now.'

'So she knew you were at Pendleton the summer before last?'

'Yes, she did.'

'Damn it!' Gerard took a turn around the room. 'We may have invited our enemy into our home, Amelia.'

'Marguerite would never harm a child.' Amelia frowned. 'If she has come under the influence of this man…'

'You think he has turned her mind…that she has been giving him information? She may be infatuated with him.'

'Perhaps.' Amelia frowned. 'I am not sure if she understands what he means to do.'

'I wish that I understood,' Gerard said in a tone of frustration. 'Everything is speculation. We have heard nothing of Northaven—' He broke off as they heard the ring of more than one person's footsteps in the hall and then the door was opened and Mrs Mowbray entered. 'Yes?'

'Excuse me for interrupting, sir—but there is a gentleman…' She had hardly finished when Toby Sinclair walked past her.

'Forgive me,' he said. 'Amelia—I must speak with Emily. It is important.'

'Toby!' Amelia gave Gerard an apologetic look and moved towards him. They were being interrupted once more, but she could not deny Toby—she knew how important this might be to Emily. 'I am glad to see you here. We were all so sorry to hear of your loss.'

A shadow passed across his face. 'It was expected and yet it was sudden. Father knew he had only a few months, but in the end we thought it would not be quite so soon. Mama was distraught. I could not leave her before this—but I must and will see Emily.'

'Of course you must. Why should you not?'

'I was told that I could not see her because she is ill.' Toby's face was white, his manner desperate. 'I cannot blame her if she hates me—but still I must see her. I know something that she must be told.'

'You have news for Emily?' Amelia stared at him, seeing the excitement, the triumph in his eyes. Her intuition told her what the news must be. 'Did Harry find the child?'

'His agents were able to help point me in the right direction, but I found her myself only yesterday. I would have been here sooner, but the circumstances…and then I heard news that delayed me.'

'You have come to tell Emily that you've found the child?' Amelia stared at him in dawning delight.

'Yes, I am pleased to say I have—but first Harry bid me speak to you, Gerard.' Toby turned towards him. 'He has learned that an attempt to murder Northaven was made three days ago. He was shot in the back, but the assassin's aim was poor and the ball merely grazed his shoulder. Harry told me that Emily was abducted and that Northaven helped her…and that may be the reason why he was shot.'

'Good grief! Has Harry spoken to him?'

'He told me that he would do so today—and then he will come here. He may bring Northaven with him.'

'Thank you for coming to me.' Gerard's mouth thinned. 'This becomes serious…if Northaven was shot because of what I asked him to do, it means they will stop at nothing.'

'Gerard…' Amelia's eyes sought his in concern.

'This is far worse than I imagined. If they would kill the marquis because he helped Emily escape...'

Gerard turned to her. 'Go up to Emily. See if you can persuade her to come down,' he said. 'I would have a few words alone with Toby.'

'Yes, of course.' Amelia glanced at Toby. 'Emily is lying down with a headache, but I will ask her to see you in the front parlour. Tell me, is the news good for her?'

'I hope she will think it excellent.'

'Very well. I shall let you tell her yourself.'

Amelia ran upstairs. For the moment her suspicions must be shelved. She was not sure when she had begun to suspect that something was not quite as it ought to be in Marguerite's manner—perhaps only in the last day or so, or this very morning. Now she was feeling concerned, for though she was certain that the woman would never harm a child, she could not be trusted if she were under the influence of a man who would kill anyone who stood in his way.

She had been unwilling to send Marguerite away until she had proof and had taken the precaution she thought necessary, but this latest news had made her uneasy. If Gerard wished to dismiss Marguerite, she could not deny him.

She paused at Emily's door to compose herself. Emily answered her knock, her eyes suspiciously red.

'Amelia...please don't ask me to see him. I cannot...'

'You would be foolish not to do so, my love. He has come here to see you—and he has something important to tell you.' She saw the doubt and fear in Emily's eyes and touched her hand. 'Do not look so nervous, Emily.

I think you must hear what he has to say. It may turn out better than you imagine. I believe he has your happiness at heart.'

Emily raised her head, a glimmer of hope in her face. 'If you think I must see him…'

'Yes, you must. He has done you a service. It was something I hoped to do for you, but Toby has news. I shall let him tell you. Wash your face and go down to him now…' Amelia paused. 'Did Marguerite bring you some camomile tea?'

'Yes, but I poured it away.'

'Good. I expected you would do so. I think you have been suspicious of her from the start. Now tidy yourself and go down to the front parlour, my love. I shall tell Toby you are willing to see him.'

When Amelia returned to the back parlour, she discovered that Toby was alone. He turned to her eagerly, smiling in relief as she inclined her head.

'Emily will come down to the front parlour in a few minutes.'

'I cannot thank you enough,' Toby said and looked awkward. 'I know I have hurt her. You must think badly of me.'

'Your apology must be to her. I trust you do not intend to hurt her again?'

'Not for the world!'

'Then you need say no more to me, sir.' Amelia smiled and glanced round. 'Did Gerard say where he was going?'

'He said he must speak to Max and told me to wait

for you here. He said to tell you that he would explain later.'

'Yes, I am sure he will, thank you. Tell me, has the child been well cared for?'

His smile faded. 'I fear she has not been treated as she ought, but she is in good hands now. I left her with my mother, who is preparing to spoil her.'

'Does Lady Sinclair know whose child she is?'

'Mama has been told all she needs to know for now. Excuse me—I must not keep Emily waiting.'

'Of course.' Amelia smiled as he left the room hurriedly. She had not asked his intentions, but she could only feel that Emily's future was assured. Toby Sinclair had acted in his usual impulsive way. His reaction to the news that Emily had given birth to a child had been one of shock, but the time accorded him by his father's death had clearly brought him to understand what was important. The fact that he had found the child and taken her to his home said all that needed to be said in Amelia's opinion.

She wished that her own affairs might be settled as easily. It would not sit easily with her conscience if she had brought danger to Lisa by inviting a woman she had thought of as a friend to this house. Yet even though her mind was tortured with doubts, she could not imagine why Marguerite would wish to harm any of them. Unless, of course, she had fallen under a man's spell...

Feeling uneasy, she decided to visit the nursery again even though it was well past the time for nuncheon.

As it happened, only Marguerite was in the small dining parlour when Amelia entered it after a brief visit to the nursery. She had discovered Beattie playing a game with strands of wool bound about the child's fingers. Lisa had been perfectly happy, absorbed in the game. Amelia watched for a few minutes and left them to it. Beattie obviously knew how to amuse children. A governess would need to be found in time, but for the moment Lisa was safe and happy.

Marguerite stood up as Amelia entered. 'No one else has come to nuncheon, Amelia. I sent the maid away for I can serve myself. Would you like me to serve you?'

'No, thank you.' Amelia went to the sideboard where an array of cold meats, cheese and bread with butter and savoury preserves had been laid out. 'I do not wish for very much. Please continue with your meal, Marguerite. I have just spoken to Emily. She told me that the tea you made for her was helpful.'

'I am so pleased. I am sure that it was the tisane that upset her before. Some people are more sensitive to herbs than others.'

'Do you often make tisanes yourself?'

'I made them for Mama,' Marguerite said. 'After Lucinda died, she often suffered with irritation of the nerves. She could not sleep without her tisanes.'

'I sometimes have nights when I do not sleep well, but Martha's tisanes have helped me.'

'I hope she does not use laudanum. It can be dangerous if you use too much. I have known it to kill.'

'No, I think she merely uses herbs.' Amelia sat down at the table with her plate in front of her. 'Is your mother better now?'

'Oh, yes. I could not have left her otherwise.' Marguerite sipped a glass of water.

'I am sure she relies on you, Marguerite. If she should need you, you must not hesitate to tell me.'

'I am sure she will not.' A closed expression had come over Marguerite's face. 'Would you wish me to take some food up to Emily?'

'Oh, no, I do not think she wishes for food at the moment.' Amelia forked a small piece of ham. 'I know that you love children, for you have told me so often— has there never been anyone you would like to marry?'

Marguerite hesitated. Her eyes did not meet Amelia's as she said, 'There was once someone I liked, but Lucinda ruined my chances. He went away and I did not see him again. Papa would not have allowed it even had he asked me.'

'I am sorry, my dear. That was sad for you. You have had a hard time of it since your sister died.'

'Lucinda was a fool.' Marguerite stood up. 'Besides, men can never be trusted. You should remember that, Amelia. Do not put too much faith in the man you marry or you may be hurt. Excuse me. I must see to some lessons for Lisa. If you need me, I shall be in my room.'

'Yes, of course.'

Amelia ate her solitary lunch. She was not sure whether or not she had driven Marguerite away with her questions, but she had felt it necessary to ask them. It was as she stood up to leave the dining parlour that she heard the ring of boots on marble tiles. She looked towards the door, waiting, expecting Gerard, and gasped as instead she saw her brother enter.

'Michael—what are you doing here?'

'Did you expect me to ignore your letter?' He glared

at her. 'You cannot truly intend to marry that scoundrel, Amelia? After all the warnings I have given you…'

'Please, come into the back parlour where we may be private,' Amelia told him. 'I would be glad if you speak in a softer tone, Michael. If we are to quarrel, it should not carry to the servants. I do not care to have my private business open knowledge.'

'It will be known soon enough if I have my way. This marriage cannot go ahead. I forbid it.'

She led the way into the small parlour she had begun to make her own. It overlooked pleasant gardens and had a French window, which she could have open when the weather permitted, enabling her to walk on to a stone terrace. The room itself was furnished comfortably with wing chairs, occasional tables and a desk where she could see herself writing letters in the future. She might make a few changes, bring some of her personal effects into the room, but for the moment it served very well. A fire had been lit and it was warm despite the bitter cold day.

When the door was closed, she turned to face her brother. His neck was red with temper and she noticed the fine purple lines mottling his nose and cheeks. His temper and his lifestyle had not improved his looks, for he had been handsome as a young man.

'I shall be honest with you. I hoped you would not come, Michael. Let me tell you at once that you cannot change my mind. I do not see why you should wish to. Gerard may not have come up to your standards when he was younger, but he is the Earl of Ravenshead now and his fortune is sufficient for his needs.'

'Can you not see that it is your fortune that interests

him now? You are an old maid, Amelia. If he wished
for a wife, he might find a dozen young girls to catch
his interest. Depend upon it, he wants your money. The
man is a scoundrel and not to be trusted.'

Amelia's expression remained unchanged despite
his deliberately hurtful words, which were uncannily
similar to Marguerite's.

'You are wrong, Michael. Gerard has told me that I
may order my fortune as I wish. We shall secure much
of it to my children; the rest will pay for the upkeep of
my orphanage and be at my disposal if I need it.'

'And you believe him? The man is a rogue. Listen
to me, sister—or you may be sorry. I have had a letter
informing me that his first wife took her own life
because of his cruelty. It was not signed, but I believe
it to be true.'

'It is a wicked lie. I know what happened. Lisette
took her own life, it is true, but it was not Gerard's
fault.' Amelia lifted her eyes to his. 'If you have a good
cause for your objection to my marriage, tell me—otherwise please leave me in peace.'

'You have got above yourself, miss. If you had done
your duty to your family and allowed me the control of
your fortune, none of this need have happened.'

'If my aunt had wished you to control my fortune,
she would have left it to you.' Amelia glared at him.
'You have not answered my questions—why do you so
dislike Gerard?'

'You will force me to tell you.' Sir Michael glared at
her. 'I have tried to bring you to your senses, Amelia.
I do not wish to break your heart—'

'Indeed? You had no such scruples when you had Gerard beaten and sent him away.'

'I had him beaten for good reason. I believed—I still believe—that he was Lucinda Ross's lover. I also think that he may have had a hand in her death…that he threw her into the river when he discovered that she was with child. Even then, you were a better match.'

Amelia staggered as if he had struck her, reeling from the shock. 'No! You accuse him of such wickedness to spite us. It is not true. It cannot be true. I shall not listen to your lies. What proof have you that any of this is true?' Her face had drained of colour and she could only stare at him in horror. 'No…it is not so…'

It must be a wicked lie and yet, if it were true, all the things Marguerite had been saying to her would make sense. She had been trying to warn Amelia from the moment she came and found her with Gerard, about to kiss.

'I do not believe it. He could not…he loved me.'

'Damn you, listen to me.' Michael scowled at her. 'I know that I saw them together in the woods some weeks before she died. She was in his arms, kissing him as if her life depended upon it—and I believe that he may have been near the river the day she died.'

'I do not believe you—this is all lies. Gerard could not…he would not…' Amelia shook her head and sat down as her legs threatened to give way. Supposing Gerard had never loved her…that he had seduced Lucinda at the same time as he had courted Amelia? He had married only a short time after their parting. He swore he had never loved Lisette…but was it all lies? Her heart would not believe it, but her mind told her that there must be a grain of truth in her brother's words. Yet still she continued to deny it. 'Gerard was visiting his uncle at that time. Besides, he would not have done such a wicked thing! Gerard would not...' A little sob broke from her. 'He would not...'

'What would I not do?'

Amelia turned her head and saw him standing in the doorway. He was staring at her, his eyes narrowed, angry. 'Gerard—how much did you hear?'

'Only your last words.' His gaze narrowed, moved to her brother. 'To what do we owe this pleasure, sir?'

'It does not please me to visit under your roof.' Sir Michael glared at him. 'Well, I have spoken my piece. I shall not linger.'

'Leaving already?' Gerard barred his way as he would have left them. 'You will oblige me by telling me what you have said to Amelia. I know that you despise me, sir. I would hear your reasons from your own lips.'

'Very well,' Sir Michael said. 'I know your evil heart, Ravenshead. You were Lucinda Ross's lover— and it is my belief that when she told you she was with child, you killed her.'

Gerard's face went white with shock. 'That is a foul lie! How can you make such an accusation? You have no proof. It is without foundation.'

'I saw you kissing Lucinda in the woods—my woods,' Sir Michael said. 'It was the kind of kiss a young woman gives only to her lover—and it is my belief that you killed her when she threatened to tell everyone that you were her lover.'

'Lucinda kissed me once in the woods—that I shall

not deny,' Gerard replied, a little nerve flicking at his right temple. He glanced at Amelia. 'I had forgot it, but it came back to me recently. She declared that she loved me and threw her arms about me. I pushed her away and told her not to be foolish. At no time was she my lover—nor did she ever threaten to reveal that I was the father of her child. She could not, for I did not lie with her. Whatever you may have heard to the contrary, I was visiting friends elsewhere when she killed herself. I returned to ask for Amelia's hand—and you were waiting for me, Royston.' He lifted his head, nostrils flared, proud, angry. 'I had no idea of what had happened to a girl I hardly knew until some time later.'

Amelia's eyes were on his face. Guilt mixed with the anger. He was hiding something from her. She felt as if a dagger had been plunged into her heart.

'Do you expect me to believe that?' Sir Michael sneered. 'I saw you together in the woods some weeks before she died. I witnessed the kiss. You did not throw her off immediately.'

'I was gentle with her,' Gerard admitted. 'I may have been flattered for she declared she loved me. I swear that I did nothing to encourage her. She meant nothing to me.' His gaze moved to Amelia. He frowned as he saw she was pale, her eyes dark with horror. 'You cannot believe his lies? You must believe me, Amelia. I was not Lucinda's lover—nor did I kill her.'

'If you tell me it was not so, I believe you.' Amelia's gaze went from him to her brother. She felt bewildered and she was hurting, trying not to believe that Gerard had lied to her. She had sensed there was something he was hiding when he had hinted that Lucinda was not as innocent as Amelia believed. Had he lain with her? No, no, she could not believe such ill of him. It would destroy her. 'You are wrong, Michael…you must be.'

'Why must he be wrong?'

Amelia spun round as she heard Marguerite's voice. She was standing in the doorway, her eyes wild, full of bitterness, her mouth curling in a snarl of hatred as she stared at Gerard.

'Lucinda told me. She boasted of it to me. Everyone thinks that she took her secret to the grave with her—but that is not true. She told me that Gerard Ravenshead was the father of her child and that she would marry him. I warned her that he was not suitable. Father would not have agreed for he hoped then that we should both make advantageous matches. It was only after her shame was known that he told us we would never be allowed to marry.'

'No!' Amelia looked at Gerard; the doubts were in her eyes now. She did not want to believe what Marguerite was saying, but Michael also believed that Gerard was Lucinda's lover—and for a moment she had seen guilt in Gerard's eyes. He had broken her heart once— how could she be sure that he was not lying to her now? 'Please—it cannot be true.'

'I tried to warn you,' Marguerite cried. 'I told you that he was not to be trusted but you would not listen.'

'Damn you!' Gerard moved towards her in a threatening manner. 'You will leave my house, witch. Your sister was a wanton, but I was not her lover. I believe that she did not know the name of her child's father, for she had more than one lover—'

'Gerard!' Amelia moved to protect Marguerite from

his anger. 'Do not speak to her thus. Lucinda was my friend. She could not have been as you describe her.'

'You would take her word above mine?' Gerard's eyes blazed with fury. 'I shall not tolerate that woman in my house another day, Amelia. I will arrange for my coach to take her home, but she leaves today.'

'Do not bother to defend me, Amelia,' Marguerite said. 'I was coming to tell you that I was leaving. Mama has need of me.' She turned and walked from the room, leaving silence behind her.

'Well—' Gerard's tone was harsh as he looked at Amelia '—do you believe her or me?'

Amelia was silent. He was so angry...bitter almost. She hardly knew him. This was not the charming man she had fallen in love with. Her tender lover of the previous night had disappeared, in his place a cold and angry stranger. She wanted to believe him, because if she did not her love became ashes—but she had seen a flicker of guilt in his eyes. He had admitted that he had kissed Lucinda.

'Gerard, I...' She faltered, the words stuck in her throat and she could not go on.

'If she believes you, she is a fool,' Sir Michael said. He glared at them both. 'I've said my piece, Amelia. If you choose to marry him now, I wash my hands of you. Do not expect me to attend your wedding.'

Amelia blinked away the foolish tears, looking at him proudly. 'You will always be welcome in my house—providing you behave as a gentleman.'

Sir Michael inclined his head, turned and walked from the room. Amelia moved away, looking out of the window at the view. The rain had stopped and the sky was getting lighter but it was as if a dark cloud hung over her.

'I am waiting for an answer.'

Amelia could not look at him. 'I am trying to believe you, Gerard,' she said, without turning her head.

'Trying!' He took hold of her shoulders, swinging her round to face him. His eyes blazed with fury. 'Good grief! You cannot think that I would ravish a young girl of good birth and then kill her when she tells me she is with child? What kind of a monster do you think I am?'

'She told Marguerite you were her lover...' Amelia drew a trembling breath. 'I know you would not kill her. I believe she took her own life, but—'

'You think that perhaps I was her lover? You think I played with her emotions, took a despicable advantage at the same time as I courted you—and then destroyed her? You believe that I drove her to her death.' Gerard's face was grey with shock, horror in his eyes. 'You swore you did not blame me for Lisette's death, but perhaps you lied? You do think me capable of these things...and Lisette did die because I hurt her, because I could not love her. I am innocent of all else, but perhaps you prefer to believe your friend?' His tone was scathing, flicking her on the raw.

Amelia shook her head. It was impossible to answer. She did not want to believe that Gerard had done the things he was accused of, but the seed of doubt had been planted. She was too shocked, too stunned to think clearly.

'I am sorry—' she began, but was interrupted by the arrival of Emily followed by Toby. One look at their faces was enough to tell the world how they felt. 'Emily…' Amelia wanted to tell her that this was not the time but before she could speak Gerard had walked from the room. 'Gerard…'

Amelia choked on the words. She wanted to call him back, but did not know what she would say if she did, because she was still reeling from the shock of Marguerite's accusation. Had it been only her brother, she would have dismissed his claim, but Marguerite's accusation had the ring of truth. Oh, but she did not want to believe her! She must be lying…

Smothering her desire to weep, Amelia turned to face Emily. She forced herself to smile.

'So, my love—is it all settled?'

'Toby has found my daughter,' Emily told her. Her face was glowing, her eyes lit from within. 'He says she has not been well treated, but she is quite healthy. She was neglected, but not harmed physically. Her adopted parents did not love her, because they had children of their own and they had long spent the money they were given to take her. They gave her up readily and Toby has taken Beth to his parents. He says that his mother will adopt her. I shall be able to see her every day. I shall look after her, love her and teach her to be happy—but her birth will remain our secret.' Her cheeks turned pink as she glanced up at Toby a little shyly. 'He has explained it is for my sake and not because he is ashamed of me…he loves me truly…'

'If you wish it, we will tell the world,' Toby said stoutly. 'But for your sake, my love, it will be better if Beth is brought up as Mama's adopted daughter. No one will think anything of it if you love her—and one day you may tell her the truth if you wish.'

'And does Toby know the truth of what happened to you now?' Amelia asked.

'When I thought about it, I guessed what must have happened,' Toby answered for her, his hand reaching to take Emily's in his own. 'I love her. I should not stop loving her whatever the truth, but when I discovered how she had been treated, I knew what I must do.'

'And how did you discover that?'

'Harry Pendleton wrote to me. He knew how I felt about Emily and once you told him her story, he thought I should be informed. It was simple enough to find the child, for no one had bothered to conceal her whereabouts. Harry's agent met me and told me what he knew and the rest was easy.' He reached for Emily's hand and kissed it. 'I am taking Emily home to Mama. We shall stay for a couple of weeks and then come back for your wedding, Amelia. Emily would not want to miss that for the world.'

Amelia wondered if there would be a wedding. She was not certain how she felt, but she could not cast a cloud over her friend's shining happiness.

'I am very pleased for you both,' she said. 'When are you leaving?'

'Almost immediately. I thought Emily could pack a small bag for now. Perhaps you would have her things sent to her at my mother's home?' Toby said with his customary eagerness.

'Yes, of course. I shall be happy to do so. Martha will see to her packing.' She moved to kiss Emily on the cheek and then Toby. 'I hope I shall be invited to the wedding?'

'You will be the guest of honour,' Emily told her. 'Toby says we shall hold a ball and announce our engagement in a few months from now. We may be married in the summer. It should not be sooner, because of his father's death. Besides, I am going to live with his mama and we shall see each other all the time...' She hesitated, looking anxious. 'You will not need me, Amelia? I know it is short notice, but you have Marguerite to keep you company now.'

It was impossible to tell Emily that Marguerite was leaving under a cloud—or that she might be forced to return home alone. 'Yes, of course. You must not worry about me, my dearest. I am delighted at the way things have turned out for you. I wish you both every happiness.'

'I am so very fond of you,' Emily said and embraced her. 'I would not leave so suddenly, but I know that you are happy and settled.'

'Yes, of course I am,' Amelia said. 'Go and pack your bag now, dearest.'

'My mother is anxious to become acquainted with Emily,' Toby said after she had gone. 'Harry told me that you intended to search for Emily's child. I am grateful, because his agent was able to save me some time in locating the child.'

'She was so very unhappy after you left. I felt I must do something.'

Toby looked a little uncomfortable. 'I did not behave well, but I must admit Emily's revelation came as a bolt of lightning. Had my father not died, I should have returned sooner. As soon as I could, I went to Pendleton and then in search of the child.'

'I dare say Emily will forgive you. She has not been well, but I believe she will soon be better now.'

Amelia left Toby to prepare his curricle for the journey. She went upstairs to her room. Discovering that the key to the dressing-room door had been put her side, she locked it. She sat down on the bed, bending her head and covering her face with her hands.

Amelia did not cry. Her distress was too deep for tears. She did not know how she felt about things at the moment. She had begun the day feeling on top of the world, but a few spiteful words had turned her world upside down. Her thoughts went round and round in her head as she tried to come to terms with what she had been told. She raised her head, a look of determination in her eyes. She must think about this calmly. It would be foolish to give way to emotion.

Michael had been certain enough of his beliefs to have Gerard beaten. He had acted in a high-handed manner to prevent her marriage at that time, but it seemed he had meant to protect her from a man he believed a rogue. He ought to have told her the story and let her discover the truth for herself. Yet perhaps he had acted as he thought best.

Amelia stood up and began to pace the room. The most terrible accusations had come from Lucinda's own sister! Marguerite was convinced that Gerard was her sister's lover. She had not been lying. She truly believed it.

Marguerite had sworn that her sister had told her that

Gerard was her lover. The evidence seemed damning. Amelia had always known it was possible that it could have been Gerard who was Lucinda's lover, if only because he was one of several men visiting the area at that time, but, as time went on, she had completely exonerated him. She had believed that Lucinda's lover was Northaven, but then she had begun to wonder if she had misjudged him too. Now two people had told her that Gerard had seduced and deserted Lucinda at the time he was supposed to be courting Amelia. A shudder of horror went through her, for if Gerard were capable of such an act he would not be the man she loved. No, no, it could not be true! Everything she knew of him denied it. Besides, something was deeply wrong here…

If Marguerite believed that Gerard had seduced her sister and then driven her to her death—why had she come to this house? She had known that Amelia was going to marry him, for she had told her, asked her to come and help take care of his child. Why would she do that if she were convinced of his guilt?

Amelia frowned as she began to revise the theory she had previously held. She had believed that Gerard's enemy was Lieutenant Gordon—that he wanted revenge because of the way Lisette had met her death. She had imagined that he was the instigator of the plot to kidnap her, possibly persuading Marguerite to help him. She had wondered if Marguerite had fallen in love with Gordon. However, if Marguerite had had reasons of her own to hate Gerard…

She would never rest unless she knew the truth!

Amelia decided she would speak to Marguerite before she left. She went along the landing to Marguerite's room, knocked at the door and then went in. She saw at once that things had been snatched from the armoire and from the chest. A stocking lay abandoned on the floor and the gowns Amelia had given Marguerite were lying on the bed—each of them had been torn with a sharp instrument, rendering them useless. The glass dressing-table set had been knocked to the floor and some silver items were missing. The mess caused had clearly been done out of spite. Marguerite had vented her anger on anything to hand.

Amelia felt slightly sick at the sight of such wanton destruction. She was seized with fear and hurried to the nursery. Relief swept over her as she found Beattie playing with Lisa while Mary stood folding a pile of clean linen and smiled as the child laughed. Lisa was safe! Amelia schooled her features to a pleasant smile.

'Have either of you seen Miss Ross in the past hour?'

'No. She came earlier, but not in the last hour,' Nurse Mary said. 'Is something the matter, Miss Royston?'

'Miss Ross is leaving us. I do not want her near Lisa again.'

'I'm glad she's gone and that's a fact,' Beattie said. 'She gave me the creeps—and that's the truth.'

Amelia didn't ask her to elaborate. She accepted that she had made a mistake in asking Marguerite to come here on the basis of a few letters. Had anything happened to Lisa because of her error she would not have forgiven herself. If Marguerite was consumed with hate for Lisa's father, she might well have constituted a danger to the child. Amelia felt guilty for having brought her to the house.

She was on her way back to her room when she saw Emily walking towards her with a bag in her hand and a cloak over her arm.

'I wanted to say goodbye,' she said. 'This is your cloak, Amelia. You were kind to lend it to me, but after I was kidnapped while wearing it I did not wear it again.'

'I do not think I shall wear it,' Amelia said. 'I may give it to one of the maids, for it is warm and comfortable.' She leaned forwards to kiss Emily's cheek. 'I wish you lots of happiness, my love.'

'I am very happy—but a little nervous. Supposing Beth does not like me...?'

'How could that be?' Amelia shook her head. 'She will come to love you, as I have, dearest. Go on now. Toby has his horses waiting.'

'Yes, I must not keep him. I shall write often—and we shall be here for the wedding.'

Amelia nodded and let her go. She took her cloak into the bedroom and threw it over a chair. She glanced uncertainly at the locked dressing-room door. As she did so, she saw the handle move.

'Amelia...are you in there? Open the door please. I would like to talk to you.'

Amelia hesitated. She wasn't ready to talk to Gerard yet because she was not sure what to say to him. Picking up the cloak she had discarded, she put it around her shoulders and went out of her room. She ran down the stairs and left the house by a side door. The rain had stopped and the wind had blown itself out, though the sky was dark and it was very cold.

She did not mind the cold. She wanted some fresh air—and she needed to be alone for a while.

Chapter Ten

Damn it! How could she think him capable of seducing a young woman and deserting her—and at the same time as he was courting Amelia herself?

Gerard was so angry when he left the room that he was afraid he might do or say something he ought not if he remained. When he saw Toby and Emily come in, he had felt there was no other option than to leave, because he could not speak as he wished with them present. Amelia was clearly in a state of shock and distress. He could only hope that she would come to her senses after a moment or two of reflection.

He was in his own bedchamber when he thought he heard sounds coming from Amelia's room. He went through the dressing closet and tried the handle of the connecting door, calling out to her. She did not answer, yet he was certain she was there. Why would she not speak to him?

It was an impossible situation! How could she believe those vile allegations? She could not if she loved him.

Gerard vaguely remembered the scene in the woods near Amelia's home some years previously. He had been on his way to visit Amelia when he met a young woman. She had been visiting her friend, for she told him that she had just come from the Roystons' house. She was carrying her bonnet by its ribbons, her long fair hair loose on her shoulders. The sunshine suited her—her skin had turned a pale gold and she wore no pelisse, her muslin gown clinging to her shapely form.

'I have been visiting Amelia,' she told him, laughing up at him with her soft ripe lips and her blue eyes filled with mischief. 'It is so warm today. I think I shall go for a swim in the river.'

Gerard struggled to recall his reply. It was something like, *'It is certainly warm enough. You should take care, Miss Ross. The river is deep and there are reeds that might catch your skirts and drag you down.'* Yes, he remembered saying something of the sort. The scene was becoming clearer now. He had dismissed it as unimportant, but now he thought it imperative that he should remember exactly.

'I shall not be wearing clothes…' She licked her lips, an invitation in her eyes. 'Why do you not come with me? We could swim and…' Her laughter was husky and seductive. 'Who knows what else we might find to do, Gerard?' She moved towards him, the perfume of roses wafting from her skin. 'I have always thought you one of the most handsome men I know.'

'You should not say such things, Lucinda.' Gerard could not help smiling, for she was a lovely young woman. He was in love with Amelia, but a light dalliance was no sin on a summer afternoon. 'Some men might take you at your word.'

Had his manner challenged her—encouraged her? He had not meant it to, but perhaps he had been at fault for her reply had been swift and bold.

'I should like you to take me at my word...' Lucinda threw herself at him, winding her arms about his neck and pressing herself against his body. He put up his hands to hold her arms and push her away, but she pressed her lips against his in a wild, passionate kiss that shocked him and for just one moment he had responded. He was, after all, a young man with red blood in his veins. 'Take me swimming...lie with me this afternoon...make love to me, Gerard.'

'No!' Gerard had pushed her away as the moment passed and he realised what she was asking. He did not want her. He was in love with Amelia Royston. This wanton girl was beautiful and he had been tempted by her kiss, but now her boldness revolted him. 'Behave yourself! Think of the disgrace to your family if you were seen swimming naked.'

Lucinda laughed mockingly. 'I do not know why Marguerite thinks herself in love with you. You are such a righteous bore, Gerard Ravenshead. I do not want you. I already have a lover and he does not scruple to take me swimming and then lie with me on a summer afternoon.'

She had laughed again and then run off through the woods. Gerard had laughed too, because he thought it the foolish boasting of a young woman who felt herself scorned. He had forgotten it until he heard about the scandal and the shocking tragedy of her death.

He had never spoken to anyone of that afternoon. He had never realised that they had been seen in what must have looked like a passionate embrace. He had certainly never thought it the true reason for the beating he had been given by Sir Michael Royston's bully-boys.

'I do not know why Marguerite thinks herself in love with you.'

Gerard frowned. He had known there was something he ought to remember from the first moment Miss Ross arrived at Pendleton.

He had not even considered Lucinda's words serious at the time. Remembering now, he thought there had been something a little spiteful in the way Lucinda had spoken of her sister. Why should Marguerite Ross have thought herself in love with him? He hardly knew her. They had danced once or twice—three times at most. He had sat next to her one evening at dinner and made polite conversation, but he had hardly noticed her. He had already been in love with Amelia.

His mind turned back to the scene earlier when Marguerite had thrown those vile accusations at him. He had been looking at Amelia, willing her to trust him, to love him as he loved her—but he had seen the doubts in her eyes.

Marguerite's accusations, the way she looked at him, had seemed angry…almost bitter. Why did she hate him? It seemed clear that she must—for why else would she meet Lieutenant Gordon and plot with him? He was certain now that the two had worked together. Gordon must have had his information from Marguerite.

Amelia's innocent letters had told her all she needed to know.

Amelia had begun to suspect it even before Marguerite's outburst. She had thought the woman under Gordon's influence but...supposing *she* were the instigator of the plot to abduct Amelia and kill her? It made perfect sense. Gordon might hate him because of Lisette's death, but he had not looked for revenge at the start. Something—or someone—had made him decide that he would punish Gerard through Amelia. If that someone were Marguerite, it explained why she had suddenly arrived at Pendleton.

Gerard felt cold. They had harboured a viper in their midst! His first thought was for Lisa, because she was an innocent, unsuspecting child. Receiving no answer from Amelia's room, he went immediately to the nursery, where he found the same peaceful scene that Amelia had found earlier. His relief was soon overcome with anger.

Damn it! He would not put up with this nonsense. Gerard returned to the master suite and opened the door to Amelia's room from the hall. A brief search told him that she was not there. He left and walked towards the stairs. Down in the hall, he asked the footman on duty if he had seen Miss Royston recently.

'She went out a few minutes ago, my lord. Perhaps a quarter of an hour. I watched her for a moment, because she seemed unlike herself—a little distracted, if you will forgive my saying so. I think she walked towards the lake.'

'Thank you.'

Gerard frowned. He was not dressed for walking.

It would take but a moment to fetch his greatcoat. He would follow her and hope that they could settle this nonsense!

The cold air stung her cheeks and eyes, but Amelia pulled the hood of her cloak over her head, determined not to be put off her walk. She knew it was foolish of her to run away from Gerard, because they would have to talk sooner or later. However, she was feeling too raw to face him just yet. Had the accusation come from just one person she might have dismissed it—but both her brother and Marguerite had blamed Gerard for Lucinda's downfall and her death. Until the previous night she had been unsure of his feelings for her, but after their lovemaking she had felt secure in his love. Now all those niggling doubts had come flooding back.

If Gerard loved her, why had he married so soon after they parted? Why hadn't he come to her and told her what her brother had done? Amelia's thoughts went round and round as she battled her tears.

Was it possible that Gerard had seduced her friend while at the same time swearing eternal love for Amelia? Could he truly be so ruthless...so cold and uncaring? Could he make love to her so tenderly if he were the man her brother and Marguerite claimed?

No, of course not! Now that she could think clearly, Amelia began to see how wrong it was. Gerard loved her. It was true that he had married another woman, and Lisette had taken her own life—perhaps because Gerard had told her that he could not love her. She had exonerated him freely of blame for that—could she not show as much faith again? She must if she trusted her own senses, her own heart—because she loved him.

She still loved him! Despite all the doubts and accusations thrown at him, she loved him. She would always love him. Without Gerard her life would be empty, a sterile pointless existence that would lead to bitter old age.

Amelia frowned. If she accepted that her brother had been mistaken in what he had seen, she must believe Gerard. He had told her that Lucinda was wanton... that *she* had kissed him. It was this that she had found so hard to accept. A light, flirtatious kiss in a moment of fun—yes, that she could accept—but Lucinda a wanton?

Was it possible that she had never really known her? They had been friends, but had Lucinda kept secrets from her? The answer must be that she had, because she had never told Amelia that she had a lover. Only when she discovered that she was with child and confessed to her parents that her lover would not marry her, had she told anyone of her shame.

Amelia wished that she knew the truth. She had always felt sad about Lucinda's suicide...but Marguerite had hinted that Gerard had killed her because she threatened to name him.

No, he would never do something like that! Amelia could not accept that he was a murderer. Everything that was in her protested his innocence. If he was innocent of her death, it followed that Lucinda had either taken her own life in a moment of despair—or someone else had killed her. So if Amelia believed Gerard was innocent of murder, she ought to believe him innocent of seduction and desertion.

She did believe him! Amelia felt the doubts fall away, a weight lifting from her shoulders as her mind cleared. Gerard would not lie to her! How could he after what they had been to one another? She had hurt and angered him because she had not instantly accepted his word. She ought to have known at once, of course, but the accusations had shocked her so deeply that she hardly knew what she was saying. She had had to deal with Emily and Toby, forcing herself to behave naturally, and it was only now that she had been able to see things clearly.

Why had Marguerite come to the house if she believed that Gerard had seduced and murdered her sister?

There could be only one answer. She was in league with Lieutenant Gordon. He craved revenge for Lisette's death and Marguerite wanted revenge for her sister's shame.

Why did she believe that Lucinda had been forced into the river? Amelia had always thought that she must have flung herself from the bridge because she could not face her shame...why did Marguerite think otherwise?

It was puzzling for until now she had never heard anyone speak of such a possibility. Even Mrs Ross had spoken of her daughter's suicide.

'I was angry with her for her foolish behaviour but I would have taken care of her. She had no need to take her own life,' the grieving mother declared. *'Her papa was angry, but I loved her.'*

Amelia recalled the mother's tears. She frowned as she tried to picture the scene that afternoon. She had gone to the Rosses' house to visit and pay her condolences. Mrs Ross had received her alone and then... Marguerite had come in. Amelia had glanced at her face and...she had been so angry...

Angry. Marguerite had not looked as if she were grieving. Her eyes were not ringed with red, as her mother's were—she was angry.

'Marguerite...' Amelia unconsciously spoke the words aloud. 'She was jealous of her sister—and angry...' Why was she so angry? Amelia could not quite grasp the last pieces of the puzzle.

She had reached the lake. She stood for a moment, staring down the steep bank at the dark grey water, which reflected the clouds above. On a summer day it would be pleasant here, but today there was a feeling of isolation as a light mist began to curl across the water. Amelia sighed, feeling lonely, uneasy. Then, as she heard a twig snap beneath someone's foot, she turned and looked into Marguerite's face. She was as angry now as she had been on the day Amelia visited her home.

'What are you doing here?' she asked her. 'I thought you had left?'

'I met someone and we decided we would wait for a while.' Marguerite's eyes flicked past Amelia to someone who had approached from the right. 'It seems we were lucky, Nanny. You said that she would walk out alone if she was upset—and you were right.'

Amelia looked round and saw Alice Horton. She was dressed in a black cloak, the hood covering her head and most of her face—but her eyes were cold, filled with malice.

A sliver of fear ran down Amelia's spine. She was completely alone here, for few were out on a day like this. Even the labourers would hurry home to eat their dinner in a warm kitchen.

'This is private land. You have no right here. The earl dismissed you.'

'Because you told him to,' Alice Horton said bitterly. 'You stole my girl's admirer and then wrote pitying letters to her…asking her to be a governess. She is a lady…better than you…'

'What are you talking about? I have stolen no one's lover.' Amelia stared at Marguerite, trying to make some sense of the accusation. 'Is she speaking about you? I did not mean to patronise you by offering you a place in my household—only to help you find happiness.'

'He liked me before you made eyes at him…' Marguerite's eyes glittered with hatred. 'Lucinda knew how I felt. She laughed at me when she told me he was courting you…but then she stopped laughing.'

Amelia felt icy cold as she looked into the other woman's face. Anger and hatred—and something more…something dangerous.

'What happened to Lucinda? Why do you think she did not commit suicide?'

Marguerite's lips curved in a sneer. 'She could swim like a fish. Lucinda used to swim in the river all the time. She learned when she was five years old. She was always laughing at me because I dare not follow her into the deep water. She had no fear of anything.'

'If Lucinda could swim, why did she drown?'

'She fell from the bridge and hit her head on an iron strut. It was an accident…' Marguerite's eyes looked strange. 'She was laughing…and then she stopped laughing because I pushed her and she fell.' A queer, high laugh escaped Marguerite. 'I shouldn't have told you that, should I? You will guess now and that means you have to die…but it doesn't matter because you were going to die anyway.' She looked at Alice Horton and giggled. 'Shall I push her in the lake? Everyone will think she killed herself because he betrayed her with that slut of a sister of mine. I got away with it once, I can do it again.'

'Now then, pet, you mustn't get so upset,' Alice Horton soothed. 'Lucinda was a silly girl, but you didn't mean to kill her. It was an accident.'

'Oh, but I did…' Marguerite's eyes blazed. 'I wanted her to die. She boasted that he was her lover. She knew that I loved him. It was why she wanted him. She had the other one—the one who had given her a child—but she wanted *him* too, because she knew I loved him. She always had to have everything, but this time I stopped her.'

'Who was the other one?' Amelia asked. She curled her nails into her palms, willing herself to keep calm. She must hear the truth now! 'What was his name?'

'Surely you know?' Marguerite glared at her. 'He was so angry because he saw her with Gerard that he wouldn't help her. He had promised to leave his wife. He was besotted with Lucinda, gave her presents of jewellery. He told her that Louisa was a nag and a scold and he would get a divorce, but after he saw her with

Gerard he raged at her, told her she was a slut and he wouldn't see her again. Lucinda told me it all before I—'

'My brother?' Amelia stared at her in horror. Suddenly, it all made sense. It wasn't to protect her that Michael had had Gerard thrashed—it was jealousy, because he believed the woman he loved had betrayed him with Gerard Ravenshead! His hatred stemmed from the belief that Gerard had taken Lucinda from him!

The sickness rose in her throat as she saw it all so clearly. Michael had been Lucinda's lover, not Gerard, but he had seen them kiss. It was just a moment of light flirtation, as Gerard claimed, but Michael had lost his head. He had had Gerard beaten and broken Amelia's heart because he was jealous.

Amelia's head was whirling as she tried to take all the new information in. Her brother had seduced Lucinda. He was the father of her child. He had promised to leave his wife, but then he'd seen her in Gerard's arms that summer afternoon and he had believed they were lovers. Amelia didn't know what had happened that day, but she imagined it was just a piece of nonsense on a warm afternoon—*because of it Michael had had Gerard thrashed and ruined her life. But what had Marguerite done?*

'Did you kill Lucinda because you believed she had taken Gerard from you?'

Marguerite's eyes had gone blank, but now they focused on Amelia once more. 'You stole him from me. I thought it was her, but it was you. She laughed at me and told me he was going to marry you. I flew at her and we struggled and then…she fell and hit her head. I saw her floating with her face in the water.'

'Why didn't you fetch help or try to get her out?'

'I couldn't swim. I'm afraid of the deep water and—' Suddenly, Marguerite's eyes narrowed, became crafty, evil. 'I wanted her to die. I want you to die. Why should you have everything while I have nothing? My father said I would never marry…it was her fault…your fault…' Marguerite advanced on her, her hands going for Amelia's throat. 'If you drown, they will blame him…and he will die too. He will know what it is like to lose everything.'

'No!' Amelia tried to throw her off, but Marguerite was too strong. 'Help me! Help me…'

Alice Horton stood for a moment, seeming undecided, then she pulled at Marguerite's arm.

'Stop this, sweeting. It isn't her fault that you can't marry. You know what your papa said—'

'Get off me!' Marguerite swung her arm back, throwing the older woman off balance so that she fell to her knees. In that moment Amelia struggled free and started to run. Marguerite came after her, grabbing her by the waist and somehow bringing her down. 'You've got to die. You can't live now that you know. *He* was supposed to help me, but he is a weak coward. So I must do it myself.'

Amelia screamed and struggled to throw Marguerite off, but she was very strong. Her hands were tightening their hold about Amelia's throat and she couldn't breathe. Everything was going black and then she heard a shout…several voices shouting. People were racing towards them.

'Damn you! You murdering bitch!'

Gerard's voice! Amelia heard it through a haze of mist, as if she were far away. Several men were shouting and there were the sounds of a struggle. She heard Marguerite screaming and then water splashing, more screaming, shouting and then sobbing. A woman was weeping bitterly.

'Is she dead, sir? My poor little mad girl.'

Amelia's throat hurt, but she struggled to sit up. She couldn't see clearly, but she knew that Gerard wasn't alone. There were other men there…some of them had guns. She thought one voice might have belonged to the Marquis of Northaven, but she wasn't sure, because it was distant, blurred. Everything was going hazy again as she fell back on the damp ground.

The woman was still sobbing. She thought it was Alice Horton. Men were talking, calling for someone to go for the doctor. Things seemed to be going on around her. She was being lifted and carried in someone's arms, but she couldn't see or hear any more…

Gerard stood looking down, his heart wrenched as he saw Amelia throw out her arm and cry out something he could not hear. Her body was drenched in sweat. However many times they changed the sheets she became wet through again and the doctor was worried that her fever would turn to pneumonia.

'If the fever turns putrid, she may die,' he had told Gerard before he left. 'All you can do is to watch over her and pray.'

'Don't let her die…' The anguished words were torn

from him. 'If I have sinned, vent your anger on me—let me take her place. I beg you, do not let her die.'

Gerard was not sure who he was praying to, for long ago he had felt that God was a myth, a fairy story. How could a gentle God allow the things he had seen in battle?

Tears trickled down his cheeks as he bent over Amelia and kissed her damp brow. 'Live for me, my darling,' he whispered. 'Live for me. I cannot bear it if you leave me…forgive me…forgive me…'

His expression was wintry. This was his fault. If he had spoken to Amelia earlier she would not have gone out alone. He should have made her believe that he'd had nothing to do with Lucinda.

Amelia opened her eyes to see a woman bending over her. The mist cleared for long enough for her to see that it was someone she knew…Susannah. She tried to speak, but the words wouldn't come. Her throat hurt too badly and every part of her body ached. Susannah touched her hand, a tear sliding down her cheek.

'You've been so ill, dearest,' she said. 'You had a fever. The doctor said it was a putrid infection of the lungs. We thought we were going to lose you. Gerard has been out of his mind.'

'Marguerite…' The word was a harsh whisper.

Susannah gripped her hand. 'Do not worry, dearest. She can't hurt anyone again. Her father has agreed to have her sent to a secure place where she will be properly cared for as long as she lives. He says he should have done it years ago, but her mother would not have it.'

'Not dead? I thought…' Amelia sighed.

'No…she tried to drown herself, but the Marquis of Northaven pulled her out of the lake. Gerard met him a few minutes earlier as he left the house to search for you. He had brought news and they were talking as they walked to the lake—and then they saw what was happening. Some of Gerard's men were already racing to your rescue, but he was the first to reach you.'

'She wanted to kill me…' Amelia's head was spinning as she tried to remember. 'She was so…strong…'

'She was ill, Amelia. Northaven has discovered the truth from Lieutenant Gordon. She is his cousin and he has always loved her, though he knew she was wild even as a girl. Miss Horton has told us more. As a child Marguerite was prone to tantrums. That is why they had a strict nanny for her. When she grew up she seemed better, calmer, but when Lucinda became pregnant their father started to forbid the girls to go anywhere—and Marguerite had become moody. She sneaked out at night, walking in the woods alone and she was prone to bouts of melancholy. Mr Ross suspected that she had killed her own sister and decided that she ought never to marry, though he was too proud of his good name to admit it to the world.'

Amelia closed her eyes for a moment. 'She was the one who planned all this, the abduction of me that went wrong and the rest…wasn't she?'

'Lieutenant Gordon says that she persuaded him; she said that he had to abduct you and kill you in front of Gerard—and then kill him. Only then would she give him what he wanted from her. He believed that Gerard was responsible for Lisette's death and agreed, because she had bewitched him, manipulated him—but in the end he couldn't go through with all the things she asked of him. When Northaven accused him of trying to shoot him in the back, he broke down and confessed that he had taken a pot shot at him, but swears it was more in the hope of scaring him off than killing him.'

'You mean the marquis forced him to confess?' Amelia's head was clearing a little. She sat up with Susannah's help and sipped a little water. 'I wonder why Marguerite decided she would kill me herself.'

'It was an impulse. You were in an isolated spot, alone—and she took her chance. She was always a little unstable…her nurse knew it. She said that both the Ross girls were inclined to be wild at times, but Marguerite got much worse after Lucinda's death. Perhaps it was her guilt because she killed her.'

'Poor Marguerite…'

'Do not pity her, Amelia.'

'I can only feel pity for her despite what she did.'

'Alice Horton was resentful because you had her dismissed, but when Marguerite tried to kill you, she attempted to stop her. She might have agreed to help with an abduction for a ransom, but she drew the line at murder.'

'Did she?' Amelia's brow wrinkled. 'I cannot remember…'

'You have been very ill, Amelia.'

'Did they send for you?'

'As soon as I heard what had happened, I was determined to come. Helene is here—and so is Emily. She put off her visit to Sinclair's. We all love you, dearest Amelia.'

'Helene should not be worrying over me. She must take care of herself and her baby.'

'We haven't let her nurse you. Emily and I have done most of it—and Martha, of course. Everyone wanted to do their best and Lisa has been crying for you. Gerard has been here much of the time, but today he had to see some people. Lieutenant Gordon has made a full confession. They are deciding what should be done with him—whether he should be sent abroad or given up to the magistrates.'

Amelia nodded. She closed her eyes. She was so very tired.

'Thank you for explaining…but I think I should like to sleep now.'

'Yes, of course,' Susannah said and kissed her cheek. 'Go to sleep, dearest. You will soon begin to feel better now…'

'Well, it is over,' Harry said as they sat together in the library. 'I am of the opinion that Gordon has learned his lesson. When he discovered that Marguerite had murdered her own sister, I thought he would be sick. The look of revulsion on his face tells me that he will not be drawn into such an affair again.'

'I still think he should have his trial,' Max said. 'You were too lenient with him, Gerard—he was behind the attempted kidnap on Amelia and the abduction of Miss Barton—and that shot outside the church at Pendleton, though he says it was no more than a warning.'

'The shot might have been meant for me. Amelia suffered no ill effects and Emily was returned unhurt thanks to Northaven. I have a great deal to thank Northaven for…and I believe we all owe him an apology.'

'Not certain of that,' Harry objected. 'His careless talk was almost certainly to blame for what happened in Spain.'

'Yes, I am sure it was—but he did not deliberately betray us and we ought to show some mercy. I let Gordon go because he is genuinely remorseful. Besides, it was Marguerite who planned it all. He was merely her tool.'

'I hope you have forgiven yourself too.' Max laid a hand on his shoulder. 'Lisette had been through a great deal, losing her lover, the rapes and then giving birth. Her mind was disturbed when she took her own life.'

'And I refused her when she asked me for love.' Gerard looked grave. 'Perhaps that is why I am being punished. If I lose Amelia…'

'Ridiculous!' Harry said. 'You cannot blame yourself for what happened to Amelia the other day. She invited that mad woman into your home.'

'If she had not, I might not have been there when she needed me. She could have been attacked at any time…perhaps months after we were married.'

'Amelia will pull through,' Max told him. 'She is surrounded by people who love her, and they will all do whatever they can to help. Just give it time, Gerard.'

'Yes, I know—thank you.' Gerard forced a smile. 'You are the best friends a man could have at such a time.'

Gerard said no more. It was impossible to explain that he was afraid that when Amelia recovered her senses, she would not wish to marry him—that she might still believe the lies Marguerite had told her.

Amelia was dreaming. She was in the water and something was dragging her down. When she looked beneath the surface, she saw the eyes of a dead girl staring at her. Then the girl's skinny claws reached out to pull her to the bottom. She could feel the air draining from her lungs…

'Amelia…' A gentle hand shook her shoulder. 'It's just a nightmare, my love. I am so sorry she hurt you. Please forgive me.'

Amelia opened her eyes. For a moment she could not focus, but then she saw Gerard. His face were pale in the candlelight and tears were wetting his cheeks. He was crying…for her. She lifted her hand as he bent over her, touching his face.

'Don't cry,' she said. 'I am better now, Gerard…' She shuddered as she remembered. 'It was just a dream… just a horrid dream.'

Gerard sat on the edge of the bed. He reached for her hand, holding it as if it were made of fine porcelain. 'When I saw what Marguerite was doing I was so afraid. I thought I might be too late. My men had held off because they did not realise what she meant to do. She was your guest, not a stranger, so they hesitated and then it was almost too late.'

'How could anyone have guessed what she would do? I had noticed small things that seemed odd, but I thought she was merely suffering from melancholy because of the life she led. Indeed, I suspect that her father may have pushed her over the edge by depriving her of her freedom.'

'She tried to kill you, Amelia. You were lying there so still... I thought you were dead.' His voice broke with emotion.

'I think I almost was,' Amelia said with a wry smile. 'If you had not come...you and Northaven and the others... I owe the marquis an apology, Gerard. I once thought he was responsible for Lucinda's death, because I thought him her seducer—but now I know that he is blameless. I know who seduced her and then left her to face her shame alone.'

'He is a rake and more, but he is blameless in this instance.' Gerard's gaze narrowed. 'You do not truly think that I...?' Amelia shook her head. 'Then who...?'

Amelia reached for his hand. 'Before she tried to kill me, Marguerite told me it was Michael.'

'Your brother...but he accused me...the morning he came here—he accused me...'

'Of seducing her and then deserting her. Yes, he did—and he drove us apart, Gerard—because he was mad with jealousy. He was besotted with Lucinda. I see it all so clearly now. Things I should have noticed when she came to the house. She pretended to visit me, but it was Michael she wanted to see. He bought her things... promised to divorce Louisa—and then he saw her kissing you. In his rage and disappointment he blamed you. He loved her, still wanted her even though they quarrelled. If she had not died, he might still have kept his word to her in the end. She may have known it in her heart. She did not take her own life.'

'You are sure Marguerite was not lying?'

'It all makes sense, Gerard—and Michael changed after that time. Before Lucinda died he was not so bad tempered. He has become worse over the years. He does not care for his wife or she for him. He is a disappointed, bitter man.'

'Lucinda kissed me. I may have let her for a moment. It was a summer day and she was pretty that day, lit up from inside—but when she wanted me to lie with her I said no. At no time did I encourage her—or Marguerite. I hardly saw either of them. I was in love with you. You do believe me?' His fingers tightened around hers.

'Yes, I do. I think that was why Marguerite wanted to kill me. In her rage, she told me that Lucinda laughed at her, told her that you would marry me—and she went for her. It may have been an accident, but in Marguerite's mind she killed her sister. I think it played on her conscience. Her father had made her a virtual prisoner and she dwelled on her wrongs. You did not want her, so you became Lucinda's murderer though she knew she had done it—but she wanted to punish you. When she suspected we were likely to marry it made her angry and somehow she persuaded Lieutenant Gordon to help her.'

Gerard nodded. 'Alice Horton came to see me this morning. She apologised for what happened and told me that a couple of months ago Marguerite's mother was taken by a stroke and can no longer speak. Because his wife was so ill, her father allowed Marguerite to help with the nursing. She took some of the sleeping draught the doctor had left for her mother and put it in her father's ale—and then she left the house to come to us. He had no idea where she had gone. She had to take the letter you wrote to her mother—if her father had known where she was, he would have come after her.'

'I suspected that something must be wrong at her home when I realised she must have taken the letter. I feel so guilty,' Amelia said. 'She might have harmed Lisa.'

'How could you know what was in her mind? Besides, she did not hurt the child. Alice told me that Marguerite desperately wanted a child of her own. I think if Marguerite had succeeded in her plans to be rid of us, she might have spirited Lisa away. We found silver from her room at Ravenshead and also some diamond earrings of yours, Amelia. No doubt she would have taken whatever she needed before she disappeared with my daughter. Imagine what might have been Lisa's fate then…living with that woman…growing up as her child.'

'It does not bear thinking of!' Amelia closed her eyes for a moment. Gerard's fingers tightened over hers. She looked at him. 'Forgive me. I had no idea that she was unstable. Her letters were so sad…so pitiful…'

'The work of a clever if deranged mind. Her father may have suspected that she had killed her sister, but no one could prove it. She had brooded on her wrongs. When Gordon came home from France and went to visit, he told her about Lisette and how she died. She saw her chance to take revenge on me.

'Gordon was angry, but he had no thought of murder until she prompted him. He says that he resisted at first, but she was too strong for him. He had loved her since they were children, and she knew how to make him do her bidding. He wanted her, but she made him promise her that he would kill us both.'

Amelia shuddered. 'And I invited her to come here.'

'You could not have known what was in her mind.'

'What will happen to Lieutenant Gordon?'

'He is to live abroad. I have given him a letter of recommendation to a plantation owner in Jamaica. I met Jacques in France and he offered me help if I should go there.'

'Should Lieutenant Gordon not go to prison?' Amelia looked at him steadily. 'Many would seek revenge, Gerard.'

'I think he has suffered enough. He lost the woman he loved.'

'Does he know that Lisa is his child?'

'No. Perhaps it was harsh, but I thought it best for her to stay with us. She could not be more loved than she is now.'

'I am glad—for her sake. You are her true papa, Gerard.'

'Yes, I am—and you are her mama. We shall both love her and care for her, and she will remain our daughter even when we have children of our own.'

'Yes, we shall always love her.' Amelia smiled. 'Can you forgive me for doubting you even for a moment? I am so sorry, Gerard. I should have known, but I was stunned…I could not think clearly. Once I had time to let my mind clear, I knew you were innocent of all their accusations.'

'Can you forgive me for letting you walk into danger? You were close to death, Amelia.'

'That was entirely my own fault. I had completely

forgotten everything else when I left the house. Besides, it is over—it is over, isn't it?' She lifted her eyes to meet his anxiously.

'Yes, my dearest. I am certain it is.'

'Then there is nothing to stop our marriage—is there?'

'Your brother…shall you tell him what you know?'

'I shall tell him all of it, Gerard. You were blameless. His jealousy and anger were misplaced. I think he may have blamed himself for Lucinda's suicide, because he told her he would not help her after he saw her kiss you—and he may find peace in the knowledge that she did not jump into the river because of his harshness. Perhaps he can find peace at last, and it may be the saving of him.'

'Yes, he may find some comfort in that,' Gerard agreed. 'He may still not forgive us—either of us.'

'If Michael wishes to remain a stranger to me, it is his choice. He may apologise and put an end to this feud if he wishes—if not…' Amelia shook her head. 'I cannot condone the way he behaved with a young woman he knew to be my friend. Besides, he made me so unhappy when he sent you away, Gerard. I have you and Lisa and all my friends—why should I need anyone else?'

Amelia stood at the church door, her arm resting lightly on Gerard's. The bells were ringing out joyfully and a large crowd of friends and local people had gathered outside to watch the bride and groom leave. Rice and dried rose petals were showered over them as they ran for the carriage.

Once inside out of the bitter February wind, Gerard

drew her to him, kissing her softly, his hand moving at the nape of her neck. His eyes seemed to search her face.

'What is it?'

'You are happy? Truly happy?'

'You know I am. How could I not be on such a day? We are married and we have our friends about us. I have all that I ever wanted.'

'Your brother did not attend the wedding.'

'No, but my nephew, John, did—and he brought me a gift from my brother.' She touched the simple but beautiful baroque pearl that hung from a fine gold chain about her throat. 'This is the pendant my mother wore when she married. Michael sent it to me. It is the closest he could come to an apology.'

'Your mother's...' Gerard nodded. 'I wondered why you chose something so simple, though it is a fine pearl.'

'Mama's jewellery was divided between us after she died. Michael was allowed to choose first. He realised afterwards that I would have liked the pendant and he told me I should have it on my wedding day. Sending it for my wedding was a symbol of forgiveness...an olive branch. I wore it to show I had accepted his offering. I shall have many occasions to wear the diamonds you gave me, my dearest.'

'You hardly need diamonds,' Gerard told her and kissed her once more. 'Whatever you wear, whatever you do, you are lovely inside and out, my darling Amelia.'

'I love you so much...'

'I am the luckiest man to have found you.' Gerard

took her hand as the carriage drew to a halt outside the house. 'Only you would have asked that Lisa should accompany us on our wedding trip to Paris. You are a pearl amongst women, Amelia. Your brother's gift was appropriate.'

'Thank you for being so understanding. Most men would hold a grudge after what Michael did...but you don't...do you?'

'I may never forgive him completely for what he did to us. It truly broke my heart and I wanted to die. I was reckless on the field of battle in the hope of death. However, I want you to be happy, Amelia. I know it would not suit you to cut your brother or his family entirely. I dare say I can greet him in a civil manner if it comes to it, though we shall never be friends.'

'It is enough,' she murmured as the carriage door was opened and a groom let down the steps. 'We must not keep our guests waiting, Gerard.'

Gerard watched as his wife moved amongst her friends at the lavish reception they had given. He felt a swelling of pride as he saw the way people greeted her. She was liked, respected and loved by everyone here. Known for her generosity, her dignity and her character, she was a truly great lady and he felt privileged that she was his to love and protect for the rest of their lives.

'Father wanted to come, you know.' Captain John Royston spoke from behind him, making Gerard turn his head. 'He is often bad tempered and lets his tongue run away with him—but he was upset when he heard what happened. Amelia looks well enough now, though.'

'Thankfully, she has made a full recovery,' Gerard said. 'You may tell your father he may visit us in Hanover Square when he chooses. I dare say Amelia will wish for a ball when we go to town next Season. I should be pleased to see him and your mother and brother—and you, of course, should you be on leave from your regiment.'

'Thank you. I'll make that known to my father.' John offered his hand and shook on it, then he nodded and moved away.

Harry Pendleton came up to him. 'So we are all three wed,' he observed. 'I think we have done well for ourselves, Gerard. There was a time in Spain when I believed none of us would ever see this day.'

'We were lucky to escape with our lives.' Gerard's mouth formed a grim line. 'And we have all had our troubles since. However, I believe we can all look forward to a more peaceful future.'

'With Napoleon safely tucked up in his island prison, I dare say England will be at peace—and I think the same may be said for us.' Harry looked thoughtful. 'I wrote to Northaven and thanked him for the part he played in this last affair, Gerard. You were right—the past is gone and should be forgotten.'

'It was harder for you to forgive, because of what happened to Susannah, but, from something he said when we talked, I believe that when he saw her fall with his ball in her shoulder it changed him. I dare say, given the chance, he may lead a better life in future.'

Harry shrugged and then grinned. 'Susannah wanted

me to write the letter. It is amazing what we do for love, Gerard.'

'Indeed, I agree with that,' Gerard said and laughed. 'Excuse me, my dear fellow, but I believe they are about to play a waltz and I should like to dance with my wife…'

Amelia turned in her husband's arms. She thought he was sleeping and she smiled as she traced the line of his mouth with her fingertip. Sometimes he could look stern, forbidding, but in sleep he looked younger and at peace, very like the young man she had first fallen in love with so many years ago. The previous night, he had made love to her passionately, hungrily, but with such tenderness that she had wept tears of happiness. She bent her head to kiss his lips softly and found herself caught in an imprisoning embrace.

'I thought you were asleep,' she said and smiled down at him.

'Were you trying to take advantage of me?' His eyes mocked her lovingly.

'Foolish man…' She tried to pull away but he moved swiftly, rolling her beneath him, gazing down at her. Her hair was loose and tumbling about her face in disarray, her skin pearly pink and smooth as his eyes feasted on her sweetness. 'Gerard…it is almost time to get up.'

'This is our honeymoon and I may not leave this bed for a week.'

'Is that a threat or a promise?' she teased, touching his beloved face. 'I think I should be quite happy to stay right here for as long as you wish.'

'I shall take that as an invitation,' he murmured huskily, bending his head to suck gently at her nipples, which peaked at his touch. 'You are so beautiful, my love. I think I can never have enough of you.'

Amelia moaned softly, her body arching, tingling as he stroked her, coming vibrantly alive as the desire pooled inside her. She ran her hands over his back, loving the satin feel of his skin, the hardness of toned muscles. His maleness felt hard and hot against her inner thigh as he sought the sweet moistness of her femininity, entering her with a deep thrust that made her cry out with pleasure.

They moved together, slowly, taking their time as their bodies matched and met in equal need—a need that took them soaring into realms of pleasure known only to true lovers. Carried and tossed by raging passion, they ended on a far shore where the soft sea spray kissed a sunlit breach and the scent of blooms wafted on a warm breeze.

'I am in paradise...' she murmured against his shoulder, tasting the salt of his sweat. 'I am truly happy, Gerard.'

'We are both in paradise then,' he murmured and smiled down at her. 'For I am in a place I never thought to be.'

Amelia lay back, content to feel him lying beside her. She thought that he had fallen asleep or perhaps he was just pretending again.

'I was thinking,' she said. 'We have so much, Gerard. We must find a way to share some of our good fortune. I realise that I made a mistake with Marguerite, but there is a young woman I know who really does need a little good fortune. Her name is Jane and I thought we might give her a Season in town this year.'

Gerard did not answer. He must truly be asleep this time. Amelia smiled. Somewhere within the house she could hear a longcase clock striking. She felt sleepy, at peace with herself. There was no hurry for anything. When they returned to England, she would write to the young woman and invite her to stay with them at their house in Hanover Square...

* * * * *